I0733938

THE WRETCHED BONES

A BEN SHIVERS MYSTERY

C.M. SAUNDERS

PO Box 67, Bridgewater, MA 02324

The Wretched Bones
Copyright © 2023 C.M. Saunders

All rights reserved. No part of this book may be used or reproduced in any manner whatsoever without written permission except in the case of brief quotations embodied in critical articles or reviews.

This book is a work of fiction. All characters depicted in this book are fictitious, and any resemblance to real persons—living or dead—is purely coincidental.

The Midnight Machinations logo was created by Jeffrey Kosh.
Cover designed by Jeffrey Kosh, http://jeffreykosh.wix.com/jeffreykoshgraphics.

Published by Midnight Machinations, P.O. Box 67, Bridgewater, MA 02324.
Midnight Machinations is an imprint of Grinning Skull Press.

All Rights Reserved.

ISBN-13: 978-1-947227-91-0 (paperback)
ISBN: 978-1-947227-92-7 (ebook)

DEDICATION

For my mother and father, who never stopped believing in me.

CHAPTER ONE

Ben Shivers slowed, then stopped his 2009 VW camper van at the gate. An overweight, balding, bad-tempered looking security guard with heavily tattooed forearms leaned out of a cubicle and motioned for him to wind down his window, which Ben did without being asked twice.

"Good morning, sir," the guard said, a look of tired suspicion etched on his face. "Welcome to the Regal Retreat."

"Thanks very much," Ben replied, forcing what he hoped was a disarming smile. "And good morning to you, too."

"Are you a guest or a visitor?"

"Just a visitor."

"Whom are you visiting?"

"The resort manager, Christine Turner."

"Just a moment, please," the guard said as he retreated into his cubicle and rifled through a stack of paperwork lying on the desk. "State your full name, please, sir."

"Ben Shivers, P.I."

"Private Investigator?" the guard cocked an inquisitive eyebrow.

"Paranormal Investigator," Ben corrected.

"Oh, okay," the security guard said dismissively.

It was a reaction Ben was used to. The paranormal didn't sit well with a lot of people. It challenged the accepted status quo, and consequently was something most didn't want to acknowledge until they had to. Nobody gave paranormal investigators an ounce of credit.

Apparently satisfied, the security guard gave Ben one last, lingering look, then pushed a button to lift the barrier. "There are car parks on either side, with a connecting road running through the complex," he said. "Feel free to park in any designated area and report to reception in the main building. Someone there will contact Miz Turner on your behalf and tell her you've arrived."

"Okay, thanks," Ben shouted out the window as he drove away. Mainly as an excuse to check out the place, he passed the first car park and took the narrow connecting road to the one at the far end of the resort, keeping his speed well below the 15 mph limit.

The first thing he noticed was the sheer size of the place. It was huge. He'd seen pictures on the website, but nothing on a computer screen could do it justice.

On one side of the streetlamp and potted plant-lined road was a large, functional-looking four-story complex of holiday apartments, which probably included a handful of permanent lets, behind which a gigantic freshwater lake rippled invitingly in the spring sunshine. A handful of what looked like continental-style, whitewashed villas lined the shore, and if he craned his neck, Ben could see a wooden jetty jutting into the water.

There was a tiny, picturesque island in the middle of the lake sporting a mass of greenery topped with several cascading weeping willows. Not being big enough to accommodate any kind of dwelling, the island appeared to serve no practical use whatsoever and looked more of a decorative feature than anything else. If that were the case, it was working. The scene looked like it had been lifted straight from a postcard.

On the other side of the road was an even bigger building, this one emblazoned with a huge green-on-white sign saying RECEPTION. A steep hill studded with trees loomed over it, the peak shrouded in mist. It looked like a hiker's dream. Snatching a glance through the window as he drove past, Ben could see that the main building appeared to house a large restaurant on the ground floor. This revelation made his stomach growl. He hadn't eaten yet.

Further down the road, he passed a compact row of shops consisting of a café, a supermarket, a pharmacy, a unisex hairdresser, a newsagent, a sporting goods outlet, and even a fishing tackle and bait store. A handwritten sign hanging in the window said they offered "full kit" rentals on an hourly basis, and there was currently a sale on.

The place was like a self-contained village, and Ben silently applauded whoever was behind the enterprise. It showed real business acumen. Create a captive market, hike up the prices to give the illusion of exclusivity, offer a service or activity that requires specialist equipment, then provide said equipment at a premium with no viable alternative. No doubt everywhere you looked there would be numerous deals and "special offers," which made people think they were getting value for money. But ultimately, the guests who had already paid to stay at the Regal paid more to partake in some activity or other, then paid still more for the necessary gear. Heck, they were probably even coerced into paying someone to teach them how to use it, too. Long live capitalism and free enterprise, because enterprise was probably the only thing you'll find free here.

And the tactics appeared to be working. Despite it being only a little after ten in the morning, people were milling about everywhere, trooping in and out of the shops and restaurant, heading down the road to unknown destinations in groups of two or three. The vast majority were guests decked out in casual attire, but the workers were easily identifiable by the smart, black trousers, shiny shoes, and branded yellow polo shirts they all wore. Some even drove what looked like golf buggies, which Ben presumed were used to ferry elderly guests between various points in the complex. They were probably charged extra for that service, too.

Ben couldn't help noticing that most of the people he saw around were older couples, probably retired, rather than young families or singletons out looking for fun and adventure. That made sense. The Baby Boomers whose kids had long-since grown up and flown the coop was where the money was, and the place positively reeked of the stuff.

The Regal Retreat was no Butlins holiday camp. It was marketed as a luxury health and relaxation facility catering to the upper end of the market, which was probably why they were so quick to reach out to Ben when things started going tits up. A bit of bad publicity could send a place like this into a tailspin, quickly resulting in complete financial ruin, and that was something shareholders were always keen to avoid.

Ben parked the VW camper very carefully in the car park at the far end of the complex between a Land Rover Discovery and a brand new, lime green BMW. A cursory check revealed the car park to be fitted with both lights and security cameras, which no doubt provided patrons with some level of reassurance. Security here was obviously at a very high level. Then he cut the engine and took a few minutes to compose himself.

As he was looking out of the front window, taking in his surroundings, there was a soft *thump* from the cabin behind him. Startled, he whirled around just in time to see that Mr. Trimble, his black-and-white tabby, had chosen that precise moment to wake up and demand breakfast, strutting out from his hiding place with his whiskers twitching and his white-tipped tail pointed straight up in the air.

"Morning, dude," Ben said.

They'd met by chance when Mr. Trimble was just a few weeks old, and they'd been inseparable ever since. Ben had been walking down a busy street in the suburbs of Southampton, minding his own business and lost in thought, when a little, scraggly ball of fur crawled out of the undergrowth and started yelling at him. Or tried to yell. He was so weak and malnourished that he could barely utter a croak.

Ben's first instinct had been to carry on walking and forget he'd ever laid eyes on the kitten. But his conscience would never allow him to do that. He couldn't just leave the poor thing there to die. Instead, he scooped it up and took it to the nearest vet.

After charging Ben £75 for a checkup and a fifteen-minute "consultation," the vet announced that Mr. Trimble, who was then known simply as "The Kitten," was severely dehydrated and suffering from pneumonia, an eye infection, and a bad case of fleas. The vet gave it a less than 30% chance of survival, even if Ben paid for treatment. This put him in an awkward position. He wasn't overjoyed about spending a fortune he didn't really have on an animal that wasn't his and was more than likely beyond help anyway. It would be throwing money down the drain.

But at the same time, he had to give the kitten a fighting chance. Every creature deserved that. Eventually, he agreed to pay for five days of treatment in intensive care upfront. That and the consultation fee wiped out most of his meager savings, but if the kitten died, as seemed likely, at least it would spend its last days in relative safety and comfort.

What Ben didn't really count on was the kitten making a dramatic recovery. After being given the all-clear from the vet, he put an ad on Facebook to try to find a new home for it. But it turned out nobody wanted a scruffy, emaciated, high-maintenance feline companion that hadn't even been vaccinated or spayed yet, so Ben was stuck with her. He'd assumed the kitten was female on account of her beautiful, pale blue eyes, but that theory was blown out of the water in the coming months when "she" grew a huge pair of balls and turned into a "he" almost overnight.

Ever since, Ben and Mr. Trimble had cohabitated and traveled around the country together in the camper van. It wasn't ideal. Most cats undoubtedly preferred a more settled environment. But the way Ben saw it, any kind of life Mr. Trimble had now was infinitely better than the one he'd had before. In fact, left to his own devices, he probably wouldn't even have a life. He would surely be dead by now.

In retrospect, Ben could see that he needed Mr. Trimble just as much as Mr. Trimble needed him. They'd met at a strange time. Just months after the event that changed everything, when nothing made sense anymore and Ben was looking for meaning in a world of shit. And that wasn't just him being dramatic. Some things really are life-changing: like losing your wife, your daughter, your job, and your house all in the space of a year. Mr. Trimble offered a chance at redemption and was a sustained presence in a world in constant flux. Something to cling to.

But he couldn't think about that.

Not now.

He could almost see the bottomless pit of depression stretching out before him like an abyss ready to swallow him whole. It would be all too easy to allow himself to fall in, or even take matters into his own hands and jump in head first.

But that wouldn't achieve anything. His life had focus now. Meaning. Even if it was only scraps of work and a stray cat, it was more than he'd had at his lowest ebb. He knew he had to keep plugging away, one day at a time, and keep the black dog snapping at his heels at bay. It was what Louise wanted.

This was recovery.

"Fuck it," he muttered. He had to stop thinking about Louise as if she was the one who'd died. She was very much still alive. She just didn't want him around anymore. Too many reminders, she said. In many ways, that was almost as hard to deal with as your daughter dying. Splitting up because of one party's infidelity was one thing, but getting divorced simply because you reminded your partner of better times was something else entirely.

"Okay, Mister T., let's get you fed," Ben said with a heavy sigh as he stepped over the mewling cat, exited the cockpit, and maneuvered into the camper van's tiny living area. Reaching into a cupboard below the tiny washbasin, he retrieved Mr. Trimble's dish and filled it with some dry food and water from the tap. The cat tucked in gratefully.

The back of the van had been customized to incorporate not just the cramped living area, which doubled as the sleeping area at night, but also a workspace with a table and a tiny kitchenette. Ben lived a simple life. He detested clutter but had all the modern conveniences he needed—his laptop computer, an electric kettle, a mini-refrigerator, and a tiny gas cooker. Every inch of the living area was utilized, and he'd installed more than enough storage space to fulfill his needs, even fitting bookshelves above the windows on both sides of the vehicle, which now sagged under the weight of his essential reference volumes and classic horror fiction collection.

Life on the road forced him to be economic in every facet of his existence. There was no room for excess baggage, and that was a good thing. He was a firm believer that the main trappings of modern life were waste and needless overabundance. People loved accumulating piles of crap they didn't need. It reinforced the idea that their existence stood for something. You had to strip all that away to find what was really important.

He and Mr. Trimble were as self-sufficient as they could realistically be. The van was equipped with roof-mounted solar panels, which provided just enough power to run the tiny refrigerator, the low-energy lamps, and Ben's laptop for a couple of hours a day when he couldn't plug into a main supply. There was even a chemical toilet in a cupboard at the back, which Ben only used when he had no other option, and a small water tank fitted to the roof that was replenished with rainwater then filtered, providing enough H_2O for washing and drinking.

Ben didn't buy into the idea that living in a van made you homeless. He had a home. It just happened to be a van. That in itself had a world of advantages. He wasn't rooted to one place, for a start. He could follow the sunshine all over Europe if he wanted. He didn't need a lot of money. To him, money was just a commodity, a means to survive, rather than a way to judge how successful someone was. The majority of the upper classes, like the people he saw strutting around the resort, were born rich and hadn't actually done anything to deserve such a privileged lifestyle. Of course, that wasn't their fault. When presented with unimaginable wealth, nobody in their right mind is ever likely to refuse it just to preserve their integrity.

Ben's biggest expenditures were petrol and food for Mr. Trimble. It was easy to live cheaply on local produce and discounted supermarket items, which he supplemented by making the most of the environment. If he parked up in close proximity to a lake or river, he went fishing, and if he was near a forest, he went foraging for wild mushrooms, nuts, and berries.

Most of his income came from his website and a Patreon that fans and followers contributed to in order to receive exclusive articles and videos. He also wrote fiction in his spare time. Horror, of course. He had a couple of books on Amazon and managed one or two news articles a month, which he sold to magazines or journals. He'd discovered that being financially independent was all about creating and maintaining multiple revenue streams rather than relying on one source.

At the last count, he'd amassed over 45,000 social media followers across platforms, which was a respectable amount, offering him a decent level of influence. But because the power supply was somewhat limited, he had to be sensible with regards to usage. On the rare occasions he was lucky enough to have a stable Wi-Fi connection, he queued up the articles for his website so it ran new material every few days. That way he created a steady stream of content for his followers to digest. He also used a plug-in to connect the website to Facebook and Twitter, which saved him posting everywhere individually, helped drive traffic to the site, and bump up the advertising revenue.

All things considered, he made a living. Just. That was fine with him. When you had enough money to live, everything else was superfluous. It wasn't as if he had his kid's college education to think about now.

And then, of course, there were field investigations like this. Ben had worked hard to build his reputation and was now recognized as one of the country's leading paranormal investigators. People contacted him when they experienced, or thought they experienced, some kind of paranormal or supernatural activity. He usually charged expenses, plus a fee determined on a case-by-case basis, and then wrote about the investigation for his site. If the clients were agreeable, of course. Most were, as it provided free advertising in the form of exposure, which made it a mutually beneficial arrangement.

He didn't always charge money for his services. Not every case had the desired outcome, and some simply couldn't afford it. Often, he accepted meals or an open bar and a few nights in a warm, comfortable bed in lieu of payment. Depending on how events unfolded, he might be able to get up to a couple of months' worth of material on any one case. That kept the revenue trickling in. However, because the owners of the Regal Retreat were so obviously obscenely wealthy, all that had gone out of the window and he'd already quoted them an astronomical figure for his services. He was optimistic about getting it, too.

Leaving Mr. Trimble greedily chomping at his brunch, Ben exited the camper through the side door and locked it behind him. He couldn't imagine theft being a problem at a place like this, but he wasn't going to take any chances. Mr. Trimble would have to wait a while for his daily exercise. Ben had an appointment to keep.

"You're the Paranormal Investigator?" Christine Turner, the resort manager asked. She was a slim woman in her late thirties dressed in business attire. Her blonde hair was pulled up into a bun, and she peered out from behind a pair of thick, black-framed glasses. She wasn't unattractive, but on first impression seemed the cold, unapproachable type who lived and breathed work. Ben couldn't imagine her getting crazy after a few cocktails and waking up on someone's floor.

They were sitting in her plush office on the fourth floor of the main building separated by a large oak desk on which lay not one but two computer monitors side-by-side, a sure-fire sign of a workaholic who simply had too much going on for one monitor to deal with.

"I am," Ben replied.

"What does that mean, exactly?"

"You should know," Ben said. "You hired me."

"I did. But it's still a very vague description. We haven't actually entered into an agreement for your services yet. Not officially. And I was just wondering, given the circumstances, what you'd be able to do for us."

"Well, I won't be able to answer that until I look further into the problem you have here," Ben explained as diplomatically as he could. "In a nutshell, I help people. Usually by finding explanations. Perhaps explanations other people might miss because they aren't exactly open to every eventuality. From there, if at all possible, I find solutions for those problems. As much as I market myself as an expert in the paranormal, you might not be surprised to know that, more often than not, the problems I face are of a decidedly mundane nature."

"That's surprisingly reassuring," Christine Turner said. "But I have to confess, I'm very curious. Is it an actual job?"

"Sometimes," Ben replied. "I doubt it will ever make me rich, but I get by." That was one of two questions he was asked most often, the other being…

"And is Shivers your real name? Or is it like…a pseudonym you've adopted?"

As if by clockwork.

"No, it's real. It's known as an aptronym."

"Excuse me?"

"An aptronym. Means a name that is especially fitting to the person it is bestowed upon. Like the poet Ezra Wordsworth, or the sprinter Usain 'Lightning' Bolt. My own personal favorite is the German football coach Wolfgang Wolf, who was once employed by a team called Wolfsburg. Brilliant."

His Wolfgang Wolf quip never failed to draw a smile. Except on this occasion. It was becoming plain to see that this woman wasn't at all interested in friendly banter. "Oh, I see. That's interesting," the resort manager said, po-faced. "Well, on to business. As you may know, Mister Shivers, the Regal Retreat is all about relaxation."

"I'm aware of that, Missus Turner, or is it Miss?" Ben said. He hoped he didn't sound flirty, but hated meeting women whose marital status was a mystery. It could turn into a horrific source of embarrassment. Of course, you could opt for the neutral, honorific "Miz," but using that always made him feel he was in an Agatha Christie novel or something. No, you had to take a gamble, one way or the other, or throw in both as he had just done to get some clarification.

"It's Miss, unless being married to a job counts," her flickering smile momentarily betrayed a deep sadness. "You can call me Christine." The woman politely held out her right hand to be shook.

Ben paused for a moment. This was the place where many so meetings went south. Whoever wanted to shake his hand, the offer of forced intimacy invariably made before they noticed his scorched, permanently disfigured appendage, usually regretted it. He was sympathetic to their plight. Who wanted to caress a stranger's angry red, misshapen, mutilated flesh? To make things easier, if he saw an opening, Ben usually made an effort to lead the handshake proposal. He did this with his left hand, something which also took a lot of people, who probably assumed he was a south paw, by surprise.

With a familiar, irresistibly mischievous flourish, he opened his palm. The fingers couldn't be fully straightened, and the thumb of his deformed hand pointed straight up in the air, which was about the best he could manage given its limited use. That was what being severely burned in a house fire did for you. The doctors said the hand would get better with time. More feeling would return as the nerves repaired themselves, he would gain more use of his fingers, the scarring would fade, and the hand would look more like a hand and less like a melted candle. But it had been three years now, and things were much the same. He'd learned to live with it. "With pleasure, Christine."

Ben was used to all kinds of reactions to what he'd come to affectionately know as his 'horrific handshake.' Some people openly grimaced, unable to contain their disgust; others swallowed hard, trying to cover up their revulsion. On one memorable occasion, a book dealer from Somerset was so grossed out he withdrew his hand completely as if being hit with an electric shock, and from then on, he flatly refused to even look Ben in the eye.

At first Ben had felt a strange sense of embarrassment or even shame, disappointed with himself for being the cause of all the ensuing awkwardness. But as time went on, he came to use his burned hand as a kind of gauge. It helped him evaluate people. He'd come to think of it as "The Scar Tissue Test."

To his astonishment, Miss Christine Turner was wholly unperturbed by the disfigurement, grasping his hand firmly and pumping it twice. She didn't flinch. Instead, she said, "How was the journey down?"

"Good, thanks. I'm used to being on the road. But I'm sure you're busy, so we can dispense with the formalities," Ben said, eager to get on to the real reason for his visit.

"As you wish," Christine Turner said. "What would you like to know?"

"Before we talk about my reason for being here, some general information about the daily running of the place would be good. Maybe a bit of history or background? Anything you feel might help me build a picture and work out how best to proceed."

"Well, the Regal Retreat, or R.R., as it's known, is a luxury health resort covering eleven acres of prime real estate here in beautiful East Anglia," Christine replied without missing a beat, slipping effortlessly into a well-rehearsed marketing spiel. "It was first opened as a lakeside hotel by a young, local entrepreneur by the name of Michael Davenport in nineteen-thirty-seven. Apart from a few lean spells during the war years, the business was an immediate success, and has been expanding ever since. Today, it is by far the biggest resort of its kind in the county. The main guest block features a hundred and twenty-four rooms, with another half a dozen four-bed villas around the lake, set apart from the main complex. They offer more privacy and are usually reserved for our more-exclusive clients. We have our fair share of celebrities stay here."

"No doubt," Ben said. He got the feeling Christine expected him to press her more in pursuit of a bit of celeb gossip, but he really wasn't interested. He was so out of touch with popular culture that even if the resort manager started dropping names, he probably wouldn't recognize many. Not unless Bruce Dickinson, Chris Rea, or a cast member from the US Office were regular guests.

"We're currently operating at between seventy and eighty percent capacity," Christine continued. "Though this rises to one hundred percent during the peak summer months. When we reach maximum capacity, we place clients on a waiting list. There's always the possibility of a cancellation. We have some long-term clients who effectively live here for large chunks of the year, and in addition, we take a lot of wedding parties and corporate events. That's the direction we'd like to steer the business in future. It's far more profitable."

"What kind of corporate events?"

"Meetings and functions, mainly," Christine shrugged. "Though we also do a popular program of company days and team-building events."

"Interesting," Ben said, even though it really wasn't. Those so-called corporate events usually amounted to being paid to humor a bunch of people who didn't like each other and coercing them into doing things they didn't want to do while they pretended to be enjoying themselves.

"The lake is our main draw," Christine continued. "We offer a range of activities from boating and fishing to wakeboarding and scuba diving for our more adventurous clients. If the water isn't your thing, there are various hiking trails ranging from easy to difficult. You can either find your own way, or partake in one of our guided tours. We also have a custom-made, nine-hole golf course on site and a lawn bowling green. There's a big tournament this week. If you would like to enter, let me know and I'll try my utmost to squeeze you in."

"Thanks, I'll keep that in mind."

"If that doesn't strike your fancy, the main building here is equipped with a state-of-the-art gym, a sauna, a wellness center, and a games room fitted with snooker and billiard tables. We also run regular yoga, Pilates, and aerobic kickboxing classes. Our instructors are among the best in the country."

"I'm sure they are," Ben said with a smile. "Just out of interest, how many workers do you employ?"

"It varies," Christine explained. "At the moment, we have around a hundred and sixty permanent members of staff, including hospitality, security, cleaners, instructors, maintenance, and administrative personnel. We run a very tight ship, but our numbers are bumped up by casual workers we recruit via an employment agency. At any one time you can expect to find between fifty and eighty staff on duty. More during peak times, of course. Most live on site, in this very building in fact, where they have living quarters. But obviously this isn't a requirement. I, for example, live about a thirty-minute drive away."

"That commute must be a pain."

"Not at all. I enjoy it. This can be a high-pressure job, and the drive gives me a chance to mentally prepare myself beforehand and decompress after a long day."

"I see."

"So would you like me to sign you up for any classes?" Christine asked with a mischievous smirk.

"I don't think that will be necessary, thanks," Ben said, unsure whether the woman was being serious or making a joke at his expense. "I would prefer to get on with the job. After I refuel, of course."

"Refuel? I'm sorry, are you referring to your vehicle or your body?"

"Well, both. But the vehicle can wait for the time being."

"Very well. You must have passed the Michelin-starred restaurant on the ground floor, which uses only healthy, locally sourced, sustainable produce. It really is excellent."

"I remember seeing it on the way in."

"But if that's not appealing to you, there is also a small Cantonese restaurant on the third floor, or we can arrange for the kitchen to deliver something to you."

"Is there a pub? Or a bar?"

For the first time, Ms. Turner's professional façade slipped momentarily, and Ben detected a note of either disappointment or disapproval. "No; this is a dry resort, Mister Shivers."

"Meaning?"

"Meaning there is no alcohol on sale anywhere on site. Not even the supermarket."

"Oh, got it." Ben didn't even try to hide how deflated he felt.

"May I remind you that the R.R. is a world-renowned health resort, Mister Shivers? Our staff go to extraordinary lengths to cater to our clients' dietary requirements and nutritional needs. For that reason, alcohol is strictly prohibited, and the same goes for smoking. If you are caught smoking anywhere on the premises, you will be asked to leave immediately. This policy operates without exception. Our clientele come here to escape such health hazards. We even discourage people from driving their cars, which is one reason we have eco-friendly on-site transport, but, of course, we accept people have to bring their cars here."

"That's very kind of you," Ben agreed. "But I can't help wondering whether the same rules apply to these celebrity clients of yours."

"Rules are rules, Mister Shivers. I don't see how that's relevant to your business here."

She was being evasive, but she was absolutely right. Ben privately scolded himself and took the opportunity to guide the conversation in a different direction. "So shall we talk about why I am here?"

"I would be happy to," Christine Turner said with what appeared to be something approaching relief. "Just let me reiterate that everything I say here is strictly off the record. I want the luxury of being able to speak freely. I believe it will aid your investigation immeasurably. But I don't want to pay a penalty for such frankness later. By that, I mean I wouldn't want anything I say coming back to bite me on the behind."

"Understood," Ben said. "Feel free to speak openly."

"I trust you aren't using any equipment to record this interview?"

"Correct." Under normal circumstances, Ben would certainly record the interview for future reference. But he found that on first meeting, what he called the consultation period, people tended to be far less restrained and intimidated than they would be if confronted with a digital Dictaphone. There would be plenty of time for a formal interview later, if it was necessary. This meeting was simply part of the feeling-out process.

"To that effect, I would like you to sign this N.D.A.," Miss Turner said, opening a drawer in the desk, pulling out a pre-printed document, and laying it on the table.

"N.D.A.?"

"Non-Disclosure Agreement. Standard practice, I'm afraid. It's just a way of protecting ourselves when dealing with the press."

"I know what an N.D.A. is," Ben said. "But I'm not sure I qualify as a member of the press."

"Mister Shivers, we performed due diligence on you. Your website, and the rest of the work you do, is very impressive. You've earned a good reputation in the field. To us, it certainly qualifies you as being a member of the press. We'd just like some security before we discuss the more-sensitive aspects of the case. I'm sure you understand."

Ben picked up the document and started leafing through it, raising a weary brow at the dense legal jargon it contained. "If I sign this, it means I can't write about what happens here. You do know the site is my livelihood and very much dependent on a steady stream of material, right? I need readers, and my readers demand, no, *deserve*, to know the truth. I'm not going to bury anything I find here under mounds of rose petals."

"Nobody is asking you to, Mister Shivers. I'm sure a man of your capabilities would be able to circumnavigate any restrictions we impose on you, anyway. But if you read the small print, you'll see that in exchange for full, unrestricted access to the Regal Retreat, you simply agree to give us copy approval before you publish anything on your site. Or anywhere else. I'm sure you know, we've suffered quite badly in recent years at the hands of hacks specializing in drumming up negative publicity. We're anxious to avoid any more. We presume your somewhat inflated fee reflects your complete cooperation."

Boom.

There it is.

The Regal would essentially be paying him extra for the right to influence the content he produced.

As much as he resented being coerced, in this instance, he felt his hands were tied. His paymasters weren't doing anything illegal or immoral; they were simply looking after their own best interests and offering him a cash incentive to fall in line. Evidently, it was the way these people did business. It wasn't entirely unexpected. He was more upset by the fact that there was no bar. Still, perhaps a few days on the wagon would do him good.

Ben scribbled his signature on the N.D.A., then leaned back in the chair and said, "So tell me what's been happening here. I need to know everything."

Chapter Two

Christine Turner suddenly winced as if in physical pain. As professional and business-like as she appeared, she obviously hadn't been looking forward to spilling the Regal Retreat's secrets. "I'm sure you've done your research, Mister Shivers. Everything that happens here… almost everything…ends up in the public domain one way or another, usually via the tabloid newspapers. It's very difficult to keep a lid on things."

"I assume you're referring to the amount of weird deaths you've had here?"

"In a word, yes."

"How many have occurred in total?"

"Well, I'm sure you can appreciate that untimely, tragic deaths occur in even the smallest of hotels. For people in the trade, it's an occupational hazard."

"Understood. But aren't the figures much higher than average?"

"I'm not sure there are any official figures pertaining to registered deaths in hotels, Mister Shivers. And even if there were, you can't fail to have noticed that most of our clientele are of advancing years, so naturally the mortality rate would be higher. This is why most statistics you see reported can't really be trusted. The numbers can be skewed and manipulated to either prove or disprove virtually anything."

"Do you want me to investigate the problem or what?" Ben snapped, a little too forcefully. He could sense the woman's defensive walls going up and wanted to put an end to it as soon as possible.

"Of course we do, or else we wouldn't have called you in. It's not what we would consider urgent business. More a low-priority kind of housekeeping we would like resolved before the summer rush.

"A rash of unexplained deaths is 'low-priority' to you?"

"Oh, they can be explained," Christine said. "Most of them, anyway. Like I said, death is a part of life. I just want you to get the facts right."

"The fact is, this place has a pretty bad reputation," Ben said.

"That depends how you look at it," Christine shrugged.

"How many deaths are we talking about?"

"You mean across the spectrum?"

"Yes. Natural causes, accidents, murders, suicides combined. Ballpark figure."

"Since the Regal Retreat first opened its doors, there have been a documented two hundred and twelve deaths on the property."

"Jesus Christ."

"We accept this figure might be higher than what you might expect, but most are a result of easily explainable natural causes, and you must also take into account one-off events like the Derry Killings."

"Refresh my memory on that."

"All the information you require is easily available online," Ms. Turner said, shifting awkwardly in her chair.

"Probably. But I would prefer to hear it from you."

"Very well. Fred Derry was a retired insurance salesman and a regular visitor to the Regal. He arranged a fortnight's stay for himself and his family in September nineteen-eighty-three. Three days into their holiday, in the middle of the night, he strangled his wife, Ruth, to death as she slept. Then he went to the room next door where his grown-up son, Adam, was staying with his wife, Elaine, and their three-year-old son, and hammered on the door until one of them opened it. And then..."

"And then he killed them all?"

"Yes. With his bare hands. Mostly. He had a little help from a bedside lamp, I believe, which he used as a bludgeoning tool."

"What happened afterward?"

"Another guest saw Fred Derry walking around covered in blood and raised the alarm. The police were here within minutes. Despite being pretty isolated out here, the R.R. is considered extremely important to the local economy. He went quietly, I believe."

"Did the case ever go to court?"

"No. Because Fred Derry hung himself while in police custody. It wasn't clear how he achieved that feat, but it's difficult to prosecute a dead man."

"Do you know if he had any history of depression or mental illness?"

"None that became public knowledge. Neither was there any mention of such things in his family history. The case drew such widespread press coverage that if there was, some bushy-tailed tabloid journo would certainly have uncovered it and splashed it across the front pages. Fred Derry didn't have any money worries, either. Or work-related stress. He was popular and successful. When the family checked into the Regal, they were in high spirits, and nobody reported any arguments the night it happened."

"So, he just suddenly went off the deep end for no reason?"

"It would certainly seem that way. Apparently, during the police interviews, he blamed nightmares and talked about hearing voices. 'The devil made me do it' kind of stuff. But isn't that what they all say to try to distance themselves from their crimes and perhaps help with an insanity-based defense further down the line?"

"It's not uncommon," Ben agreed. What he didn't divulge was his belief that perhaps not every murder suspect was lying when they suggested the devil, a demon, or some other paranormal entity, made them commit violent acts. Obviously, some used 'the voices' as an excuse, and others were mentally ill. But Ben knew there were forces at work in the universe influencing our lives and actions in a range of subtle and not-so-subtle ways, whether we acknowledge it or not. He decided to change his approach. "So why do *you* think he did it?"

Christine paused. "It's not for me to speculate. I'm just the resort manager."

"Fair enough. What else has happened here?"

"Mister Shivers," Christine sighed. "Please think of the Derry case as an example. A case study. I can't tell you about every incident in detail; I will be here all day and, as I am sure you can appreciate, I have other things to do. You can put your journalistic skills to work, and I'll be on hand for any specific questions you might have."

"I see. So, what do you want from me, exactly? Do you think I'm going to patrol the place like some kind of accident-awareness officer?"

"Oh, no. Our health and safety protocols are solid, and believe it or not, we do have staff patrolling the grounds acting as troubleshooters on the lookout for people getting into potentially hazardous situations. We want to know why these things happen with such regularity. Is there a root cause? Why all the death and tragedy? Apart from anything else, it ruins the atmosphere. If there isn't a natural explanation, we want you to explore the possibility that what's happening here might be classed as… supernatural."

"Is there anything else?" Ben asked. "Something you're not telling me?" What may have seemed like facetiousness on his part was, to him, an essential part of the investigation. He pushed buttons to see what would happen. People with something to hide generally didn't cope with cross-examination well.

The resort manager simply sniffed contemptuously, as if aware of Ben's motives and was fully prepared to fight fire with fire. "Haven't I given you enough to get started?"

"You have indeed," Ben conceded. "I was just wondering why you chose me, in particular, with my background and reputation. Simply by bringing me in, you are virtually admitting something paranormal is at work here."

"That's as may be. I certainly can't think of anything 'normal' that could lead to so many deaths."

"Do people ever report any other kind of paranormal activity?"

"Such as?"

"Ghosts or spirits?"

Christine hesitated, letting out a chuckle that turned into a guffaw as it died in her throat before it could be fully formed. Then she sniffed and glanced furtively away.

Ben studied her reaction closely. Under such scrutiny, people were easy to read, and this woman's reactions intimated that whether by accident or design, Ben had hit the nail right on the head.

"Of course, we get those kinds of reports," Christine said. "I think most hotels do, as well as places like museums, pubs, and even amusement parks. Am I right?"

"Absolutely."

"I just don't see what relevance it has. By definition, ghosts and spirits are not physical things. As far as I am aware, they can't influence or affect people, so to us it's an unrelated matter. Unless you prove otherwise, of course. Until then, we'd like you to concentrate on what could be causing all these deaths. It can't just be coincidence."

"I wouldn't go so far as to say ghosts can't affect people," Ben said. "But I take your point. The more streamlined the investigation, the better. I can always broaden it if necessary. So let's talk about that somewhat inflated fee."

"We're prepared to pay you three times the daily rate stated in our correspondence. Plus, you will be allocated a guest room and given full use of the facilities. All free of charge. We'd like to hire you for three days minimum, with the option to extend. Additionally, if we find the work satisfactory, you will also be subject to a completion bonus of fifty percent of the total fee. This, as I already stressed, is all under the proviso that the Regal is given copy approval on any related content you publish, and that applies to all media."

Ben quickly ran the figures through his head. By his calculation, that amount of money would be enough to finance him, the van, and Mr. Trimble, for several months. Which reminded him, "It's a deal. Can I bring my cat?"

"Your what?" Christine looked horrified. "Regrettably, Mister Shivers, pets are not allowed at Regal Retreat. They make a mess."

"No pubs, no off-licenses, no pets… What do your guests do for fun around here?"

"As I've explained, we have an impressive range of health and fitness-based—"

"Yeah, yeah," Ben interrupted. "I know. But my cat's already here. What if I kept him in the van? He won't be any trouble. You won't even know he's here."

"I-I guess that would be acceptable."

"Great. I guess I'll get going, then. I'm assuming I have the run of the place?"

"Absolutely," Christine acknowledged with a shrug. "Within reason, of course. Ask questions, by all means; we appreciate that you have an investigation to conduct. But do be discreet, and try not to bother either the staff or the guests too much."

"Discretion is my middle name," Ben said, rising to his feet. It really wasn't. Ben didn't actually have a middle name. And if he did, something like "Sarcastic" or "Prickly" would be more fitting, but he recognized the need to tell Christine what she wanted to hear. She also had a job to do, and needed to feel as if she was doing it. At least in that sense they had something in common.

East Anglia, 1645

Elizabeth Thrower sat alone in her tiny hovel, hunched over the yellow and orange flames leaping as if alive in the tiny stone fireplace. That was all she had in the way of luxury. She didn't need much. Outside, the wind screeched and howled, and she pulled her woolen shawl tighter around her frail shoulders to ward off the pervading chill.

They would be coming for her. Of this she was certain. The hunters, for that's how her mind perceived them, would come and snuff out her life like a candle. Maybe tonight, maybe tomorrow, maybe the next day. She didn't know when they would take her, just that they would. Something else she knew was that she was too old and tired to run. All she could do was wait and plead her case when the time came, if they gave her a chance.

These past few years had been hard. Catholicism was sweeping through the land like a plague, laying waste to everything that lay before it and imposing its own set of laws and beliefs. There was no place in the new world for people like Elizabeth who refused to conform.

The hunters were close.

Just yesterday, they'd got hold of old Maggie Reid, who'd lived on the other side of the village. They stripped her naked and dragged her through the streets crying and screaming while they beat her with sticks, leaving a crimson trail on the cobbles. They took her to the common, where they lashed her to a wooden pole, blindfolded her so she couldn't strike anyone down with the evil eye, and built a pyre of dried wood around her.

And then they lit it.

They said that if she was human, she would burn. But if she was aligned with the devil, he would save her from harm. If that happened, they would simply find some other way to kill her. Ether way, she was doomed.

In the autumn stillness, Maggie's shrill, agonized cries could be heard for miles around, and it wasn't long before the air was filled not only with those awful shrieks, but also with the stench of roasting meat as her withered flesh crackled and burned. It took a long time for her to die.

When the grisly deed was done, the villagers raked out her bones from the ashes, ground them to dust, and cast them to the wind to deny her a final resting place. The final insult.

This, they said, was punishment for being a witch.

A witch?

These philistines knew nothing.

Powerless to intervene, Elizabeth had watched from a distance, a scarf covering her lower face to conceal her identity. But still, some of the villagers knew who she was. She saw the recognition in their eyes as they jostled for position among the others overcome with bloodlust, ferocity, and misguided fury.

They didn't understand, these hardline fundamentalists. They were unwavering in their beliefs and unwilling to accept anything that didn't neatly fit in with their narrow world view. Everything they didn't condone was deemed to be the work of the devil, and they then sought to crush it in the name of God. To Elizabeth, it was almost as if they were lashing out against things they didn't understand, as if in some perverse way dispensing punishment for their own ignorance.

Two patches cut from the same quilt, Elizabeth and Maggie had been valued members of the local community not that long ago, their skills and knowledge in high demand. People summoned them to ease their sicknesses or to help the gravely ill purge themselves of their life's misgivings and regrets before passing on. In this guise, they became known as sin eaters and were forced into exile, away from the main flock, as if their very presence was somehow poisonous.

Some of their number branched out into fortune-telling or selling blessings and trinkets to hunters, farmers, and fishermen. True enough, sometimes they were called upon to deliver curses, which they did at their own discretion, always trusting in their morals and refusing to do anything for the lure of riches alone. This was the way it had always been done. Elizabeth didn't need money. True practitioners of the ancient arts rarely did because the natural world had a way of finding balance and taking care of its own. In her mind, that would be misusing her gift. The villagers looked after her, made sure she had enough wood for the fire and food in her belly, and this was all she needed. It was an honor system. She catered to the villagers' needs when called upon, and they catered to hers.

But then, almost overnight, in this new culture of creeping fear, she'd been cast aside. Not just sent to live alone, but ostracized. It had been ten days since she'd last had a visitor. Little Sally didn't bring her eggs from the farm anymore, and Tom the baker didn't send his apprentice with any leftover loaves of bread. For the first time in a long time, her food cupboard was almost bare. It was worrisome. As the specter of hunger arose, her stomach gurgled and she squirmed in her chair, pulling her shawl tighter.

She was used to being alone. She liked her own company, having made peace with herself long ago. But there was a world of difference between being alone and being lonely, and recently the latter had taken hold and sank its cold talons into her. Added to this was the constant anxiety. She could feel change in the air and knew something terrible was coming. Worst of all, she also knew there was nothing she could do about it. Whatever the future held, she was going to have to face it by herself.

CHAPTER THREE

$\mathscr{A}$t the conclusion of their meeting, Christine Turner had given Ben some meal vouchers and a laminated gold-colored resort pass called an R.R. card with the number 327 printed on it, which she said doubled as a key card for his room over in the main block. He couldn't decide what he wanted to do first. It was like being given the keys to the kingdom. Having spent most of the last three years living in the camper van, the temptation was to just chill out and take advantage of the comparative luxury. But he knew he couldn't do that. There was work to do.

As he was passing anyway, he opted to make the impressive-sounding restaurant on the main building dubbed GROUND ZERO, stylized in block capital letters, his first port of call. It was now after eleven, that strange twilight time between breakfast and lunch. It was probably too late to even be adequately covered by that catch-all term "brunch," but he thought he should investigate anyway.

On entering through the huge set of double doors off the reception area, he was confronted with a smiling young woman with a generous spread of freckles and lush, shoulder-length red hair standing behind a reception desk. A chest-mounted badge pinned to her yellow blouse said her name was Beth.

"Good morning, sir," the girl said brightly. "Can I see your R.R. card, please?"

"Good morning," Ben replied, handing it over. The girl took the card, peered at it, and typed something into a machine behind the counter. Then Ben remembered the vouchers and fished them out of his front pocket. "Are these any good?" he asked.

Beth took the vouchers, flicked through them, took one, and handed the rest back to Ben. "Sure, they're good, sir. They're platinum vouchers, which entitle you to pretty much anything you want in the restaurant at no additional charge. The breakfast buffet service is from seven to ten, lunch is midday to two, and dinner is six to eight-thirty."

As she talked, the girl used a hand-held machine to punch a hole in the corner of the voucher, then handed it back to Ben.

"Here. You're good to go. Just bring that with you next time you come. It's valid all day. Tomorrow, use the voucher marked with the corresponding date. I see you have three, so you're covered for the next three days."

"Pretty cool," Ben said. "Thanks for the help. But it seems I've missed breakfast and I'm too early for lunch."

"No worries, sir. The set times are just for the buffet service. You can order a meal any time you want. Well, until we close at ten, anyway. And even after that, you can always call room service and they'll be happy to bring you some snacks. We all get struck by midnight hunger pangs from time to time!"

"That's true," Ben said through a grin of his own. He was already warming to the girl. In the service industry, a smile and a good-natured demeanor go a long way, and she had an abundance of both.

"Just head on over to a table and choose from the all-day menu you'll find there."

"Wonderful. Thanks again," Ben said, pocketing his R.R. Card and vouchers as he entered the restaurant.

It was obviously a cut above your local gastropub. Decked out in warming shades of orange and brown, his feet sank into a thick, plush carpet as he paused to take in his surroundings. To his surprise, there were still several tables of diners dotted around, their relaxed chatter creating a low, welcoming hum.

The moment he located an attractive table next to the window, pulled out a chair and sat down, a young waiter with spiky black hair, making him look like a lost member of Good Charlotte circa 2004, appeared and handed him a faux leather-bound menu emblazoned with the restaurant's name in gold leaf. Ben thanked him, and the young waiter smiled, nodded politely, and walked away.

Just reading the quintessentially British menu made Ben's mouth water. It was simple and uncomplicated, like most high-class establishments, but undeniably impressive. The choice of mains included rod-caught trout and potato wedges, veal steak with seasonal roasted vegetables, Angus beef in red wine sauce and creamed mash, Cumberland sausage and black pudding, and roasted duck with orange and mango. Given that the last meal he'd eaten was tinned spaghetti hoops on toast, it was a tough choice. As he wasn't going to be paying for it, he briefly entertained the thought of ordering two mains, before eventually opting for the Angus beef with a runny-yolk Scotch egg starter. Difficult decision made, he placed the menu on the table in front of him as a signal to the waiter that he was ready to order.

Twenty-five minutes later, he was tucking into one of the finest meals he'd ever eaten. In the absence of any sense-numbing alcohol, the seared meat teased his taste buds before mercilessly beating them into submission. The food was so delicious he had to force himself to save a few morsels of beef for Mr. Trimble, which he wrapped in a paper napkin and stuffed into his pocket when nobody was looking. He wasn't sure what the cat would make of the sauce, but he was certain to appreciate the snack.

After his meal, Ben decided to take a stroll to his designated room in the residential block across the road. It was a fine spring morning, and the sun warmed his face and bare forearms as he walked out of the restaurant and onto the tree-lined thoroughfare bisecting the resort. He crossed the road, entered the building through the open main doors, and was immediately struck by how spacious and well-maintained everything was, not to mention spotlessly clean. There was no reception desk; instead, a phone hung on a wall next to a row of vending machines filled with soft drinks and snacks, which he guessed provided a direct link to the desk in the other building. The entire ground floor had apparently been converted to provide disabled access, with gradients instead of steps, wider doors to accommodate wheelchairs, and even strategically placed grip bars. Nice touch.

There was a bank of three elevators in the lobby. Ben pushed the button and waited, arms folded. Seconds later, the doors of the middle elevator opened with a loud *ping!* and an elderly couple wearing matching white shorts and sky-blue T-shirts bearing the slogan GO FOR IT! spilled out.

"Good morning!" the couple announced in unison.

Ben returned the pleasantry, offered what he hoped was a warm smile, entered the newly vacated lift, and pushed the button for the third floor.

As the doors slid closed, cool air conditioning and piped music flooded the metal box. The whole experience was, by design, calm and relaxing. Given all the greenery, pristine surfaces, and sunny dispositions, it was hard to imagine someone going on a murderous rampage in such tranquil surroundings. But it had happened, and things of that nature apparently happened with alarming frequency. He couldn't wait to do some more research, but he needed his laptop for that, which was safely stored in the camper. First, he wanted to check out his room. Van life was liberating, but taking sponge baths in lukewarm water every other day was no substitute for a hot power shower or a relaxing bath.

Swiping the gold R.R. card over the electronic reader outside the room, Ben stepped back as it deactivated the lock and pushed the door gently open. Stepping foot into a hotel room for the first time always filled him with a sense of excitement tinged with trepidation, almost as if he were an intruder.

He wasn't surprised to find the sparse, modern-looking room immaculate. It was dominated by a huge, queen-sized bed facing an oversized, wall-mounted plasma TV, and a set of patio doors opened onto a balcony overlooking the road and the main building containing the restaurant he'd just left. A kettle and some assorted sachets of tea, instant coffee, sugar, and powdered milk were placed on a side table, and there was a separate shower room. The only thing missing was a mini bar.

Sliding open the patio doors, he stepped out onto the balcony, leaned over the railing, and gazed out at the street below, where he saw the friendly old couple in matching T-shirts he'd just passed in the elevator walking down the street.

Whenever Ben saw an older couple who had probably been together most of their lives, it always set off a chain-reaction of emotions. Firstly, seeing such displays of affection was heart-warming. It reinforced the romantic notion that love could not only exist in such a cold, materialistic world, but flourish. And if love was real, anything was possible. Wasn't it? Even if, by its very nature, it couldn't last forever.

However, that warmth soon gave way to something more akin to cynicism. Were they really that happy? Or were they just putting on a show? Maybe they'd both given up on ever actually finding true happiness and settled on the convenient option instead. And if that were the case, who were they really trying to convince? Onlookers or themselves?

Underpinning everything else was an undeniable sliver of cold jealousy. Ben wanted that. He wanted to love and be loved again. Even if it hurt. Shit, he would take the fake kind if genuine love was beyond him. Sometimes, he wondered if he wanted it, *especially* if it hurt. It was as if something inside him needed the pain. Thrived on it. It made everything else he experienced brighter, more scintillating, and somehow relevant, adding meaning and resonance to an otherwise drab and empty existence.

Ronald and Marjorie Brand had been holidaying at the Regal Retreat since Ronald's retirement in 2006. They booked two weeks every year at the beginning of the holiday season, except in 2014, when Ronald had that persistent prostate problem and was in and out of the hospital most of the year.

The Regal Retreat was open to visitors all year round, but the Brands liked to come in spring. If they came any sooner, the English weather would probably confine them to their room. Not that that would be such a bad thing. There were worse rooms to be confined to. The rooms at the Regal Retreat were more than adequate and boasted practically every modern convenience you can imagine. But knowing how important it was to stay fit and healthy in their advancing years, the Brands liked to stay as active as they could. They enjoyed the facilities: the senior fitness classes, the Pilates, the senior competitions, and the walking tours around the lake.

One of Ronald's proudest moments was winning the Regal Retreat Lawn Bowling Singles Tournament Winner's Cup last year. The winner's trophy, as cheap and tacky as it was, meant the world to him. It was almost symbolic. So much so that he brought it back here with him to offer some incentive and motivation when this year's tournament kicked off in two days. The standard wasn't what you'd call world-class, but everyone wanted to win, and there was nothing like some healthy competition to keep the mind sharp.

If all they wanted to do was watch TV, it wouldn't be worth coming, and they still had the timeshare in Majorca for their sunshine breaks. It wasn't as if they couldn't afford it. When Ronald sold the property-development firm he'd founded in the glorious eighties, he'd pocketed a tidy sum. Plus, he made sure to keep his hand in by becoming a silent partner and picking up the quarterly dividends. This, coupled with his retirement fund and some shrewd financial investments along the way, ensured he and Marjorie were well-looked-after in their old age.

There might even be enough money left over when they popped their clogs to set up their son, Mark, in business. With a bit of luck, by then, he might be mature enough to know what to do with it. Right now, he was on the payroll of the property-development firm, one of the conditions of Ronald's sale, but it was common knowledge Mark would never make senior partner. He was still too precocious and reckless to ever be trusted in a position of seniority.

For the Brands, this annual visit to the Regal Retreat was more of a tradition, and like most old farts, Ronald and Marjorie were sticklers for tradition. Without history, what did any of us have?

An extra three grand a year, that's what.

Ronald had been trying to silence that ultra-conservative, joy-killing voice ever since he'd retired. But you don't get to be this wealthy without being thrifty, and some habits are hard to break.

"Are you ready to go, Ron?" Marjorie's voice cut through his reverie. "What the heck are you doing?"

"Dear Lord, woman. I'm in the bathroom. Do you want diagrams?"

"Of course not. But sometimes, I do worry. Anything could happen to you in there with the door locked. I wouldn't even know about it until it was too late. You might collapse or drop dead. How am I supposed to help you then? You tell me how, hmm? How? I won't be able to even open the door. Do you really want to die in a toilet? Do you?"

Ronald pulled the chain and sighed. He hadn't even done his business. Not properly. He'd squeezed out a turd the size of a peanut, if that counted. Even pooping loses its charm when you get old. It's either all or nothing. You get peanuts, or you get a river of molten lava. He just liked sitting on the throne for a few minutes at periodic intervals. It gave him time to think. The bathroom was his quiet place, usually, and he'd been getting increasingly philosophical in his old age. It wasn't such a bad thing. After a lifetime of doing stuff, you should at least get some time at the end to dwell on it.

Standing upright, he pulled up his shorts and washed his hands in the tiny basin, catching sight of his reflection in the mirror as he did so. He quite liked his new GO FOR IT! T-shirt. It suited him. Bizarrely, the same sky-blue color also suited Marjorie.

Both closer to seventy than sixty, they had been married almost half a century. That was a long time. He wasn't exactly sure when they'd started dressing alike. It was neither planned nor discussed. It was something they just sort of fell into. They had similar tastes. Isn't that one of the things that keeps couples together after those lusty initial few years have passed? Similar tastes, mutual interests, and shared values? They were the cornerstones lasting relationships were built on.

Obviously, it hadn't all been smooth sailing. How did the song go? Life is a rollercoaster? That much was true. And every marriage has its share of ups and downs. You couldn't properly appreciate the highs, or even recognize them, without experiencing the accompanying lows. They put things into perspective. Like Marjorie's affair with that young gardener they'd employed when they'd lived in Shirebrook back in the 90s, for instance.

That certainly put things in perspective.

Ronald had always known about the trysts. A doting partner always knows on some level, whether they choose to confront it or not. You can just sense it, some barely perceptible change in the dynamics of your relationship. The furtive glances, the evasiveness, and the over-compensating in certain departments. They were all tell-tale signs, and it didn't take very long for the private detective agency he hired to confirm his suspicions. That was money well spent.

He'd never talked to Marjorie about her affair. There was no point. By the time he found out about it, according to the detective agency, it had all but ended. All he had to do was ensure it stayed that way.

He wasn't completely blameless. He'd been neglecting Marjorie for years, working long hours and staying late at the office. There are only so many hours in a day, and nobody can be everywhere at the same time. Sacrifices have to be made.

Every woman has needs. And if you don't cater to those needs, she'll find someone who will. It made him question whether you should give a relationship everything and put every ounce of your heart and soul into it, or if you'd be better served to always hold something back, giving the impression that you could always do better, and maybe someday you will? It's human nature to want more than you have, to keep striving. It shows progress and upward momentum. The moment you think you have everything and extracted all you can from any given situation is the moment you start taking it for granted. And from there, you were only ever one step away from losing everything.

The real irony was that if he'd spent more time with her, he wouldn't have been able to afford the Shirebrook spread, and they wouldn't have needed a gardener. Life was funny like that. It teaches you important lessons, and then in the next breath lets you know in no uncertain terms that the universe was openly mocking you.

Man plans, and God laughs.

Indeed.

Getting older didn't help. His libido started waning long before Marjorie's did. This was pre-Viagra, when becoming impotent was a very real danger for stressed-out men nearing retirement age. The stress only really affected those who worked hard to build a life for themselves and their families. The ones that didn't invest as much time in their jobs never seemed to be afflicted with such concerns. Ironically, they were usually the ones who kept all their own hair, too. Strange to think that these days, a quick consultation with his GP would have changed everything.

Finding out that your wife was having an affair is difficult to process initially. You turn bitter and begin to question everything. During petty squabbles, Ronald lost count of all the times he almost played his trump card, the one thing guaranteed to swing any argument or disagreement firmly in his favor.

But he always resisted, knowing that if he went there, everything would change. Once that bomb was detonated, the damage it would do could never be undone. There was no putting that genie back in the bottle. It would certainly mean the end of his marriage, and what was he to do then? Live out his final years alone? If that happened, he would be the one suffering every day. The loneliness would be crushing. Why should he be the one punished? He didn't even have any close friends, another consequence of working 14-hour days most of his adult life.

So, he put up with it, buried his emotions, and time marched on. Before he knew it, years had passed. It would be ridiculous to even bring it up now after sitting on the knowledge for so long and saying nothing about it.

Hey, let's talk about that affair you had twenty-five years ago!

Ronald made his peace with it. In fact, if he was brutally honest with himself, in the deepest, darkest corner of his mind, the thought of Marjorie making love with some toned, muscular young buck even turned him on a little. In that respect, it had actually done their marriage some good. Who needed Viagra?

It was the dreams he couldn't stand. The dreams that brought everything flooding back night after night.

"Ronald? Have you fallen down the pipe?" Marjorie's voice came drifting through the door again. She sounded impatient.

"No, love. Just coming!"

Putting on his best "I'm okay!" face, Ronald unlocked the bathroom door and stepped out to find Marjorie, resplendent in her sky-blue GO FOR IT! T-shirt and white shorts, waiting for him with her arms folded. You would think they were running a marathon rather than going to their pre-booked Pilates class.

The couple stepped into the corridor, letting the door close softly behind them, and then got the lift to the ground floor, where they saw a nondescript guy of average height and slightly stocky build wearing a black polo shirt waiting. He appeared to be alone, which made him stand out from the other guests. While trim and reasonably good-looking, he was unshaven and slightly scruffy. Most notable of all was the brooding sullenness that seemed to emanate from him, as if he was carrying the weight of the world on his shoulders.

He's probably a worker or some kind of contractor, Ronald thought to himself as he mirrored Marjorie's reaction and gave the stranger a friendly greeting.

He could only hope the guy wasn't a fucking gardener.

Opening the door to the shower room, Ben let his eyes roam over the sparkling chrome fittings, a stack of fresh, crisp white towels, and a matching dressing gown, all monogrammed with the distinctive R.R. logo, until they settled on the small selection of expensive-looking lotions, shampoos, and soaps sitting on a glass shelf beneath a polished mirror. There was even a mini-shaving kit. That was the clincher. He decided on the spot that a hot shower and a close shave would work wonders.

Without another thought, he stripped off and turned the tap until scalding hot water cascaded out of the shower head. In truth, it was probably a little too hot. Within seconds his skin was reddened and tender. But Ben welcomed the slight discomfort and closed his eyes as the grime was cleansed from his body. He couldn't deny he needed this, and he was sure the people he planned to interact with during his stay at Regal Retreat wouldn't disagree. Deodorant can only take you so far.

Dripping wet, Ben wrapped one of the soft, oversized bath towels around his midriff and cracked open the mini-shaving kit. After wiping the condensation off the mirror, he studied his reflection as he lathered his lower face. He felt much better after the shower but still looked tired. His skin was pallid, and crow's feet pulled at the skin around his eyes. He had to get with the program and project a good image.

All in all, on first impressions, the Regal Retreat seemed like a classy establishment, and he felt he'd totally lucked out in landing this gig. It wasn't just the cash injection and the opportunity to cultivate some content for his website he welcomed; it was also the opportunity to recharge his batteries. For him, van life was a choice rather than a necessity. But after several weeks cooped up with only his books and Mr. Trimble for company, he could do with a break. He was already looking at this venture as a kind of working holiday. The sooner he could get back to his laptop and start doing some research, the better. He just needed a little lie down first.

CHAPTER FOUR

*T*here was a fire.

Acrid smoke assaulted Ben's nostrils, and the air around him was filled with the sound of angry crackling and the snarl of hungry flames as they devoured everything in their path. Fear, panic, and an awful sense of helplessness began to consume him as he suddenly came to his senses.

Where were Louise and Amy?

Louise should be in bed with him, and little Amy should be in the crib in the corner of the bedroom.

One—or both—of them should be screaming.

Why weren't they screaming?

Expelling lungfuls of hot, sour-tasting smoke, he tried yelling their names, but all that came out were coughs and splutters.

His airways burned, and he couldn't see. Couldn't even open his eyes. They seemed welded shut.

Forcing his burning eyelids open a fraction, he frantically looked around the room. But between the smoke and the darkness, he could see nothing except white and orange flashes.

Flames.

Struggling to suppress the growing terror, he reached out to feel around.

Then came the pain.

The white, searing waves of agony shot up his arm as flames licked his flesh.

He knew on some level that this couldn't be happening. Not again. It had to be a nightmare.

More like a flashback.

It was less a dream and more being transported back in time to the night three years earlier when he had awoken to find the house aflame around him.

Then, as now, his own safety and well-being faded into insignificance. All he cared about were Louise and Amy. They had to be okay because they kept him grounded and gave his life meaning. They were a constant, steadying thread in all the chaos. Without them, he was nothing. Nothing at all.

Strange how when you love someone so completely, it clouds your judgment.

Choking, coughing, spluttering, and crying out in pain and confusion, Ben's eyes suddenly snapped open.

Where the fuck was he?

He wasn't in the van.

He was lying on a luxurious, soft bed clutching his scarred right hand, a scream caught in his throat where it morphed into a sickly gurgle.

Was he still sleeping?

Could this be some kind of dream within a dream?

As he looked around at the wall-mounted TV, the still-open balcony door, and the dressing gown he was wearing embroidered with the letters R.R., he remembered.

The Regal Retreat.

He was on a job. Or, more accurately, he was *supposed* to be on a job.

He hadn't been planning on falling asleep. But the combination of fatigue and the relaxed surroundings had conspired to throw him off the edge of reality into the abyss of sleep. The fire had just been a dream. A horrifically vivid dream. It must have been brought on by the decadent brunch he'd had. His system was more used to convenience food.

Rubbing his eyes, Ben sat up in the bed and found his torso covered in a thin film of sweat. He hoped he wasn't coming down with something. All he needed right now was to be laid low with a cold or a virus. He checked his phone and noted that he'd been asleep for less than an hour. Not as bad as it could have been.

This wasn't the first time he'd dreamed about that night. For a while, he relived it whenever he closed his eyes. Even when he was awake, The Event, as he came to know it, was never far from his thoughts. It was always there, like an immovable boulder in a stream, making all his other thoughts, all the mundane day-to-day stuff, go around or over it. Ordinarily, he did a pretty good job of papering over the cracks. But that was exactly what he was doing, papering over the cracks. They say time is a great healer, but no amount of time or therapy could ever put him back together again. Not completely.

As if he needed his memory jogged. He was reminded of it every time he looked at his scorched and disfigured right hand. What he didn't need was to experience it again in excruciating detail.

Thank you, dream.

It felt unnatural and somehow wrong to put dirty clothes on after a shower, almost like he was undoing all his good work, but since he hadn't taken a change of clothes with him to the meeting with Christine, the black polo shirt and faded denim jeans represented the only option he had. At least until he could pick up some fresh clothes from the camper and arrange for his laundry to be taken care of, which shouldn't be too much of a problem in a place like this.

For now, the dirty clothes would have to suffice.

Over the years, Ronald had noticed a pattern in his dreams. Strangely, they came more frequently and were much more intense whenever he and Marjorie were staying at the Regal. He knew it couldn't be anything to do with the place itself. How could it? Your surroundings might influence your dreams a little, but to what extent? Everyone knew that dreams were linked to the subconscious mind. In daily life, you can actively push away the things you didn't want to think about. Force them to one side and focus on something else, or even bury them beneath a pile of rubble. But at night, you're at the mercy of your own imagination.

The dream was always the same, and it played out like a movie. First, he saw himself kissing Marjorie goodbye in the morning and heading off to work. They were both much younger. Next, he saw her on the phone with someone. There were only landlines in those days. Then he saw her opening the door to the newly employed gardener, his toned, tanned body filling the door frame and his long, blond hair shining in the summer sun. He ran his fingers through it and grinned like he'd just stepped out of a Levi's commercial.

Next, in his mind's eye, Ronald would see them fucking, but the positions were different. Sometimes the gardener was on top, other times Marjorie was on top, her face contorted in ecstasy and eyes half-closed as he pawed at her breasts and she took him inside her. But it was usually doggy style, the gardener thrusting away feverishly behind his wife on the marital bed. The grin was back, pulled wider over his brilliant white teeth whenever he delivered a firm slap to Marjorie's bum cheek.

That was only the beginning. At this point, all Ronald wanted was to extricate himself from the dream in order to spare himself the agony of what was to follow. But he never did. He was powerless to stop the movie from playing out to its bloody conclusion. And some tiny, masochistic part of him wanted to see it.

He saw himself at a coffee shop meeting the guy from the detective agency he'd hired and being handed a phone number scrawled on a piece of paper. Then there was another man. This one faceless. Threatening and intimidating.

Dangerous.

Ronald gave the stranger an envelope full of cash, and they parted company. The next time they met, the man handed Roger a different envelope, this one slim and brown. Heart thudding in his chest, Ronald opened it. He didn't want to see what was inside, even though he already knew.

But he wasn't in control anymore. He was at the mercy of some strange cosmic force much bigger than him, bigger than everything. All he could do was watch and try to grasp at branches and twigs as he was swept away on the current.

Hands trembling, he took the envelope and opened it.

The envelope contained photographs. This was the age before the digital revolution, and these photographs weren't the kind that needed to be developed, either. That would leave a trail. Evidence. Witnesses. These were Polaroids. One shot and done.

The pictures showed a dead body lying face-up in a pool of blood on some debris-littered ground somewhere. It was a young man, fit-looking, with tanned skin and long, blond hair now matted with blood. His throat was slit and gaped open in what could almost be a sick, contorted grin some way below his mouth, revealing to the world its grisly inner workings.

The gardener.

That was usually when Ronald woke up in a cold sweat. It signified both the end and the beginning of the nightmare because he would be on edge all day after one of those dreams, turning things over in his mind and trying to separate the fiction from the reality.

He tried to behave normally but knew Marjorie suspected something. She probably wouldn't link him with the disappearance of her precious lover boy, but it would get her thinking—and that was never a good thing. She was very astute and could easily jump to conclusions. She might add two and two and get five, but even that was too close to the truth.

He could find it within himself to forgive her infidelity. But not that slimy, disrespectful prick. Of all the gardeners and handymen in England, Ronald had chosen him. Given him work, money, and a reason to get out of bed in the morning. And he repaid him by fucking his wife?

No, that kind of behavior just would not do, and punishment was the only recourse.

There were many perks to being wealthy, just one being able to hire people to solve your problems so you didn't need to get your hands dirty. Ronald had hired the gardener to take care of the overgrown rose bushes and tulips, and then he had hired someone else to take care of the gardener when he became a problem. Just another example of life's sweet irony.

Despite being haunted by the dreams, Ronald wasn't sorry about what he'd done. There was no guilt. He would make the same decision again in an instant. Being young, dumb, and full of cum was no excuse. The only regret he had was using that particular person to solve the gardener problem.

He should've known it wouldn't be that easy.

Every couple of years since, the man he'd hired problem resurfaced and demanded more money, saying he would go to the police if Ronald didn't comply. Blackmail, extortion, whatever you wanted to call it.

Ronald wasn't sure if he believed the threats. If the guy went to the police, he would only be implicating himself. But he could do it anonymously or arrange some kind of plea bargain and get away with a lighter sentence. He was only gambling with his time, and at his age, he had time to burn. The amount of money he was fleecing from Ronald justified the risk. At the opposite end of the scale, however, Ronald was too old to take chances, and he had no desire to live out his last years in prison. He was thankful Marjorie wasn't too involved in their finances. If she saw the missing money, she would demand answers.

He'd tried numerous ways to fix the problem. He'd moved house and changed his phone number several times. But somehow the murdering bastard always managed to find him. That was what he did. Ronald wasn't a difficult man to track down, and in the hitman's line of work, you attain a certain skill set.

Ronald even considered hiring another hitman to kill the hitman, fully aware that he would not only be compounding the problem but would also be taking twice the risk. He'd been lucky to pull it off the first time. Anyway, he didn't even know the first guy's name. He'd been very careful about giving up any personal information. It wasn't necessary, he'd said. Ronald, meanwhile, had been an open book.

Fucking stupid.

The bottom line was that Ronald lived in perpetual fear of his crime being exposed. If that happened, he would lose everything: his reputation, his wife, his assets, his money.

But he wouldn't go down without a fight, even knowing that the legal fees would consume his life savings. What's done is done, and he couldn't turn back the clock. All he could do was make his peace and live with the decisions he'd made, even if it meant paying until the money ran out or he found some other way of dealing with it.

Upon opening the door of the camper van, Ben was greeted with a chorus of accusatory meows and some decidedly dirty looks as Mr. Trimble leaped up from his preferred resting place on the bench and came to investigate the disturbance.

"Hey, dude, did you miss me? Or are you just annoyed because lunch is late?"

Ben already knew the answer to that question. They say that while dogs have owners, cats have staff, and it was difficult to argue the point. Then he remembered something and put his hand in his pocket to see if the steak he'd saved from his posh meal at Ground Zero was still there. It was, though by now the juices had seeped through the napkin and it was beginning to stink. Just how Mr. Trimble liked it.

Ben unwrapped the meat and fed it to Mr. Trimble from his hand. Treat polished off, the cat sniffed around for second helpings, and when none were forthcoming, he pointed his white-tipped tail straight up in the air and went prancing around the tiny living space in a dramatic show of apparent distaste.

Ben used the roller to manually raise the van's roof, which allowed him to stand to his full height and stretch when he needed—standard practice whenever he parked up anywhere for an extended period—and plonked down on the L-shaped bench that ran one length of the van. Then he picked up the clockwork radio from the nearest shelf, which, apart from a framed photo of Louise and Amy, was by far his most treasured possession. Quite often, Ben found himself with only his radio, his thoughts, and Mr. Trimble for company as the wind and rain buffeted the van in some secluded outpost or other. At first, the idea of being alone with his thoughts terrified him, but he'd made his peace as best he could. As long as he didn't allow it to drift too far into the shadows, he got by.

The clockwork radio was permanently tuned into a digital classic rock station because the background noise, which was usually something familiar, helped him find his writing groove. When he flicked the switch and turned it on, it immediately started belting out an old AC/DC classic from the Bon Scott era. The combination of razor-sharp guitar licks and shameless tongue-in-cheek lyrics instantly transported him right back to his teenage years. Bon Scott had shuffled off this mortal coil before Ben was even born, but he left behind a legacy that would never die.

Humming along softly, Ben fired up his laptop. Noticing the battery was hovering slightly below thirty percent, he plugged the cable into the power cell, which, when not attached to an external supply, was topped off by solar panels fixed to the roof. The cell didn't completely fulfill his requirements, and it sometimes felt like he was locked in a perennial battle with a dwindling electricity supply. Today, it would only give him a couple of hours of working time, but it would be enough to update his socials and make a start on his research. Rooting through his pockets, he found the R.R. card and flipped it over. Conveniently, on the reverse side was printed a list of "useful" phone numbers and the resort's Wi-Fi code. Minutes later, Ben was in business.

People brainwashed by reality TV shows tended to think that being a paranormal investigator was all about dramatic confrontations with demonic entities and being chased through abandoned lunatic asylums by angry ghosts. The truth was rarely that exciting. Ben spent the bulk of his time researching, information-gathering, and interviewing witnesses and experts in various fields. Most of what happened in the present had some kind of connection with the past, and he knew from experience that if he could find and follow the signposts, they often led to the source of the problem. Whatever that problem was. Luckily, over fifteen years as a journalist in London in a previous life had taught him the necessary skills. Obviously, it wasn't an actual previous life. The jury was still out on whether or not reincarnation was real, and despite his occupation, Ben was a natural skeptic. But the two spheres of being were so different, it felt like an entirely different existence. Like many others, he'd spent most of his time in the Big Smoke chasing money and dreams, which always dangled frustratingly just out of his reach.

In a way, it was almost a relief when the print industry collapsed in on itself and the vast majority of traditional journalists lost their jobs in the face of declining readerships and diminishing returns. Even though the publishing executives still went to meetings by private helicopter and took long business lunches at luxurious five-star establishments much like the Regal, they opted to cut costs by streamlining editorial teams and increasing workloads. It wasn't a sustainable business model. The quality of the product suffered, leading to further decreases in circulation, which only compounded the problem.

The rock music magazine Ben worked on lost readers month-after-month for years and ended its life in such a steep decline that it was forced to shut its doors entirely. After that, he transitioned to freelancing for a succession of websites, but they paid less, and no matter how hard he worked, he could barely keep his head above water. He certainly couldn't afford to continue living in Zone 1. That left little option than to sell up and move to a leafy suburb in Hampshire, taking Amy and Louise with him.

There they enjoyed an idyllic existence for a couple of years. Ben continued freelancing, dipping his toes into the media-consulting business when opportunities arose. Then came The Event, and his life was torn apart. There were two distinct states of being: before the fire and after. Before, he'd been a family man, a dedicated worker, playing the game and getting by. After, he became a truth-seeker, an adventurer, and a disillusioned loose cannon with a chip on his shoulder and a penchant for craft ale.

He wanted answers, and he would stop at nothing to get them.

He'd lost everything he ever valued and sold almost everything he had left so he could buy the camper van and reset his life.

And here he was. Three years into his new, stripped-down existence, and still trying to get used to it. Still trying to make his way. Still trying to start again. Sometimes, it felt as if everything before The Event had happened to somebody else, and, in a sense, it had. He was a different person then.

The good thing about van life was the ability to go almost anywhere at a moment's notice. There was nothing quite like getting out in the field, immersing yourself in the environment, and interacting with people in pursuit of a story. But the internet was such a vast resource, it provided the perfect starting point. Besides, as per Christine's instructions, he was trying to keep a low profile around the resort. At least for now.

Surprisingly, despite all the stories and alleged negative press Christine had mentioned, when he Googled the Regal Retreat, the first page of results were almost exclusively booking agents and review sites. The reviews were universally positive. He couldn't find a single disgruntled customer, which was impressive. In truth, it was a little too impressive, almost as if the resort had paid a PR company to tamper with the SEO algorithms in order to bury specific results and promote others. Which, when Ben thought about it, was not just possible, but very likely.

All the juicy stuff was to be found after that heavily commercialized first page of results, and the deeper he dug, the more alarming stories he found. As expected, many of them were focused on the Fred Derry killings. Four people, including a baby, butchered senselessly, followed by a suicide in police custody, had all the elements the tabloids loved, right down to the neat ending. There were countless articles examining various aspects of the case, but another story dominated the search results.

Michael Davenport himself, the founder and owner of R.R. no less, was found dead at the on-site villa where he was staying in October 1994. He was alone when he died, and there were no suspicious circumstances. By all accounts, his heart just stopped. He was eighty-nine, so there shouldn't be much of a mystery attached. Yet there was. He was considered to be in exceedingly good health and had passed a stringent medical exam just the week before.

Anything or nothing could have brought on the heart attack, Ben mused. Old age is the time when your body begins to fail and things just stop working. But it was odd that Davenport had died at the resort.

In a state of semi-retirement, he spent most of his time looking after his other business interests in London, which included a casino in Mayfair and a chain of upscale hotels. That fateful visit to the Regal had been his first of the year, and his last ever.

Being a kind of local celebrity, not to mention an esteemed member of the aristocracy, meant that more than one newspaper helpfully carried a detailed obituary. They all stated the same facts. Michael Davenport was born to a wealthy family in 1905. Traditionally, the Davenports had been farmers and landowners before moving into property development. They made much of their fortune during the Industrial Revolution, when they traded in factory units and warehouses in the southeast of England. They also had a financial interest in a very profitable, privately owned coal mine in south Wales and a sideline in workhouses, where the young and poor were callously exploited. In 1937, Michael Davenport had pooled the family's resources and realized a "long-standing dream" of opening an exclusive resort, which became the Regal. He was married three times, most recently to Catherine, an American antiques dealer, who had died in 1981 after a protracted battle with cancer. Upon his death, Michael Davenport's fortune and all his assets were transferred to his closest surviving relative, his son Glenn.

There was something there. Ben could sense it. Something in that potted history could go some way to explaining the sequence of macabre events at R.R. Perhaps some piece of the puzzle had been gently shoe-horned into place to make a pretty picture, even though it didn't quite fit.

But what could it be? On the face of it, Michael Davenport didn't seem like a particularly nice guy. But that wasn't a crime. Most successful people had a ruthless streak. It was one of the things that made them so successful, often at the expense of others.

Elsewhere in the Google results, there was a litany of murders, suicides, and accidents. Even a cursory glance confirmed that the resort was a hive of misery, tragedy, and despair. There was so much to get through that it seemed only logical to start at the beginning and work chronologically. Through careful referencing and cross-referencing sources, Ben would be able to piece together a timeline of events that would hopefully edge him closer toward finding out what the fuck was going on here.

As far as he could tell, the drama began even before the place opened for business when one construction worker died and another was paralyzed when a wall collapsed on them. Just a few months later, a foreman was found hanging from a beam at the property. The verdict was suicide, though there were rumors that he'd been the victim of some kind of uprising amongst his workforce, who killed him and staged the suicide. One thing was clear from the outset; there was no shortage of intrigue at the Regal Retreat.

Just a few months after it officially opened, a lady by the name of Bethany Walters slit her wrists in a bathtub, and the year after that, a ten-year-old boy drowned in a boating accident on the lake. That incident drew severe criticism amid safety concerns, and a public inquest was conducted. The inquest found no one individual accountable but recommended a new set of safety measures and insisted they be enforced.

In 1940, at the beginning of the Blitz, when the cities of England were decimated by German bombs, a stray incendiary device landed on the main building and virtually demolished it. Amazingly, there were only six casualties, of which two were fatalities, but nobody could work out just how the Nazi bomber responsible had diverted so far from its flight path. Its intended target was probably London, or perhaps the docks of England's south coast, both sites over two hundred miles away. The bomber should have been nowhere near East Anglia, the general consensus being that the crew simply got lost and ejected their load at random to lighten the load.

The damage from the blast, combined with the widely implemented austerity drive, put an end to business until the property was re-opened after the war in 1946. However, it would be another three years before it was open to the public. In those grim post-war times, the severely damaged cluster of buildings was used for an entirely different purpose: they'd been converted into a low-key hospital for servicemen and women wounded during the war. Hundreds of thousands came home injured, and most were simply not ready to re-enter society. Some were blinded by shrapnel or deafened by bomb blasts; others had limbs blown off or other disabilities. They needed not only treatment, but care and time to adjust. To help in this regard, they were often kept segregated with their "own kind." Because of its remote, serene location, the Regal Retreat was utilized as a facility to treat the mentally ill, those who'd come back with severe psychological problems. Most were suffering from a condition that would now be diagnosed as Post-Traumatic Stress Disorder. Back then, it was simply called "shell shock."

During the 1940s, treatment for the mentally ill was still in its infancy. While now seen as radical, barbaric, and counterproductive, the lobotomy, when the connections to and from the prefrontal cortex of the brain were severed, was considered the peak of scientific innovation. One of the many downsides was that following the operation, the patient's intellectual or emotional capacities were often compromised. They became unresponsive or slumped into a permanent state of inertia, sometimes regressing to a borderline catatonic state. Even that wasn't the worst of it. A smaller percentage retained their faculties but lost their self-awareness and self-control, along with their inhibitions. Many of these patients became violent, which is why the events of February 4th, 1948, shouldn't have come as much of a surprise to anyone.

Lieutenant Archie Smith of the 1st Battalion, Royal Fusiliers, had been recuperating at the Regal Retreat for nearly eleven months after a short stint at a POW camp in Danzig. It's unclear what happened to him while he was incarcerated, but an article in *The Times* newspaper said that upon being freed by allied forces, he was "in an exceedingly fragile physical and mental state, prone to sudden rages and loss of temper."

In all likelihood, the lobotomy was intended to correct this. However, rather than pacify him, the operation seemed to tip Archie Smith over the edge. First, he smothered his roommate to death with a pillow; then, he took one of the resident doctors and a young nurse hostage. In the sensationalist style of the day, the article focused on how he had tortured and dismembered the doctor with his own medical instruments before raping the nurse and eventually being shot dead by military police.

It was a testament to the severity of the crimes that the newspaper went into such salacious detail. Too often, criminal acts committed by current or ex-service personnel were painted over or sometimes completely swept under the carpet. They had to present a united front, and the establishment didn't want to be held responsible for creating monsters. Also, they knew that such stories might dissuade people from joining the war effort in the future, and it wasn't good for morale. Looked at more than seventy years after the event, the Archie Smith case highlighted glaring inadequacies in a system that trained men to be robotic, emotionless killing machines, then expected them to seamlessly conform into productive, law-abiding members of society when their purpose had been fulfilled. Such a transition was rarely smooth. The human mind was a brittle thing and could only take so much before it shattered.

The Times article even recorded Archie Smith's last words, verbatim, which he apparently yelled from the rooftop where he made his last stand moments before being shot dead. "It was her. She made me do it. She won't let me rest. She haunts my dreams. I see her everywhere, though I know it can't really be her. She can't be real. I did things of which I am ashamed, but she was just a young servant girl. Who cares about her? It was war, I tell you. War! We *all* did things of which we are ashamed. Isn't all fair in war?"

At first, it was assumed he'd been talking about the nurse he'd abducted. But when questioned, the young nurse maintained that she'd had no dealings with Smith prior to the incident. For most of his stay, she'd been stationed on a completely different wing and hadn't even given him so much as a bed bath. A cursory investigation revealed no links between the two whatsoever. It was never determined which "young servant girl" Smith had actually been referring to. Or if it was, it was never disclosed to the public. In keeping with the prevailing attitude of the day, which hadn't changed much over the years, following the tragedy, the authorities and the facility staff closed ranks and the incident soon became part of Regal Retreat folklore.

As Ben was slowly learning, there was a lot of it.

CHAPTER FIVE

arjorie Brand was feeling apprehensive. Well, it was more a creeping sense of unease, really. She couldn't put her finger on why she felt that way, but she hadn't been "right" all day. It started with Ronald's thirty-minute toilet break. She didn't know what he did in there, but she knew it was more than the usual toilet activities. Had to be. And he did it three or four times a day. Not that she was keeping track. Except she was. Kind of.

Over the years, the time he spent in the bathroom had gradually increased. Nobody pooped for that long. Did they? He didn't even take a book or a newspaper with him, so she knew he wasn't reading. Did he just sit there on the throne the entire time, staring into space with his trousers around his ankles?

It just wasn't normal. If she didn't know better, she might think he was trying to hide from something.

And it wasn't just the extended toilet breaks. Ronald was keeping something from her. It was written all over his face. You don't stay married to someone for half a century and not know when something was wrong. When Ronald returned from one of his increasingly frequent and lengthy toilet breaks, he was a different person. Since he'd taken "a step back" from the business, he'd been generally more easygoing and less stressed. Nothing really got him excited except watching England play rugby. But immediately following one of his marathon bathroom sessions, he became sullen and moody. Several times, his eyes had been red and his cheeks blotchy as though he'd been crying in there. Worse than that, he tried to disguise his foul mood with fake smiles and forced humor. A wafer-thin, saccharine-sweet, and obviously insincere veneer. Ronald probably thought he was doing her a favor by not being open about whatever was on his mind, but the reality was she felt excluded and disrespected.

A few times, she'd asked him point-blank what the problem was. Whatever the issue, she could take it. She was always more resilient than Ronald gave her credit for. She wasn't this delicate little bird that had to be kept in a cage. Health scares were always a cause for concern later in life, and if something was bothering him on that front, she wanted to know about it so they could face it together. He sometimes seemed to forget that his future was inexorably linked to hers.

But in response, he would just flash one of those plastic smiles, avoiding eye contact as he did so, and change the subject. "What's on telly, love?"

A typical male response. Bury your head in the sand and hope everything works out.

Once or twice, she'd asked herself whether he knew about Hugo.

It couldn't be possible, could it? They'd been so careful, and it was over almost as quickly as it started. It really was no more than a summer fling and barely qualified as an affair. It was just physical.

Surely, if Ronald knew, he would want to talk about it. Knowing him, he would want to know every last detail. Pull it apart and analyze it. He wasn't the type to keep such a thing to himself. He would use the knowledge like a weapon, taking it out every now and again to sharpen it and jab her with the pointy end. Perhaps using it as leverage to get what he wanted. He'd always been a master of manipulation.

But no. There was nothing. Not even so much as a hint. And that made her question whether there really was anything wrong with Ronald or if she was just being paranoid.

She allowed her eyes to roam around the room. They were nice here at the Regal. Plush. She especially liked the robes. Her eyes settled on a little trophy on the bedside table. Ronald's Regal Retreat Lawn Bowling Singles Tournament Winner's Cup. As trivial and meaningless as that thing was, it seemed to hold an almost symbolic importance to her husband. Marjorie thought perhaps it was the only material prize he had ever won, apart from her of course. It had come late in life, and therefore took on exaggerated importance. He spent hours polishing it, and sometimes he just stared at it with a faint smile on his face.

If he knew about the fling, it wouldn't make any difference to Ronald that it was long over. That Hugo had dropped her like a hot coal, stopped replying to her clandestine messages, and simply disappeared off the face of the earth. Perhaps that's just how things were done these days. There was practically a whole generation between them. She'd read something in a woman's magazine about the modern trend of simply disappearing from people's lives instead of talking things through. Was it called ghosting? What a terrible habit. So cold and impersonal. Perhaps Hugo had been an early proponent.

She'd been disappointed with how it ended, but she'd never expected, nor wanted, anything more than sex and maybe, if she was brutally honest, some attention. With their son Mark off to university and Ronald spending every waking moment at work or with clients, she was alone a lot. That was no excuse for what she'd done, of course. She knew it was wrong, and if she ever had to, she would own up to it. But until then, she saw no need to rock the boat.

The whole thing was difficult to process. It wasn't like she planned to have an affair. It wasn't in her character. It just happened. Looking back, she thought she just might've wanted one last fling. She wanted to feel beautiful again. Didn't everyone make bad decisions from time to time? Well, that was hers.

Perhaps these night terrors she endured were a consequence of her guilty conscience. Some kind of coping mechanism. With no real friends, nor anyone she could confide in, Marjorie was full of brooding, broiling emotions for which she had no outlet. Instead, they festered within her subconscious mind like rotting teeth. These awful dreams might be the only way the guilt could manifest itself. She grew to accept them as a kind of punishment and could only hope they were just figments of her imagination.

Unbeknownst to her, Marjorie's nightmare was a lot like her husband's. She'd had one just the night before, the very night they arrived at R.R., so it was still fresh in her memory. The most remarkable thing about it was that it was so lucid and well-defined. The colors were sharp and vivid, the sensations and emotions vivacious and all-consuming. It was more like playing a part in a movie than dreaming, the experience filled with significance and layers of hidden meaning. She could only hope the awful events it depicted were purely metaphorical and not rooted in reality.

She couldn't pinpoint exactly how long ago they'd started. It seemed as if the dream had always been part of her. Strangely, she only ever had it when she and Ronald were staying at the Regal. She could never understand why that was. Maybe the change in surroundings or the improved air quality made her inner self more receptive. Sometimes, snatches or fragmented scenes turned up in other dreams like echoes, but she only had the full, immersive experience here.

At first, she'd been confused and frightened, and even questioned her sanity.

What was happening to her? Was it possible for someone to be driven insane by guilt?

But these days, she looked forward to the dreams with a kind of perverse apprehension, as they were her only link to the past. To Hugo.

The dream usually began with him knocking at the door one afternoon to ask for a glass of water. She invited him in, they talked for a while, and the next thing she knew they were kissing and his hands were all over her. It was so clichéd, like something out of a tacky romance novel or a low-budget porno film.

Other times, the dream skipped the introduction and dropped her right at the point where they were about to have sex for the first time, with her on the living room floor ready to accept him into her. It was like an assault on the senses. She could smell Hugo's sweat, feel his skin on hers, and even the touch of his rough, calloused hands. Sometimes, she saw his sharp blue eyes boring into hers and felt him part her legs to penetrate her. That was the highlight, but in her haste to be filled, her feverish mind sometimes skipped that part.

The rest of the dream was always the same.

First, she saw Ronald give a thick envelope to a shadowy stranger. Later, when she tried to recall his face, she found she couldn't. It was just a featureless mass. While most of the other details remained fresh in her mind, that aspect was the first to melt away. She had an elevated view of the proceedings, as if she were watching a television drama play out from a position on the ceiling, and though she couldn't quite see what the envelope contained, she knew it was full of money. Sometimes in dreams, you just know things. She also knew what the money was for.

By this point, the creeping unease was growing, chilling her bones and forming a tight knot in her stomach. She knew what was coming but remained powerless to prevent it, the sense of helplessness debilitating.

Despite her best efforts to avoid it, events skipped to another scene where she saw the same shadowy stranger with the envelope approach Hugo from behind. Without so much as a word, he cupped a hand over her lover's mouth and drew a thick silver blade across his throat. Hugo's brilliant blue eyes widened in horror, and he tried to escape the clutches of the stranger as the lifeblood ran out of him and drenched his clothes, painting them crimson. After what seemed like an age, the struggles grew weaker. Then, with a cough and a pained grimace, Hugo sank to the ground as the stranger stood over him admiring his work, bloody knife in hand. As Marjorie watched him die, she couldn't help wondering what was in Hugo's mind. Was he, by any chance, thinking of her the moment he slipped away? Were his last thoughts occupied by someone else, someone more special to him than she was? Or was his mind full of so many different women that no one person was deemed important enough to rise above the others? That would be a tragedy in itself, though he probably wouldn't see it that way.

From the beginning of their relationship, if you could call it that, a part of her was fearful that Hugo was some kind of silver-tongued Lothario who just wanted to bed her, and when he had his way, he would be gone with barely a backward glance. He was charming, affable, and ruggedly handsome, the kind of man most women, especially bored, middle-aged housewives, would fall over themselves in pursuit of. He probably had a dozen women on the go, and she would only be fooling herself if she really thought she was special.

Then Marjorie asked herself what *she* wanted, because that was what was really important to her. It sounded narcissistic, but when people are honest with themselves and everything is stripped away, that's all that is left. You. Your needs, and your desires. She didn't want to marry the guy. She already had a perfectly adequate husband who took care of most of her needs, especially the material ones. She liked her life. Without Ronald financing it, she would be in a hole ten-feet-deep. She might even be forced to find a job.

Hugo was just a gardener. He had the body of an Adonis, but the brain of a dormouse. He could barely look after himself, let alone someone else. He could, however, perform in certain areas where Ronald was now lacking.

And therein lay her quandary. She was mature enough to know that you couldn't have everything. Life just didn't work like that. She'd already decided to sever ties with Hugo, so, in a way, his dropping off the radar made things easier. But she resented the fact that he'd taken the initiative and been the one to end things. If you could call it that. It wasn't only embarrassing, but insulting. That should have been her decision, not his.

Now, alongside the burrowing guilt, Marjorie was left with this nagging uncertainty. Had Hugo dumped her? Or had something more sinister happened?

The dreams couldn't just be a coincidence. They felt constructed, contrived, even. Almost as if they were trying to tell her something.

As she and Ronald strolled down the central road of Regal Retreat dressed in their matching sky-blue GO FOR IT T-shirts, she turned her head to the side and whispered into the breeze so softly that nobody else could hear, "Message received, Hugo. Loud and clear."

Hunched over his laptop, Ben stretched and rubbed his eyes. The nap in his fancy room had reinvigorated him, but only temporarily. Now the weariness was back, making his arms heavy, slowing down his brain, and tugging at his eyelids. He'd covered barely more than the first decade of the Regal Retreat's history, and already the amount of death and misery was almost overwhelming. However, as yet he could find no discernible pattern. Apart from the location, there appeared to be no links or commonalities whatsoever between the events. There was just the sporadic, not-so-occasional bout of manic, unrestrained violence without rhyme or reason. Frustratingly, there was no way of knowing if he was even getting the full picture. It was common knowledge that due to a lack of resources, newspaper coverage dropped off significantly during and after the war. Other things may have happened and not been recorded.

Added to this were deaths from natural causes that weren't deemed newsworthy except on slow news days. But, of course, there was no way of knowing definitively whether they were indeed natural. It was entirely possible that some murders might have been overlooked. It has been suggested that English serial killer Harold Shipman, also known as "Dr. Death," could be responsible for the deaths of over 250 people, making him one of the most prolific murderers in history. But the true figure will never be known because he preyed on the sick and elderly, and when they died, it didn't always come as a surprise.

It was unclear whether the Regal Retreat continued in its role as a makeshift sanatorium after the Archie Smith episode in 1948. Though Ben searched every available local and national newspaper archive, plus some other relevant websites and databases, he could find no more mention of the place until April 1955, when the senseless violence literally returned with a bang.

As England was approaching something resembling normality in the postwar years, one of the most popular pastimes amongst the upper classes was clay pigeon shooting. Given the wide expanses of open countryside in the vicinity and the kind of clientele it was striving to attract, R.R. was eager to embrace the sport. Tom Dobbs was the proprietor of the Dobbs & Sons grocery stores, which flourished in Britain when rationing and other restrictions were lifted. At their peak, they had two dozen stores throughout East Anglia, ensuring that Tom, from humble beginnings, was gleefully accepted into the aristocracy. He was a keen sportsman, playing cricket at counties level in his younger days, and later taking up game shooting. Well into his fifties and with business booming, he led a good life. Which is why it came as such a shock to all concerned when, on an otherwise unremarkable Sunday morning, he turned his favorite twelve-bore shotgun on his shooting partner, a textile mill worker named Fred Dickie, giving him both barrels.

Poor Fred was killed instantly, which is what usually happens when you are cut in half by shotgun pellets. Tom Dobbs was subsequently wrestled to the ground and disarmed by bystanders, stood trial, and was given a life sentence for murder. In this particular case, life really did mean life because he never tasted freedom again, dying in jail of natural causes some years later.

When asked to explain his actions, Dobbs used phrases like "moment of madness," and "blackout," and nobody ever found any ulterior motive. Clay pigeon shooting was immediately discontinued at Regal Retreat.

It didn't stop the death, however. Or even the shootings. Six years later, in March 1961, there was some kind of "gangland hit," as it was described by the tabloids. Underworld figure Roger Crankston, who operated illegal gambling dens and a loansharking business in Liverpool, was enjoying a weekend break in one of the lakeside villas with a moll half his age when the door was kicked in and he was shot six times by men assumed to be members of a rival gang. The moll, a woman named Daphne Ness, was also shot twice, once in the head, but miraculously survived.

Perhaps concerned about a second, more successful attempt on her life, she never ratted out the murderers, maintaining that she'd only seen their backs as they left the villa after having dispatched her beau. One of the intruders turned on his way out and shot her as she came down the stairs, she said, but claimed she never saw his face. Or at least, couldn't remember enough to give the police a description.

"Must be amnesia," she'd said.

How convenient.

Daphne Ness emigrated to Australia the following year. Not surprisingly, Roger Crankston's killers were never caught, the general consensus being that his untimely demise was no great loss to society.

And the hits just kept coming. Pardon the pun. In 1963, two people died in separate accidents: an electrocution and another drowning. In both cases, after lengthy inquiries, the resort was absolved of all blame. Then, in June of the following year, a man by the name of Thomas Woodhouse, a regular guest, went home after their annual holiday and strangled his wife to death for no apparent reason. Afterward, a few of the more smutty newspapers started linking the grisly events, bestowing the retreat with the title of "Murder Hotel." The name didn't stick, however. Ben could just imagine Michael Davenport using the Old Pals network to keep his going concern as viable as possible.

This was hard going.

Sensitive to his human's plight, Mr. Trimble raised his furry head and gave a silent meow from his position on the bench. Ben reached across, smoothed the cat's head, and gave him a little tickle behind the ear. He was grateful that Mr. Trimble had opted this time to let him work in peace rather than trample all over his keyboard in search of attention. It wasn't unusual for him to have a go at typing, though his meanderings never amounted to more than strings of random letters as his paws molested the keyboard.

Thysnll;lmjuuusntpmuchsyfnysiendoskeeeeeeeee.

On several memorable occasions, Mr. Trimble had attempted to send emails to valued clients or newsletter subscribers, hitting the "Send" button prematurely as Ben typed. It had been an absolute Godsend when Outlook introduced the "cancel send" function, giving him a short window to recall the email before it landed in people's inboxes. That spared him a few blushes. Once, Mr. Trimble had even succeeded in initiating a video call with a prospective business partner, his wide-eyed, furry face filling the screen as a prim and well-dressed, though slightly confused man accepted the invitation for an unscheduled video call.

Today, though, he seemed strangely subdued, content to sleep away the hours until his next meal. How grand life must be if you were lucky enough to be born a feline. Ben bookmarked the last site he was browsing, scribbled the date he had reached into the notepad he always kept close at hand, then rose and pulled his keys from his pocket. He needed some air. And maybe some exercise. Perhaps a stroll around this famed lake was in order.

CHAPTER SIX

East Anglia, 1645

After they killed Maggie, as expected, the savage eyes of the community fell on Elizabeth. They called her a witch, as well as other vile things. They knew nothing. If they did, they'd know she was no witch. Her primary role in the village was that of sin eater. She took evil and consumed it so others didn't have to suffer. Traditionally, her kind were called to visit people on their deathbed so that they may depart this earth free of guilt. But increasingly, the living wanted to be absolved, too.

Sin takes many forms, and Elizabeth knew them all. She knew every lie and crossed word, every form of treachery, betrayal, and infidelity, every wrong-doing and breach of trust.

It was her regular clients, also the biggest sinners, who supported her by sending food and goods. Tom the baker, who'd been having secret trysts with Maggie Phipps next door for over fourteen years, sent bread most days. Lynette the farmer's wife, who made a lover out of almost every young, fit stable hand her husband took on, often two or three at once, gave her a steady supply of hen's eggs. Elizabeth also had a good relationship with William Murdoch, the thatcher, who harbored unnatural, impure thoughts about his own brother. Thoughts he wouldn't want others to know about. In exchange for her silence, William was happy to keep her humble dwelling well-maintained and weather proofed.

Yes, the sins she consumed on behalf of others were many and varied. Human beings were imperfect creations, and the more people realized that and embraced it, the better it would be for everyone. It was a sign of how deep the sins ran in the village that until recently Elizabeth's cupboards were never empty. Quite the opposite. She sometimes found herself with a surplus of food, which she gave to the poor and needy before it spoiled. That was her own way of paying penance.

While she saw most of her clientele regularly, others were one-time callers who had succumbed to temptation and committed one foolish, yet damaging deed. Like Francis the Cobbler, who had burned down young Maizie Clark's shop when it began to threaten his own business, not realizing young Maizie was spending the night there. She had no chance of escape. Elizabeth felt some sympathy toward Francis. Setting the fire was wrong, but he hadn't meant to kill anyone.

When they wanted to make their peace, the villagers would send for her, and she would visit them in their homes under cover of darkness. They would prepare a lavish meal, the bigger and more sumptuous, the greater the sins, and she would eat it in their company. They often sat wordless, conversation unnecessary, but sometimes they talked while she ate. They treated her like a confessor and told her everything they had done, every bad thing that lurked in their depraved, twisted minds, knowing she was duty-bound to never tell another living soul.

By the time she left them, her belly would be full of food, her head full of secrets, and her soul full of sin. Sometimes, it was difficult to tell which was heavier.

Too bloated to walk, she often purged herself as she traversed the narrow, cobbled streets on the way back to her hovel next to the lake, her body rejecting the influx of rich food. But she couldn't let the sins escape. She had to catch them before they were absorbed back into the world. So, she would sink to her knees and use her hands to scrape the barely digested meat, bread, and vegetables off the cobblestones and shovel them back into her mouth. A few steps later, she would succumb to another vomiting fit, and the process would be repeated. Each time, the chunks would be smaller, more slimy.

If anyone saw her, they would undoubtedly think she was a starving street urchin. But it wasn't greed or hunger that drove her; it was a sense of duty. Her bloodline had served the community for generations, taking the pain and suffering upon themselves for the good of others. There were aspects of her existence, her role, that she didn't enjoy, but nobody's life was perfect. Tom the Baker would probably prefer to sleep in instead of getting up before dawn every day to fire the ovens, and Lynette the farmer's wife probably didn't like going out to work the fields in the pouring rain. But everyone pulled together, took the good with the bad, and did what communities needed to in order to survive.

Elizabeth didn't have many regrets in life, but at times like this, she wished she'd taken a husband in her younger years. If only for the companionship such an arrangement would bring. Though now old, haggard, and covered with blemishes and moles, she'd been beautiful once. The problem always was that no suitor could find it within himself to accept her fiery independence and stubbornness.

There had been men. Of course, there had. But rather than embrace her qualities, they'd always tried to change her. Subdue and mold her into the timid servant girl they wanted. And that would never do.

Only one man had even spent longer than a single night with her.

Gideon.

They had one perfect, glorious summer together almost thirty years ago, after they'd met at the local market when he was down from Dorset on business. What kind of business, she was never sure. It didn't matter. He went home with her and didn't leave until the nights drew in months later.

Living in sin made her and Gideon the talk of the village, but she didn't care. It wasn't as if the sinners around her were in any position to judge anybody. At times they seemed to forget that she knew everything about them.

That summer, it felt as though time had stopped in its tracks. It was the first and only time in her life she had known true happiness. She was so committed that she even took Gideon's last name. She never liked her own, anyway.

Then, one frosty autumn morning, she awoke to find him gone. There was no explanation. Not even a note. One day he was there and everything was good, the next he was gone.

In his eagerness to depart, Gideon had even left behind his meager belongings, which Elizabeth burned in the fire. She never saw nor heard from him again. Some people say it is better to have loved and lost than never to have loved at all. Those people didn't understand the gut-wrenching, all-consuming pain of loss.

She couldn't deny that the experience changed her. Made her more cynical and bitter and less sympathetic toward the philanderers and perverts that populated the village. On occasion she muttered cryptic warnings as she forced the last morsel of food into her mouth as they sat together.

"You are not fit to have a family. No more. This ends now."

She remembered doing just a thing whilst sitting with Ezra Davenport, the landowner who had earlier confessed to not only lavishing far more attention on his teenaged daughters than he did on his wife, but also to having sexual relations with the family pets. Human or animal, no living creature was safe from his attention. He was an insatiable beast.

She saw him stiffen in his chair as her words broke the uncomfortable silence that had been festering between them. She didn't speak out just to soothe her own splintered heart, but in the hope of preventing others from more persecution or suffering. Some men were simply evil, and she wanted this one to know that a plate of liver and onions would not be enough to satisfy her next time. Therefore, it was best to ensure there would be no "next time."

Sitting in her simple wooden chair, a shiver racked her frail body. She flexed her legs, wincing at the memory and the dull ache that had taken up residence there, and hoped the storm would blow over. She didn't want to end up like Maggie Reid.

Perhaps the hunters would forget about her, she thought.

But, of course, that would never happen, and it was foolish to even contemplate it. She had "wronged" too many people by exposing their wicked ways, as was her calling.

Ezra Davenport, for one, would surely have an ax to grind, and wouldn't hesitate to throw her name in the hat to silence her and even the score. Probably worried she would spill his sordid secrets to the rest of the village, he'd tried to stop her leaving his home that night. He was a huge man, towering at least a foot over her. She remembered his painful grip on her arm, and the look of contempt on his face as he growled, "What a man does behind closed doors is nobody's business but his own, witch."

Only Elizabeth's quick thinking had saved her. She scratched at his face, her sharp nails carving gouges down one stubbled, pock-marked cheek, and when he recoiled in pain, she made a break for the door. He wouldn't dare go after her. Someone in the village might see and ask questions.

But he made a plan for her that night. Elizabeth knew it. And Ezra Davenport and his cronies would be coming soon.

"You can join the queue," Elizabeth said aloud to herself, the utterance immediately followed by a brief cackle and a succession of heaving dry coughs. Her mouth filled with sour phlegm.

And then there was a bang on the door.

They were here.

Ben took a spot at a bench beneath a willow tree next to the expansive, gently rippling lake. Its outer reaches were a tranquil, almost Mediterranean blue/green in color, and it is in these areas that most people had congregated. They fished, paddled, or simply sat along the bank like Ben, enjoying the waning sunshine. It was hard to believe this body of water had been the cause of so much terror and abject misery over the years.

The center of the lake was altogether less inviting. The darker, choppier mass signified deeper water, but there was something else. Something less immediate and more pervasive. It looked ominous. Ben noticed that consciously or otherwise, the people in the handful of boats on the lake gave the middle section a very wide berth.

He watched as an elderly couple strolled along the pebbled path that courted the lake's edge hand-in-hand, wearing matching white shorts and sky-blue T-shirts. Cute. They looked somehow familiar. But how? He'd only spoken to several people since he'd arrived.

Then it came to him.

The elevator.

He'd passed them on the way to his room at the residential block.

Ben guessed the couple had been together most of their lives. They walked in silence with that slightly jaded, yet contented air, as if they'd both said and done everything they had to say and do and all that remained was reflection and quiet contemplation.

After The Event, he'd made life as good as it could be, with the camper van and Mr. Trimble. He pretty much did what he wanted with minimum responsibilities. His only commitment was to his readers, and they were a fairly understanding bunch. Compared to his previous incarnations, it was a stress-free, depressurized existence.

But as much as Ben hated to admit it, a small part of him still yearned for a more conventional life with a house, a mortgage, a steady job in a nice office, and a two-week package holiday in Spain every year. A wife and kids.

But you had that before, and you fucked it up.

True, he'd fucked it up. But it wasn't all his own doing. He'd had help with the fucking up. Doesn't anyone get a second chance at life? At happiness?

Get over it, you whiny bitch.

That was easier said than done.

Ben gave himself a mental kick in the ass. He couldn't afford to get sucked into this rut of self-loathing. There was work to do. He was lucky. These were the times he should cherish, when there was something else to focus on, something to take his mind away from all the shit.

It wouldn't last. There would be times when he found it hard to breathe, when it felt like the walls were closing in, crushing the life out of him. Not just the walls, but the entire world. He would feel helpless again. Lost, useless, cast adrift. A man with no direction, no self-worth, and no ambition. He'd already achieved all he wanted in life and had no desire to go back over the same old ground. It was difficult enough the first time. There was nothing left to accomplish. That was why he threw himself into these jobs, these investigations, with such vigor. They gave him something to sink his teeth into. As much as he tried to keep it all in check, he sometimes became obsessive, stopping at nothing until he found answers.

He let his eyes roam over the lake and onto the whitewashed villas studding the perimeter. He counted six, just as Christine Turner had said, each segregated by a network of hedges and fences. There was room for a lot more villas, and knowing R.R.'s thirst for profit, it surely wouldn't be too long before they were built. There was no doubt about it; the villas were beautiful. Facing the lake and designed in traditional Spanish art deco style, they were two or three stories tall, and each boasted a well-maintained garden and a private drive that doubled as a parking area. From his vantage point, Ben thought he could also make out a hot tub in one of the gardens. This truly was the lap of luxury.

More to satisfy his curiosity than anything else, he decided to take a walk up to the villas. As he approached, he looked for signs of life. Two appeared to be empty while another two had vehicles parked in the drive. There must be some kind of gathering or meeting in a third because the drive was filled with three cars parked bumper-to-bumper and another was positioned on the road outside. Another villa had all the curtains drawn, meaning that the occupants had taken the privacy thing to the next level. Must be one of those celebrity guests Christine had talked about.

The ghoul inside him couldn't help but wonder which of the villas Michael Davenport had died in back in 1994. Something about the man put Ben on edge. Heck, there was no denying it; something about this whole place put him on edge. There was nothing he could positively identify. It was just something about the atmosphere.

He walked slowly past the short row of detached buildings, trying to act casually so as to not arouse suspicion, knowing that the mere act of doing so would probably arouse suspicion. Luckily, the road running through the complex snaked around to serve the villas before morphing into a footpath that apparently encircled the lake, so, if challenged, he could just say that he was out walking the path. There were no signs to the contrary, so he assumed he was within his rights to do so. After all, Christine did say he had the run of the place.

There was a flame-red Plymouth Fury parked in the drive of one of the smaller villas, and Ben couldn't help but stop for a second to admire it. As he was doing so, a tall, slightly rakish man sporting glasses and a mop of blond hair stepped out of the doorway, wiping his hands with a tea towel. "Beautiful set of wheels, isn't it?" he said with a local accent.

"Indeed," Ben agreed. "A Fury?"

"Sure is. You know your cars."

"Not really," Ben shrugged. "But it's just like the one Stephen King wrote about in that novel. I forget what it was called."

It was Christine, his inner voice said, sending a chill down his spine. Could that just be a coincidence?

"It is? I'm not familiar with it."

"You should look it up," Ben said. "They made it into a movie, too. Early eighties, I think. John Carpenter directing."

"Which is better? The movie or the book?"

"I don't think it's right to compare art forms," Ben replied. "I mean, it's like asking which is better, music or beer. As far as I'm concerned, there's a place in this world for both."

"Very true!" the man guffawed. "I never thought about it like that."

"How long have you had it?"

"Nine years or so. I have three at the moment. I buy 'em as junk and do 'em up. Takes up all my free time, which doesn't please the wife. But it's my passion, you could say. We all have one, don't we?"

"I never understood the expression, 'free time,'" Ben mused aloud. "Time is far from free. In fact, it's the most valuable thing we have. To say time is 'free' does it a great disservice."

"So true," the blond-haired man said, his smile wavering for the first time.

"Must be an expensive hobby," Ben said, anxious to get the conversation back on track. He found that whenever he talked to a stranger, it made them more receptive if he talked about something that was important to them.

"Not as expensive as you might think. I pick up most of the parts at junk yards for cheap. It's just a case of ringing around. There are a few people in my circle who call me up when something comes in they think I might want. Like I say, it's more time-consuming than anything else. Between this and the Am-Dram Society I belong to, it's a wonder Sheila puts up with me at all."

"Am-Dram?"

"Amateur dramatics!" the man said with a dramatic sweep of the arm. "We rehearse every Thursday night and put on three or four shows a year to support local charities. Once, we even went on a nationwide tour. That was madness. Blackpool, Dudley, Rhyl, Bromsgrove. But what's on tour stays on tour, as they say. None of us are West End material, of course. And it's doubtful you'll ever even see any of us on daytime T.V. Apart from Lionel, obviously, who once had a speaking part in The Bill. He played a burglary victim. Most people take Lionel with a pinch of salt. One week he'll tell you he had two lines, the next he'll tell you he had a five-minute monologue. His story changes so much, some of us wonder if he even knows what the truth is himself. Loves to name drop, too. So much so that someone has to walk behind him picking them all up. He's on Andrew Lloyd Webber's Christmas card list, apparently. But even if that's true, one has to wonder how many names are on that list. It might run into the thousands, and I bet he doesn't even write them himself."

"So, are you retired?" Ben asked, trying to build up a picture of his new acquaintance.

"Heavens, no. I wish! I'm a historian and lecturer at U.E.A. The University of East Anglia. I have another twenty years or so to put in before I can even think about retirement. Twenty-five, if this government has its way. I'm on a year's sabbatical and thought I'd kick things off with a week at Regal Retreat. I grew up 'round here, see, and always said I'd treat myself to this one day if the opportunity ever arose."

"Well, I'm happy to see that it has!" Ben said, genuinely impressed. Anyone who could wangle a year off work, probably on full pay, won his admiration, and it was refreshing to find someone so passionate about his hobbies.

"Thanks a lot," the man said, stepping forward and offering his hand. "Pleased to meet you."

"Likewise," Ben said, accepting the handshake and feeling himself flush slightly as the familiar stab of self-consciousness went through him. Though his new friend must surely have noticed Ben's disfigured hand, he didn't baulk at the contact as so many had before him. That meant he had unwittingly passed the Scar Tissue Test.

"The name's Tim Norgood."

"I'm Ben Shivers."

"Say, Ben. I'm about to take this little baby out for a little spin. Just a couple of miles through the lanes to blow some cobwebs off. Would you care to join me? It's not often I meet a fellow Fury enthusiast."

"I'm actually more of a Stephen King enthusiast than a Plymouth Fury enthusiast."

"Well, by all accounts that makes you a Fury fan by default. I'd love to hear more about this book and, to be honest, I'd love to show off a little."

"In that case, sure, sounds good!" Ben said as a shiver of child-like excitement went through him. He couldn't deny that it was a great-looking car. Doused in nostalgia, it called to mind street races, muscle tops, and 1950s Americana.

"Wonderful. I'll just pop in and tell Sheila."

Ben waited patiently outside the villa. He could hear Tim addressing someone inside but couldn't quite make out what was being said. This was already taking on the surreal, life-affirming qualities of one of those days when anything could happen. But still, there was a seed of doubt. Was this kind of behavior…normal? Did men often invite other men they barely knew out for an afternoon drive to "blow some cobwebs off?"

Maybe the years had made Ben cynical, but he was pretty sure that had he been a child, there was no way he'd accept a ride in a stranger's car. In fact, he would actively campaign against it and tell others to do the same. Strangers cannot be trusted. Yet, here he was, a grown man preparing to do just that. It was hypocritical and reckless but wildly exciting.

Tim reappeared dangling a set of car keys from his fingers. "Okay, here we go!"

"Wonderful," Ben said, trying not to let his growing apprehension show.

He needn't have worried. They drove slowly down the road between the two main buildings, through the security-controlled gate at the far end, and minutes later were whizzing down one of the country lanes, crisscrossing the area around the resort as the last of the sunlight streamed in through the windows.

The engine purred, and Tim handled the car expertly, braking for bends and swerving to avoid potholes that could damage his pride and joy. To complete the illusion, the Rolling Stones boogied out of the eight-track car stereo, which Ben noted with surprise.

"I didn't know they still made those," he said, nodding to the over-sized piece of kit positioned low on the dashboard between the driver and passenger seats.

"The eight-track? Oh, they don't. They were phased out in the early eighties, though RadioShack continued selling them right up until nineteen-ninety. They were probably hoping for a comeback, and when they realized that wasn't going to happen, they started catering to the retro crowd instead. But much like old video recorders and cassettes, they were so popular in their prime that they aren't exactly hard to find at car boot sales and the like. You can pick them up in good condition, and they aren't too difficult to refurbish. It adds authenticity. Now, finding new music to play…. In fact, anything post-nineteen-eighty-three, that's far more difficult. It leaves you with limited options."

"Well, it wouldn't seem right if you played Grime."

"Who's that?"

"Never mind," Ben said. "This is the Stones, right? Which album?"

"Their finest, in my humble opinion. *Let It Bleed*, from nineteen-sixty-nine."

"The one with 'Gimme Shelter' on it?"

"The very same."

"Classic. You said you're a historian?"

"That's right."

"What kind? I mean, history is a big topic. Do you have an area of special interest or expertise?"

"I do indeed. Local history, pre-William the fourth."

"Why pre-William the fourth? What did he do?"

"Nothing much, comparatively speaking. He was a son of George the third, who ruled from eighteen-thirty until his death in eighteen-thirty-seven. It's just a convenient cut-off point. As I said, I grew up in the area. My family has lived here for generations. I believe everyone should have more of an appreciation about where they come from. In the words of Terry Pratchett, 'If you do not know where you come from, then you don't know where you are, and if you don't know where you are, then you don't know where you're going. And if you don't know where you're going, you're probably going wrong.'"

"I agree with that. Didn't East Anglia have its own royal family at one time?" Ben asked, remembering something he'd read online that had caught his eye that afternoon.

"Sure, as did most parts of the British Isles. East Angles, as it was known, was one of the traditional seven kingdoms. From the sixth century to the year seven-forty-nine A.D., it was ruled by members of the Wulfingas Dynasty, named after Wuffa, which in turn means 'descendants of the wolf.' All these kingdoms, and a bunch of outside influences, were all involved in a titanic power struggle. The last king of East Anglia was Guthrum the Second."

"What happened to him?"

"Killed in battle," Tim said without an ounce of sympathy. "Like all the best kings."

"Tim?" Ben began. "You said something earlier which piqued my interest."

"Oh yes? What was that?" Tim replied, glancing at Ben out of the corner of his eye. "Was it that thing about *Let It Bleed* being my favorite Stones album? I mean, I realize it may be a controversial statement. Most people tend to favor *Exile on Main Street* or *Sticky Fingers*. You could even make a case for *Beggar's Banquet* or *Goat's Head Soup*. Heck, once, I met a guy at a classic car convention who swore *Between the Buttons* was their best moment. I mean, I can accept most people's opinions, even if they differ from mine. But *Between the Buttons?* Come on!"

"No, it's nothing to do with the Stones," Ben said.

"Then what is it?"

"You mentioned that you always promised yourself you'd treat yourself to a stay at the Regal Retreat. I was just wondering why. I mean, there must be a million other places you could go. In your position, you could probably go anywhere in the world. So why here?"

"Fair question," Tim Norgood said, appearing to settle down in the driver's seat again after his Rolling Stones outburst. "When you grow up around here, the Regal has some kind of…pull. It's where the rich and successful come. Even if they only come once a year and half-bankrupt themselves doing it. If you can afford to come here at all, it means you've arrived. You're at the pinnacle of your chosen profession. As a kid, I would see the Rolls Royces and Bentleys driving all these movie stars, sporting icons, and captains of industry through the village on their way to and from here, and I promised myself I would experience it one day. Except, of course, I would be driving a Plymouth Fury rather than a Rolls or a Bentley."

"Movie stars, sporting icons, and captains of industry?" Ben interjected. "In my research so far, I've found it was mostly gangsters and army officers with undiagnosed P.T.S.D. who visited."

"Oh, there's been plenty of those, too. And reality T.V. stars. It's probably fair to say the place attracts all sorts. So, what are you researching?"

"Just the history of R.R. for an article I'm working on. I'm a journalist." Ben hesitated, debating how to proceed. He often found it was in his best interest to not give too much away too soon after meeting some-one. Not telling them everything was vastly different from lying. Ben just didn't feel the time was right to divulge that he was a paranormal investi-gator. That usually sent the conversation down a different, not always beneficial, path.

Tim glanced into his rear-view mirror to check if it was safe, then he slowed the Fury and pulled into a lay-by to let another car pass on the narrow lane. The other driver beeped his horn in appreciation. "What kind of article is it?"

Ben thought he saw a shadow cross his new friend's face. "It's an investigation into some of the mysterious deaths that have occurred here," he said. "The murders, accidents, and suicides."

"Is that right? Well, there's plenty to choose from. When I was a kid, we used to call the place Horror Heights."

"Horror Heights? I like it. I might use that in the article, if you don't mind?"

"Not at all. It's not like I personally named the place. It scared the shit out of us, to be blunt. We used to dare each other to sneak in here at night."

"And do what?"

"Nothing, really. Just slope around looking for ghosts and whatever."

"Did you ever find one?"

"Nah. I remember getting chased once by this big, brutish security guard. That's probably the closest I have ever personally come to the afterlife. So far, anyway."

"Close enough," Ben said with a laugh.

"Too right."

"So, what do you think is causing all these deaths? Any ideas?" Ben asked, eager to garner someone else's opinion on the subject.

"Definitely."

"What?"

"Life," Tim said simply, putting his foot on the accelerator and pull-ing off.

"What do you mean?"

"Death is a consequence of life. You can't have one without the other. There's a lot of life at the Regal, so its stands to reason death will follow in its wake."

"That's true." It wasn't the answer Ben wanted, but the man was absolutely right.

"What else could possibly be a cause? You think there's something else going on?"

"It's worth thinking about," Ben said. "There are just so many. A much higher percentage than the law of averages legislates for."

"That might be true. But what could that cause possibly be? Tragic as they are, these deaths have occurred over a period of decades, to all kinds of different people, and in all kinds of different ways. I can't see any connection, apart from the obvious."

"What would the obvious be?"

"The location. They all came to Regal Retreat. Do you think there's something in the water?"

"Note to self: Must wear tin foil hat more," Ben said. Though his remark was light-hearted, the moment Tim mentioned the water, Ben's mind immediately went to the lake—the dark, seductive, brooding lake—and he wondered if the remark could be closer to the truth than either man suspected. Maybe there *was* something in the water.

Tim slowed the car, steered into another shallow lay-by, expertly performed a faultless three-point turn, then started driving back the way they'd come. "Better get back before Sheila sends out a search party. She worries, you know."

"Of course. Is Sheila your wife, did you say?"

"Wife and rock. She has a dual role. Or my 'better half' as she maintains, and I am loathe to disagree. One thing I've learned is that women are always right, even when they're wrong."

"Copy that," agreed Ben. "Whoever coined the phrase, 'Happy wife, happy life' absolutely nailed it."

"Indeed. Are you married yourself?"

"Used to be," replied Ben. "It didn't last."

"Sorry to hear that."

"It wasn't your fault," Ben said. "You weren't even there."

The two men then fell into an easy silence as the gently purring vehicle ate up the few remaining miles between them and the resort. When they arrived back at the gate, Tim wound down his window and showed the security guard his guest pass emblazoned with the R.R. logo, and the gate was opened.

"This place is harder to get into than Fort Knox," Ben said, thinking aloud. "Not that I've ever been there."

"Yeah," Tim said. "I mean, I get the safety and security aspect. There's a lot of moneyed people here. But what the top knobs fail to understand is that virtually all crime that has ever been committed here, including the murders, were committed by people with guest passes, rendering that gate practically useless."

"That's a great point," Ben agreed.

Minutes later, Tim guided the Fury into the parking spot outside the villa and both men exited the vehicle.

Ben made sure he remembered to manually push the button down on the door to lock it, old school-style. "How long are you staying here, Tim?" he asked.

"Full disclosure; we got a heavy discount on a five-night stay on Trivago," Tim said with a smirk. "Gold Star member. One of the few perks of being a fixture on the lecture circuit for over a decade is that I stay in a lot of hotels. Other perks being all the coke and groupies."

Ben chuckled aloud at the man's sarcasm.

"What about you?"

"I'm not really into coke and groupies. I'm more of a craft beer and horror movie guy."

"I meant, how long are you staying?" Tim said with an exaggerated roll of the eyes.

"Not sure," Ben started. Suddenly realizing how suspicious it sounds when people check into hotels for undetermined lengths of time, especially exclusive places like the Regal, he hastened to cover his tracks. "I mean, my plan was to just stay here a night or two. Unwind a little, have a look around, take some snaps, maybe grab an interview or two.

Any longer than that and the article won't pay for itself. My outgoings would outweigh my incomings. This place is expensive. But who knows? If I like it, I might stay a little while longer and try to write it off on my tax returns as expenses."

"In that case I might just be seeing you around," Tim said with a broad smile. "I hope you enjoyed the run. These Plymouth's are outstanding machines."

"I certainly did. Thanks again for your hospitality, and I do hope to see you again before you or I leave. I might want to pick your brain some more." One thing most academics had in common was the innate desire to wax lyrical about their chosen topic, and if Tim's area of expertise was local history, it would be a wasted opportunity if he let all that knowledge slip away untapped.

"Any time," Tim said agreeably. "I mean I say I'm on a break, but there's nothing I like better than chatting about history. This part of the country is just so rich and diverse. It's also a bit dark sometimes, not to mention bizarre. We have a saying that sums it up quite well. N.F.N."

"N.F.N.?"

"Normal for Norfolk," Tim said. "Meaning that whatever crazy things happen here are probably normal to us. It's said the phrase was coined by doctors who often wrote it on patient's records to describe people who were, shall we say, intellectually challenged. From there I guess it leaked out into the wider world. So yeah, feel free to give me a knock if I can help out in any way. I might even leave out the Rolling Stones chat next time."

"Oh, you can leave that in."

"Well, you know where I'm staying. Sheila and I don't have any plans other than to take some long lunches and chill out here. Be seeing you." With that, Tim Norgood turned and entered the villa.

What an interesting guy, Ben thought, turning and walking back the way he'd come. He was already thinking about his next move, but he didn't have to think about it for long. It was dinner time.

CHAPTER SEVEN

fter their Pilates class, Ronald and Marjorie Brand had a quick bite to eat at Ground Zero, then retired to their room to relax and watch a late-afternoon movie. It had become something of a routine. Ronald was a huge Humphrey Bogart fan and had been watching and re-watching his repertoire most of his life. When you're thirty, fifty-seven seems so old but at any point after you reach that age, it seems so young.

The Big Sleep and *The Maltese Falcon* were among Ronald's favorites, and he knew the former was available on one of the movie channels piped into their room. It was the Lawn Bowling Singles Tournament tomorrow, and he wanted to be well-rested so he could defend his title. Nobody was taking that trophy away from him. Not that there would be much in the way of competition. There wasn't last year. But he could only beat what they put in front of him, and he intended to.

Marjorie couldn't stand Humphrey Bogart. She called him overrated and pug-ugly, which was disrespectful in the extreme. She much preferred Paul Newman. It was pretty obvious to Ronald that what Marjorie really meant was she would rather watch Paul Newman movies because he was better looking. Marjorie could be so shallow sometimes. When did someone's looks become more important than their acting ability?

"Since around the birth of Hollywood," was Marjorie's standard reply, and unfortunately, she wasn't wrong. But that didn't mean Ronald had to agree with it.

Over the years he'd come to accept that being in a long-term relationship, let alone a five-decade-long marriage, meant losing your identity to an extent. You grew to learn what your partner liked and sacrificed the parts of yourself that didn't gel so well with certain parts of the other until the two of you became one amorphous mass. You become washed out and jaded, a poor imitation of your old self. The matching sky-blue GO FOR IT! T-shirts they wore were symptomatic of that condition, as was settling down to watch a Lack Lemmon film instead of either Bogart or Paul Newman. Jack Lemmon occupied some kind of middle ground, a happy medium. But Ronald wanted to watch *The Big Sleep*, damn it. Why was that so hard?

He used to be able to justify the constant compromising by telling himself that was what love was all about. Nothing was perfect, you have to work at it, and every other cliché under the sun. It all served to temporarily conceal the fact that if he and Marjorie really were in love, he wouldn't mind not being able to do what he wanted. Simply spending time together would be enough.

But that kind of idealistic attitude will only carry you so far. Sooner or later you had to face reality, and reality wasn't always that great. One thing was for sure. If Ronald was going to spend the rest of the evening doing things he didn't want to do, he needed a toilet break first. Probably a long one.

Given the limited options available on site, and the gratuity meal card burning a hole in his pocket, Ben thought it would be foolish to go anywhere else for dinner other than Ground Zero. It was just a short walk from the lakeside villa where Tim and his wife Sheila were staying, and by the time he arrived, dinner service was in full swing.

As he approached the doors, he suddenly began to feel self-conscious about his casual attire. There was no formal dress code, not that he could see, but he noticed many of the men wearing dinner jackets as they walked arm-in-arm with their partners, most of whom sported evening dresses topped off with expensive jewelry. Like on a cruise ship, in such an enclosed environment, dinner must represent the highlight of the day for many, and Ben felt hopelessly inadequate in his faded Levis and black polo shirt.

He fully expected to find Beth at the desk, the young lady with red hair and freckles who had so adequately looked after him on his previous visit, but he was surprised, and a little disappointed, to find that she wasn't there. In her place was a tall, young, dark-haired guy. "Oh, no Beth?" Ben said as he walked up to the counter. "Is her shift over?"

"Excuse me, sir?" the young man replied in a heavy Eastern-European accent.

"Beth," Ben repeated. "I just thought she might still be working."

"Beth?"

"Yes, I met her here this morning."

"I'm not sure to whom you are referring, sir."

"Oh? How long have you worked here?"

"Er… A little over two months, sir." The young man remained poker-faced, but his eyes narrowed slightly as if he were silently assessing Ben. "Are you here for dinner?"

"Yes. Yes, I am." Ben was momentarily confused. How could the guy not know who he was talking about? The girl's name was Beth, wasn't it? He remembered her name tag. Then he pushed the doubt to one side. Christine Turner said hundreds of staff worked here. Maybe they were rotated around, or one was just filling in for an absentee. It was entirely possible for two people to work at a place this size and hardly ever meet, wasn't it? Besides, he hadn't asked how long Beth had worked at the Regal. She might have started just the day before for all he knew.

"How will you be paying, sir?"

"With this," Ben said, producing one of the meal vouchers he had in his pocket.

"Very well. And your R.R. card?"

"No problem." As he passed it over, Ben noticed that the restaurant employee, whose name tag said "Alex," gave him a slightly wary glance.

Was he just not accustomed to answering questions? Did he have something to hide? Or was Ben just being paranoid?

The young man used a hand-held device to scan bar codes on both the meal voucher and Ben's R.R. card. Something about the action felt unusual. At first, Ben didn't realize what the issue was. Then, the penny dropped.

The process was different.

Earlier that day, Beth had used a hole punch to mark the voucher and entered the serial number or whatever manually into some machine tucked behind the counter. Now, Alex was using some fancy electronic device.

"Oh, you had an upgrade? That must make things easier," Ben said, nodding at the hand-held device.

Alex stopped and looked at the contraption he was holding with a look of mild confusion. "I'm not sure what you mean, sir."

"That thing you're using. Last time I came in here, the girl had to enter all the info by hand. Took a while. This way looks much smoother."

"Oh, right," Alex said. "When was the last time you came? Must have been a while ago. We've used this system ever since I've worked here."

"Actually, it was earlier today. The girl punched a hole in the voucher. Look."

Sure enough, there was a neat, round hole in one corner of the used voucher, plainly visible to them both.

"I don't know what to tell you, sir." Alex the Edgy Restaurant Worker said with a shrug. "Your meal voucher has a hole in it. I don't know what to tell you, other than if these vouchers have been damaged, we're not actually supposed to accept them. I'm doing you a favor."

Ben was taken aback. He didn't know what all this could mean, but most of all, he didn't want to pay for the meal. "Okay, then. No worries. I guess I must be mistaken."

"No problem, sir," the worker said as he handed back Ben's R.R. card and meal voucher with a perfunctory smile. "Have a nice day."

Ben took them, offered a perfunctory smile of his own, and headed into the restaurant in a state of mild confusion. He wasn't mistaken. Beth had used a different system to book him into the restaurant, and the hole in the voucher was proof. Something didn't add up. That guy Alex couldn't be mistaken. He was an employee. But why would he lie about something so innocuous?

He tried to shrug it off. What did it matter?

Maybe there had been some kind of electronic glitch this morning that temporarily rendered the electronic system unusable, and the glitch had since been fixed. Glitches happened all the time. Whatever, he didn't have time to obsess over it.

Puffing out his chest, he made his way through the bustling room to an empty table in the far corner. As he walked, his feet sank into the lush carpet and the gentle hum of conversation washed over him like warm water. Again, inexplicably, his mind was dragged to the lake and what it must feel like to drown in it. That awful, helpless sensation of suffocating, slipping away, and all the connotations that came with it. The overriding emotion must be one of regret and unfulfilled potential. Missing out. Dying when there was still so much to do.

Damn. Why so morose?

If he hadn't been in public, at that point Ben would have gladly slapped himself across the face. Still, even thinking about drowning in the lake was a damn sight better than thinking about either the hole in his meal voucher, The Event, or the horrible burning dream he'd had that afternoon.

By the time he gratefully flopped into the chair at the table, his appetite had deserted him. Beads of sweat stood out on his forehead, and he was on the verge of having a panic attack.

What the hell was going on?

He felt on the brink of something. Some precipice. He sensed danger, instinctively knowing that it wasn't too late to back away, but it soon would be.

With Ground Zero being so busy, he accepted it might take longer than usual for the waitress to appear. He was dimly aware that most of the activity seemed focused on the middle of the room, where there appeared to be some kind of self-service option. Hadn't Beth mentioned something about a buffet earlier?

Beth.

He could still picture her face, her lush red hair, and her toothy smile. But now, her image gave him chills.

Just then, a voice brought him back to reality. "Not interested in the carvery option this evening, sir?"

"Huh?" He looked up to see a fresh-faced young waitress with blonde hair neatly tied up in a bun.

"Would you like the carvery option, sir? Or did you have something else in mind?"

Caught by surprise, Ben said, "What does the carvery involve?"

"It's very popular," the waitress replied, motioning toward the gathering in the middle of the room. "You can find a wide selection of seasonal roasted vegetables, along with turkey, beef, pork, and all the trimmings. You can help yourself."

Ben considered this for a moment, looked again at the throng of people, then said, "I'll just order something off the menu, if that's cool?"

There was a flicker of…something…on the waitress's face as she retrieved a pad and pencil from her breast pocket. *Disappointment? Impatience?*

"No problem, sir. So, what'll it be?"

"Toad-in-the-hole, please," Ben said without consulting the menu on the table. He'd earmarked the dish on his previous visit, and right then he thought it might be the only thing he thought he could stomach. Bland, stodgy, unspectacular. Just the way good British food should be.

The waitress gave a contemptuous sniff and left. As Ben watched her weave her way through the crowd of diners, he didn't feel the least bit guilty for making her work harder. The girl came across like a snot-nosed little cow, and besides, if this place really was as luxurious as it tried to be, he expected to be waited on, not be coerced into getting his own dinner. That's what the buffet and carvery options essentially amounted to, and places like this loved to push them on their clientele knowing that it was both more economical for them and easier for the staff.

When the food arrived, plonked on his table by the waitress with a fake smile, it was excellent. Ben just wasn't hungry. Instead, he excavated the sausages from their Yorkshire pudding home and pushed them around his plate with his fork for a while, deep in thought.

There was something he just wasn't getting.

Something he was missing.

He knew the answer wasn't going to just fall in his lap. It wouldn't be that easy. He was going to have to work for it. He needed to get back to his computer. Still, it would be a pity to waste such good-quality bangers, so he carefully wrapped them in a napkin for Mr. Trimble.

Looking up, he realized it would also be a shame to not at least take a closer look at the carvery on the way out, if only to satisfy his curiosity. Ben angled toward the middle of the room, exchanging smiles with an elderly woman in a white evening gown using a serrated knife to slice into a fat, succulent-looking turkey. As she did so, juice flowed from the tender white meat. Her plate filled, she handed him the knife. Ben smiled and thanked her.

Then he realized he had neglected to pick up a plate of his own. Stuck in an awkward moment with a queue already forming behind him, he decided he had no other option than to style it out. Using the knife the woman had given him, he cut off three thick slices of meat. Stuffing one in his mouth with his fingers, he smacked his lips noisily and said, "Mmm! Delicious!" then put the other two slices in the napkin already containing the sausage and calmly walked out of the restaurant.

En route to the door, he passed the blonde waitress who'd served him; her fake smile now twisted into what was either an expression of disgust or bemusement. Either she had been watching him sample the turkey or something else about him offended her. It didn't matter. He probably wouldn't even be here for long. The Turkey Incident was the most punk thing he'd done in a while, and it felt damn good.

It was now just after seven. As Ben made his way back to the van, gazing up at the star-studded sky featuring an immaculate full moon as its centerpiece, he plotted the next steps in his investigation. He was no closer to solving the mystery, but having talked and interacted with some of the workers and guests, he felt he now had a slightly deeper understanding of the Regal. There was the expected selection of holidaymakers and workers to be found, some of whom were undoubtedly happier to be there than others, but it was a similar situation everywhere else. On the face of it, there was nothing glaringly obvious about the Regal that made it such a magnet for death and misery. No chanting hordes or homicidal maniacs running around. Not tonight, anyway. But putting all the accidents, deaths, and injuries down to coincidence or plain bad luck was ridiculous. The statistics showed that something was seriously amiss. He just didn't know what.

Chapter Eight

Ronald was sulking again. Marjorie knew it was because he wanted to watch a bloody Humphrey Bogart film, like he always did when he was in a bad mood. He just didn't have the guts to come out and say it. Instead, he'd spend twenty-five minutes doing God knows what in the bathroom, then emerge with that plastic smile plastered across his face and pretend to enjoy the Jack Lemmon movie they would undoubtedly end up watching despite the fact that she would much rather be watching *Cool Hand Luke* again.

The worst part about it all was his sanctimonious, holier-than-thou attitude. She was talking about Ronald. Not Jack Lemmon. Ever since they'd first got together, he had a funny way of making her feel like he was doing her a favor and she was somehow indebted to him for something.

As the minutes crawled by and Ronald did whatever he did in the bathroom, Marjorie changed out of the sky-blue GO FOR IT! T-shirt into a clean, white blouse and sat on the edge of the bed. It seemed this was how she'd spent most of her marriage. Sitting and waiting, while a little nugget of guilt, shame, and fear throbbed somewhere deep inside.

It was draining. She could never relax, nor let her guard down for a minute. No evidence of her affair with Hugo remained, but she was hopeless at keeping secrets. What if she talked in her sleep? Or had too much to drink one night and let something slip? Constantly being on your guard was exhausting. At least R.R. was a dry resort, so she didn't have to worry about that.

Picking up the Catherine Cookson novel that was perpetually placed on the bedside table, Marjorie tried to immerse herself in another epic tale of fraught, unrequited love. But it was no use. The words just washed over her. She couldn't take anything in.

Nighttime was creeping up, and not long after darkness fell, she would have to go to bed. The idea filled her with dread because she knew she would either spend most of it lying awake, or she would be forced to endure the awful dream sequence again where she watched her lover, sorry, ex-lover, be murdered. Neither option was particularly attractive, and she wished for a third. But there was only the devil and the deep blue sea to choose from. Giving up on the novel, she put it back in its rightful place on the bedside table next to Ronald's precious Regal Retreat Lawn Bowling Singles Tournament Winner's Cup.

The trophy caught her eye, and she picked it up, turning it over and feeling its weight. It fit snugly into one hand and appeared to be fashioned from brass and stained wood. It was cheap, the kind probably bought in bulk and engraved to suit. Somewhere at the Regal there was probably a storeroom filled with the things. If Ronald wasn't so preoccupied with "defending" this shitty, little, worthless trophy, maybe he would notice how much Marjorie was hurting inside. How forlorn and defeated she was.

Did he ever look around?

Their marriage was so empty it had become like a void, sucking up any positivity she'd once had. She'd been suffering silently for so long now it was the only existence she knew, and that wasn't right. In fact, it was downright unfair. Ronald was too wrapped up in himself and what he wanted to pay any attention to her. Even after he retired, when he'd promised things would be different, she was always playing second fiddle to something else. For most of their marriage it had been work, and now the latest thing more important than her was this sodding bowling tournament. Proof positive that he didn't really give a shit about Marjorie or their marriage, and she had wasted most of her life joined at the hip with a weak-minded, self-centered, runt of a man.

Marjorie could feel the rage beginning to course through her veins like liquid fire. All the pent-up frustration of being confined to a long, largely uneventful marriage finally finding an outlet. She started shaking, and then hyperventilating, shocked by the sheer strength of emotion she was experiencing.

It actually felt good. She threw back her head and took a deep, quivering breath to savor the moment.

Just then, the bathroom door opened out stepped Ronald. Poor, pathetic, self-absorbed Ronald.

He stopped half in and half out of the bathroom, a look of utter bemusement on his face. "Marj?" he said.

For the briefest moment, Marjorie thought he might redeem himself by showing some concern. But no. The only concern he had was for that damn worthless trophy. A fact underlined by the next thing he said, which ironically also turned out to be the *last* thing he said.

"What are you doing with my Regal Retreat Lawn Bowling Singles Tournament Winner's Cup?"

When Marjorie didn't answer, he must have known something was wrong because he began to retreat back into the bathroom.

Too late.

From her seated position on the edge of the bed, Marjorie launched herself at him, swinging Ronald's prized trophy as she did so. Her husband's mouth dropped opened in terror, probably realizing that this exchange wasn't going to end well for him.

Marjorie let out a primal grunt of rage and threw every ounce of energy into the first blow, which landed squarely on Ronald's forehead, snapping back his head. The look of surprise on his face morphed into a confused frown as a single drop of blood ran down his face from the point high on his domed forehead where the skin had split.

Marjorie took a small step back, shocked by her own actions. She'd never hurt a living thing before. Not even so much as an insect. If she found a spider in the house when she was cleaning, she simply closed the door to contain it and waited for Ronald to come home. It suddenly occurred to her that she wouldn't be able to do that anymore. After this, she would have to make other arrangements if she found a spider. In fact, after this, nothing would ever be the same again.

She was surprised to realize that she didn't care. This felt good, like a release. It was almost sexual, the intensity powerful enough to bring back all the sweet memories of Hugo. And that only fueled her anger.

The next time she struck Ronald, she didn't grunt; she moaned, and couldn't help her free hand momentarily going to her crotch, where it stayed for several glorious seconds, applying just the right amount of pressure in just the right place.

Ronald staggered back into the tiny bathroom and collapsed to the floor, arms flailing. His head cracked off the porcelain toilet, and there he lay, on his back, staring upward from a spreading pool of blood contrasting against the white tiles as a thick vein in his neck throbbed.

Marjorie moved in on him, a pleasant, warming sensation radiating out from the center of her being. Standing over him brandishing the Regal Retreat Lawn Bowling Singles Tournament Winner's Cup, now dented and flecked with blood, she brought it crashing down on Ronald's head once more.

This time, a small jet of blood spurted out of his left ear. Something inside his head must have broken.

There was going to be blood everywhere. Thinking about cleaning up the mess made Marjorie irrationally angry until she realized that she wouldn't have to clean up after Ronald again. Not now, not ever. Nobody would, for that matter. This was the last mess he would ever make.

She didn't stop battering her husband until his face and head were smashed beyond recognition. His lower jaw hung at a sickening angle, having been all-but separated from his face; his features were flattened so much that white shards of bone were visible through ripped skin, and his skull was horribly misshapen, a landscape of dents and discolored bruises and swellings, with rivers of blood flowing through, around, and in between them.

The trophy itself had been reduced to a crumpled, deformed lump of scratched wood and twisted metal from the constant pummeling she had inflicted. Evidence, she noted, that it was such low quality, it wasn't even worth the fuss.

Finally, as Ronald lay dying on the floor, a series of odd clicks and gurgles coming out of his face, Marjorie sank to her knees beside him, suddenly overcome with a sense of relief. As she did so, her husband's failing body let out a low, grumbling fart, and the stench of fresh defecation flooded the bathroom.

That's it, Marjorie thought. The final insult. *Thanks for that, Ronald. Thanks for everything.*

Meanwhile, Ben's grim research continued. Upon returning to the van and giving Mr. Trimble his meaty treats, he logged into the resort's Wi-Fi and opened the pages he'd bookmarked earlier. News reports said there was a serious accident in 1966, two years after Thomas Woodhouse murdered his wife, when some kind of gas explosion in the boiler room of what he guessed was now the administration block. One worker was killed, and another so seriously injured he needed to have a leg amputated. The investigation found that a faulty valve had been to blame rather than human error.

A faulty valve? Hard to believe that a simple valve could be the cause of such devastation. The building was closed for several months as it underwent structural repairs.

Then Ben stumbled across something especially interesting. In the summer of 1969, the site was utilized as a film set. Fittingly enough, the movie was a Hammer Horror rip-off called *From the Depths.* Interest piqued, Ben quickly opened another window on his browser and went to the IMDb website to see if there was a listing. There was. The film appeared to be some kind of *Creature from the Black Lagoon* clone about a humanoid monster living in a lake and surfacing periodically to drag unsuspecting victims into the water. Pretty standard fare. But... There it was again.

The lake.

Christine Turner hadn't been kidding when she'd claimed it was the center of activity at the resort. So much activity focused on such a dubious place was a recipe for disaster. And so it proved when one of the extras was seriously hurt when he was accidentally shot with a gun that was supposed to be loaded with blanks rather than actual bullets. Something similar had happened to Bruce Lee's son Brandon years later when he'd been filming *The Crow*. R.R. proved that even that unlikely event wasn't without precedent. In the aftermath of that particular tragedy, conspiracy theories abounded. There was less public attention when the person working on *From the Depths* was hospitalized. Nobody seemed to care very much about an extra working on a low-budget, British B-movie. But you have to wonder how these things happened. Even in the Swinging 60s, there must have been health and safety checks.

Into the 70s, and things went unnaturally (for R.R.) quiet, which must have been a pleasant surprise for the bigwigs. It was business as usual. Either there were no incidents at all, or none were deemed sufficiently serious to be recorded.

The peace wouldn't last.

On March 27, 1973, there was a bizarre double tragedy. Firstly, at around 6:00 a.m., a panic-stricken, fourteen-year-old boy by the name of Tim Marsden ran to the front desk saying he'd been out on an early morning fishing trip with his father Roger when he'd lost his footing on the tiny boat they'd rented and fallen into the lake. The man disappeared beneath the surface, leaving young Tim to row to the shore alone and raise the alarm.

The truly strange thing was that, despite an extensive search, Roger Marsden's body was never found. Sometimes, if people fall into rivers, they get carried out to sea, and from there they can get taken by the currents and end up almost anywhere. But for a body to go missing in an enclosed space like the lake was a real mystery. It was speculated that the body must have either become entangled in submerged debris or found its way into an underwater tunnel or cavern but that was all it was. Speculation.

The second tragedy happened later that same afternoon, while the search was in full swing. The weather took a sudden turn for the worse, which isn't exactly unusual in the British Isles, and it was decided the search should be suspended until it cleared As one of the many search boats was making its way back to shore, it struck a diver, killing him instantly. It was probably scant conciliation for his family, but at least the diver's body was recovered and given a proper burial.

It was always assumed that the body of Roger Marsden would turn up sooner or later, but as far as Ben could tell, it never did. That meant it must still be down there, somewhere in that huge expanse of water. It would now be a skeleton, stripped of flesh and tissue, locked in a watery purgatory as people swam and went boating or fishing around it, all blissfully unaware. Ben shuddered, the images from the Hammer Horror movie still fresh in his mind.

And that wasn't the only strangeness he found regarding the lake.

Whilst trawling through the archive of a local newspaper called the *East Anglia Gazette*, he found not one, but three reports of people seeing disembodied, multi-colored lights over the water. More specifically, in the vicinity of the uninhabited little island. What's more, one of the articles referenced several other, older reports, and an old legend indicating that the lights were an omen of death. There was speculation that they could be the result of swamp gas or some kind of barely understood atmospheric phenomena. The most recent report, made in 1994, suggested aliens could be at work. This was a typical reflection of popular culture, Ben thought. In the days of *The X-Files*, when alien abduction and cattle mutilations were all over the news, people were keen to relate any unexplained event to aliens, whereas a hundred years ago they would blame everything on fairies.

Ben yawned and rubbed his eyes with the heels of his hands. Ten more minutes and he would call it a day. Overall, he enjoyed being his own boss and working for himself, as opposed to dancing to someone else's tune. Nobody ever got rich working for someone else, not that getting rich was his priority. The downside was that there was no safety net and very little wiggle room. You couldn't afford to have a day off or be unproductive for long because then you didn't get paid. Ben didn't need much. He looked around at the money-soaked clientele at R.R. and had no desire to be like them. Money wasn't his main motivation. He was driven by something else, something more profound: a thirst for knowledge, a desire to solve the unsolvable, to succeed where others had failed. These were the things that spurred him on, made him fight through the darkness to find those little shards of light that made everything worthwhile.

Mr. Trimble lazily rousing himself from his usual spot on the bench made Ben switch focus.

"What's up, dude?"

The cat gave a grizzled meow in response and stalked his way to the rear of the camper van, tail twitching, to where his litter tray was kept. This was followed by the sounds of digging, scratching, and beads of litter being strewn across the floor.

"Oh, wonderful. That turkey and sausage went straight through you, huh? Consequences of living like a king, I suppose."

Ben was familiar with the signs and knew that it was time for Mr. Trimble to evacuate his bowels. Pretty soon, the confined space they shared would be contaminated with the eye-watering stench of cat poop. It wouldn't be so bad if Mr. Trimble didn't insist on making eye contact while he did his business.

Look at me, human. I'm pooping. You will watch, and you will admire.

To take his mind off the unfolding drama, Ben pulled out his phone and scrolled through his contacts until he found Christine Turner's number. He didn't want to be a nuisance. He knew she was a busy woman. But he liked to maintain a channel of communication with his clients, and now that he'd uncovered a bit more history, he wanted to touch base and provide a progress report. Not that there was much actual progress to report.

Deciding against a phone call, which could be considered intrusive at that time of night, he typed out a text message instead. That way, the resort manager could reply at her leisure. To his surprise, Christine replied almost instantly, and they arranged a meeting at her office for the following morning.

By now, Mr. Trimble had finished his business and came fussing around Ben's ankles, all headbutts and purrs. He wasn't the most sociable of animals, but for some reason he always sought attention after using his litter tray. It was almost as if he craved the recognition.

"Nice dump?" Ben said as he tickled a white spot on Mr. Trimble's upturned chin. "Suppose I'd better clean that up before it stinks the place out."

He went to the litter tray, strategically placed as far away as possible from where he usually sat, and used the handy poop scoop to fish out two good-sized turds and a chunk of soiled litter.

Then he was presented with a conundrum. If he was in the countryside, or bedding down in some other secluded spot, he would simply toss the excrement out of the nearest window. After all, it was natural fertilizer. But that was something you couldn't do at most campsites for obvious reasons, and something you certainly couldn't do at a place like the Regal. Not if he wanted to keep his privileges.

Instead, he dug around in the junk drawer beneath the sink, the place where he kept old receipts, pens, boxes of Paracetamol, and various other odds and ends, until he found an old plastic bag. Poop scooped and bagged, he looked around for something to do with it. He couldn't dump it in the waste-paper basket. If he was going to do that, he may as well as left it in the litter tray. There must be a litter bin of some description outside.

Sliding open the van's side door while still holding the plastic bag at arm's length, he stepped outside into the peaceful, still night.

From the car park he could see the main residential block, where many of the rooms still had lights on, the occupants probably either watching TV or preparing for bed. Knowing he had a room reserved was not only a comfort but a privilege he planned to make full use of, and he'd already made up his mind to retire there before midnight for a well-earned sleep.

Spying a bank of industrial-sized rubbish skips at the far end of the car park, he headed in that direction, his mind already on that warm, soft bed.

Suddenly, the peace was shattered by the wail of sirens. Several, by the sound of it.

What the hell?

The cacophony of noise was still quite a distance away, but it was getting closer by the second. Ben stopped and looked anxiously up the road toward the main gate. He could imagine a convoy of emergency vehicles winding their way through the network of country lanes Tim Norgood had introduced him to earlier.

The noise grew louder and louder until a white vehicle sporting a blue light appeared, skidded to a momentary halt, paused for the gate to be opened, then continued into Regal Retreat.

At first, Ben couldn't tell if it was a police car or a paramedic, but he could discount a fire engine on the simple basis that the vehicle wasn't big enough to be a fire engine. Plus, nothing appeared to be on fire. He couldn't see any flames, smell any smoke, or hear any shouting. Quite the opposite. An expectant hush had settled over the entire resort. He could feel the anticipation and could almost see the blinds twitching in the residential block across the road.

As it traveled up the narrow road toward him with its top-mounted blue light flashing, the vehicle killed its siren. Ben could now see it was a police car. It was closely followed by another, and then an ambulance.

Something had happened.

Something big.

Chapter Nine

East Anglia, 1645

"Do you, Elizabeth Thrower, admit that you lie with the devil? That you, willfully and consciously, did agree to be his instrument here in the Kingdom of Earth?"

It was Ezra Davenport speaking. That kiddie-fiddling, sheep-bothering, bastard. Who else? He'd had it in for Elizabeth ever since he'd started confessing his multitude of sins to her, and it was clear he didn't think she could keep them to herself. The less people knew about his sordid activities, the better.

Behind Davenport hovered another figure she didn't recognize. It was shrouded in a long, dark cloak topped off with a large-rimmed hat above a face partially concealed with a thick, black beard.

Elizabeth opened her mouth to deny the awful accusations. She didn't believe in God, not their God anyway, so how could she possibly be in league with the devil? That was a Christian creation, a religion to which she did not adhere. The charge was akin to accusing an owl of trespassing.

But all that came out of her mouth was a shrill scream as she writhed in the chair to which she was lashed.

The pain was too much.

She could feel her insides ripping and tearing as the cold metal thing they'd pushed inside her seemed to grow with every movement. Each time Ezra Davenport turned the screw, often at the instruction of the mysterious stranger at his side, fresh bolts of agony racked her quivering body and more blood gushed out of her onto the floor between her feet to gasps from the assembled audience.

She was in a room crowded with people swimming in and out of her view. It was hard to move her head, and it was a long time before she realized they must have strapped her head to the chair.

Some of the faces she recognized. There was Davenport, of course. She also saw Lynette the farmer's wife, Francis the Cobbler, and Tom the Baker, who was rarely seen at social events. Maggie Phipps, the woman he was having an affair with, was also in attendance, though Elizabeth noticed they kept a polite distance, each of them grinning manically and taunting her as the torturers gleefully went about their gruesome business.

Once, she thought she caught a glimpse of Gideon in the crowd. Her lost love. Had he come back for her? After all this time? She always suspected he'd left her for another woman. Why else would he leave the sanctity of the home they'd built together without so much as a parting word? For the past thirty years she had resented him for it and wished him only misery. She even kept his surname to remind her every day of his wickedness.

Her hope was crushed when she realized she was mistaken. He wasn't there. Why would he be?

Elizabeth longed for the serenity of eternal darkness to take her, if only to put an end to the pain and humiliation. But every time she neared unconsciousness, someone would douse her with freezing water and bring her back to this awful reality. They wouldn't let her rest. For days, it continued. And nights.

After dragging her from her hovel after dark, they'd brought her here to this cottage on the edge of the village. The same village she'd grown up in. First, they beat her and tied her to a chair. Then cut off all her hair whilst bombarding her with questions.

After that, they'd started cutting and chopping at her flesh with a sharp silver dagger, thinking that would be enough to make her confess to doing deals with the devil.

It wasn't.

So they cut and chopped more, and more. Soon, most of the skin from her arms and legs had been flayed and lay strewn around the little room in pale, gore-streaked clumps. In a moment of clarity, she saw a fly settle on one and instinctively knew the creature was tasting her. The torturers were careful not to cut too deep. They wanted her to confess, not die. Her confession would validate their crimes and reinforce their twisted ideology.

By then, Elizabeth was almost delirious from the pain, but still she refused to bow to their demands.

Then, as their frustration got the better of them, they brought in the instrument. Elizabeth caught a glimpse of it and saw that it looked like an oversized metal pear with a long, wooden handle attached to it. She wondered what purpose it could serve and what they were going to do with it. The moment they forced open her legs and ripped off her undergarments, she knew.

The pain was unimaginable. Elizabeth thought about succumbing to their whims and fancies just to make it stop.

What did it matter?

She was going to die anyway, by one means or another. She may as well save herself this ordeal.

But some obstinate, resolute part of her character refused to be swayed. Let them do what they wanted. The body was just flesh. Her spirit would remain strong, and she would laugh in the face of hardship the way she'd always done. She wanted to die with her dignity intact, not bend to the whims of others. She'd done enough of that in life, and this is what it had brought her.

Untethered and free to roam, her brittle mind drifted away from her pain-filled body in search of blessed relief. She was a little girl again, playing catch in the sunshine with her friends in the village. She was innocent, happy, and carefree in a much simpler time.

It wouldn't last. The world was waiting to envelope her in misery, blackening and corrupting her soul. Even at such a young age, Elizabeth was never like the other kids. She knew things. Things she shouldn't, and sometimes couldn't, know.

Yet, she did.

She didn't even have to go looking for it. The knowledge just appeared in her mind as if planted by some external force. Sometimes it was quiet and barely perceptible as if being glimpsed through a veil. Other times, the knowledge was loud and brash, demanding her attention.

The ability lent itself well to being a sin eater, for she was never shocked. Not only because she was used to dealing with the worst aspects of the human character, but because often she could see the sins in her mind's eye even before the sinner confessed.

When she came of age, her grandmother told Elizabeth she had the "gift." She was a seer, and she should be proud of the fact. It was rare. The gift had skipped her mother. Neither did it imbue itself on either of her elder sisters. Nobody knew where or upon whom it would manifest. That was as much a mystery as its origins. But everyone was in silent agreement that it didn't strike without reason or cause.

Having something very few people had was both a blessing and a curse. It made Elizabeth feel special, but she was glad that her grandmother wasn't alive today to see what had become of the world and what these charlatans were doing to her and her kind.

And then there was a new pain, unbearably hot and searing, dragging her back to the dreadful present. The cottage, the chair, the villagers.

Compared to her other wounds, the pain seemed small at first, almost insignificant. More of a minor annoyance than anything. But it steadily grew in intensity until the hurting in her woman parts, as anguished and severe as it was, almost paled in comparison.

They were ripping out her fingernails.

All the while, Davenport shouted at her, dousing her face with his vile spittle. "Admit your deeds, witch!"

Elizabeth remained stubbornly silent. Oh, she wanted so much to yell and scream and tell the assembled crowd of all this man's wrong-doings.

She wanted to spill all their secrets, one after the other. Every last one of them. Let them all wallow in their filth and then tear each other apart. It was no less than they deserved.

But she knew nobody would believe her. They would think she was lying out of a thirst for revenge. In other words, doing the devil's work. It would only help them justify their actions. So no, she would bide her time.

It would come.

As her body finally relinquished its hold and each nail was wrenched free from the flesh that had housed it, it made a strange popping sound. Elizabeth wasn't sure if it was an actual sound or just something she could hear in her head. Each time a nail came away, the assembled masses roared and cheered their approval, then fell silent again to await the next.

By the fourth or fifth nail, Elizabeth didn't even have enough strength left to scream. Her head, clumps of matted hair still clinging to it, lolled uselessly atop her neck, held in place only by leather straps as her swollen eyelids drooped.

Darkness.

Another splash.

More cold water.

And she was awake again.

The end was near. She could feel its shadow descending on her.

And she was glad.

So glad.

"She is obstinate," Ezra Davenport said. Not directly to Elizabeth, but rather to himself or one of his cohorts. The disappointment in his voice was clear. He wanted to see her buckle and break.

"Indeed," came another, unfamiliar voice.

She was too far gone to raise her head, but Elizabeth knew it was the cloaked stranger who spoke. His voice, gravelly and thick like treacle, matched his demeanor.

"Obstinate she may be. But let us see if she passes the final test. Untie her."

Early on the morning after R.R. was overrun with emergency vehicles, Ben was in Christine Turner's office, as previously arranged. The resort manager looked haggard and drawn, as if sleep was a distant memory, and her eyes kept flicking anxiously toward her office phone and mobile, which lay side-by-side on the desk. She was expecting calls, and probably lots of them. "Can we keep this brief?" she said, her voice hoarse and harried.

"Sure thing," Ben replied. "I won't take up much of your time."

"So, what can I do for you?"

"You can start by telling me what happened last night?"

"What do you already know?"

"Absolutely nothing. I was working in the van when, just after eleven, a paramedic and several police cars showed up. Being of a naturally curious disposition, I hung around for a while. But it became increasingly difficult to keep a low profile, and when a cop asked me to go back to my room, I retired to the van instead. I thought that might be easier. When I woke up this morning, the whole place was crawling with police. Crime scene investigators, forensics, people taking statements and asking questions. I'm sure I spotted a couple of news crews buzzing about, too."

Christine sighed. "Yes. This is exactly what we wanted to avoid. In fairness, I believe the emergency services were as discreet as they could be, but the damage had been done, I suppose. As for the news crews, that was unavoidable, too. I have no idea how the news leaked out so quickly, but those people are good at their jobs. They have their methods. Maybe they patch into police scanners or something. Did you talk to the press?"

"No, and I don't intend to."

"What about the police?"

"In all honesty," Ben said, "I find it better to not talk to police unless they talk to you first. Call it a life rule."

"Well, I doubt you'll be able to avoid it much longer. They have lists of all our workers and guests. It seems they're working their way through everybody, and they'll be eager to interview as many as possible."

"Regarding?"

"I really don't want to go into detail."

"But if the news is already out, it's only a matter of time before it becomes a matter of public knowledge. I could go home and Google it."

"Are the names Ronald and Marjorie Brand familiar to you?" Christine said, sighing.

"No, I don't believe so. Are they guests here?"

"Yes," Christine replied before hastily correcting herself. "Well, maybe I should use past tense. They *were* guests here. Now one of them is dead and the other is a guest at the local police station."

"Jesus. What happened?"

"The police are still trying to work that out."

"Accident? Suicide? Murder?"

Christine looked awkward. "If you don't mind, I'd prefer not to speculate. Anything I say would be little more than conjecture, and this is not the time for that. But let's just say we can probably take 'accident' off the table."

"I understand," Ben said, suddenly feeling a rush of sympathy for the woman, who was obviously trying to keep it together and remain professional under difficult circumstances.

"Was there something else you wanted to discuss this morning, Mister Shivers?"

Ben thought about it for a moment, before saying, "You said you brought me here to investigate the inflated death rate."

"That's right, we did," Christine replied.

"There was no other reason?"

The woman hesitated, and in that instant Ben knew beyond doubt that the resort manager wasn't being entirely straight with him.

"Christine, if you want me to get to the bottom of whatever's going on here, you're going to have to come clean and tell me everything."

"Fine. It's this so-called ghost problem."

"What about it?"

"It's perhaps a little more serious than I made out yesterday. We've even had T.V. crews from those big American paranormal T.V. shows asking to film here."

"So what?" Ben shrugged. "Lots of hotels claim to have ghosts. In fact, many of them use it in their marketing. The public love the idea of staying in a haunted house."

"Not here. People come here to relax. Not to have the shit frightened out of them. All the attention is bringing in the wrong kind of clientele. Between that and the mysterious deaths, it's like we're fighting a battle on two fronts. And it's a battle we're losing."

"So have people always reported seeing ghosts here?"

"Obviously, I haven't been here forever, but as far as I can tell, it isn't a recent problem. However, the…sightings? Experiences? Seem to be increasing both in frequency and intensity."

"Like whatever is here is getting stronger?"

"Precisely, Mister Shivers. And we'd like the matter dealt with once and for all.

"Unfortunately, hauntings are rarely that simple," Ben explained. "It's not like I'm a plumber called to fix a leaky tap."

"We understand that. I just wanted to stress the urgency, especially in light of last night's incident."

"You think it might be connected to a haunting?"

"As I said, I don't want to speculate," the woman replied, her eyes drawn once again to the pair of phones on her desk. "To me, that sounds like a leap. All I know for sure is that neither this growing paranormal reputation nor the events of last night can be good for the Regal. And that's my main concern."

"I get it," Ben said. "I'll ramp up my efforts."

"Please do that. Do you remember at our first meeting I described your business here as being 'low priority'?"

"I do."

"Well, the status has changed. You can now consider it high priority. Code red, in fact. If such a thing exists outside disaster movies. Whatever is happening here, whatever is causing these…incidents, we want it stopped. As soon as possible."

"Message received. In fact, I might be onto something," Ben said.

"Care to share details? I could use a lift."

Under different circumstances, the look of pure relief on Christine's face might have been comical. As it was, it just made her look more troubled.

"Actually, it's still a little early in the investigation. Like you, I wouldn't want to speculate."

"Touché, Mister Shivers. Touché."

As Ben bid farewell and exited the office, he heard the office phone ring. It was going to be a busy day for the resort manager.

So there had been another of Regal Retreat's infamous "incidents." Somehow, Ben wasn't surprised. They happened with such frequency that by the law of averages, if he stayed long enough, something was going to happen. Of course, you could say that about anywhere. But the fact that a guest had died within twenty-four hours of his arrival spoke volumes.

On his way out of the administration building, he plucked his mobile phone out of his front pocket and quickly scanned the local news sites. There was nothing online yet. Local newspapers, underfunded and stretched to breaking point, were rarely the best source of information. Most of the journalists they employed simply sat in their offices scanning the nationals waiting for someone else to break a story, which they then reproduced and followed up if it was considered to be of local interest.

That morning, Ben had noticed two marked police cars in the car park, along with a couple of immaculate dark blue Audis. Detectives. That suggested that whatever fate had befallen the Brands warranted investigation. Of course, every death warranted some form of investigation, but in this instance, the police presence was unnaturally heavy. That the incident had happened at such an exclusive location probably had some bearing on proceedings. In the company of so many rich, influential people, the police had to be seen to be proactive.

The police cars and Audis were still in the car park. What was more, some of the uniformed officers now appeared to be having some kind of debrief. Four of them were standing in a semi-circle around a stocky, middle-aged man with unkempt, sandy-colored hair and a 1970s-style pornstache.

Must be a detective, Ben thought as he deliberately slowed his pace in order to eavesdrop. The mustached guy seemed to notice and shot a glance in Ben's direction.

"Fuck," Ben muttered to himself. He immediately quickened his pace and pretended to ignore the gathering, as if finding a group of police officers having a meeting in a public car park was a common occurrence. Apart from a few parking tickets and teenaged transgressions, he had always been a law-abiding citizen, but police still made him nervous.

He briefly considered using the police presence to his own ends. Maybe he could latch on to their coattails and get some interviews from the staff and guests. If he used the right approach, he probably wouldn't even need to identify himself. Everyone would just assume he was with the police.

He immediately discounted that plan. What if someone challenged him? Even worse, what if the real police got wind of his activities and charged him with impersonating a police officer? At the very least, they would surely take a interest in him and what he was doing at the R.R. Not that he was doing anything illegal; it was just best to keep a low profile and wait for this, whatever "this" was, to die down a little.

On letting himself into the camper van, he fired up his laptop and with some trepidation settled down for another research session. What he found was more of the same.

After the double lake tragedy of 1973, there appeared to be another lull, this one stretching right up to October 13, 1979 when there was an apparent murder/suicide at one of the villas. Roger Tilbury, fifty-eight, strangled his wife Mary, then hung himself from the rafters. Jesus Christ.

As Foreigner faded out and gave way to Bon Jovi on his clockwork radio, Ben made some notes, then moved on up the timeline. In February 1981, a worker was killed in some kind of accident while tending to the grounds. Further research suggested that he had somehow managed to run himself over with a diesel-powered lawnmower. The chopping blades severed an artery in his leg, and he was dead before anyone could reach him.

Two years later, a summer concert was held on the grounds; a stage collapsed, putting three people, two performers and a member of the audience, in the hospital. Judging by the lack of follow-up stories, Ben assumed they all survived. Interestingly, an article in the online archive of the *East Anglia Gazette* dated March 7, 1982, suggested that a concert promoter had applied for a license to hold a folk music festival the following year, but the application had been rejected amid safety concerns.

Ben was just beginning to think about what he would get for lunch when he stumbled across something that stopped him in his tracks. It was another article from the *East Anglia Gazette*, this one dated March 7, 1987.

GIRL FOUND MURDERED AT EXCLUSIVE RESORT

It wasn't the headline that grabbed his attention; he was fast becoming desensitized to all the death and violence.

The thing that made him first lean closer to the computer screen to make sure his eyes weren't deceiving him, then recoil in horror when he realized they weren't, was the accompanying photograph. It showed a pretty, young, fresh-faced girl with a smattering of freckles and lush red hair cascading over her shoulders sporting a huge, toothy smile. In the picture, she was still wearing a school uniform, so she couldn't have been older than sixteen when it was taken. The caption said simply, "Beth White, 17, was found dead yesterday morning."

He knew the face.

Beth.

The smiling redhead who'd welcomed him to Ground Zero not long after he arrived at the R.R.

Was it really just the day before? So much had happened since then. It seemed as if a lot more time had passed.

There was a chance he could be mistaken. It could be a coincidence; someone with similar looks, a similar name, who worked at the same place?

No, that was stretching things a little too far. If that was the case, Ben could write a whole article on the synchronicity of it all. No. He knew in his bones that this was the same Beth he had met. And that picture. It was her.

But she was dead—and had been for over thirty-five years. That could only mean one thing.

Ben had seen a ghost.

And not only had he seen a ghost, but he'd interacted with a ghost. Conversed with one. She'd punched a hole in his voucher, which now sounded like an excruciatingly bad pun.

He swallowed hard and covered his mouth with his hand. No wonder Alex, the Eastern European guy he'd talked to, had no idea who Beth was. When she had been murdered, he hadn't even been born.

1987. The year Def Leppard released *Hysteria* and Andy Warhol died.

This was it. Exactly what Christine was talking about. The paranormal was merging with the normal. He'd walked right into the heart of the mystery and hadn't even realized it.

Ben suddenly felt sick to his stomach.

What the Christ had he got himself into?

Just then, there was a firm rap on the driver's side door.

Chapter Ten

The knock almost made Ben jump out of his skin.

Who the fuck could that be?

He wasn't expecting anybody. Nobody here even knew where he was parked.

Craning his neck, he peered in the direction of the door, but the curtain separating the camper's cockpit from the living area blocked his line of vision. He wouldn't be able to peak through without whoever was knocking seeing him.

He could lay low and pretend not to be home, but that was just ridiculous. Whoever it was would be able to see the light. He might be a little on the anti-social side, but he had nothing to be afraid of. Plus, not knowing who was knocking and why would tear him apart. He had to know.

Mr. Trimble shared Ben's trepidation. Having been rudely awoken from his latest slumber, he now stared straight at the source of the noise, eyes wide and ears pricked. Once, he glanced at Ben, and then back again.

Are you going to handle this or what?

Taking a deep breath, Ben leaned back and used his arm to sweep aside the curtain. A face stared back at him through the driver's side window. Unkempt, sandy-blond hair, awful porn-star mustache.

The detective he'd seen earlier. The one who had thrown him a dirty look.

Ben had obviously made the guy's "To Do" list.

Rejoice.

Ben smiled as the man made a turning motion with his hand. The meaning was clear: open the window.

Ben did better than that. He squeezed between the two seats into the cockpit and opened the door, forcing the policeman to take a step back to avoid being knocked over. "Help you?"

"Good morning, sir," the visitor said, flashing an open wallet displaying a police badge and warrant card. "Detective Carter, Norfolk Constabulary. Could I have a few moments of your time?"

"Why?" Ben said, instantly on the defensive.

The detective paused and looked Ben up and down. "Is this a bad time, sir?"

"Not at all," Ben replied.

I swear, if he says, "You look like you've seen a ghost," I'm going to fucking lose it.

"Looking a bit peaky, is all," the visitor said with a slight West Country burr. "Heavy night?"

"Nope. Have you tried getting a drink here?" Ben replied, again a little too defensively.

This wasn't going well. When he thought about it later, he wasn't even sure if the detective was implying what Ben thought he was.

"Well, I can assure you this won't take long."

"You'd better come 'round to the side door then," Ben said, trying hard to keep the agitation out of his voice.

The detective disappeared from view, but when Ben slid open the camper's side door, there he was. By no means a small man, he must have been six feet tall and edging toward eighteen stone. The van shuddered and re-settled as he hoisted himself inside while Ben was forced to retreat to make room for him. Stooping slightly, the detective cast his eye around the cramped living quarters. "Nice place," he said, his tone almost believable. He smelled faintly of old coffee.

"Thanks," Ben replied, motioning to the bench that represented the only place to sit. "Have a seat."

With a noticeable hesitation, as if he believed the bench would give way under his weight, which it very well might, the detective cautiously lowered himself down next to an unimpressed Mr. Trimble, who stood his ground while keeping a firm eye on the new arrival. "Is that a he or a she?"

"It's a he," Ben replied. "Meet Mister Trimble. Picked him up as a stray. The vet told me he was going to die. The vet lied, Mister Trimble got better, and I've been stuck with the little fleabag ever since."

"Friendly?" The way the detective said the word made it sound halfway between a question and a command.

"Usually," Ben said. "Unless you happen to be a rodent, in which case, he might tear you to pieces and leave your organs on the floor at my feet as an offering. I wouldn't take it personally."

Mr. Trimble chose that moment to cock his head slightly, suggesting firstly that he understood what his human was saying about him, and secondly that mutilation and dismemberment was entirely acceptable behavior.

"Beautiful animal."

"It might not show, but he appreciates it," Ben said, tickling Mr. Trimble's chin as he carefully positioned himself on the bench in between the cat and the detective. He wasn't falling for the policeman's fake platitudes, and he was pretty sure his cat wasn't, either.

Their knees were almost touching. God. Being in such close proximity to a total stranger was awkward, but it was unavoidable given the size of the detective and the relative dimensions of the camper van.

"As I said, I won't take much of your time. I just have a few questions."

"Fire away," Ben said, a knot of something between apprehension and excitement growing somewhere in his midsection.

"So, you're a paying guest here?"

"No. I suppose you could call it sort of a working holiday," Ben replied.

"And what kind of work do you do?" The detective produced a small notebook from his jacket pocket and began scribbling in it with a stubby yellow pencil.

"Journalist. Sort of. I run a website."

"Always fancied that kind of gig myself. Maybe some day I'll write a book, eh? They say there's a book in everyone, don't they?"

"They certainly do," Ben replied, hoping the detective wasn't about to ask him how to go about it or, even worse, collaborate. No doubt he would expect the service for free. People outside the industry rarely understood that writers didn't all do it for fun. To some it was a job, and professional people couldn't afford to fritter away their time. You would never dream of asking a builder you just met to build you a wall for free simply because they knew how.

For the first time, Ben noticed the detective's pale blue eyes. They were emotionless, and unnervingly cold. As they talked, they periodically flicked between Ben and some random spot elsewhere in the living area. He was looking for clues, or anything that might be amiss, and not being very subtle about it.

"Name?"

"Ben. Ben Shivers."

"S. H. I. V. E. R. S?"

"Correct."

"What kind of website did you say you ran?"

"I didn't say. But it's a paranormal investigation site."

"Hmm. And what does that entail?"

"Paranormal investigations, mostly." Ben wasn't deliberately trying to be facetious, but stupid questions sometimes warranted stupid answers.

"Ghost hunting?"

"Sometimes."

In Ben's experience, despite their profession, many police officers and other public servants were more receptive to the paranormal than most. They saw and experienced a lot in their working lives, some of which could not be adequately explained by science. They saw people at their worst, and in the most extreme situations. He'd once interviewed a paramedic who attended the scene of a car accident where a minibus carrying a group of school children had collided with a tree.

Three of the kids died, and more suffered catastrophic injuries. The paramedic became convinced that as she worked on the survivors in the road, the ghosts of the dead formed a protective cordon around her.

I could see them out of the corner of my eye, watching me. But when I turned to look at them, there was nothing there.

"Have you had any luck in chasing ghosts yet?"

"I don't know if I would call it 'luck,' but I leave most investigations with some kind of evidence, or at least closure for my clients. It's not like going fishing, you understand. There are rarely definitive, quantifiable solutions to these kinds of problems. Often, all people want is a reason. Any kind of resolution is a bonus."

"Of course, of course. So that's what you're doing here? Hunting ghosts?"

"Not in so many words," Ben said. "That's a very simplistic way of looking at it. A bit like me dismissing all police work as 'catching the bad guys.'"

"But that's precisely what it boils down to." The detective laughed a cold, humorless laugh. "That's a good analogy, though. I'd love to spend more time bending your ear, but unfortunately we have more serious business to attend to."

"We do?"

"Indeed. Could you tell me whether or not you've seen these people before?" the detective asked, producing a small color photograph from an inside pocket of his jacket with a deft flick of the wrist.

The picture showed an elderly couple standing arm-in-arm on a beach somewhere, white sand and green sea stretching out behind them. Their tanned, lined faces contrasted starkly with their white hair, giving the impression they were no strangers to exotic holidays.

Almost as a reflex, Ben opened his mouth to say no, he'd never seen those people before.

But then he hesitated.

Because he had.

In hindsight, he might have known who would be in the picture even before the detective showed it to him, and he silently thanked Christine Turner for the heads up. He could feel the detective's eyes trying to burrow into his mind and knew that the policeman would have spotted the recognition on his face even if he'd tried to conceal it.

"I don't know their names, but yes, I think I have seen that couple before. When I was checking into my room in the main block yesterday, I saw them coming out of the elevator. We're staying in the same place, I believe."

"The residential block?"

"Yep."

"What time would that have been?"

"I'm not sure exactly. It was after I'd eaten. Maybe around midday."

"Could you be any more specific about the time?"

"Sorry, no, I don't recall. Between twelve and one is the best I can do"

"Did you notice anything…unusual?"

"About them?"

"Yes."

Ben thought for a moment. "No, I can't say I did. Unless you call wearing matching T-shirts unusual."

"Matching T-shirts?"

"Blue, with GO FOR IT! written on the front in big letters."

"Why does that stick in your mind?"

"It's not every day you see people parading around in matching T-shirts." Ben was slightly alarmed, though not surprised, at how quickly the conversation had morphed from a friendly chat into something approaching an interrogation.

"I suppose not. Did anything about either one's demeanor strike you as odd?"

"Not at all. They just seemed like an old, happy-go-lucky couple on holiday. All smiles and pleasantries."

"Did you talk to either of them?"

"I believe we exchanged 'hellos.'"

"Who said it first?"

"I can't remember. Them I think."

"Which one?"

"Like I said, I can't remember. It was the kind of interaction you have dozens of times a day."

"Nothing noteworthy about it?"

"Nothing."

"Did they say anything else?"

"No, I don't think so."

"And did you see them again?"

Ben thought for a moment. "Actually, I did. I saw them later that same day, which would make it early yesterday evening. They were walking near the lake. At least, I think it was them."

"How sure are you?"

"Almost positive."

"What time would that have been?"

"Again, I'm not too sure. Around dinner time."

"You really need to get better at telling the time, Mister Shivers." The detective made no attempt to hide the irritation in his voice as he scribbled more notes in his notebook. "You don't wear a watch?"

"Who does these days?" Ben protested. "I'm not stupid. I have a mobile phone instead. I don't carry a flashlight either, in case you were wondering. Or a map. My phone comes equipped with both those things, too." Even as the words passed his lips, he noticed a chunky silver watch affixed to the detective's wrist.

Damn.

It wouldn't surprise Ben to learn that he carried a flashlight, too. And maybe even a map. "What's all this about, anyway?"

"The couple in the picture are Ronald and Marjorie Brand. At some point late last night, Marjorie murdered Ronald in their room. Bludgeoned him to death."

"What? That's terrible!" Thanks to Christine, Ben had had prior knowledge. But hearing the gruesome details, and which one had died, rammed everything home.

"Indeed, it is."

"What happened, exactly?"

"It's a police matter, Mister Shivers. The investigation is ongoing, and I'm not at liberty to discuss specifics."

"Of course."

"So, you have a room here, you say?"

"Yep."

"Why?"

"What do you mean?"

"Well, it seems you have a perfectly adequate living arrangement here. Cozy but adequate. But you say you met the Brands in the main accommodation block?"

"That's correct."

"So, what were you doing there?"

"My room is there. It's part of the deal. I use the van to work."

"To hunt ghosts in?"

"Sometimes."

Ben detected a note of condescension in the detective's voice.

"Why work here when there's a nice, comfortable room at your disposal?"

"Habit, I guess," Ben shrugged. "This place doubles as my office. Plus, I don't like leaving Mister Trimble here alone for too long. He gets bored. Then he's liable to chew the curtains or piss on the floor to show his displeasure."

"Lovely. I bet you're glad not all your guests do that. So what kind of arrangement do you have?"

"Well, I feed him and give him a place to sleep and he shits in the corner, hopefully in his litter tray, and sits on my keyboard to distract me from time to time."

Despite Ben's attempt to diffuse the situation, Detective Carter was unmoved. "I was referring to your arrangement with the Regal Retreat, sir."

"Sorry. Of course, you were."

"What's the nature of the work you're doing for them?"

"I am not at liberty to discuss specifics," Ben said, relishing the opportunity to turn the tables on the detective. "It's a matter of client confidentiality. Plus, I was made to sign an N.D.A."

"In the event of a criminal investigation, such agreements are usually rendered null and void, Mister Shivers."

Ben could feel himself begin to soften. The man was just doing his job. Who was Ben to stand in his way? Solving the crime should be everyone's priority. "I'm just doing some research with a mind to writing some articles about the place. I guess you could say it's for marketing and promotion purposes."

"Who did you arrange this with?"

"The resort manager, Christine Turner, commissioned me. You can check up with her."

"Thanks. I will," the detective said, still scribbling furiously in his little notebook.

"What room are you staying in?"

"Room three-twenty-seven."

"Third floor?"

"That's usually where you find rooms beginning with 'three.' Hotels and resorts are funny like that."

"Is that so?" Detective Carter said, fixing Ben with his cold, dead eyes. "Mind if I check on that, too?"

"Of course not," Ben said, knowing the detective was going to check every element of his story whether he agreed to it or not. That was what detectives did.

"Would you mind telling me where you were last night, Mister Shivers?"

"Not at all. I was here until just before midnight. Then I went outside to dump some litter in the bin, saw some police cars arrive, and thought it better I spend the night here out of people's way instead."

"Why would you think that was better?"

"You boys seemed to have your hands full without me parading around interfering with crime scenes or something."

"Why did you think there was a crime scene?"

"All the flashing lights kinda gave it away."

"And you slept right through until this morning?"

"I did."

"Can anyone corroborate that?"

"Sure. Mister Trimble was here with me the entire time."

"Any human witness?"

"Unfortunately not."

"Did you, at any point, consider leaving the resort?"

"No. Why would I?"

Ignoring the question, Detective Carter plowed on. "Did you see or hear anything out of the ordinary before or after the police arrived?"

"Apart from all the police cars and ambulances? Nope."

"So, what were your first thoughts when you realized there had been an incident?"

"My first thoughts? I can't remember. By that point, I was just thinking about bed. I knew that whatever was happening, or had happened, you guys would have it under control."

Ben found that when talking with people, especially people with an elevated sense of self-worth, a little flattery went a long way.

"Fair enough. What time did you say you first saw the Brands?"

"Around midday."

"What did you say to them exactly?"

"Just hello."

"And what did they say?"

"Erm…hello back, I think. Haven't we already covered this?"

"Just clarifying some details, Mister Shivers. Did they seem to be in good spirits to you?"

"They did. They were all smiles."

"And what time did you say you saw them after that?"

"I told you I wasn't sure."

Detective Carter pretended to consult his notes. "Ah yes, that's right. You did."

Ben knew the detective wasn't as bumbling and absent-minded as he was making out. If he was, he would never have attained the rank he had. He'd seen enough episodes of *Columbo* on Channel 5 to know that asking the same questions repeatedly was a tactic designed to check a story for holes. If the answers differed, it was an indication of guilt.

There was a short, awkward silence as both men looked at each other. Ben got the feeling that Detective Carter was waiting for Ben to break it, and soon enough, he did. He didn't appreciate being made to feel uncomfortable in his own home, even if his "home" was just a van. "Would that be all, Detective?"

Detective Carter studied Ben for a few more seconds. "How long did you say you'll be staying here at the Regal Retreat?"

"I'm not really sure. Maybe a few more days."

"No schedule to speak of?"

"Open-ended."

"Great. So would it be okay to drop by if I have any more questions?"

"Absolutely. Anything to help, Detective. You know where I'm staying, and where I'm parked. I promise I won't leave town without your say-so, Sheriff."

The detective remained stone-faced, Ben's latest attempt at humor falling just as flat as the others. As he stood, stooping to avoid bumping his head on the roof, Detective Carter motioned to Ben's computer, which was still open on a news archive. "Doing a spot of research?"

"Just reading up on the history of the place. All part of the service."

"Well, there's plenty of that," said the detective as he maneuvered his bulky frame closer to the door. "History, I mean."

"Can I ask you something?" Ben said, sensing an opportunity. "Maybe you can save me some legwork."

"Ask away."

"Who killed Beth Hughes? Back in eighty-seven?"

The detective stopped, turned his head, and regarded Ben with his cold, piercing blue eyes once again. "Why do you ask?"

"Just researching an article."

"About Beth Hughes?"

"About the Regal Retreat."

"It was before my time, I'm afraid. I might look it, but I'm not that old. The details of that case are a matter of public record, should you go down that route. I wouldn't be able to tell you anything Wikipedia or that news archive couldn't."

"So just to clarify, her killer was never found?" Ben pressed, determined not to be sidetracked.

"As the murder of Beth White remains officially unsolved, I would say no, we didn't. That's what 'unsolved' means, Mister Shivers. But you know what they say; never say never. New evidence might come to light any time. Police work has come a long way in the past three decades, and we are solving more historical cases each year."

"Were there any suspects?"

"Excuse me?"

"Suspects. Were there any…suspicions? Did you take anyone in for questioning?"

"There are always suspicions," the detective said. "But that's exactly what they are. Suspicions, until proven otherwise. Without solid, irrefutable proof, they don't mean much. Why the sudden interest? She hasn't come back, has she?"

Assuming it was rhetorical, Ben didn't dignify the question with an answer. Instead, he let Detective Carter have the last word and watched him, with some difficulty, turn and exit the vehicle.

As the door slammed behind him, Mr. Trimble turned his head to look at Ben as if to say, "What the fuck was all that about?"

Reading the cat's expression, Ben said, "I'm not sure, dude. I'm not sure."

Chapter Eleven

East Anglia, 1645

There was overwhelming relief as the cold, metal, pear-like instrument, now slick with blood and fluids, was pulled out unceremoniously from the space between Elizabeth's legs. Then the ropes binding her to the chair were cut, finally allowing her to slump to the floor, sobbing and shivering. She gagged and vomited, the hot sour liquid running down her chin and on to her chest as a grayness lurking on edges of her vision encroached and she began to slip into the abyss.

Suddenly, her face and head were once more drenched with icy cold water, and the villagers were on her immediately, pulling and grasping at what was left of her hair and withered limbs, their grip slipping and sliding on her mangled, bloodied flesh.

"Get the witch to her feet!" someone shouted.

And then the chorus started, dozens—or maybe hundreds—of disparate voices all coming together and chanting as one, "ON HER FEET, ON HER FEET, ON HER FEET!"

Too weak to fight back, Elizabeth was hoisted into the air and held aloft like a trophy.

Amidst the chaos enveloping her, two voices stood out. Her nemesis Ezra Davenport and the cloaked stranger. They were openly discussing what to do with her, their voices somehow floating above the din.

"Let the fire decide," Davenport decreed menacingly.

"No," the stranger protested. "The weather has not been kind to us. There is no more dry wood. There are other ways."

"May I remind thee that you are only here because I summoned you." Davenport's tone took on a darker tone. "I also made a sizable donation to the cause you recommended, if you remember."

"'Tis true. Indeed, I remember. You did both those things."

"Then should I not have a say in the woman's fate?"

"If that were indeed the case, what would you desire?"

"I want to see her burn. We all do!" There were eager exclamations from the rabid crowd of villagers.

"I said no," the stranger's voice remained calm, but bristled with a barely suppressed fury.

"Fine, then. We will crush her with weights. Let the force of God expel the evil from her body. Rain does not dampen the weight of a boulder!"

More raucous cheers.

"Again, no. I have other plans."

This seemed to anger Davenport, who, through more foul means than fair, had accumulated great wealth and become a prominent member of society because of it. He was not accustomed to not having his own way, nor having his authority questioned. "You," he seethed. "You come to my village, take my money, and think you can tell me what to do? Remind me, remind us all, who are you again?"

The cloaked stranger, evidently accustomed to dealing with such unruly characters, raised his voice assertively. "I am Matthew Hopkins, Witchfinder General, and by order of the crown, I have been given the task of scouring these green lands in search of witches and the Devil's familiars. Largely because the local dignitaries such as yourself are incapable of doing so. Or, of course, are they themselves in league with the devil. Whenever and wherever such examples are found, I interrogate them and act accordingly."

"With respect, in this instance, you are not acting in accordance with the will of the people. As you can see, they want her to burn. Isn't that right?"

There was a cheer of approval. The loudest yet.

"I work to appease the crown," the stranger who called himself the Witchfinder General said, his tone both firm and weary. "Not the people, and certainly not you."

"The crown? And what if we reject this notion and carry out justice our own way?"

"Then you yourselves will be tried."

"For what crime?" scoffed Davenport.

"Treason. Or perhaps murder and abuse."

"But you are the one abusing this worthless witch!" As if to emphasize his point, Davenport lashed out with his palm and slapped Elizabeth across the jaw. Despite her awful injuries, the fresh bolt of unexpected pain made her wince. "You brought tools and erudition!"

"I did indeed," the man calling himself the Witchfinder General said. "The difference, Mister Davenport, is that I am paid by the King to do this work. It is both my occupation and my calling. It seems you just do it for fun, which is more akin to the Devil's work than the good Lord's."

Following this condemnation, Ezra Davenport, perhaps sensing that his foe could not be swayed, fell silent and let the stranger have his way.

Alone again, Ben sat on the bench in the van and ran his hands through his hair as he waited for his heart rate to stabilize. He felt almost violated, as if his insides had been taken out, examined, then put back in.

He tried not to take it personally. Detectives made a living violating people in the legal sense. It wasn't personal. Right now, Detective Carter was probably making someone else feel uncomfortable and probably getting a perverse kick out of doing so. Ben had nothing to hide, and therefore nothing to worry about. Not knowing the exact time you did something wasn't a crime. Unhelpful, maybe. But not a crime. Had he known there was going to be a murder, he would've taken notes.

Ben tried to put his run-in with Detective Carter out of his mind and returned his attention instead to Beth White, sourcing several other news articles so he could compare details and build up a more-detailed and -rounded picture of what had happened. Most articles rehashed the same information, but there was the odd nugget to be found.

It was widely accepted that Beth had been found by a walker early on the morning of March 6, 1987, lying in a pool of blood outside one of the villas next to the lake. None of the reports specified which one. That meant there was a one in six chance the body had been found outside the villa Tim Norgood and his wife currently occupied, where Ben had been just the day before. He could even have walked over the exact spot where Beth had been found.

The poor girl had suffered multiple stab wounds, mostly to her back and torso, and there was evidence she'd been sexually assaulted. She had only worked at the resort for three weeks.

Because she'd lived on site, in the staff quarters in the administration building, the assumption was that she had either been out walking alone or been enticed out of her room by a person or persons unknown. Her roommate said she'd been acting strangely that night, more withdrawn and sullen than usual, as if something was on her mind. The roommate remembered Beth going out at around 10:00 pm, saying she was going to "Clear her head." The roommate never saw her again. By the time she woke up the next morning, Beth's body had already been discovered.

In the aftermath, the R.R owner, Michael Davenport, was quoted as saying, "This is indeed a terrible tragedy, and the thoughts of myself and all the staff here at the Regal Retreat go out to the poor girl's family. Though we didn't have time to see the best of her, she was a valued member of the team, and she will be greatly missed. We have complete faith in the justice system to find the culprit and bring them to trial. Rest assured, we will be making a donation toward funeral costs and associated expenses. We feel it is the least we can do under the circumstances."

How conscientious of them, Ben thought. Davenport seemed like the kind of guy who grabbed every opportunity to see his name in print. It was both ironic and somehow fitting that he himself would die at one of the very same villas just a few years later.

In the wake of Beth's murder, there was a lengthy police investigation. Numerous witnesses and suspects were brought in for questioning, but all were released without charge, and soon enough, the story faded away to make room for others. Just another unsolved murder. Ben was left with the impression that it was in a lot of people's best interests to see it sink into obscurity, not least of all the Regal Retreat, who didn't need any more bad publicity, and the local police, who'd been again found wanting. You would think they'd be more adept at solving serious crimes, given the practice they got around here.

One of the most poignant pieces Ben found online was an appeal for information by Beth's heartbroken parents. They were barely in their forties, but the experience had prematurely aged them. They were broken. In the accompanying photograph, they held onto each other for support as they stared grimly into the camera with washed-out eyes swollen from crying. Despite that, there was still an air of defiance about them.

Ben could sympathize. To have a child ripped from this world was the most brutal thing imaginable. It just wasn't right, and it fucked with the natural order of the universe. People grow up, have kids, get old, then die. And somewhere along the way, their kids have kids. That was what was supposed to happen, so when it didn't, people naturally felt some kind of injustice. More than that, they wanted someone to blame.

Unfortunately, Beth's parents got neither. At least in Ben's case he could blame bad luck, the fire, or, at a push, his own inadequacies at being a father. Who or what could these poor people direct their anger at? Some faceless murderer who was never even identified, let alone punished?

By now, Ben was convinced he'd met an actual ghost. The question that most irked him was why had Beth chosen to show herself to him of all people? It hadn't been a fleeting glimpse of a shadowy figure, a stolen insight into another world. This was no case of mistaken identity. There had been an interaction, a conversation with a girl who'd been murdered decades earlier. They had bonded.

Ben had experienced some weird shit in his life, some of which couldn't be rationalized or explained away by science. But contact with the spirit world to this extent was not just rare; it was practically unheard of. They had talked, had an intelligent interchange, and while they did so, Beth White had appeared as solid and real as anyone else at the R.R.

If not an encounter with a ghost, maybe he had been the victim of some kind of time slip? Had he somehow traveled back in time to some point prior to Beth's murder in 1987? That seemed even more unlikely.

The only other possible explanation was that someone was playing a practical joke on him. But who? And more importantly, why? If that were indeed the case, it was extraordinarily well-planned and executed, and involved an entire cast of characters. Who on earth would be cruel enough to hire someone to play the victim of an unsolved murder in the name of a prank?

No. He had met Beth White. Somehow, he had met her.

Perhaps he wasn't the only one. Maybe the interactions were so frequent and lifelike that most people didn't even realize she was a ghost. Or maybe some did, but only on a subconscious level. Frowning, Ben searched several different terms on the internet.

Beth White ghost, Regal Retreat time slip, Regal Retreat time travel.

The time-travel stuff yielded no results whatsoever, and any search term containing "Beth White" redirected to one of the articles written about her murder. Nothing new there.

Thinking perhaps not everything made it into the newspapers, he had an idea. He picked up his phone and dialed Christine Turner's office.

She answered on the second ring. "Ben," she said, her tone slightly irritated. "What is it? I've been fending off the press most of the morning."

"I just have a quickie," Ben replied.

"Okay, go."

"You said before that several people had reported seeing ghosts at the R.R.?"

There was a brief, uncomfortable silence, during which Ben could almost visualize the resort manager figuratively, or even literally, banging her head against her desk. "Yes, I did. Why do you ask? Has anything else happened that I need to know about on this day of days?"

"Not to my knowledge. Although I did receive a visit from a Detective Carter, who will probably be checking up on my story with you at some point."

Christine sighed. "Yes, I've already met Detective Carter."

"Charming fellow."

"Totally. But as long as he does his job, I'm prepared to put my personal feelings aside," Christine said, as if this was something she had already discussed, either with someone else or herself.

"So, about those ghost sightings."

"What about them?"

"Do you keep a database or ongoing record of such reports?"

"Of course not." Christine's tone had now transcended impatient and was quickly heading toward derisory. "Who does that? We keep records of tangible events and quantifiable facts, not gossip and hearsay. Anyway, people tend to go right to the papers with that kind of thing to try to make a quick buck. Everyone loves a ghost story, don't they?"

"They do indeed. So, are you familiar with the Beth White murder?"

"Yes. It's one of the more famous— Sorry, infamous, ones."

"Why didn't you mention it before?"

"Mister Shivers, there are a hundred other murders and unexplained deaths I didn't mention. I was economizing our time, not deliberately trying to keep something from you. That would be futile, considering everything is so widely documented anyway."

"Point taken. So, what are your thoughts on it?"

There was a long pause, presumably while Christine collected her thoughts. Ben could hear her breathing and could almost hear the wheels of her mind turning. But, in addition, he sensed something else. Some undercurrent he couldn't quite identify. Finally, she said, "We all have thoughts and opinions. I'm not sure how relevant mine are."

The words came out slowly, as if having been carefully selected. Maybe a little too carefully.

Ben decided to push, just a little. "Well, do you know if anyone here has ever seen her ghost?"

"The ghost of Beth White?" Christine's tone suddenly went up a few notches, as if she couldn't quite believe she was having this conversation.

"Yes."

"I don't... I can't think of any off the top of my head. Have you tried searching online?"

"In the process. I just thought I'd go straight to the horse's mouth, so to speak. I was kinda hoping you would have that ongoing record."

"Well, I'm sorry I can't be more help." Her tone was dismissive, the conversation almost over.

"Not a problem. I just have one more question."

"Make it fast. I have a reporter from *The Times* waiting outside."

"Is any one ghost reportedly seen more than any other at the Regal?"

"That's an easy one. Yes."

"Who?"

This time there was no pause. "That would be the Gray Lady."

Chapter Twelve

East Anglia, 1645

As Elizabeth was held aloft, she felt hands all over her, grabbing, clawing, pinching, slapping. Everyone wanted a piece. She didn't know where she was being taken. It didn't matter anymore. She knew the end was near, and that was enough. This would all be over soon. In her fractured mind, death would be a blessing. At least the pain would stop. But even the physical agony and the awareness of her body being systematically ravaged and mutilated as her assailants sought to break her down wasn't the worst of it. That was the betrayal.

She'd been a valued part of the community once. But now these very people she'd served for so long had been seduced by this new ideology taking over the land and turned their backs on her. Not only that, but they wanted to destroy her. All the times she'd helped them in the past, all the relationships she had built and nurtured, counted for nothing. The pain this knowledge caused cut her deeper than any blade ever could.

She was suddenly glad she'd never taken a husband or borne a child, for if she had, they surely would also become targets. She didn't want to see her loved ones suffer this kind of trauma. This was a battle she had to fight alone.

It was fitting, she thought. She'd been born alone, had lived her life alone, and now she would die alone. And in the very same place. She'd never traveled far, her entire life played out within a few square miles.

As she was carried out of the dwelling into the night, the chilly air bit into her, prickling her flesh and making her shivers more intense. She gazed up at the night sky studded with beautiful stars like pin pricks of light in a heavy blanket, her eyes full of questions that would never be answered.

These people were doing this in the name of their God. What kind of deity demanded such sacrifice? What had she done that could be considered so wrong?

She hadn't hurt anybody. She was just a lonely spinster trying to make her way through life as best she could. The only people she spoke ill of deserved it. Who is really at fault, the sinner or the one who holds the sinner to account?

Elizabeth subscribed to the old ways and bowed before the plethora of ancient gods. The ones that had always been, and always will be. Not this perverse Christian sham that promoted only intolerance and suffering. How many people had died already in the name of this so-called God? And how many more must die before the remaining populace were battered into submission? This religion was nothing but a tool that enabled the wicked to ply their awful trade and be revered for it by legions of unseeing buffoons.

"Where are we taking the witch?" a faceless minion shouted, one of the many who sought his God's affection by persecuting another human being.

Elizabeth knew the answer even before the one calling himself the Witchfinder General could voice it. Sometimes, her foresight was a curse rather than a blessing.

"The lake."

Elizabeth could contain herself no longer. Summoning all her reserves of anger, she harnessed it and used it as her driving force. From her lofty position, she yelled, "Davenport? Where are you? Can you hear me? How was Polly last night? Polly, your youngest? Did you enter her room, put your hand over her mouth, and take her while her mother slept? The way you did last week and the week before? On the Sabbath, no less? And after the deed, did you not swear her to secrecy once more? And threaten her very life should she ever speak out?"

The raucous sounds of the baying crowd dropped by just a few notches, the villagers keen to learn more secrets about their brethren even in the throes of bloodlust.

"Silence! Silence, you witch!" Ezra Davenport raged.

"But what a man does behind closed doors is nobody's business but his own. Isn't that right, Ezra? Isn't that what you told me that night you attacked me? I wonder what your little Jack Russell would say if he could speak our language. Would he perhaps tell us what happens on those late-night walks you take him on? Or of your tiny manhood? With a pee-pee that size, it really is a wonder you were able to make children at all."

There was an audible gasp from the onlookers.

That time, Davenport didn't slap her with his open palm. He made a balled fist, swung, and punched her.

Elizabeth grunted as the blow landed square on her chin. One of her teeth popped out and her mouth filled with blood as her lower jaw hung dislocated.

"See how many cheap lies you spread, whore," Davenport said. Then he leaned in closer, until his face was mere inches from hers. "One more thing for you to know before ye go," he growled. "Do you remember that lover you took? The name escapes me. Oh! Gideon? The man you lived in sin with all those summers ago?"

"L…left me…" Elizabeth croaked, each syllable sending shockwaves of pain through her shattered jaw.

As the crowd started cheering and moving in unison once more, Ezra Davenport laughed. "That's where you're wrong. He never left you. All this time, he's been closer to you than you think. That's what ye get around here for being a liar and a cheat from away, see? Treating us village folk like simpletons and looking down his nose at us. But don't you worry, you'll be reunited soon. And your reunion will be sweet, I'm sure."

The Gray Lady? It was hardly original, but Ben didn't recognize the name from his research. He checked his notes to make certain and found that in all the dozens of people he'd come across so far in this investigation, none had so much as mentioned any kind of ghostly lady, be it gray, blue, or pink with yellow spots. He quickly typed the name into Google and hit "enter."

The search yielded quite a few results and it soon became apparent why this Gray Lady hadn't cropped up before. Until then, his research had been focused on actual events. Documented, historical occurrences. Everything had been rooted in reality. Anxious to explore all other possibilities first, he'd been actively avoiding the esoteric route. But things were about to take a sharp left turn. It was often the case that paranormal activity became concentrated in places where there had been a lot of misery and suffering. This extended to sites where natural disasters had occurred, or even accident black spots. It was almost as if the ghosts, or whatever else was causing the activity, were drawn to it, possibly even fed off the negativity.

This new line of inquiry revealed that the Gray Lady was synonymous with the Regal Retreat. A typical account was to be found in a local publication called *East Anglia Argus*, which, though now defunct, was archived in an online database Ben subscribed to. A Halloween-themed article dating from October 1979 read, in part:

> One of the most enduring ghost stories in the entire county is that of the Gray Lady, who has been sighted frequently on the grounds of the Regal Retreat over the years. She is usually seen in a tattered gray dress, which led to her nickname, but her real identity is believed to be that of the doomed Elizabeth Thrower who was tried as a witch. On occasion, the ghostly Gray Lady has been seen in such vivid detail that she was mistaken for a living person, and only when the witnesses

look down and see her gliding with her feet making no impression, nor even touching the ground, do they realize they are in the presence of a supernatural entity. Her favorite haunt is said to be along the banks of the lake, where she has been frequently spotted by visitors.

There were a few other reports of sightings on blogs and in the local press, but the Gray Lady, aka Elizabeth Thrower, was usually only mentioned as part of a larger article about something else. One piece he found described her as a "local witch," and another as a "famed ghost." Though evidently not famed enough to have much written about her over the years. Ben made a mental note to put that right before his time at the R.R. was up, or shortly thereafter.

Would Christine have any useful information about this woman? He decided that even if she did, it probably wouldn't be in his best interest to bother her again today. He understood that recent events had knocked him way down the pecking order and didn't want to push his luck.

Then he had an idea.

Opening the side door of the camper, he peered outside. It was cloudy, and the temperature seemed to have dropped a few degrees. It was quiet, with very few people around, and tiny pellets of drizzle hung in the air. A stiff breeze blew in off the lake and the air seemed oppressive and thick, all of which fit the general mood. There were still police cars, both marked and unmarked, in the car park, but now there was just one of each, leading Ben to assume that the bulk of the police presence had already moved on to something else.

Perfect.

Ben grabbed a lightweight jacket and headed out.

As he passed the lake, he stopped to study it for a while. It was captivating. Apart from several walkers skirting the perimeter and whatever creatures existed within its depths, it was completely devoid of life. Without people and sunshine, the vast body of water took on a foreboding deep blue hue, and clouds of wispy, translucent mist rolled across the rippling surface, enveloping the tiny island in the middle. He half expected to see a display of disembodied colored lights like those he'd read about, but all was silent. Under these conditions, the scene took on an eerie, otherworldly quality, making it look like some kind of fairy kingdom.

Ben's mind flashed back to what he'd read about the horror movie that had been filmed here, and in that moment, it was easy to believe that the murky water played host to some kind of bloodthirsty, supernatural creature. Not just the metaphorical kind, but one of flesh and bone. With a shiver not caused entirely by the chill in the air, he pulled up his collar and continued on his short journey.

He feared Tim and Sheila Norgood might have gone out for the evening, or perhaps they had checked out of the Regal by now. Anyone hoping to have a quiet break was shit out of luck given recent events. So it was with no short measure of relief that, as Ben approached the villas on the banks of the lake, he saw Tim's pride and joy, the red Plymouth Fury, parked in the same place he'd last seen it. Stealing himself for what could be a very awkward conversation, Ben approached the door and knocked.

There was no reply.

He waited a few seconds, then knocked again. He was about to cut his losses and come back later when the door opened a crack, and Tim peered out.

"Yes?"

The man looked terrible. His eyes, narrowed to slits, were reddened, and deep wrinkles lined his face. It looked like he'd aged a decade in a day. Most alarmingly, he appeared not to remember who Ben was.

Confronted with such an unexpected sight made Ben retreat a step. "Tim?"

"Yes?"

"It's Ben. We met yesterday. Do you remember? You took me for a spin in the Fury?" He motioned to the classic car positioned on the drive behind him.

That seemed to spark something in Tim, and his mouth formed an "O" of surprise as recognition crept over his face. "Oh, of course I remember. Hi, Ben! Sorry, I'm a bit fuzzy. I was just taking a nap. Is there something I can do for you?"

"Er... Is this a bad time?" Ben started hesitantly.

"N-not at all. Just haven't been sleeping too well these days."

"Okay. Well... I was hoping I could pick your brains about something."

Tim looked unsure. "What would that be?"

"You said you're a local historian. I'd like to ask you some questions about... Well... Local history. Specifically, someone called Elizabeth Thrower? Does the name mean anything to you?"

Tim's eyes suddenly widened slightly before he regained his composure. "It... It does, yes."

"So could we have a chat? About her?"

"I-I guess that would be okay."

"Great!" Ben said, doing his best to inject some enthusiasm into his response and hoping it would somehow transmit to Tim. The guy looked half dead. "So how about I treat you to lunch? You can, of course, bring your wife, Sheila?"

"S-Sheila, yes," Tim replied, still hovering behind the door and emanating waves of suspicion. "When were you thinking?"

"How about now?"

Tim hesitated for a moment. "Actually, we already have plans for lunch. I'm afraid it's too late to renege."

"No problem," Ben smiled. "We could do dinner instead?"

"That would be better for us."

"Fine, you know Ground Zero?"

"Of course. It's about the only place to eat around here."

"Shall we say around seven?"

"Perfect," said Tim with obvious relief.

Ben couldn't decide whether the man was pleased to have made dinner arrangements or if he was just glad the awkward exchange was finally over.

Chapter Thirteen

East Anglia, 1645

Some time later, they arrived at the lake, on the shores of which Elizabeth had spent virtually her entire life. As if on some signal, all at once, the multitude of grasping hands let go of her, and she fell to the hard, unforgiving ground with a thump. It should have hurt, but instead, she took some quiet relief from the coolness of the pebbles and clods of damp earth pressing against her ripped and maimed flesh. Once more, her eyes began to close.

Somebody kicked her in the back. Hard. She felt the booted foot strike her spine and then a sudden numbness. She knew the blow did her serious damage. But she didn't flinch. Not only did she not have the energy to expend on such a futile task, but she didn't want to give her assailant the satisfaction. What did one more wound matter?

"Away, away!" someone yelled. It sounded like the one who called himself the Witchfinder General.

Was he going to save her? Perhaps experiencing a change of heart? Seeing the error of his ways?

Elizabeth didn't really think that was the case. But for one moment at least, a flame of hope ignited within her, and she began to dream of freedom. Of being permitted a return to her old life, as if all this were just a dream or some terrible mistake.

She knew it was too good to be true.

"Where is the rope? Get me the rope!" the voice said with authority.

Elizabeth's eyes fluttered open and she saw that yes, it was him. The Witchfinder General. For a moment his bearded face, now twisted into a bloodthirsty leer, swam in front of her, filling her vision, before swiftly disappearing.

Then she felt hands on her again. Pulling and manipulating her limbs.

She wanted to tell these people, *her* people, to go back to their wicked, sinful lives and leave her alone. But even if she did tell them that, they wouldn't listen. They'd worked themselves into a frenzy. Fragile, weak-minded underlings that they were.

Someone held her while someone else lashed her hands together tightly, the rope cutting into her wrists and opening up new wounds on top of old.

It's just flesh, she told herself.

"Now her feet!" the Witchfinder General shouted.

"Why, pray tell, are we doing this?" asked Ezra Davenport, his voice full of scorn. Elizabeth would know that voice anywhere.

"It is the final test!"

"Why waste our time? She should burn like the witch she is!"

"I said no! This is a trial by water. We shall bind her hands and feet and pitch her into the lake. If she is indeed laying with the devil, make no mistake, he will not let her die. He will come to her aid and make her float!"

There was a chorus of boos and jeers.

"And then?"

"And then, the trial will be over. We will know the truth, and she will hang."

"What if she isn't laying with the devil?"

"Then she will sink to the bottom of the lake and drown. Have you ever tried swimming with your hands and feet tied?"

"So either way she dies?"

The Witchfinder General didn't answer the question put to him. He didn't need to, and Ezra Davenport and his cronies seemed happy with the silence.

Once again Elizabeth was hoisted crudely into the air and carried closer to the murky depths of the lake. She was now so close she could smell it and hear the caw of birds as they swooped overhead. Moments later, she also heard the sounds of frenetic splashing and involuntarily recoiled within the grip of a dozen pairs of hands as ice-cold water sprayed her face and exposed skin.

There was nothing she could do now.

She almost smiled as the irony of the situation dawned on her. The God these people followed was supposed to preach mercy and forgiveness, yet here they all were caught up in a ruthless, murderous attack. She could only hope that one day things would change and these people and others like them would see the error of their ways.

The deities she worshiped touted no such duplicity. They advocated only the laws of nature and the universe, where every element must be perfectly kept in line or the whole system collapses. It was a delicate balance, but these were rules of life based on the natural order of things. The way things have always been.

When these simple rules were flouted, the deities were capable of exacting ruthless retribution. The universe and life itself were the backdrop to an ongoing battle between the forces of light and dark, good and evil. A battle that had been raging for all time.

A new emotion began to bubble within Elizabeth. Resignation gave way to pure rage, and this time she did smile.

Then she laughed aloud.

Soon, she was whooping and bellowing hysterically. Some of the sounds she made sounded like words, but not from any recognizable language.

There were murmurs of confusion and puzzlement all around her as the villagers struggled to comprehend what they were seeing. It was almost as if they could sense a change, a tipping point, a shift in the balance, and a wave of uncertainty swept through the crowd as Elizabeth continued to writhe, her body contorting and convulsing, her head thrashing from side to side.

"Fear not!" the Witchfinder General yelled above the building cacophony. "I have seen this behavior many times before! It means the Lord is winning the fight. Light is overcoming dark. Too late for her, the evil is being expelled from her body. This is how it manifests! Shut your mouths or else the devil may leap inside and find himself a new home!"

How stupid these people are, was Elizabeth's final thought as she was finally pitched into the freezing depths of the lake.

The breath was sucked crudely from her body, and every orifice was filled with silty black water as the numbing coldness engulfed her.

Still, she didn't struggle. There was no fear or panic. Instead, she simply allowed herself to be swallowed. All the pain left her ruined body and she was weightless, as if resting on clouds.

As she floated away, she grinned. This wasn't the end.

It was just the beginning.

Ben couldn't move. He struggled, his body heaving and muscles flexing with the effort, but it was useless. He was frozen with terror, the paralysis so complete that it took him a while to realize that his hands and feet were bound with what felt like thick lengths of rope.

It was pitch black, and he could barely open his eyes. Every time he did, they stung unbearably. All around him was a feverish hissing, crackling, spitting noise.

Fire.

He felt flames lick his feet and lower body. The pain was excruciating, and he opened his mouth to scream. He could hear a repulsive popping, bubbling sound.

With horror, he realized it was his skin.

It was cooking.

He was cooking.

He could smell it. The sickly, pungent aroma of his own flesh as it sizzled like a pork chop on a barbecue.

Was this the dream again?

It felt different.

Where were Louise and Amy? They had to be close. Ignoring the stinging sensation, he forced his eyelids open and willed them to penetrate the darkness.

He couldn't see anything.

Now he heard something else above the roar and crackling of the flames.

People. Hordes of them, shouting and…chanting?

Burn! Burn! Burn!

There was exhilaration in their voices, the noise building to a riotous crescendo. It was bedlam.

And the pain was intensifying.

He was surprised to realize that being tied up didn't matter because, on some deep subliminal level, he knew that the ropes only bound his body. They could never control his spirit. The body was weak. It was just flesh and bone. With time, flesh and bones grew old and frail, ultimately turning to dust. But the spirit only grew stronger and yearned to be set free of its physical constraints.

As his spirit left his dying body, he heard a tune playing somewhere off in the distance. A jaunty tune he knew well.

It was getting louder.

Closer?

And louder still.

Ben's eyes snapped open.

He could see again, and the pain was gone.

He was lying on the bench of the camper with Mr. Trimble curled up next to him, purring softly, and the calming sound of raindrops hitting the roof filling the gloom.

He'd been dreaming again.

Fucking hell.

But he could still hear that annoyingly joyous tune.

Then he realized the tune was the ring tone on his phone. Someone was calling him.

He sat bolt upright on the bench, drawing an accusing look from Mr. Trimble, and grabbed his handset off the table.

"Hello?"

"Mister Shivers?"

"Yes?"

"It's Christine. I'd like to schedule another meeting at your earliest convenience."

"No problem," Ben said, rubbing his eyes. Something in the woman's voice bothered him. "What's this regarding? Anything in particular, or would you just like the pleasure of my company?"

"It's certainly not that, Mister Shivers."

"Bummer. Then what's on your mind?"

There was a lengthy pause, as if Christine was silently debating something. Finally, she said, "I have something I think you'd like to see."

Any lingering vestiges of drowsiness evaporated, and Ben was suddenly fully alert. "What… What kind of thing?"

"I'd prefer not to discuss on the phone, if that's okay. Just come to the office as early as you can tomorrow. I'll be on site around seven-thirty."

"I will," Ben said. Then teasingly added, "Can't you at least give me a hint?"

"It's regarding that girl you mentioned. Beth White? The one who was murdered back in the eighties?"

Ben was stunned into silence. "What about her?"

"Tomorrow, Mister Shivers."

And with that, the line went dead.

Rude.

Ben thought about heading over to Christine's office right that minute to try to catch her before she left, but she'd called him from her mobile, which meant she was probably already on the way home. Plus, he'd made plans with Tim and Sheila, and he had no way of letting them know he wouldn't be able to keep their appointment. To stand them up on their first date, so to speak, would be exceedingly bad form, and he was counting on Tim to tell him more about this Elizabeth Thrower character. But what information could Christine possibly have about Beth? He would just have to wait to find out.

Sighing, he ran his hands through his hair. His heart was still racing. He was used to having nightmares. His therapist said it was due to survivor's guilt. But that one had been a doozy. Two dreams of burning in two days? That was unusual, even by his standards. It was strange how the dreams seemed to bear little relation to each other, but Ben couldn't help thinking they were somehow linked.

It was troubling. Even looking past the metaphors and symbolism some people would have you believe dominates the subconscious, two dreams so intrinsically similar seemed too much to be a simple coincidence.

But while the first burning dream was less a dream and more a memory, a flashback to something that had mentally and physically scarred him, the second was a complete mystery. He had been lashed to something and burned alive. Like a witch.

Could it have something to do with his research? Had something he'd read lodged in his brain like a splinter?

He couldn't even remember falling asleep. After he'd gone to visit Tim Norgood, he'd come straight back to the camper and started outlining some articles. At some point he must have just dropped off.

Damn it.

Tim!

He checked the time on his mobile. It was just after six. He must have been out of it for three hours or more. What a way to waste half a day. He needed to pull himself together and get ready for dinner.

Judging by the state of Tim earlier that day, Ben wasn't entirely convinced he'd turn up, but he had to give him the benefit of the doubt. Ben was a lot of things a lot of the time, but he was never late.

Shit. He stank. A mixture of grime and sweat. There was no escaping the fact. That was what sleeping in your clothes did for you. Not having a washing machine didn't help, either.

Leaning forward on the bench, he reached a hand between his legs. His fingers found a catch, which he slipped open to allow the front of the built-in storage compartment to drop down with a soft thump, eliciting a bad-tempered meow from Mr. Trimble, who jerked awake and looked around, startled, as if anticipating some kind of attack.

"Sorry, dude," Ben said, reaching into the cavity. This is where he stored most of his clothes. He liked to keep things simple and was by no means a fashion junkie, so most of his attire was strictly functional: comfortable jogging pants, jeans for when he went outside, long- and short-sleeved T-shirts, a couple of sweaters. When you worked mainly from home, and home was a camper van, you didn't need an extensive wardrobe. Shit, Ben didn't even have a wardrobe; hence, the storage compartment.

He rummaged around until he found a pair of slightly creased beige slacks and a white polo shirt. The polo shirt smelled musty. Everything smelled musty. But it was the best he could do on short notice, and he hoped a quick burst of Lynx Africa would carry him through.

Swearing under his breath, he hurriedly changed into the slacks and polo shirt, then transferred as much of the contents of the storage space as he could into a black refuse sack. A place like this must have a laundry service, or at least a laundromat where he could wash his clothes himself. He should really have done it sooner. No matter. He'd just stash the bag in his room in the main block until he could ask Christine about it in the morning, grab a quick shower, then head out for dinner.

It was still raining outside.

Shit.

But it wasn't as if he had to dress to impress. He grabbed the lightweight jacket hanging by the side door, shrugged into it, then picked up the bag of clothes and headed out into the early evening.

The police cars were all gone. He guessed that meant their inquiries had been concluded, for now at least. They would no doubt set up an incident room, or more likely an incident desk, at the local police station and spend a few days sifting through all the information they'd gathered, comparing stories, tracing timelines, checking for inconsistencies, and trying to piece together what exact fate had befallen Ronald Brand. Bludgeoned to death by his own wife, according to Detective Carter.

Wow.

What the police had to work out was why. Ben didn't envy them. The "why" didn't really concern him. Marjorie must have had her reasons. What he had to find out was how the murder fit in with the grand tapestry of tragic events at the R.R.

It must take incredible effort for a little old lady to beat someone to death. How could a relationship deteriorate that much? The couple must have been in love at one time. They still looked to be in love when Ben had seen them in the afternoon. It just proved no matter how happy people seemed on the outside, nobody really knew what was going on behind closed doors. Or even behind closed eyelids.

Stepping into the lift in the main block, the same place he'd exchanged smiles and greetings with Ronald and Marjorie Brand, was an eerie feeling. In that moment they'd both looked so happy and content that cold-blooded murder must have been the furthest thing from either of their minds.

Ben was still deep in thought as he made his way to Room 327 and swiped his R.R. card on the lock. The door obediently clicked open, and he slipped the card into the slot on the wall to activate the power. The dim room flooded with soft yellow light.

Housekeeping had been by. The bed had been changed and a new branded dressing gown lay on top. That probably meant there were fresh towels, too. Fantastic.

At first glance, the place looked immaculately clean. Outstanding service. He dropped the bulging refuse bag on the floor and turned to close the door behind him.

That was when he saw it—a piece of paper on the floor, stark white against the polished brown tiles. It appeared to have been slipped under the door, and he must have stepped right over it when he'd entered the room.

What the heck?

Stooping to pick it up, Ben wondered what it could be. Some kind of advertisement? If so, it was a little intrusive. Who slid leaflets under hotel doors in this day and age? Most people would prefer to spam your email instead. They didn't even have to go out to do that.

Maybe it was for some kind of adult service, he reasoned. He was a man of the world and knew you often received such propositions, even in fancy establishments, and usually in the form of fliers or business cards. The escorts bribed the hotel staff to let them in, and probably passed on a share of the profits.

Call this number for a good time!

Was this something a place like the R.R. would condone? He doubted it. It didn't fit with their wholesome image, and it was a little far into the sticks for prostitutes to come on the off chance someone might require their services. The nearest town was miles away.

He could now see that what he held in his hands wasn't a business card at all, nor a flier. It appeared to be a page ripped out of a notepad and neatly folded into quarters. With a building sense of dread, he slowly opened it. There, scrawled in the middle of the page in looping handwriting were the words:

You are in over your head.

Get out of R.R. and stay out.

Chapter Fourteen

Despite the race against time, Ben was at Ground Zero well before seven. He didn't like to keep people waiting. The same Eastern European guy, Alex, was manning the front desk, and this time he appeared a little warmer and more receptive. Ben refrained from asking him about Beth White again. Or anything else. Instead, he waited patiently as Alex used the handheld machine to scan Ben's R.R. card and meal voucher, then found an empty table in the corner where he took off his wet jacket and draped it over the back of the chair before sitting down. He was trying to act normally, but his heart thudded in his chest so loudly he was scared other diners might hear it and he couldn't help constantly surveying his surroundings. Was anyone surreptitiously watching him?

There was no getting around it; he was rattled. He couldn't stop thinking about the note he'd found in his room. It was obviously a warning, like something out of a Victorian murder mystery, but who from? And why?

The delivery method was intended to be threatening. It was also a power play. Whoever sent it wanted him to know that they knew exactly where they could find him. More worryingly, they didn't seem overly concerned about being caught, even with all the security measures in place at the resort and the conspicuous police presence. What if they'd initially gone to his room not to slide a note under his door, but to confront him face-to-face? Who knows where that might have led.

So many things about this situation troubled him. For starters, how had the aggressor known which room he was staying in? He replayed conversations he'd had with everyone he'd come into contact with since arriving at the resort to see if he'd let something slip. He didn't think he had. It wasn't something you casually brought up.

Oh, by the way, I'm over there in Room 327 if you or any of your associates want to come over and threaten me at any time. If I'm not there, just slide a note under the door…

Had he pissed off anyone? Maybe Alex or the blonde waitress at Ground Zero? They might have the means and opportunity. Maybe even a motive if they thought he was being a dick. But they were staff and surely wouldn't be in the habit of warning off guests, no matter how much of a dick they were being. They must meet dicks in a variety of guises on a regular basis, and Ben doubted they cared about him that much. They wouldn't want the hassle. They were just trying to make a few pounds in lousy catering jobs on their way to something more fulfilling.

No, this smacked of a bigger conspiracy. He was getting too close to something.

But what?

As far as he could ascertain, the only person who knew precisely where he was staying was Christine Turner. That said, the entire place was probably monitored by CCTV, and anyone of considerable standing would be able to track his every move at the touch of a button.

Heck, they might even be watching him right now.

Ben pulled out his phone and pretended to scroll through his messages, the way most self-conscious people sitting alone in restaurants, or anywhere else, did to make themselves look slightly less pathetic. Because she'd been the last person he communicated with, the first name he saw on his contact list was Christine's. He thought back to the phone call earlier. She definitely hadn't sounded herself. Something had been off. And what could she possibly have to say about a murder that happened over thirty years ago?

All this weirdness had to be connected. There was just too much happening for it not to be. And in all likelihood, it was also in some way connected to the Brand murder, and possibly even his reason for being here. Ben's head began to swim. This was big. Too big.

"Okay if I sit?"

The voice startled Ben so much he almost dropped his phone. His head snapped up to find Tim Norgood standing next to the table.

"Sure, sure. Please do," Ben replied. "Sorry, I was lost in my own little world there."

He was pleased to find Tim was looking much better now than he had earlier. His eyes were less reddened, his face less weathered, and his endearing grin was back. He was dressed in a pair of brown cords and a yellow windbreaker, with the rollneck of a cream-colored sweater visible at the top. He couldn't look more like a middle-aged university lecturer if he tried.

"Shame they don't serve alcohol here," Tim said, taking off the windbreaker and pulling out the chair opposite Ben. "I could really do with a Scotch on the rocks."

"Me, too," Ben agreed. "And I'm not even a whiskey drinker."

"Tough day?"

"You could say that," Ben said. Then he realized Tim was alone. "No Sheila?"

"She won't be joining us, unfortunately," Tim said, picking up the menu. "She's staying at the villa to rest. She's exhausted and isn't feeling in top form. She might be coming down with something."

"Sorry to hear that," Ben said, suddenly acutely aware that he'd never even laid eyes on the elusive Sheila. He might just be paranoid, his thought process influenced by recent events, but for all he knew, Sheila might just be a figment of Tim's imagination. Worse than that, right now she might be lying dead in the villa and Ben might be settling down to dinner with a murderer. "I hope she's okay," he heard himself say, as if from afar.

"To be honest, she isn't one for socializing at the best of times, even on holiday," Tim replied. "She'd much prefer a simple meal at home in front of the telly. Speaking of which, I'm starved. Are you hungry?"

Ben was surprised to discover that he wasn't just hungry, he was famished. He called over the blonde waitress and he and Tim each ordered the sirloin steak. Both noticed the look of distaste on the waitress's face when Ben asked for his to be well done.

"You know that kind of treatment burns all the flavor out of the meat?" Tim said after the waitress had taken their order and left. "The only way to eat good steak is rare."

"So they say," Ben replied with a shrug. "Although I'm convinced most people only get rare steak because they see other people do it. They fall for the hype. Call me old-fashioned, but personally, I prefer my food to be cooked."

"Cooked, yes. But not incinerated."

"If you knew how common tapeworms were in cattle, you'd ask for your steak to be incinerated, too."

"Jesus Christ. Did you have to go there?"

"Why not? People need to be aware of things like that. Taeniasis is no fun."

"What's that?"

"The name given to the intestinal infection in humans caused by an adult tapeworm. One of the main causes is eating undercooked beef."

"I'll take my chances," Tim said dismissively, clearing his throat.

"You have no choice, unless you ask them to take your steak back to the kitchen and ask them to cook it some more."

"Can we move on from this topic, please?" Tim said, grimacing slightly. "Sorry if I seemed kind of out of it when you came by this afternoon, by the way. I appreciate the visit. I made the mistake of taking an afternoon nap. They always hit me for six."

"Yeah," Ben replied. "You said you haven't been sleeping well recently. Why is that?"

Tim suddenly looked edgy. It was almost a return to the furtive demeanor he'd displayed earlier that day. This time, however, he appeared to catch himself and put a lid on it. "It's nothing you can help with, unfortunately. It's nothing anyone can help with. Life is a long journey, and we all pick up baggage as we go. It gets heavy after a while. So remind me, what can I do for you again?"

"I'm not really sure," Ben began, searching for the right words. "I've been researching the history of the R.R. and came up with a name. Elizabeth Thrower? It's popped up more than once, actually. Some sources refer to her as a famous witch, others as a ghost who now haunts the grounds in the guise of a Gray Lady, though I couldn't find any reports that were remotely plausible. All I can find online are a few anecdotes and second-hand stories. More troublesome is the fact that there's no record of this woman dying, or even being born. I checked this afternoon."

"Really? That's odd. Where did you look?"

"The usual places. I searched the parish records first, which you can access online, then some of the local newspapers that have databases stretching back centuries. I also trawled through the National Archive."

"I bet that was fun."

"It was."

"And you found nothing?"

"A few near misses but nothing that matched. It's almost as if she's been scrubbed from history, or never existed at all. I remembered you saying you were a university lecturer and a local historian, so I wondered if you'd be able to help me out. At least point me in the right direction or fill me in on what you know of it."

Tim nodded sagely as he placed his hands on the table and laced his fingers. "I see. Well, I must admit I haven't researched Elizabeth Thrower through any official channels, but I'm more than familiar with her story. So, what, specifically, would you like to know?"

"Firstly, was she an actual person? Or just some kind of myth."

"She was certainly real," Tim continued. "At least, I've always accepted as much. Though now that you've cast doubt on it, I'll have to look it up myself for my own sanity. If what I've come to believe is true, she once lived in the area. Not far from this very spot, in fact. I wouldn't care to speculate if she's now a ghost or not, but the witch part is supposedly true. Actually, let me rephrase that. I doubt whether we will ever know if she really was a witch, in the sense that she used magic, but she was tried as one, found guilty, and executed right here at what is now the Regal. In the lake, to be precise."

The lake.

After everything that had happened in the past few days, this news shouldn't have come as much of a shock to Ben, but it did. His muscles tensed, and his hand went to the back of his neck where the skin suddenly started prickling. Everything seemed to point back to that body of water. "She was murdered?"

"Nope," Tim said patiently, as if explaining a complicated mathematical equation to a difficult teenager. "She was accused of being a witch and underwent what was considered in those days a fair trial. Of course, this being the seventeenth century, what they did to her was tantamount to torture and would never be allowed in this day and age. Not even in Guantanamo Bay. Probably. In those days, though, it was all legal and above board. The story goes that they wanted to extract a confession, but Elizabeth Thrower wouldn't give in. Apparently, she held out for days while her captors did the most awful things to her. The whole unsavory episode culminated in a trial by water."

"Isn't that the one where they just chuck you in a river, or in this case a lake, and watch you drown?"

"Sort of," Tim said. "If you were a true servant of the devil, it was said he would intervene and use his evil powers to make you float. Believe it or not, records show that on occasion, that *did* happen. Of course, nobody knows if the devil really was intervening. Probably not. But something made those people float. Not that it did them much good. If they had the audacity to float, it was seen as proof of guilt and they were either stoned to death or fished out of the water and burned at the stake instead. If, on the other hand, they were innocent and had no such power, they simply sank like a stone and drowned."

"So they died either way."

"Precisely. To make escape even more unlikely, they usually tied their hands and feet before chucking them in. Witch trials were rife in this area," Tim continued, hitting his stride. "I'm sure they've cropped up in your research. Salem, Massachusetts is the most famous case, where more than two hundred people were accused. Ultimately, nineteen were hanged, one poor soul was pressed to death, and at least five died in prison. Most modern scholars agree it was a case of mass hysteria. But all that nonsense was prevalent throughout Europe, not just across the pond. Some countries didn't even keep records of how many they killed. Or if they did, those records were destroyed. Combined, the figure certainly ran into the thousands, if not tens of thousands. All, would you believe, in the name of religion."

"Nothing has started more wars," Ben said.

"Actually, that's a misconception. Ideological differences and power grabs are the main causes of war. By the way, which two countries do you think have had the most wars with each other?"

"No idea," Ben confessed. "China and Japan?"

"Not even close."

"England and France?"

"Wrong."

"I give up. Or should I say, 'I surrender?'"

"Sweden and Denmark. They've had around thirty full-scale wars since the fifteenth century."

"Really? That's bizarre."

"Isn't it? Back to the topic at hand. Did you know Elizabeth Thrower was one of the last known victims of Matthew Hopkins?"

"I've heard of him. What was his deal?"

"He called himself 'Witchfinder General' and assumed great powers. But there is no evidence that it was a legitimate title bestowed on him by Parliament or anyone else in authority. It may have been done covertly, or more likely he just took it upon himself and nobody disputed it. He traveled the country seeking out what were thought to be witches and putting them on trial. Hundreds of people were killed on his say-so. In fact, it is said he was responsible for more deaths than every other witch hunter in history put together."

"Wow."

"Wow indeed," Tim said. "Of course, the system was wide open to manipulation. If anyone had a personal grievance against you, all they had to do was accuse you of being a witch and make up a few unsavory stories.

If they greased the palm of the local clergy or the visiting witch hunter, or perhaps even paid off a few false witnesses to perpetuate false rumors, paranoia would do the rest and your enemy wouldn't be around much longer."

"Do you think that's what happened to this Elizabeth Thrower?"

"There's nothing in the history books to suggest it. I'm just surmising. But you know most of history was unwritten. A lot happened behind the scenes, so it's certainly a distinct possibility. She had a reputation as a seer and sin eater, so perhaps those skills were misinterpreted. Or..."

"Or what?"

"Or maybe she knew too much and was silenced."

"What did sin eaters do, exactly?"

"It's a custom usually associated with Wales and the Welsh Marches, though it did spread to a few pockets in England. Nobody is quite sure how or why. Traditionally, they were sent for after a death in the community. They would consume food or drink over, or sometimes on, the deceased as a way of appropriating the sins of the departed so they could continue their journey into the afterlife unburdened."

"That's fascinating," Ben said. "But assuming she had that ability, if the people whose sins she consumed were already dead, how could any knowledge she had affect them?"

"The dead could be guilty of such heinous crimes that the stigma might affect their surviving relatives. Plus, there is evidence to suggest that here in East Anglia, the powers of the sin eater were extended somewhat beyond their traditional parameters."

"How so?"

"It's believed that in some cases, sin eaters like Elizabeth Thrower consumed the sins of the living, not just the dead."

"Two steak dinners, gentlemen! Who ordered the well done?"

Ben and Tim both looked up at the interruption.

"Impeccable timing," Tim said.

For one terrible moment, Ben expected to come face-to-face once again with the ghost of Beth White. If that happened, he was convinced the thin, taught thread keeping him tethered to reality would finally snap and he would float up, up, and away to a land of madness and make-believe.

Thankfully, this waitress bore no resemblance to the murdered girl. But, Ben thought, who was to say that this girl wasn't a ghost, too? Maybe they all were. The concept of a luxury holiday resort staffed entirely by ghosts was something straight out of a Stephen King novel.

"Everything okay, Ben?" Tim asked with what sounded like genuine concern as he set about his still-bleeding steak with a serrated knife. "You've suddenly gone a bit pale. Are you having second thoughts about that charred lump of meat?"

"W-What? No. I'm fine. It's nothing," Ben replied. "Please continue."

"Well, that's the sum of my knowledge, really. Probably as a consequence of her sin-eating activities, poor Elizabeth Thrower was tried as a witch and drowned in the lake. The end."

"And what happened to the Witchfinder General?"

"He came to a sticky ending, too," Tim replied, stuffing a forkful of bloody meat into his mouth. "The story goes that he contracted tuberculosis and died shortly after the Elizabeth Thrower incident. A penance for his evil deeds, some said. A lot of people died from T.B. in those days, but I wouldn't rule anything out. If memory serves, the witch trials continued for a time after his death. What is often claimed to be the last one occurred in seventeen-twelve when a Hertfordshire woman called Jane Wenham was sentenced to death. By then, the courts were becoming more clued-up about the whole witch thing being open to manipulation and had started being more lenient."

"What happened to her? Did she get off with it?" Ben asked.

"Indeed, she did. During the trial, she was accused of conversing with the devil and flying. But the judge quite correctly pointed out that even if it were true, there was no law against flying and overturned the conviction."

"That's such a British thing to do," smirked Ben. "Tim, you know all these tragic events that happen here?"

"Like that poor Ronald Bond guy?"

"Ronald Brand," Ben corrected. "But yes, like him."

"What could possess someone to do such a thing to their own husband? I mean, Sheila and I sometimes have minor disagreements. Usually about me spending too much on broken eight-track tapes or other accessories at boot sales. It's not the expense she complains about; it's the room they take up in the house. It's only a modest semi-detached, and the garage and drive are already full of cars and bits. I commandeered the spare bedroom to keep records and tapes in. It used to be an office, but neither of us ever did much work in there. She calls me a hoarder and claims that, if left to my own devices, I'd fill every little nook and cranny with what she calls old tat. A smidge unfair if you ask me, but I can see her point. Sort of."

"Tim," Ben began hesitantly. "Have you noticed how many of these incidents and accidents involve the lake?"

"Can't say I've thought about it that way. This new one didn't involve the lake, did it?"

"Not exactly," Ben agreed. "Though I did see the old couple walking along the shore just a few hours before all the shit went down. I saw them more than once yesterday. I even said hello to them."

"You did? That's trippy, man."

"Think about it," Ben said. "In your professional opinion, do you think there might be some connection between Elizabeth Thrower, the lake, or the R.R. in general, and all these weird, violent happenings?"

"Seems like a bit of a leap. What kind of connection could there be?"

"I don't know. That's one of the things I wanted to talk to you about. You're far more knowledgeable in local matters than I am."

"For a moment there, I thought you were going to tell me you believed the curse."

Ben stopped chewing and stared across the table at his companion. "There's a curse?"

"You didn't know about it? I thought that's what you were getting at. It's more of an old wives' tale, really. And it's pretty localized, so I doubt it has ever been reported at length in the wider media, except in passing maybe. You could be forgiven for missing it completely if you don't live around here. We all know curses are about as real as witches, right?" Tim tried to force a chuckle, but it died on his lips.

"Tell me more."

"Well, the story goes that when Matthew Hopkins and his cohorts tossed her into the lake, Elizabeth Thrower didn't drown. Even with her arms and legs bound, she somehow managed to make it to the little island you can still see."

"What then?"

"Personally, I'm not sure I believe that part. I mean, how could she survive in the water long enough to get to the island and evade capture at the same time? It doesn't make sense. Unless the Great Horned One really did intervene, of course. In any case, she made it to the island and survived just long enough to invoke whatever strange magic she was into and curse the villagers who'd been so intent on killing her."

"So…she was a witch after all?"

"If you believe the story, it would seem that way. Though, personally, I believe the word 'witch' is a very loose description. The word was used as a kind of slur against anyone who rejected Christianity. Those people were shunned and generally mistreated. It was basically discrimination. I doubt anyone even knew she'd survived the trail by water until weeks later, when Elizabeth's body was discovered on the island by a couple of fishermen."

"Couldn't she have just washed up there after she drowned?"

"Possible," Tim agreed. "But when they found her, the fishermen said she was lying at the water's edge in a pool of her own blood, surrounded by strange symbols she'd etched into the mud."

"Where did the blood come from?"

"The implication was that it was from a self-inflicted wound. It could've been some form of blood sacrifice. And in the absence of any other living creature, she used her own. Might even have killed herself in the process. The grisly details weren't recorded. But there's one other thing that was."

"What's that?"

"When they found her, she was smiling."

"Well, that could be natural. A result of cadaveric spasm. Muscles stiffening and contracting post-mortem. In some cases, it makes it appear that the corpse is smiling. Thank your lucky stars she wasn't demonstrating postmortem priapism."

"I know I'm going to regret asking," Tim said. "But what's that?"

"It's also known as 'angel lust,'" Ben explained. "In layman's terms, it's when someone has an erection after death."

"How does that work?"

"Unknown. But it does. Ironically, it was said to be common among crucifixion victims, and there are numerous Renaissance-era paintings depicting Jesus in such a state."

"Well, if Elizabeth Thrower did have an erection, either before or after death, it would certainly be newsworthy."

"Certainly."

"How do you know all this anyway?"

"When you're a journalist, you make a living stockpiling tons of useless information. The trick is retaining it all."

"It's not proving so useless at the moment."

"Yeah, well," Ben said, "I also know far more than is healthy about poisonous fungi. I hope I never have to call upon that."

"You know, it's possible that smile was a result of…"

"Cadaveric spasm?"

"Yes. That. Though it's also a possibility that that part of the story was embellished after the fact. It's the role of historians like myself to try to strip away the padding and get to the root of the story. Sometimes it's easier said than done."

"What kind of symbols were they?"

"Who knows? The fishermen only recognized the few words written in English."

"And what were they?"

"'Never forget history repeats.'"

"That's it?"

"That's it."

"It sounds…ominous."

"Perhaps," Tim agreed. "Without context, who knows? It's been suggested that they were so eager to cover up their dirty deeds and put the unsavory incident behind them, the villagers held a meeting when Elizabeth's body was discovered, during which it was agreed to never speak of it again. They essentially tried to airbrush her from history. That's what makes those words she left behind even more sinister. Prophetic, even."

"They did a pretty good job of the airbrushing," Ben said. "Is that why I haven't I come across this in my research? I mean, even if half of it isn't true, it sounds like such a pivotal historical event, you would think that someone would write up an account."

"That's one question I might be able to answer more definitively," Tim said.

"How?"

"I have a friend who once worked on the picture desk of the *East Anglia Gazette*. He told me that a few years ago the paper was all set to run a double-page spread about the legend of Elizabeth Thrower to commemorate some anniversary or other, but the story was pulled at the last minute. He was pissed off because he had to work overtime to fill the gaping hole."

"Why was the article pulled?"

"Commercial pressures."

"Like what?"

"You're a journalist, Ben. You must know something of the politics involved. My friend said that someone at the paper tipped off Davenport. Not Davenport Senior. He was already dead by then. I'm talking about his son, Glenn. The family heir. Being a successful entrepreneur means he has a hand in controlling the purse strings of a lot of successful businesses, both large and small, not just the Regal Retreat. When he got wind of it, he made it abundantly clear that if the story went to print, he would personally see to it that every enterprise he was involved with would pull out of any advertising deals they had with the *East Anglia Gazette* and take their business elsewhere. That would certainly have meant the end of the newspaper. As I'm sure you know, the majority of local newspapers are run on a shoestring budget. They simply couldn't afford to lose the advertising revenue."

"The rotten bastard. So, they pulled the article?"

"Quicker than you could say, 'Yes sir, no sir, three bags full, sir.'"

"But why would he care so much about one measly article? I mean, people all over the country write about the R.R. whenever something happens, which is often. He can't gag them all."

"Nor is he trying. I guess even he acknowledges that once it's out, there's no way you can stuff a genie back in the bottle. I understand what you're saying, though, and for me it all ties in with the agreement the villagers made after they found Elizabeth's body. The Davenports have been a prominent family in the area for generations. It's entirely possible that one of their ancestors was among those villagers and the current head of the family is simply honoring the original gagging order by never allowing anyone to speak of the witch and her curse."

"But what about the public interest?"

"You could argue that unless a definitive link between Elizabeth Thrower and contemporary events is established, there is no public interest. It would simply be a case of rehashing salacious gossip, centuries-old salacious gossip at that. It would also shine a light on some rather nefarious activities that most people around here would prefer to forget. East Anglia was a hotbed of witch trials."

"Could that be because it was a hotbed of witches?" Ben interjected. "Just playing devil's advocate."

He winced at his own choice of words.

"It could indeed," Tim replied. "But even that is besides the point. If any of this could potentially have a negative bearing on the Regal's reputation, you can understand Glenn Davenport's desire to keep it buried."

"You don't think he was just protecting his own best interests? Rather than the resort's reputation?"

"Oh, definitely. But those two things are intrinsically linked. I'm not painting him as some kind of saint. As a brood, the Davenports have a long history of being utter bastards. You don't get to be that rich and powerful without being cunning and ruthless."

Ben thought back to one of his earlier conversations with Christine.

"Coal mines and Victorian workhouses, wasn't it?"

"Precisely. Among other ventures. You know how cutthroat the business world can be. By all accounts, the Davenports are not the kind of people you want to get on the wrong side of."

"So, what's the nature of the curse?"

"Huh?"

"I mean, what punishment did this Elizabeth Thrower invoke on those who'd wronged her? Did she turn them into frogs or something."

"That isn't so clear. But I doubt it was anything so dramatic."

"Where do you stand on all this?"

Tim paused to consider the question, pushing the decimated remnants of his steak around his blood-streaked plate with his fork as he did so. "Hard to say. Do I believe Elizabeth Thrower was tried and executed as a witch? Yes. Do I believe the whole messy business has been suppressed and almost eradicated from the history books? Yes. Do I believe she really was a witch and used magic or whatever to put a curse on the people who wronged her? That one is more difficult to answer. Without any supporting evidence, I'm inclined to go with my rational side and say it's highly unlikely."

"But what if all the death and tragedy blighting this place is the supporting evidence?"

"Meaning?"

"Consider the Ronald Brand murder for starters. What if making seemingly nice, level-headed people lose their shit and do terrible things to each other is the witch's revenge?"

"How the heck would she achieve that?" Tim scoffed. "Demonic possession?"

"Well, no. Only demons are capable of demonic possession," Ben said. "But what if she can somehow influence people's actions from beyond the grave? Never forget history repeats. That's the message she left behind, isn't it? Could those words be committing the place to some kind of…cycle of tragedy?"

Tim was silent for a moment, then said, "Nah. I don't buy it. Terrible things happen everywhere, all the time, in every corner of the world. Are you saying Elizabeth Thrower is responsible for all of it?"

"Of course not. But you have to agree that there are far more incidents and accidents here at the Regal Retreat than any comparable place. Statistically speaking."

"How do you know that?" Tim said. "Have you studied every other location in the same detail? People said the same thing about the Bermuda Triangle. True, some strange occurrences did happen there…"

"Like Flight Nineteen, when five American bombers disappeared, along with one of the rescue planes sent to search for them. No trace of the planes or the pilots was ever found," Ben interjected. "No bodies, no floating wreckage, no oil slick, nothing."

"For one," Tim said. "There was the USS Cyclops, too, which disappeared in nineteen-eighteen with the loss of over three hundred lives. But people forget that the area known as the Bermuda Triangle is one of the busiest shipping lanes in the world. The fact is that given the amount of traffic using the water and air space, there isn't statistically anything unusual going on. These disappearances and disasters are just as likely to happen in any other given geographical location. But the mystique took over and influenced the way people thought and talked about it. Whenever something odd happened in the area, which covers anything from five hundred thousand to one and a half million square miles, depending on who you ask, it was immediately attributed to the 'curse' and became a sort of self-fulfilling prophecy. The same thing could be happening at the Regal. At the very best, what we might have here is a spike, a statistical anomaly, not aided by the fact that everyone's just waiting for the next weird thing to happen."

"Interesting point of view," Ben said. Despite the overly simplistic explanation, Tim might just be right.

The historian shrugged and looked down at his now almost-clean plate. It was clear to see something was on his mind.

"Tim, what is it?"

The man looked awkward and anxious, like a boy called into the headmaster's office to explain himself. Finally, he said, "Now we've covered that, can I ask you something? Off the record?"

"I didn't know we were ever on the record," Ben said. "But sure. Fire away." It would be a refreshing change to be on the receiving end of a grilling.

"Have you had any strange dreams since you've been here?"

Ben's mouth dropped open as he thought back to the two nightmares about burning he had endured. "Yes. How on earth could you know that?"

"What kind of dreams?" Tim continued, ignoring Ben's question.

"I lost my daughter in a house fire three years ago. My marriage disintegrated as a result. That's how I ended up living in a van. I dreamed about the fire, not for the first time, but the first time in a long time. And then today I dreamed of another fire. But it was different. This time, I was lashed to a pole or something, being burned alive."

"Like a witch?"

"Like a witch," Ben agreed. "What's that? Some kind of crazy coincidence?"

"Seems as though there are a lot of crazy coincidences around here," Tim said. "I'm sorry to hear about your daughter."

"Ancient history," Ben replied. To him, it wasn't ancient history. Not at all. He re-lived the tragedy and its myriad consequences every day of his life. But he didn't want to burden a comparative stranger with his morosity. "Both dreams were so...vivid. Much more so than most of my other dreams. I could smell the smoke; I could *feel* the pain."

"It's just funny you should dream of burning witches," Tim said, laying his knife and fork on his plate and pushing it to one side. "Given the history of this place."

"Funny is one way of describing it. You think this curse or whatever is somehow dictating what I dream about?"

Tim didn't answer. Instead, he said, "When I was ten years old, my brother Terry and I were playing on some train tracks near my house. We weren't supposed to, of course, which is probably why we did it. Boys will be boys. Being the older one, I should have known better. And I should have taken better care of my little brother. He was my responsibility. There were so many things I should have done that day but didn't. Another thing I should've done was see or hear the train coming. To this day, I have no idea why I didn't. We were just playing. I wasn't paying attention, and the train just seemed to come from nowhere. Before we knew it, it was upon us. A towering, screeching metal monster, billowing smoke, and bigger and more terrifying than anything my mind could comprehend. It was all I could do to jump out of the way. Terry wasn't as quick as me. The train… The train…"

"Hit him?"

"Yes."

"That's truly awful," Ben said, noticing tears filling the corners of Tim's eyes. This was obviously difficult for him to talk about.

"After it happened, I dreamed about it," Tim continued. "Sometimes once or twice a month. I even saw a shrink in my twenties who put the dreams down to survivor's guilt. Over time, the gaps between the dreams grew longer and longer until I was only having one or two a year. Until I came here. The thing is, *here*, the dreams are more powerful than they ever have been. And they come every night. Every time I close my eyes, in fact."

"How do they make you feel?"

"Kinda weird," Tim replied. "There's such an intense mix of emotion. There's the things you would expect; anger, regret, sorrow. But there's also an element of comfort because I feel somehow close to my brother again. I always get to experience the precious few moments before the train hits, before everything changed. I cherish them. Only now, I know what's coming and I still can't do anything about it. You can't change history, right?"

"Never forget," Ben said. "What if that *is* the curse? What if Elizabeth Thrower used magic to somehow mark this place, using dreams as a medium, and whoever stays here is forced to remember things they spend the rest of their lives actively trying to forget."

"Wow. Wouldn't that be something? You make her sound like a witchy Freddy Krueger from the *Nightmare on Elm Street* movies," Tim said.

"Maybe that's not so far from the truth. Except, instead of appearing herself, she uses our own memories as weapons against us. Could these dreams be her seeking justice?"

"What do you mean?"

"The dreams could serve as a kind of retribution. Seeing as she's supposed to have been a sin eater, an occupation so closely linked to guilt, it makes sense."

"But what did we do?" Tim threw up his hands in exasperation. "We weren't even alive when the villagers killed the woman."

"Collateral damage," Ben shrugged. "Perhaps it's the place itself she's raging against, rather than whoever happens to be here."

"Possibly," agreed Tim. "But I don't think whatever's causing the dreams is so selective. I mean, I don't think it has the ability to distinguish between acts of good or evil. Those things are subjective, anyway. More than likely, it somehow draws on painful memories buried in our sub-conscious, things that left a scar or things we've hidden, and brings them back into the open to persecute us. It wasn't your fault your daughter died, and deep down I know I wasn't responsible for my brother's death. The one common element we both share is the mistaken belief that we could have prevented the tragedies. Something like that could drive a person crazy. Send them over the edge."

"It could," Ben agreed. "And there's no telling what they might do then. All those unhealthy, destructive thoughts of guilt and revenge. It's probably different for us. I mean, we're both forced to re-live acci-dents. There's guilt, sure. Definitely on my part, and probably yours, too. But we don't really have anyone else to blame. There's nowhere to direct the anger, so we internalize it. But imagine if there *was* someone we held culpable for whatever we're trying to escape? Any little gripe or grievance would be highlighted, emphasized, and possibly blown out of all proportion."

"Do you think that's what happened to the Brands?"

"It's certainly plausible," Ben agreed. "Do you think the people who murdered Elizabeth spent the rest of their lives dreaming about it? About her?"

"I would put money on it," Tim replied. "Knowing what we know

now, I would imagine the nightmares ran through the villagers like a plague. And that was how Elizabeth exacted her revenge. She literally drove those who wronged her crazy. But her revenge didn't have a shelf life. So even after all those responsible for her death were dead, the curse continued. It's lasted generations. She isn't just taking it out on the townspeople, but also their children, and their children's children."

"But why do you think it affects visitors? People just here on holiday with no emotional connection to the area?" Ben asked.

"I think, over time, local people adapt and learn to live with whatever the curse makes them dream about, to an extent. They make their peace with it. Like I did with Terry's death. So perhaps the dreams, or the curse, assuming they are related, don't affect locals quite so profoundly. But imagine you are a visitor, completely new to the place, and never experienced anything like it before?"

"I don't have to imagine," Ben said. "I am a visitor completely new to the place."

"And there you are. I can see you're having trouble coping. It's written all over your face. Picking up on what you suggested earlier, perhaps lake is the epicenter, so the closer you are to it, the greater the effects of the curse."

"Given everything else we've discussed, that seems entirely plausible."

"Hey, you know what we should do?" Tim said, mischief dancing in his eyes.

"What?"

"We should just dig up the old witch and ask her. Assuming the legend is true, the fishermen who found the body buried her on the spot. On the island in the lake."

"What? And she's still there?"

"I don't think anyone would be brave enough to try moving her."

"You're right," Ben said. "You're right."

Chapter Fifteen

East Anglia, 1645

As the icy water of the lake took her in its grasp, Elizabeth had a realization. She wasn't going to die like this. No way.

She wanted justice.

Not just for herself, but for all the others who'd wanted nothing more than to live their lives on their own terms, not those set down by bureaucrats in ivory towers who had no concept of her struggles.

The water drenching the rags she called clothes, seeping through to her skin, and filling up her lungs did nothing to quench the flames of rage burning within her. With a superhuman effort, she strained against the ropes binding her wrists and ankles, placed there by the villagers she once served.

Anger helped. In its purest form, it gave you strength and courage, enabling you to reach plateaus you had never before thought attainable.

Her mind was filled with vicious, vengeful thoughts. Vivid and blood soaked. She envisioned the Witchfinder General's tongue skewered with a roasting fork, Ezra Davenport's steaming insides wrapped around a wooden stake, Lynette the farmer's wife's head lopped off and lying in the street, and Tom the Baker's eyes carved out and impaled on poles for the crows to peck at.

Elizabeth had always known of the inherent wickedness permeating the village. Of course, she had. Being a sin eater, she was privy to it all. Whether every village was the same or not, she couldn't say, for she only knew this one. Instead of biting her lip, she should've spilled everyone's secrets. Warned others. Tried to change things and be a force of good. How much misery would have been avoided had she forsaken her oaths and broken her silence?

But what was the use?

Being the sin eater was her role, and no role came without its struggles. Besides, she knew only too well that you can't force people to change. They have to see the faults in themselves before they can do that, and these people were just too conceited.

Little by little, strand by strand, the ropes binding Elizabeth's wrists and ankles unraveled until they finally gave way completely, allowing her to move freely once more. Even though she was still submerged in the icy water, the sense of achievement she felt was almost euphoric and gave her fresh impetus.

She was free!

Nothing was going to stand in her way now.

She pushed herself up from the lakebed, her hands sinking in silt right up to her bony wrists. Then she opened her eyes and looked up. At least, she thought it was up. It was difficult to tell in the swirling, all-encompassing darkness. She relied on the little bubbles of air she caught sight of, stark in the inky water, to show her the way. They didn't come from her mouth, as she was fighting to keep all the air she had inside her where it was, knowing that if she should let it out, she would never get it back again. Instead, she assumed that the tiny bubbles emanated from her clothing, having been trapped between the layers of petticoats and undergarments she wore to guard against the winter chill. It was almost as if they'd been sent by some higher force to guide her. Save her, even.

Little tiny bubbles.

They told her which direction represented certain annihilation and which direction offered the slightest glimmer of hope.

Her limbs were heavy, and her entire body screamed for oxygen.

She could feel herself fading away, the very life force being sucked out of her, and fought to suppress the panic and clarify her thoughts.

She might be free of her shackles, but she still had to be careful. The villagers would be looking for her, scouring the surface of the lake with lanterns and torches. Maybe even patrolling the waters near the shore in boats. They would want to make sure she really had drowned and would cause them no more grief.

Lungs screaming, Elizabeth gave up trying to swim and instead began lurching through the water like some grotesque flightless bird, an abomination of nature. The thing that should not be. Her feet sank ankle-deep into the silt on the bottom of the lake, and she had to use all her power to pull them free and propel herself another step.

She instinctively knew which way the nearest shore was. She mustn't go there. They would be waiting. And if they caught her again, there would surely be no escape.

No, she had to go forward.

Always forward.

At times it almost felt like she was being pushed through the still waters by some mysterious unseen force at her back, like a stiff breeze.

On she went, further.

Now the water was so deep it pressed down on her from above, pushing her deeper into the silt. But it didn't stop her.

Nothing would.

Then, in the deepest part of the lake, something suddenly loomed out of the gloom, coming within inches of her. Something foreign that she knew should not be there.

What's that?

Her heart leaped into her mouth when she realized she was looking at a grinning human skull.

The skull was still attached to the skeleton of what was once a human body that had long since been stripped of any skin and tissue. Now, the only thing clinging to the bones was weeds. The skeleton stood upright in the water, blocking her way, its arms and legs jerking and spasming as if performing a grim dance. A dance just for her.

When she looked down, she could just about see that one of the skeleton's legs was affixed to a chain, and the other end of the chain shackled to a huge, rusted iron weight.

Stunned, Elizabeth stumbled over some unseen obstacle and lost her balance, falling in slow motion until her languid body became suspended in the water.

Somehow, she knew the skeleton belonged to Gideon, her lost love.

Unable to scream, she opened her mouth and unleashed a torrent of air bubbles. The last of her oxygen. The grief was insurmountable, indescribable, but at the same time there was a nugget of vindication, even joy. Gideon hadn't abandoned her for another woman after all. All those years ago, the wicked villagers, or a faction of them, had killed him and thrown him in the lake.

That was what Davenport was talking about when he'd said Gideon was closer than she knew.

He always had been because he'd never really left.

The despair turned into rage. Now she didn't just want revenge for herself and her kind, but also for Gideon.

For love.

These villagers had ripped out her heart, destroyed her livelihood and systematically crushed her. They needed to pay.

With great effort, she slowed her racing heart, got her bearings, and was away again, inching forward through the mud and silt one determined stride at a time.

One more step.

Another.

Soon her feet found firmer purchase, and the weight bearing down on her lessened. She was close to salvation.

So close.

Then, her head broke the surface of the lake.

She gulped in grateful gasps of air, while simultaneously looking feverishly around her. She could hear them, the villagers. But their voices were muted and came from a long way away. She turned in the water and saw them lining the far bank of the lake, torches and pitchforks in hand. The fools couldn't see her.

Where was she?

The island.

She'd found the island in the lake, or she'd been guided here. Perhaps the only place in the world that might offer her sanctuary that night.

When the meal was finished, Ben and Tim headed out into the evening drizzle. Tim said he was in a hurry to check on Sheila, while Ben had to feed Mr. Trimble and get back to his research. The two men walked down the street together in the direction of the villas until they arrived at the main car park, at which point Ben announced, "This is me," and veered off.

"The Volkswagen?" Tim asked. "Outstanding feat of German engineering."

"Indeed," Ben confirmed. "More comfortable than it looks, too. But just as cramped as it looks. It's not a Tardis."

"How unfortunate," Tim chuckled. "If you had a Tardis, I might even consider trading my Fury for it. It would undoubtedly be better on fuel." Then he shook Ben's hand and went on his way, pausing only to shout over his shoulder, "Good luck with the research, and let me know if you have any more questions. By now you've probably realized how passionate I am about the most obscure things, and it's always good to be of service."

Only after he'd left did Ben realize that they still hadn't exchanged contact information, and he didn't even know how long Tim and Sheila intended to stay at the R.R. Still, being a noted historian and lecturer would mean that Tim shouldn't be that hard to track down. Everyone was on Facebook, Twitter, or Instagram these days. Most people were on all three, and more besides. Social media could be a bewildering hodgepodge for the uninitiated, but a valuable tool if you knew how to use it.

As Ben unlocked the driver's side door of the camper and climbed in, a far more unsettling thought occurred to him.

What if it had been Tim who'd left the note in his room?

If that was the case, he had just inadvertently led his persecutor right to his doorstep. Literally.

Good work, Ben.

That was a ridiculous assumption, he told himself. He hadn't told Tim which room he was staying in at the main block, and what would he stand to gain from scaring Ben away? If he was on the R.R's payroll, he hid it very well, and had revealed much more tonight about his private life than he needed to. No. Ben trusted his instincts, a journalist's best weapon, and they told him Tim was on the level. A little off-center and eccentric perhaps, but on the level.

Speaking of weapons, before entering the living area, Ben opened the glove box in the VW's cockpit and pulled out his extendable baton. It wasn't the most practical of weapons to use in a confined space, but he would feel safer having it close at hand just in case he had an unexpected visitor at some point. He would much rather have a handgun at his disposal, but as he didn't know how to use one, and they were illegal in Britain anyway, a baton would have to do. Under the Prevention of Crime Act of 1953, batons were illegal, too. As was any offensive weapon. But he was far more likely to escape prosecution for owning a baton than a firearm.

There was a lot in his mind to sift through. He couldn't shake the feeling that he had all the pieces of the puzzle, but he just couldn't put them all in the correct order. Not for the first time, he began to wonder what exactly he was doing at the Regal Retreat. Was his involvement a simple public relations exercise? If all they wanted was some positive re-inforcement, or someone to improve the online reputation of the place, there were specialist marketing companies for that. He was just a lone wolf with a limited reach.

At first, he thought he'd been handed a fantastic opportunity. Now it felt more like a poisoned chalice. It crossed Ben's mind that if anyone was to question why the R.R. hadn't done more to combat the chain of violent incidents, they could always say they'd employed him, but he'd been unable to solve the mystery. Was he being set up to be a scapegoat? The gnawing paranoia distracted him, which was probably exactly what they wanted, whoever "they" were.

Mr. Trimble was afflicted with no such concerns and welcomed Ben with an accusatory series of meows while he weaved around his legs. Dinner was late.

"No extras for you tonight, fella," Ben explained. "I have to 'fess up and admit I had the most delicious steak but forgot to save you some, so it's dry food only for you."

In response, Mr. Trimble turned around, lifted his tail, and showed Ben his ass.

Charming.

As Ben emptied the cat's litter box and filled his dish with food, he tossed around his options. Where would he sleep tonight? He no longer felt safe in Room 327. It was almost as if the room had been corrupted or tainted somehow. The other option was to bunk down in the camper. He was no stranger to that, but would he truly be safe here? If whoever sent the note knew where his room was, they could probably find out about the camper. It wouldn't be too difficult. At least Room 327 was in close proximity to other people.

He knew he mustn't let himself be consumed by fear and doubt. Fear, or some derivative of it, was something everyone had to deal with to some degree on an almost daily basis. Fear of crashing your car, fear of doing something wrong at work, fear of losing a loved one, fear of the un-known. It wasn't such a bad thing. It kept you alert and was vital for self-preservation.

Nevertheless, it was important to control it and not let it control you. For that reason, Ben decided to put the warning note out of his mind and carry on about his business as if nothing had happened. At least for the time being. It would send a message to anyone watching him that he wasn't going to be intimidated.

As he switched on the kettle to make a cup of coffee and went about his chores, he couldn't stop thinking about what he and Tim had discussed over dinner.

Never forget history repeats.

It seemed outlandish. Fantastical, even. But what if the theory they'd begun to formulate was correct? What if this Elizabeth Thrower had found a way to permeate the dreams of people who visited the R.R., the place where she'd been so callously and brutally murdered centuries earlier?

It was difficult not to feel any sympathy for the woman. More than likely, as with so many others back in the days of the witch trials, she was just a harmless oddball. In days gone by, too many people were scared or distrustful of anything they considered different or out of the ordinary. There was comfort and solidarity to be found as part of a pack, and anything that challenged that ideal was considered a threat.

Of course, the very idea that she had the innate ability to manipulate people's dreams long after her death, or even at all, suggested that she may not have been quite so innocent. If anything could be indicative of some kind of supernatural power, that was it.

Ben picked up where he'd left off with his online enquiries, but now he began looking at everything from a different angle. Glancing back over his previous research, he found that there was scant evidence of sleep disorders in any of the news articles and reports he'd read. But why would there be? Unless you were specifically looking for evidence of it, as he was now doing, it wasn't something automatically linked with violent acts. And that was assuming any suspects or witnesses confided in them that much. Given their sensitive, personal nature, they'd probably prefer to keep any nightmares they had to themselves.

However, the more he thought about it, the more it made sense, and there were a few random quotes and snippets of information scattered through the ages that seemed to feed into the idea. What had Archie Smith, the soldier, said back in 1946?

"She won't let me rest. She haunts my dreams and makes my waking life a nightmare."

Had he really been talking about some Polish servant girl in the war, as it had been assumed, or was he referencing Elizabeth Thrower? Regardless, reliving literally your worst nightmare night after night would certainly take its toll, not only physically but psychologically, and could have played a significant role in a lot of these accidents and incidents. Even in the absence of any crushing guilt, when people's sleep patterns are interrupted, they get sloppy and careless, which might also be a contributing factor in some cases.

But how did the ghost of Beth White fit into it? Was that the witch's doing, too? Influencing someone's dreams was one thing, bringing someone back from the dead to punch a hole in his meal voucher was something else entirely. Could it be that the teenaged murder victim's spirit had transcended space, time, and even death, to make contact with him? If so, what could she possibly want?

He pulled up the last article he read about the murder and read it again, convinced there was something he was missing, some small detail that would tie everything together.

Beth White was found by a walker early on the morning of March 6, 1987, lying in a pool of blood near one of the villas next to the lake. She had suffered multiple stab wounds to her back and torso and had been sexually assaulted. Her killer was never caught.

Her killer was never caught.

Ben remembered the assumption that murderers eventually always returned to the scene of their crime and wondered if it meant that not only was the killer still at large, but could possibly still be at the Regal, either as a worker or a regular visitor.

He or she could be here right now.

It could even have been them who left the warning note in his room.

As far as he could tell, there was another lull after the Beth White murder, this one lasting right up until 1997. This time, it was a double suicide. Abigail Haus and her husband Heinrich were visiting from Germany. On the morning of June 2nd, they were due to check out and continue their European tour. They'd already purchased tickets for a flight to Bruges later that day, but when they failed to check out, housekeeping was sent to check on them and found them both dead in bed.

The inquest ruled Ricin poisoning. Apparently, they'd both ingested it, probably orally. Nobody could piece together what had happened, and for a time there was talk of the whole thing being an assassination plot to silence Heinrich, who had once done some kind of security consultancy work for a shadowy Russian millionaire. The whole affair was very odd, as were many of the cases at the R.R., and left many questions unanswered.

Two years later, there was another boating accident in which a teenager lost his life, and a year after that there was yet another murder. Ben scoured the article hoping to find a connection with the Beth White case that perhaps everyone else had missed, but there were no similarities whatsoever. Ernest Bradley and Thomas Stevenage were golfing buddies and business associates. By all accounts, they had a monumental falling out somewhere around the seventh hole of the Regal's then newly fashioned nine-hole course and Ernest beat Thomas to death with a five-iron in front of scores of horrified witnesses. It was an open-and-shut case. But in another strange twist, Ernest never stood trial. The sixty-eight-year-old died of a massive heart attack before things could get that far.

In 2004, a twenty-three-year-old worker by the name of Jack Whatmore dropped dead on the premises from a suspected brain hemorrhage. Ben noted, with some discomfort, that it had happened at the Ground Zero restaurant, which only raised more questions. Why was it the ghost of Beth White he'd seen and not the ghost of Jack Whatmore? Beth worked at the restaurant but had been murdered somewhere else. Who in their right mind would return for all eternity to their place of work?

None of it made sense. However, if there was one thing Ben had learned in all the time he'd been investigating the supernatural, it was that there were very few hard and fast rules, apart from the unwritten one that decreed that paranormal activity never happened when you were expecting it.

Much like our own reality, the supernatural world was random, chaotic, and unpredictable, a reflection of a world so fucked up that parents outlived their children and anyone could carry the sum of human knowledge around on a device so small that it fit in your pocket. Ben wondered how people in Elizabeth Thrower's world would react to such wonders. No doubt they would consider it the work of the devil and probably try to destroy it, along with you for possessing it. The real tragedy was that most people used said device mostly to look at pictures of cats (nothing wrong with that) or argue with people they didn't know about things they didn't care about.

Ben, still trying to decide where he was going to sleep that night, could feel his eyelids growing heavier and leaned back to rest his head. In some ways he dreaded the onset of sleep. He didn't want to submit to that shadowy, alternative existence for fear of what it may hold. The more he thought about it, the more he believed dreams played some role in everyday life, if only in forming tenuous links between past and present, bridges traversing time and space. As his mind fogged up, he prepared to let himself drift away and see where his next adventure took him.

Suddenly, a tentative banging sound shattered the heavy silence. He sat bolt upright on the bench, fingers tensing around the handle of the baton he still held.

Was someone knocking on his door?

The knock came again, slightly harder this time.

It was the side door, which was unusual. When most people came knocking, they tended to overlook the side door, unless it was open, and headed for the cockpit, specifically the driver's side just as Detective Carter had done.

He glanced at his phone, which showed a time of 10:48 p.m. Too late for visitors. Perhaps it was the detective with another round of questions. But surely even the police would wait until morning, unless it was some kind of emergency.

Baton in hand and trying to prepare himself for anything, Ben slowly opened the door. What he found there both shocked and relieved him.

Tim Norgood.

Their eyes met, and Tim gave a sheepish smile. "I hope I'm not interrupting anything," he said, tousled blond hair blowing in the wind.

"Not at all," Ben replied, quickly slipping the baton into the waistband at the back of his jeans so as not to alarm his visitor. "Is something wrong?"

A fine drizzle was still coming down, causing the streetlights lining the road outside to reflect off one side of Tim's face, leaving the other side in perpetual shadow. He looked both nervous and excited. "Since our talk at dinner, I've become more and more convinced that you're absolutely right. Something is wrong here," he said. "Not to sound too dramatic, and I have no idea whether or not it qualifies as a curse, but I think some kind of otherworldly force is definitely at work."

"You and me both," Ben replied. Then he noticed for the first time that Tim was carrying something bulky and awkward-looking. From his body shape alone, it was clear that whatever the thing was, it was heavy and Tim wasn't used to all the exertion. "What do you have there, Tim?"

"A shovel and a pick."

Ben cocked his head and instinctively retreated slightly into the confines of the camper, his paranoia going into overdrive. "Why are you walking around at night with a shovel and pick?"

"I thought we could make a concerted effort to solve this mystery once and for all."

"How?"

"By heading over to the island in the lake and looking for Elizabeth Thrower's grave. At least that way we'll find out whether or not that part of the legend is real and we can take it from there. Do you have a flashlight, by any chance?"

Chapter Sixteen

It just so happened Ben did have a flashlight. He had several, in fact. Artificial light sources didn't just come in handy when living in a van; they were an essential piece of a paranormal investigator's kit. There were a lot of dark places to explore.

He opened the storage compartment next to the one where he kept the bulk of his clothes and rummaged around amid the battery packs, candles, and other miscellaneous items until he found two compact, military-grade Maglite flashlights. Each was no bigger than a cigar but consideration, he stuffed an extra battery pack into his pocket, grabbed his lightweight jacket, and joined Tim outside. "Where did you get that shovel and pick, anyway?" he asked.

"Did I mention I'm an amateur archaeologist?"

"Amateur dramatics, yes. Amateur archaeology, I'm not sure," Ben said.

"Well, you never know when you might need them, so I always keep a few tools in the boot of my car," Tim said.

Something passed between the two men; quiet suspicion on Ben's side and a noticeable defiance on Tim's, as if driving around with a full complement of digging tools was perfectly normal.

"In case you want to dig something up?" Ben asked, as if doing such a thing was a common occurrence. And who was he to judge? Maybe it was, and he was the unusual one for not doing it.

"Pretty much. You know what they say..."

"What's that?"

"It's better to have a shovel and not need it than need a shovel and not have one. Take this, will you?"

Tim handed Ben the pick. It felt reassuringly heavy in his grip. "No problem," Ben said as the two men began walking across the car park in the direction of the lake. He discreetly checked to see if the baton was still tucked in the back of his waistband. It was.

There was a short, slightly uneasy silence before Tim said, "So, Ben, I have an update on Elizabeth Thrower for you."

"Splendid! What did you find out?"

"I skimmed through some notes and did some digging, if you'll excuse the pun. I discovered that early in her life, she had a common-law husband."

"So?"

"So, do you know what that could mean?"

Ben stopped in his tracks. "She changed her name?"

"Correct. Not through any civic duty, but it was more a gesture to symbolize loyalty. Her given name was actually Elizabeth Grange, not Thrower. That would explain why you couldn't find any birth or death records. She would've been registered under her given name. I didn't check. Thought I'd leave that to you. I'd like some credit for the assist if it leads anywhere."

"What happened to the husband? Was he there when she was killed?"

"It seems not," Tim replied. "Details are scant, but apparently he was a fly-by-night philanderer from 'away.' Whether the split was amicable, or whether one of them was left heartbroken, it undoubtedly had a profound effect on Elizabeth."

"No doubt," Ben agreed, trying to imagine the implications of such a life-changing event in that long-ago time. Apart from the psychological trauma of a break-up everyone has to experience at some point in their lives, there was also the social stigma that was much more prevalent in Elizabeth's time. In the simplest terms, she was probably seen as discarded. Unwanted. It could be part of the reason she became a social out-cast, the sin-eating stuff coming as more of a convenience than a calling. What else was she going to do?

"Ben, what kind of journalist did you say you were?" Tim asked.

"The paranormal kind."

"Excuse me?"

"I'm more of a researcher than a journalist these days. I used to write for a rock magazine, hence the encyclopedic knowledge of the Stones and dozens of other tired, old rock bands. Now I run a website and write the odd feature, so the two disciplines kinda merge into one."

Tim looked surprised. "You're a ghost hunter? Like on T.V.?"

"Most of the people you see on T.V. are charlatans," Ben said. "They have no option but to hype things up and exaggerate to get high ratings and keep their contracts."

"So, they're all fake?" Tim looked as if someone had just told him Santa Claus wasn't real. "Isn't that…fraud?"

"Not if they include a disclaimer at the start of the program that explicitly tells you that what you're watching is for entertainment pur-poses only. That basically gives them free license to do what they want. None of it has to be 'real,' so to speak. Most of the action is implied, all in the name of entertainment. I'm not saying they don't find any evi-dence of the paranormal at all. No doubt, some of them do from time to time. There's plenty out there. But some of those so-called investiga-tions last for days, and it's all condensed into a convenient forty-five-minute episode to fit the programming schedule. Trust me, if you record eighteen or twenty hours of footage of you and your mates stumbling around a creepy, abandoned mental hospital in the dead of night, you'll find enough material to fill the time, even if it's only the odd unexplained noise or fleeting shadow."

"What about all that fancy gear they use?"

"Apart from thermometers and things like E.M.F. meters, most of the bits of equipment you see on T.V. are just gimmicks with barely any scientific basis. Anyone could rig up a little hand-held electronic device with some flashing lights and whistles on it and claim the lights will turn red if a ghost comes within ten feet. They might spin a few tech-heavy lines to add some authenticity, but essentially, it's nonsense."

"What does an E.M.F. meter do?"

"Measures electromagnetic fields. Paranormal activity is said to trigger fluctuations, causing readings to spike."

"Wow," Tim said, sounding impressed. "This is a whole new world. Where would one acquire such a device? If one were to, I don't know, consider keeping one in the boot of his car? Are there any specialist outlets for this kind of thing?"

"Sure," Ben said. "Or you could just get one off Amazon like everyone else."

"That simple, huh?" Tim said, sounding somewhat disappointed. "On the topic, did you bring any equipment with you?"

"Of course," Ben said, reaching into his pocket and taking out his smartphone.

"Your phone? What are you going to do with that? Call the vengeful spirit hotline?"

"If there was one, I would," Ben said. "It worked for *Ghostbusters*. Fact is, the average smartphone has all the equipment you need built into it. A high-res camera with a range of settings and a flash, a video camera, and audio-recording software. It even has a flashlight," he added with a wink.

"But does it have an E.M.F. Meter?" Tim countered.

"Sadly not. But there's probably an app for that. The dream is to obtain proof that the paranormal exists. Verified, documented, irrefutable proof. Audio is good. Pictures and video, even better. But even if I took a thirty-second clip of a headless ghost levitating right before our very eyes, it would still be almost impossible for it to be accepted by the masses. Human beings are hard-wired to be skeptical. Too much trickery around these days. Accessible, easy-to-use technology has a downside. Anyone with a smartphone can take a picture of a ghost. But equally, anyone with a smartphone can mock up something that *looks* like a ghost. You don't even need any training. Just a filter."

"Aren't there ways of verifying whether captured footage is real?"

"Yes. But that kind of analysis is expensive. Fake footage shows up so much now, when they see it, people just assume that's what it is. The worst thing that can happen is if someone comes forward with some impressive evidence that's later found to be faked because that discredits the whole field. But most material doesn't stand up to scrutiny. And even if it did, it would simply be brushed aside by mainstream science or, even worse, buried. Science deals with facts. Things that can be readily explained. If you presented solid evidence of life after death, for example, it would challenge the accepted status quo and put a lot of people in very precarious positions. Most accepted religions would crumble overnight, and mainstream science would be confronted with a barrage of questions it wouldn't be able to answer. All this would lead to an unprecedented period of upheaval and social change. Have you ever heard of Charles Fort?"

"The ancient fortification in Ireland?"

"What? No, the man."

"Name rings a bell," Tim admitted. "Who is he again?"

"Who *was* he. He shuffled off this mortal coil in the nineteen-thirties. Bonus points if you get the reference."

"I don't."

"Didn't think you would. I know not everyone is obsessed with magazines as I am. Anyway, I guess you could say he was part scientist, part philosopher, and part writer. He collated anomalies, freaks of nature, and weird occurrences that science couldn't explain. His entire ethos hinged on the fact that mainstream scientists were only interested in reinforcing their own rigid beliefs rather than assessing on balance what evidence actually presented. Data that didn't fit their criteria was either ignored or discredited."

"Interesting. I never thought of things that way," Tim said.

"To an extent, selective thinking is something we are all guilty of. We all compartmentalize things to suit ourselves. It makes this crazy world we live in easier to navigate."

As they chatted, the men left the road and took the gravel path skirting the water. "We're almost at the lake," Ben said, suddenly feeling apprehensive as the reality of what they were doing dawned on him. "What's the plan, then?"

"Can you swim?" Tim said, looking at Ben from the corner of his eye.

"Yes. But surely, you can't..."

"Relax, Ben. I'm joking. Call it gallows humor, if you will."

"I'd rather not."

"We'll borrow a boat. I came out earlier and had a little look around. I found just the thing. And...here it is," Tim said, stopping and looking around furtively.

Ben looked down to see a tiny two-man rowboat. It had been hauled up out of the water and was now lashed to a post. "We're going to steal it?"

"Steal it? Heavens, no. We're just going to borrow it. When we've finished, we'll put it back where we got it from and nobody will be any the wiser."

"What if someone comes? There's a big security presence here, and presumably they're going to be extra vigilant given recent events."

"We'll be quick," Tim said. "It's unlikely anyone will be patrolling much in this weather, anyway. But the longer we stand here discussing it, the more chance there is of us being caught."

It sounded like a challenge. For a moment, Ben felt like a child being egged on to do something naughty or dangerous by a friend, and he wondered if the situation was some kind of action replay of what had happened the day Tim's brother was killed. It felt like a watershed moment. But Tim was right. If they were going to solve this mystery, exploring the island was a crucial step.

Ben looked out across the lake, which rippled gently in the wind, the dark water reaching out and lapping at the rowboat as if trying to reclaim it. The island, barely visible, loomed out of the shadows.

Was he doing the right thing?

Of course, he wasn't. This was completely the *wrong* thing to do, on so many levels.

It crossed his mind that if anyone wanted to silence him, someone like Tim, for example, this would be the perfect opportunity to do so. They could just push him off the boat and watch him drown. Maybe hit him over the head with an oar to be sure. His body wouldn't be found until the next day, maybe not even then, and his death would probably be marked down as an accident or suicide. He could see the headlines now:

> *Paranormal Investigator Ben Shivers, 39, becomes latest fatality at the Regal Retreat. The ex-journalist, who had struggled following the tragic death of his daughter and the subsequent breakdown of his marriage and lived in a camper van with a stray cat called Mr. Trimble, was found drowned in the resort's lake. The death is unexplained, but there are not believed to be any suspicious circumstances.*

"Ben?"

"What?"

"I said help me untie her and get her in the water."

With a final sigh of resignation, Ben set down the pick he'd been carrying into the bed of the rowboat, next to a pair of oars, and turned to examine the moorings.

The boat was held in place with just a rope and a simple knot. It took no time at all to release, and between them, he and Tim began heaving the small craft into the water. It was more difficult than it looked; their task was made all the more awkward because they kept losing their footing in the mud. At one point, Tim lost his balance completely, slipped, and found himself planted on his rump at the lake's edge, grimacing as the cold water began to seep through his clothes. He was lucky not to whack his head on the side of the boat on the way down, and when he got up, his lower half was caked with mud.

With one final shove, the boat slid off the embankment and into the water with a gentle splash. Tim jumped in and grabbed an oar, motioning frantically for Ben to follow.

After a last moment's consideration, he did so, fully aware that this could rank as one of the stupidest things he'd ever done. Perhaps more stupid than the time as a twenty-one-year-old when he'd spent the last of his money on beer and attempted to walk the nine miles home from a club he'd been at. He stopped for a rest halfway and woke up the next morning, freezing cold and covered in bird shit.

Bird shit may well be involved again, but this situation could potentially pose an even bigger hazard to his health. Even if Tim didn't try to murder him, two inexperienced, middle-aged men stealing a rowboat and taking it out on a lake in bad weather at night was a recipe for disaster.

When Ben got in the boat, it lurched sickeningly to one side, then to the other as both men adjusted their weight and attempted to balance each other out through a fraught process of compensation and over-compensation.

Once settled, the first thing he did was look around for a life jacket. There wasn't any.

Nor did there seem to be much in the way of other survival equipment: no flares, life rings, or even so much as a whistle. The inside of the boat was bare. "Have you done this before?" Ben asked hopefully.

"What? Take a boat out to an island in the middle of a lake at night with a virtual stranger to look for the grave of a supposed witch?"

"Well, yeah," Ben said. "That. But I was thinking more about just the rowing part."

"Nope. Never done it before," Tim said dismissively. "But how hard could it be? You just dunk the oar in the water and use it to propel the craft in the direction you want to it go while simultaneously trying your best not to fall in. For the most part, it's simple physics. Force versus resistance."

"I'm sure there's more to it than that. There must be a certain level of skill involved. We can barely see the place we're supposed to be going."

"We will see it soon enough. We just need to get a bit closer. Now come on, let's get this show on the road."

To Ben's surprise, Tim was right about two things: though the rowing business was exhausting, it wasn't as technically challenging as it looked, and when they reached what he estimated to be the mid-point of the lake, the island did become visible again, looming gradually into view like an oasis in the desert. The fact that Tim didn't appear to have any murderous intent toward him, at least not yet, was a considerable bonus.

"I see it," Ben gasped. The way they were positioned in the boat, facing each other with him peering over Tim's shoulder, meant that he took on the extra responsibility of navigator. They'd been rowing for over fifteen minutes, and after a rocky start had settled into a rhythm that was now seeing them cover a distance at a respectable speed. Neither of them were likely to ever make the GB Olympic rowing squad, but they were getting the job done.

Tim excitedly swung his head around, the sudden motion literally rocking the boat.

"Steady, steady," Ben warned, laying the oar across his lap and gripping the sides of the tiny craft as it wobbled.

With their destination in sight, both men began rowing again with renewed enthusiasm, and Ben could barely contain his excitement as the shadowy landmass got bigger and bigger. He felt like a character in a boy's adventure novel.

In no time at all, the tiny boat drew up to the island, which looked and felt much bigger than it did from a distance. The bottom of the craft scraped on the lakebed, which was Ben and Tim's cue to jump out and plunge knee-deep in freezing water so they could drag the vessel safely up onto land.

They'd kept the rope, but there was no fixed mooring to tie it to, so instead, they maneuvered the boat into a small clearing on the edge of the island and lashed the rope to a tree to prevent it from sliding back into the water. The last thing either of them wanted was to be stranded somewhere they shouldn't be.

Job done, Ben stood in the overgrown clearing flexing his aching shoulders and surveying his surroundings. He drew one of the Maglite flashlights from his pocket and shone it into the stifling gloom surrounding them. The island was not only bigger now they were actually standing on it, but a lot more intimidating, too. It had been left to nature, and nature had done its work in reclaiming it. Directly in front of them was an impenetrable wall of dense foliage, sagging tree limbs, and broken trunks. Gnarled roots protruded from the earth like grasping hands.

How the heck were they supposed to get in there?

Finally, the probing light from Ben's Maglite picked out an overgrown, barely distinguishable path leading from the comparative safety of the clearing deeper into the untamed tangle of trees and bushes.

"Tim, I don't suppose you remembered to bring a machete?"

"Unfortunately, no," Tim replied, joining Ben in staring at the natural barrier in front of them. "Until now a machete hasn't really been a required part of my excavation kit."

"So, what's the plan? Are we going to dig up the entire island? I know it's not very big, but it's big enough for that to not be an option."

"Don't be silly; that would take days. No, we have clues."

"What kind of clues?"

"Several accounts state that Elizabeth Thrower is buried on the east side of the island, with her head facing west."

"Why?"

"In orthodox Christian tradition, it was believed that burying people in this manner would allow the deceased to witness the second coming of Jesus. The fishermen also buried her with a bible and a crucifix, simply to make a point," Tim explained. "They believed she was in cahoots with the devil and were trying to make things right. For all we know, they might have just been making things worse."

"You can say that again. What happened to respecting other people's way of life?"

"That didn't happen much in seventeenth-century England. The good news is that by all accounts the fishermen helpfully marked the spot where they buried her with a cairn and a wooden cross."

"That was nice of them," Ben said. "But surely the cairn and the cross won't still be there?"

"Unlikely. But there might be some remnant of one or the other. As far as I can ascertain, the island has been left virtually untouched ever since. As you can see, it isn't really big enough to house any buildings, apart from maybe a couple of sheds, and the ground probably isn't firm enough for building on anyway. It's still surprising the Regal hasn't used it in some fashion, though."

"True," Ben agreed. "They utilize everything else. I don't see any evidence of vandalism or trespassing, either. It's almost like people have been actively avoiding coming here. Even this little path looks more natural than man made. Nothing more than an old rabbit trail or something. So where do we start?"

"The east side of the island is directly opposite our current location," Tim said. "Looks to me like this path you found will take us directly there, as the crow flies. It's certainly heading in that direction."

"Wouldn't it be easier to just take the boat around?"

Tim considered this for a moment, then said, "What if there's nowhere to park? I mean, tie it up? Also, I think we got lucky on the way here. There might be any number of submerged rocks around this island. We'd never see them in the dark. One could easily bash a hole in the bottom of the boat, and if we go in the water, there's not much chance of us being rescued until morning. I don't think either of us has it in them to swim to the shore. Best-case scenario, we might be able to make it to the island. But do you really want to spend the night here, wet and shivering, and then face the consequences of our questionable actions in the cold light of day?"

"Since you put it like that…"

With a last look at each other, the two men set off.

Chapter Seventeen

East Anglia, 1645

lizabeth knew just how close she'd come to death the moment they threw her in the lake. She'd felt its sharp, frigid claws reaching for her and smelled its fetid breath.

She also knew she wouldn't be able escape its clutches for much longer. The only clothes she had were ripped and sodden, forcing her to remove them and expose her pale, puckered skin to the elements. It was impossible to dry them, or even make a fire, and the weather was bitterly cold.

Her forced nakedness should be the ultimate humiliation. But now, the shedding of her clothes was an almost symbolic gesture representing a total denunciation of society's laws. The social order had rejected her, so she rejected it. An eye for an eye and a tooth for a tooth, as it said within the pages of the book they all revered so much.

The island was tiny. There was nothing to eat, save for a few wild berries, mushrooms, and roots. Not enough to sustain her. But she wasn't hungry, and she didn't have to keep herself going for long. Just long enough to do her work. Remaining undetected was of far more importance.

Worst of all were her insides. That metal thing they'd shoved up her had done a lot of damage. Ravaged her. She could feel how wrong things were, and the insides of her thighs were permanently sticky with congealing blood. It was all she could do to stand upright, and she found it much less painful to walk hunched over, arms crossed protectively over her abdomen. Now and again, something would work its way loose and slide down her leg. Some mangled piece of flesh, or perhaps a part of one of her organs.

She didn't let it worry her.

She made a bed of reeds, and for the longest time, she slept to give her body time to gather its strength. Hours passed. The line between dreams and reality melted away.

Though her appetite was largely absent, after an undeterminable time in hiding, Elizabeth felt she needed something more substantial than a handful of half-rotten berries. Out of desperation she thought about eating one of the clotted, fleshy lumps that fell out of her. Truth be told, she even picked it up and put it to her lips, her cracked and blackened tongue flicking out to sample the offering. It tasted like copper.

But she couldn't bring herself to do it.

It would be tantamount to eating herself, and where would that lead? Her body would never be able to repair itself as quickly as she devoured it.

She knew she was dying. If the cold or hunger didn't get to her, she would surely succumb to her injuries sooner rather than later.

But the rage still burned within her, keeping her alive, and she wouldn't allow herself to be taken until her task was completed.

She wanted retribution.

As she recuperated, she entertained herself with fanciful daydreams about swimming across the lake to the village to hunt down the men and women who had wronged her. Ezra Davenport would be first, followed by the one who called himself the Witchfinder General. Next would be Tom the Baker and Lynette the farmer's wife. One by one, she would make them all pay.

But she was weak and broken. Any able-bodied man or woman would easily overpower her. Her physical body had almost served its purpose.

There were other ways to get what she wanted. She would call on the

Ancient Ones. The true gods, who ruled this planet before man invented the absurd fallacy of one all-seeing, all-powerful entity. They would help her.

There was a lot to be done, but she worked with grim determination and surprised herself by remembering all the necessary incantations, even those in obscure, dead, foreign languages, though she didn't have access to any of her books or scriptures. Like others of her ilk, she had committed what she could to memory then burned her books rather than be caught with them. Even so, her recollection was so exhaustive that it was like tapping into some vast bank of collated knowledge.

She hid during the daylight hours to avoid being spotted, during which time she would fall into a kind of fugue. Almost a state of suspended animation. Hunger pangs deserted her, and she didn't even feel the cold. Faces danced before her eyes. Faces she knew. Faces she had once respected, even loved. But now all she wanted was to see those faces skinned, smashed, and stamped into the ground.

At night she came alive, working feverishly until the break of dawn, always fighting against the coming of the light.

Fighting against the cold.

Fighting against death.

Always fighting.

So often she wanted to lie down and drift into the eternal blackness. She knew something else was waiting for her and would gladly accept whatever afterlife she was granted, free of all this fear, pain, and hatred.

But she wouldn't allow it.

Couldn't allow it.

Not yet.

Soon, all the spells had been cast, the promises made, and all that remained was one final task, the crowning glory.

With the last of her energy, she took a rock and used it to sharpen a stick to a point, which she used to carefully scrawl an elaborate set of symbols in the mud bank. Among the symbols were four words written in her native language.

NEVER FORGET HISTORY REPEATS

When she was finally done, Elizabeth Thrower lay on her back in the midst of her work with a satisfied, heart-rending sigh. Upon doing so, she immediately felt at peace. A warm, comforting sensation enveloped her, and the ghost of a smile tugged at her thin, pale lips.

For the first time in a long time, she felt safe. At ease. This was it, the culmination of her efforts. It was as if her entire life had been leading up to this point, every other step of her journey just another marker on the course some higher power had plotted. She'd been serving her purpose, and now that purpose was almost fulfilled.

As the first shards of yellow sunlight fell over the rippling surface of the lake, she gazed toward the heavens and raised the sharpened stick above her head. It was almost a relief when, still smiling, she brought it down with all her might and felt the unyielding tip pierce her throat. As the crimson blood poured out of her and trickled down into the black water of the lake, it ran over the symbols she had drawn, calling them into action and giving them life.

Her last words were barely a whisper.

"Never forget history repeats..."

It was tough going. The path, what there was of it, was so narrow that Ben and Tim had to walk in single file, lifting their knees higher than normal in an exaggerated stomping motion to avoid being tripped by the undergrowth. Ben took the lead, hacking at the encroaching branches and vegetation with the sharpened blade of the shovel as Tim walked behind him, carrying the pick and shining one of the Maglites so they could see where they were going.

However, the shovel was too heavy and cumbersome to wield with any accuracy, leading to a lot of wasted energy, and within minutes, Ben's hands, already blistered and sore from the rowing, were oozing blood and fluid from open sores. Then he had an idea. Reaching into his waistband, he withdrew his telescopic baton and flicked his wrist to fully extend it.

"Bloody hell," Tim said from somewhere near his right ear. "What are you doing with that?"

"Can't be too careful," Ben replied, passing the shovel to Tim for him to carry. "Better to have a telescopic baton and not need one than need a telescopic baton and not have one."

"I see what you did there," Tim replied.

Ben briefly considered telling Tim about the warning note he'd found in his room but didn't think it was the right time or place. It could wait, not least because he wasn't totally convinced that Tim wasn't the one who'd sent it.

The baton proved just as effective as the shovel in chopping down the vegetation, but much easier to use. Even so, at one point, one of the thick, sinewy branches he attacked didn't break under his onslaught like it should have. Instead, it sprang back at him with a vengeance, striking the side of his head. It felt like an open-palmed slap, as if the island itself was trying its best to repel them, and immediately afterward Ben felt something warm and sticky trickling down the side of his face and wondered whether it was sweat or blood. If it was the latter, he'd probably end the night looking like the last survivor in a slasher movie.

After ten minutes or so of hacking and slicing his way through the impenetrable foliage, Ben had to stop for a rest, bending over and placing his hands on his knees to help him get his breath back.

"Okay there?" Tim said, a note of what sounded like genuine concern in his voice.

"Sure," Ben replied. "Just having a breather."

"Let's spread the workload and swap places for a while. You take the torch and bring up the rear," Tim said, shooting an admiring glance at Ben's baton. He seemed to consider saying something else before overruling himself and wiping the sharp edge of the shovel, where sap, leaves, and various detritus had built up through Ben's misuse of it, on the ground. The university lecturer and amateur thespian then set about thrashing a path through the untamed vegetation with an unsettling level of aggression, grunting loudly as he went. Ben followed a safe distance behind with the flashlight, still holding the baton and questioning his life choices all over again.

The two men continued in this manner until they fought their way to the far eastern side of the island, their task gradually becoming easier as the vegetation thinned and they eventually stumbled into a narrow clearing at the water's edge.

As if on some kind of signal, the moon chose that moment to peek out from behind its shield of clouds and flood the area with its spectral white light. They were on the blind side of the island, meaning nobody from the R.R. would be able to see them unless they happened to be taking a midnight stroll around the lake, which, while not impossible, was extremely unlikely.

On reaching the clearing, Tim immediately broke out into an excited, lolloping happy dance. "This looks like it could be something!"

"I hate to be a killjoy, but I don't see anything."

"Let's spread out, starting at the water's edge and working backward. If you see anything that resembles a grave, shout out."

"You can count on that," Ben said, producing the other Maglite from his pocket and using his hand to shield the beam, just in case.

He did what Tim suggested, bending over and systematically examining small sections of the earth in front of him with the flashlight while using his other hand to brush away the layer of topsoil as he worked his way steadily backward.

Close to the water's edge, the ground was sandy and soft, allowing Ben's feet to sink into it. He didn't think anyone would be so stupid as to try to bury a body there. It would be a pointless task. If you even succeeded in digging a hole, the ground would undoubtedly spit the corpse back out.

But the more he retreated, the firmer and more solid the ground became, the probing roots from the wild vegetation covering most of the island, doing their work and knitting the earth together. Common sense suggested that the sweet spot would be on the verge where the vegetation began to take over.

There was remarkably little litter, apart from a few customary supermarket shopping bags and crisp packets washed up by the tide or blown onto the island by the wind. At one point, he thought he'd found something interesting: a foreign object half embedded in the soil. But it was nothing more than a discarded plastic bottle. When mankind finally succeeds in obliterating itself, our legacy will be a few empty buildings and mounds and mounds of cheap plastic.

As he retreated further back toward the tree line, Ben began to lose hope. This was like looking for a needle in a haystack. A needle you weren't even sure was really there. He paused, straightened, and flexed his muscles.

How long had they been on the island?

It felt like forever, but in reality had probably only been an hour or so at most. He didn't check the time because it wasn't important. They were going nowhere until they'd either found the grave of Elizabeth Thrower—or scoured every inch of the island.

Then his foot scuffed something. Something hard and immovable. He assumed it was a pebble, or another plastic bottle, and twisted his body around to see, but what he saw was neither of those two things. Instead, it was two rocks, placed on top of each other.

How did that happen?

Rocks didn't stack themselves on top of each other in nature, did they?

He stooped to have a closer look, shining the Maglite on the tiny structure. The rock on the bottom was about the size of a paperback book, while the one on top was about half the size and flatter, as if carefully selected for its ability to sit snugly atop the other. It looked as if it had been placed there deliberately and a thick layer of dirt suggested it had been there a very long time.

Off to the side was another, slightly smaller rock of similar appearance. It was possible that at one time all three rocks could have been part of the same mini-structure. Would three rocks constitute a cairn? Not that it mattered. There could have been many more rocks at one time, these three being all that remained.

Suppressing a sudden rush of excitement, Ben said, "Tim? Would you come here a moment, please?"

Tim appeared at his flank, stooping to get a better look at Ben's discovery. "What's that?"

"I was about to ask you the same question. Does it look…constructed to you?"

"The way they're positioned like that?" Tim replied, his voice trembling slightly. "It certainly does. And it looks as if that smaller one could easily have fallen off the top."

"So, this is what's left of the cairn the fishermen built?"

"Might be."

"But would it stay undisturbed for so long?" Ben asked. He was still having problems processing all this.

"Who's going to disturb it? The island has been off-limits. Not only that, but inaccessible, too. Nothing bigger than a rabbit has stepped foot here for centuries."

"Seems reasonable," Ben agreed. "So, what do we do now?"

"We start digging."

"And what do we do when…*if*…we find her?"

"Not sure. But we could at least start solving this mystery and hopefully put an end to this whole sorry saga."

"Sounds good to me," Ben said. "The sooner we clear this up, the sooner we can get off this bloody island." He picked up the shovel and thrust it into the damp earth, using his foot to drive it deeper.

"Hey! Careful!" Tim hissed, placing a firm hand on Ben's arm to restrain him. "She was buried without a coffin, remember? If you carry on like that, you're going to dismember what's left of her. With all the weathering, tidal shifts, and resettlement, there's no telling how far down she might be. It could be ten inches or ten feet."

"Good point," Ben agreed as he slowly withdrew the spade, half expecting it to contain the remnants of a human skeleton. Thankfully, it didn't.

He emptied the sandy soil onto the ground, and from then on was much more careful, sensitive to any kind of resistance that might indicate the spade had come into contact with a corpse.

As Ben worked, the chilly breeze grew into a stiff wind accompanied by a mournful howl, almost as if the elements were providing a sound-track to his clandestine activities.

After he'd cleared a patch of land about a meter squared and a few inches deep with no visible sign of anything unusual, Ben stopped for a rest. The moment he did so, Tim fell to his knees and started combing through the soil with his bare hands.

"What are you doing?" Ben asked, mildly horrified.

"Looking for fragments."

"Fragments of what?"

"Elizabeth Thrower. Bits of bone, if there's any left. Maybe some scraps of clothing."

Ben let him rummage around for a few minutes while he caught his breath before saying, "Anything?"

"Don't think so," Tim replied, sounding disappointed as he picked something up and held it between his thumb and forefinger to examine it by the flashlight's beam before deeming it worthless and throwing it over his shoulder. "Let me dig for a bit."

Ben, glad of the break, passed the shovel over to Tim and took a few steps back to allow him room to work. As his friend scraped and gouged at their fledgling excavation, Ben decided to take a walk around the clearing to stretch his legs. Stopping on the edge of the island a few feet away from the water's edge, he paused to admire the dark expanse stretching out before him while flexing his aching back and inspecting his blistered palms.

The lake. It had undoubtedly provided an untold amount of happiness and pleasure over the years, but at the same time, it had been the source of infinite despair, proving you couldn't have one without the other. Looking at it now, in all its serene beauty, it was easy to believe the lake held secrets. Was it possible for a body of water to be haunted? If places, people, and even things could be, he didn't see why not.

His thoughts once again turned to Beth White. In the past day or two, no matter what else was on his mind, everything seemed to circle back to her. She was the thread holding all this together. What was she trying to tell him?

Ben was a firm believer that some people were more sensitive or receptive to paranormal phenomena than others, and therefore more likely to have unexplained encounters. His path in life ensured that he was exposed to such things more than most, which at times left him wary of building up some kind of tolerance. But in fact, the opposite was true. Now, he felt more dialed in to mysterious goings-on than he ever had before.

Paradoxically, he also found himself becoming more skeptical and less susceptible to bullshit. He understood now more than ever that everybody had an agenda. Nobody did anything for nothing, and Ben hated being taken for a ride. In both his business life and his relationships, he strived to be transparent and make everything he did mutually beneficial. If he wrote an article for his website about a supposedly haunted hotel, for example, he was paid a modest fee, the hotel received publicity, and his readers were given some material. Everybody got something.

What Ben couldn't accept was duplicity and people lying and manipulating others for their own ends. That included unscrupulous businesses falsely claiming their premises were haunted to appeal to the dark tourism crowd who spent most of their time visiting Chernobyl or Aokigahara, Japan's so-called Suicide Forest, for fun.

If he ever encountered anything untoward, he would expose their racket quicker than he would cash a winning lottery ticket. He had no time for that self-serving crap. However, the Regal Retreat seemed to be doing the opposite. They were anxious to suppress any spooky goings-on for the simple reason that they wanted to corner the luxury market and couldn't be bothered with ghost hunters and grief junkies.

"Er… Ben?"

The muted yet emotion-filled tone of Tim's voice derailed Ben's train of thought and made his head snap around. "Yeah?"

"Would you come here for a moment, please?"

Ben hurried over to where Tim had apparently frozen in motion, slightly stooped with the shovel half-buried in the earth. He was staring at something.

"What's up?"

"Look down there and tell me that's not a human skull."

Ben wished he could do that.

He really did.

But one glance at the freshly turned earth, where the top of a bone-white dome had been exposed, told him otherwise. "Fucking hell," he said. "Is it her? Elizabeth?"

"The fuck should I know?" Tim snapped. "Most skeletons look the same to me, you know, when they're all stripped off flesh and skin and stuff." The last few words rose in tone so much he hit an accidental falsetto.

For some reason, hearing such a vulgar outburst from Tim jarred a little with Ben and rammed home the gravity of the situation. It sounded so unnatural, and emphasized the fact that both men's nerves were shredded.

Eager to move things along, Ben dropped to his knees and began carefully helping Tim brush the soil away with his hands.

The skull was positioned in the earth at an angle and soon, an oversized eye cavity filled with mud appeared, followed by a concave cheekbone, and finally a row of teeth. The skull boasted no obvious cracks or holes, which suggested two things: whoever the body belonged to hadn't died from a blow to the head, and it hadn't inadvertently been damaged while Ben and Tim had been digging around.

Next, several stark-white vertebrae appeared, which in turn gave way to a slender collarbone.

With Ben and Tim so engrossed in the task at hand, neither of them noticed the trio of men approaching from their blind side. They remained blissfully unaware of the new arrivals until their leader, now standing mere feet away, said, "Would one of you mind explaining what the hell you are doing?"

Chapter Eighteen

Ben instantly whirled around to face the newcomers. He felt like he'd been caught smoking behind the bike sheds by his old comprehensive school headmaster, a sadistic bastard if there ever was one. The man was a huge advocate of corporal punishment, even after it was banned in British schools in the late Eighties. That ruling took quite a long time to reach the provinces, and Mr. Watkins would think nothing of bending you over his desk and whacking you six times with a sturdy bamboo cane he kept in his office.

The voice that shattered the silence of the island was authoritative, threatening, and sounded vaguely out of place. But bizarrely, Ben recognized it from somewhere.

He slowly turned to see Detective Carter standing over him, the man who had previously visited his van. This time he was flanked by a uniformed police officer.

"Mister Shivers," the detective said. "I had a suspicion that our paths would cross again. I must be psychic. Maybe you could write an article about me."

"At least I didn't leave town, Sheriff," Ben replied, knowing his facetiousness wouldn't be appreciated but powerless to stop himself.

"It may have been better if you had. Now, let me run that by you again. What the hell are you two doing out here?"

"Would you believe we just came out for a midnight stroll and got lost?" Tim interjected with very little conviction.

In addition to the police presence was a tall, gaunt, smartly dressed man with a hooked nose, who was so intimidating he could put Christopher Lee to shame. He stared at Ben with rage burning in his eyes and said, "I want these men arrested and escorted from the premises immediately. Throw the book at them. Do you hear me? The book."

"Excuse me for asking," Ben said. "But who are you?"

"Glenn Davenport," the man replied with a haughty smugness. "I own this piece of land you're digging up. And everything else around here."

The latest in the never-ending line of Davenports. Of course. Ben could only hope the man's ancestors had been more likable, but he seriously doubted it. This man radiated contempt and toxicity, and those particular qualities didn't appear overnight. They were honed and cultivated over the course of a lifetime.

"Mister Shivers I'm already familiar with, and… I'm sorry, who are you?" Detective Carter began, turning his attention to Tim.

"I'm Tim. Tim Norgood." In what must be a reflex action, Tim made a forward motion as if to shake his hand before evidently thinking better of it and shrinking backward.

"Are you a guest at the Regal?" Detective Carter demanded.

"I am indeed. It was always on my bucket list, so to speak. This year my wife and I finally took the plunge."

"And where's your wife at the moment?"

Somewhat disconcertingly, as he asked the question the detective's eyes flicked down to the recently desecrated patch of ground.

"She's back at the villa. Probably fast asleep by now. Her partying days are long behind her."

"You call this a party?"

"Not exactly, Officer."

"Detective. Not Officer."

"Apologies, Detective."

"So do you always leave her alone in the middle of the night and go around digging up…" Detective Carter stopped, edged closer to the grave site, and said, "What is that? A body?"

"More of a skeleton, really."

"Mind telling me who it belongs to?"

"We believe it's the remains of Elizabeth Thrower," Tim replied.

"How long has that been there?" the detective said, stooping and peering closer at the remains.

"About four hundred years," Tim said with a shrug. "Give or take."

"How did you pair of idiots manage to stumble across it?"

"Believe it or not, it was a largely scientific process. The biggest stumbling block was navigating that bloody path across the island," Tim said.

The statement didn't strike Ben as being strictly true. There was precious little science involved. It was more a case of connecting dots and seeing where they led. But it was clear Tim wanted to attach a degree of legitimacy to the operation, even if the operation was illegal.

Detective Carter was unmoved. "In that case, I'm arresting you both under the Burial Act of eighteen-fifty-seven. You do not have to say anything. But it may harm your defense if you do not mention when questioned something which you later rely on in court. Anything you do say may be given in evidence."

"You're arresting us under the what now?" Ben asked nobody in particular.

"The Burial Act of eighteen-fifty-seven."

"Is that even…a real thing?"

"Oh, it's real," Tim said sheepishly, interlocking his fingers and placing his hands on his head like a prisoner of war, entirely unprompted. "Under the Burial Act of eighteen-fifty-seven, once a person has been buried, it is unlawful to disturb or remove the body without the correct authority."

"What?" Ben exclaimed. "You knew all along that we'd be breaking the law didn't think to tell me?"

"Well, I knew about the Burial Act," Tim admitted. "Most archaeologists do. Even amateur ones. But I didn't know we'd get caught. It seems we might be in a spot of bother now."

"A spot of bother? Really? Do you think?" Ben was enraged. "Do you think we're in a spot of bother now, Tim? Jesus. I had you down as one of those by-the-book academic types. Turns out you're a fucking liability. Just try not to say anything else until we both speak to a duty solicitor," he said, remembering what little he knew about the law. Most of his knowledge of the British justice system came from watching repeats of the Bill and Inspector Morse.

"And don't forget to charge them with theft as well, Officer!" erupted Glenn Davenport, jabbing a finger at them. "Theft of one of the company vehicles."

"It's Detective, not Officer, thank you very much, Mister Davenport. And if you're referring to the rowboat, it's hardly a luxury yacht, is it? They probably could have bought it for a hundred quid. And it's yet to be determined whether they stole it or not."

"Luxury yacht or bicycle, theft is theft. And how bloody else do you think they got her?" Glenn Davenport said. "Teleportation?"

"If we place them under arrest, it could only be 'suspected' theft at this stage, and the charge we already have them on is sufficient to take them down to the station for questioning. I'm sure everything will come out in the wash."

"Very well," Glenn Davenport grumbled. "You know best. I suppose."

"That's correct," Detective Carter said dismissively. "I most certainly do."

The detective didn't deem it necessary to handcuff either Ben or Tim, saying he didn't want either of them "doing themselves a mischief" by falling over on the uneven ground. Ben thought perhaps the fact they were trapped on a tiny island might also have something to do with it. Even if one of them made a break for it, there was nowhere to escape to. As the uniformed officer gathered up Tim's tools and the small group prepared to leave the clearing, Ben noticed each of them in turn glancing down at the corpse that had been partially exhumed, no doubt wondering what it would lead to.

At Detective Carter's instruction, the uniformed PC led the small, unlikely procession of men back along the same path bisecting the island that they had all come down.

In his eagerness to see justice being done, Glenn Davenport was next in line, stomping angrily through the undergrowth and constantly urging the lead officer to pick up the pace. Ben and Tim followed immediately behind him, with Detective Carter bringing up the rear. The wind was now biting, and Ben was secretly glad he wasn't going to have to row back to shore on the flimsy little boat he and Tim had "borrowed." Every cloud had a silver lining.

The boat the second group had arrived on was indeed bigger than the rowboat. But only marginally, and Ben had serious doubts that the thing would be able to safely accommodate all five of them. It did have an outboard motor, however, the noise of which must have been masked by the elements when they made the initial journey over. As the boat slowly chugged its way to the jetty, Ben gripped the sides with both hands and stared off into the distance.

His mind was in turmoil. Most of all, he felt embarrassed. What had he and Tim been thinking? So much for Christine Turner's instructions to keep things on the down low. He'd be lucky if she even retained his services after this. Heck, after this latest development, he'd count himself fortunate if he didn't end up in jail.

Still, maybe parting ways with the R.R. wouldn't be such a bad thing. The place was not only proving dreadful for his reputation, but also his mental health.

A stolen glance at Tim suggested that he shared Ben's discomfort. He sat with a morose look on his face, no doubt considering the possible implications of the duo's misguided actions. He did, after all, have a responsible job and a wife to think about, which was more than Ben had. At least his bad decisions only affected him and a cat.

It seemed to take an age for the boat to arrive at the jetty. There was little conversation, a solemn atmosphere settling over the craft. Detective Carter did the bulk of the talking, and only then to give the uniformed officer, who looked like he'd just graduated from the police academy, instructions. For the duration of the journey, Glenn Davenport sat with his arms folded glaring at Ben and Tim and doing little to disguise his animosity.

Upon their safe arrival on the bank of the lake, the five men exited the boat and walked down the jetty to the road, where a dark blue Audi and a marked police car waited.

Less than half-an-hour later, Ben and Tim had arrived at the nearby Victorian-style police station and were booked in by a weary-looking custody sergeant. They each signed multiple pieces of paper and were searched, the contents of their pockets catalogued and stowed in clear plastic bags. They were also fingerprinted, photographed, and provided DNA samples. The whole process was demeaning, which Ben supposed was part of the point. He was thankful he didn't still have his baton. He didn't know if it qualified as a weapon—it was hardly a grenade launcher— but he doubted the police would look favorably upon it. Nobody had mentioned it, so he could only assume it had been missed by Detective Carter and his cohorts and was still on the island. No doubt someone would find it eventually, and Ben would be banged to rights should they carry out fingerprint testing. But he would ride his luck until then.

After the formalities were taken care of, Ben and Tim were led off to separate but adjoining cells on the first floor of the police station. As they were led down a corridor and up a flight of stairs, Ben looked over his shoulder at Tim and said, "Don't forget to request a duty solicitor, and don't say anything until you chat with him first."

He'd learned in his career as a magazine journalist that a bit of bravado often went a long way. If the people around you thought you knew what you were doing, even if you didn't, they tended to treat you with slightly more respect. In professional terms, it was known as "blagging it."

Ben hadn't been in a police cell since his late teens, the culmination of a few questionable life decisions, yet nothing much seemed to have changed in the intervening years. The basic premise was that you were locked in a bare, sterile room and left there for a while to think about what you'd done. Of course, the potential consequences were much more severe, but for all intents and purposes, a holding cell was the adult equivalent of a naughty step.

He couldn't help wondering whether Marjorie Brand had been brought to the same station after she'd battered her husband to death. Probably. In fact, depending on how things were done in this backwater town, she might even still be here.

As the heavy metal door slammed shut behind him, Ben slumped onto the hard single bed in the corner of the room, still marveling at his own stupidity, and settled in for a long wait.

As it happened, he didn't have to wait too long before the cell door opened again and an unshaven man in his mid-twenties with spiky black hair and carrying a battered brown briefcase ambled in. "Nick Foster," he said by way of introduction. "Duty solicitor on call."

"I thought it would take you longer to get here. At least until the morning," Ben said, standing to greet his visitor.

"You're in luck. The bigwigs at Norfolk and Suffolk constabularies recently issued new directives. They got tired of people with warrants out for their arrest handing themselves in in the middle of the night when they knew there were no senior officers on site. In the past they mostly worked office hours, and by the time they clocked in the next morning, a smart criminal would have already knocked eight or ten hours off the time they can legally be held before being charged. It meant the police were instantly in a race against time and usually only had half a day to gather evidence, so they implemented what is essentially a shift system to ensure there's a senior cop on site around the clock at most stations. If these senior cops want to formally interview suspects, they need duty solicitors present. So, presto! Here I am."

Ben could tell Nick Foster was thrilled about it.

"I understand you were brought in at two-twenty-three a.m. under the Burial Act of eighteen-fifty-seven."

"Something like that."

"It's an unusual one," the young solicitor said, sitting on the bed beside Ben and leafing through a handful of papers he'd withdrawn from his suitcase. "I can't wait to hear this story. Tell me everything. Not just what was happening at the time of your arrest, but also the events leading up to it. Try not to leave anything out."

And that was exactly what Ben did. He told Nick Foster about his arrival at the Regal Retreat, his research into the sordid history of the place, the meetings with Christine Turner, seeing Ronald and Marjorie Brand, the ride in the Plymouth Fury with Tim, the visit he received from Detective Carter at the van, even the warning note slipped under his door. He finished with how Tim had come to find him at his camper and persuaded him to pay a visit to the island in the lake to see if they could locate the body of Elizabeth Thrower. The only part he left out was his encounter with the ghost of Beth White. He didn't think the duty solicitor needed to hear about that.

As Ben talked, the young duty solicitor scribbled in a notebook and nodded at intermittent intervals to show he was keeping up. Otherwise, there was little reaction. No disbelief, shock, or disgust. Ben came to the conclusion that despite his comparatively tender years and obviously limited experience, Frost must have already heard many worse stories than his.

When Ben had finished, the younger man said without looking up, "Okay. A lot to unpack here. So you don't deny the theft of the boat or digging up the corpse?"

"Is there any point?"

"Not really. Unless you wanted to go to Magistrates court and take your chances. The odds would be against you, but you'd have a chance to plead your case. Do you have a criminal record? Any prior offenses?"

"I've had a couple of bumps along the way," Ben admitted. "Nothing too serious."

"No convictions?"

"Nope."

"In that case, I think you'll be better off taking the plea bargain they'll surely be offering you. You'll probably get off with a stern warning, or maybe a nominal fine. It will go on your record though, so you'll have to keep your nose clean in future."

"What would a plea bargain entail?"

"As it stands, you're essentially being charged with theft and disturbing a body without lawful authority. Neither offense is especially serious, and you and Mister Norgood are both fellows of reasonably good standing. All things considered, I might be able to get the charges reduced to simple trespassing. It's the less serious charge."

"Sounds good."

"Of course, that's assuming the plea bargain is even an option. We'll establish that during your formal interview."

"When might that be?"

"Very shortly, I imagine."

Despite his tender years and slightly disheveled appearance, Nick Foster was very thorough, and efficient. Just a few minutes with him reassured Ben immensely, and he was feeling much better about the situation by the time the cell door opened again and the desk sergeant who'd booked Ben in said, "Mister Shivers? This way, please."

Accompanied by Nick, Ben was led back down the staircase and along a brightly lit corridor deeper into the station. It smelled like disinfectant and was deathly quiet, which he imagined was only to be expected given the very late—or very early—hour.

The men were taken to a room marked **Interview Room 2**. The first thing Ben noticed was the desk behind which sat Detective Carter, closely followed by the bars on the window. On top of the desk was a large tape recorder. As they entered the room, the detective pressed the RECORD button.

"For the tape, this interview will be carried out by myself, Detective Carter, warrant number two-seven-zero-three-seven-four, and Ben Shivers. Also present is duty solicitor Nick Frost."

"Not gone digital yet?" Ben said in an attempt to break the ice.

"We still do things the old-fashioned way 'round here," the detective replied, motioning for Ben and Nick to take a pair of chairs on the opposite side of the desk. "I'd like to crack on with things, if it's all the same to you."

"By all means," Ben agreed. Police stations made him nervous. It was like being a fly trapped in a spider's web. And he had no desire to spend a moment longer than he had to in the company of the unpleasant detective.

"For the tape, you and your accomplice are charged with stealing a boat at the Regal Retreat last night," Detective Carter began after dispensing with formalities. "And using it to gain access to a restricted part of the complex where you then proceeded to desecrate a grave. For this, you were arrested under the Burial Act of eighteen-fifty-seven. Do you accept the charges?"

"No comment," Ben said.

"Is this going to be a 'no comment' interview?" the detective asked, looking crestfallen.

"No comment," Ben said again, purely for his own amusement knowing he was well within his rights to continue in this manner for as long as necessary. Detective Carter made the charges sound serious, but that was his job.

Still, Nick had also made it known that cooperating with the police scored massive brownie points and would benefit him in the long run. Criminals often used the "no comment" approach in an attempt to frustrate and slow down legal proceedings, hoping the police would get bored and move on. The problem was, that never happened. For his part, Ben would be quite happy to carry on "no-commenting" until the detective tired of him and abandoned the interview, but he wanted this to be over as soon as possible. Plus, there was something that bothered Ben. "I have a question," he said.

"Excuse me?" the detective said, looking up from his notes.

"A question."

"The way this works is I ask the questions and you answer. But if this will ease things along, by all means ask."

"How did you know we were there? You and your band of merry men just appeared out of nowhere. Were you having me followed?"

"Nothing so dramatic, I'm afraid," the detective said dismissively. "We don't have the manpower for that. We were alerted by Glenn Davenport, who'd received a call from one of his security guards. They'd seen lights on the island and thought somebody was lamping out there, which, if you didn't know, is the practice of using lights to hunt rabbits and other game. While this isn't illegal in itself, hunting and all use of firearms is strictly prohibited at the Regal Retreat. Their house, their rules. When the security guard went to investigate, he found one of the resort's boats missing and reported it as such."

"Since when have detectives been interested in things like lamping and petty theft?" Ben asked.

"Well, as you already know, I'm the detective in charge of the investigation into the recent murder of Ronald Brand. As a matter of routine, I am made aware of any further incidents possibly pertaining to the case, however insignificant they may appear to untrained eye. You'd be surprised what turns up after a murder."

"No doubt."

"So would you mind telling me how you acquired that wound near your left eye? I didn't notice it last time we met."

Ben's hand immediately felt for the injury. "I walked into a branch tonight."

"Does that happen often, Mister Shivers?"

"Not really," Ben replied, noticing how the detective brazenly studied his hands and knuckles looking for defensive wounds. He was obviously trying to ascertain whether or not Ben had been in an altercation recently.

"By the way," the detective said. "You'll be relieved to know that a murder charge is temporarily off the table. We still have to run some tests, but it would appear that the body we found you with has been there a considerable amount of time."

"No shit, Sherlock. How long did it take you to work that out?" Ben said.

The response drew an angry reaction from Nick Foster, who admonished Ben with a stern "Mister Shivers, please try to be respectful!"

Ben sighed. "Very well. But it doesn't take a degree to see that body has been in the ground a while. Four hundred years or more, if it is who we think it is."

"And just to clarify, who do you think it is?" Detective Carter asked.

"Elizabeth Thrower. If your search throws up no results, try looking for Elizabeth Grange instead. One person, two names, and a lot of stories."

"And who might that be?"

"You really don't know?" Ben found that hard to believe. A detective of Carter's experience must have heard the name before. It was a time-honored police tactic to simply ask as many leading questions as they could and just let suspects trip themselves up.

"Pretend I don't."

"Apparently, she was an old woman tried and executed as a witch, when that was a popular pastime in these parts. It's refreshing to see not that much has changed. I'm sure your investigation will yield more information than I could ever give you."

"Are you saying she was murdered?"

"Executed. I'm not sure of the legal ramifications."

"How did the body end up on that island?"

"Your guess is as good as mine. I'm just a journalist working on a story."

"Ah yes, a journalist," the detective said, with barely any attempt to hide his derision. "Remind me how you came to know where this body was buried?"

"We didn't know where it was buried. Not definitively."

"So your stumbling across it was just a happy accident?"

"Pretty much, though I can't imagine many people being happy about unearthing a long-dead corpse."

"Do you often go around fully kitted-out, randomly digging up plots of land in the middle of the night?"

"Of course not."

"Then I repeat the question, how did you know the body was there?"

"As I said, I'm a journalist. I follow leads and chase stories. Build articles, one brick at a time. When we went to the island, we didn't know we were going to find a body. We suspected. But we weren't sure about anything."

"Erm... If I may interject," Nick said, as he shuffled a handful of printouts. "You say my client is being charged under the Burial Act of eighteen-fifty-seven?"

"That is correct," Detective Carter agreed, his eyes narrowing. Evidently, the only people he disliked more than murderers and journalists were duty solicitors.

"I assume you're referring to Section twenty-five of said act, which makes it unlawful in England and Wales to disturb human burials without a license from the Secretary of State, or on ground consecrated by the rites of the Church of England, without the permission of the church."

"Again, that's correct." Perhaps suspecting trouble, the detective's gaze narrowed even further.

"When was the site declared sacred or holy?"

"Excuse me?"

"The meaning is clear, Detective. Unless you have information to the contrary, that patch of ground has never been consecrated."

"So?"

"So unless I am very much mistaken, that renders the charge null and void."

"What about the license?"

"The license of exhumation?"

"If you say so."

"It can be acquired after the fact, Detective. You should know this. We just have to apply to the Ministry of Justice. I think they open at nine. If we apply online and stress its importance then agree to collect it in person, we should be able to have the license for you by lunch time. Instances like this are relatively common. Construction workers and the like inadvertently unearth long-buried bodies all the time. Consequently, the process has been simplified."

Ben couldn't resist giving the duty solicitor an admiring sideways glance, which was undoubtedly caught by Detective Carter.

"But…we still have to run tests to determine exactly how long the body has been in the ground."

"Detective Carter, if that body is centuries old, as we all suspect, it means the perpetrators of any foul play, if there was any—which will probably never be proved, by the way—will be long dead. You know as well as I do that the grave is a place of historical interest rather than a crime scene. You admitted yourself my client is not under suspicion of murder. It's on the tape."

"That still leaves the theft," Detective Carter said, his face beginning to turn an angry shade of red.

"Of that, you have no standing proof. Did my client admit any wrongdoing?"

"No. But if he didn't nick a boat, how did he get to the island? Swim?"

"That's something we can neither confirm nor deny at this stage. The onus is on you to prove my client's guilt, rather than on him to prove his innocence. That's a cornerstone of the British justice system. Everyone is innocent until proven guilty. Do you have any witness statements or C.C.T.V. footage of him or his alleged accomplice committing the crime? Or any other evidence? Because without any of those things, and in the absence of a confession, it will be the word of the arresting officer against the word of my client. I don't think the Crown Prosecution Service would go for that. It would be the very definition of an unsafe conviction."

"Your client was found on private property. Restricted private property at that…"

"Great. Then charge him with trespassing, give him a caution or a fixed penalty fine and let's call the matter closed. I'm sure you have more important things to do right now, as do we all."

Detective Carter blinked a few times in rapid succession and stared at Nick Foster with his mouth slightly agape, as if silently contemplating the sheer nerve of the young man. Then followed a mercifully brief silence as the detective weighed up his options. Finally, he nodded sagely and fixed Ben with a stony glare. "You can consider this a final warning. One place you don't want to be is on my radar."

Ben wanted to point out that he was already on Detective Carter's radar. Instead, he summoned his best regretful expression, and said, "Understood, Detective. And I'm truly sorry for any inconvenience my actions may have caused."

"Are we free to leave?" Nick Frost said, standing up and breaking the tension.

"You are," the detective replied, a note of frustration ringing in his voice. "Interview concluded at five-fifteen a.m."

Ben and Nick Frost left the interview room and went back to the front desk, where Ben was asked to sign yet more forms and given back his bagged-up possessions.

As day broke outside the station, the two men paused. "Thanks for the advice, and the help," Ben said. "If it hadn't been for you, I might have punched him in the face and be looking at a charge of assaulting a police officer by now."

"Violence is never a solution," Nick said. "If you lose a fight, you probably go to hospital, and if you win, you probably go to jail."

"True. You did well in there."

"You sound surprised."

"More relieved."

"Just doing my job, Mister Shivers," Nick said. "There's just one thing you should know, for future reference."

"What's that?"

"In order to be valid, an exhumation license from the Ministry of Justice has to be signed by the deceased person's next of kin, which might complicate matters if the situation changes and you're required to produce one later, or should you ever find yourself in this situation again. If that woman really has been there a couple hundred years, you'd be hard-pressed to find a next of kin at all, let alone at short notice. Just something to keep in mind."

"Certainly," Ben agreed. "But wait, if it would've been so difficult to get one of those licenses of exhumation things, does that mean you were…bluffing in there?"

The young duty solicitor grinned widely. "Of course not. That wouldn't be morally correct, would it? Let's just say I was making use of every available opportunity. It's my job. If the police around here don't read up on the law as much as I do, then that's their problem."

"Well, thanks again. You know your stuff."

"Thanks for the compliment," Nick Frost said. "Can I give you a lift anywhere? This village is in the back of beyond."

Ben thought about the offer for a moment, then said, "No, thanks. I've put you out enough already. It looks like it's going to be a nice day. I need to clear my head, so I'm going to walk back to the Regal. Not far, is it?"

"A couple of miles," Nick said, reaching into his pocket and producing a business card, which he handed to Ben. "Give me a call should you require my services again. I've crossed swords with Detective Carter before. He can be like a Rottweiler once he gets his teeth into something."

"Will do," Ben replied, turning away and walking into the rising sun. He had another early morning meeting with Christine Turner, and there was a lot to discuss.

Chapter Nineteen

It was over four miles from the police station back to the R.R. and the walk took almost a full two hours. When he arrived, the first thing Ben did was stop by the van to feed Mr. Trimble, who wasn't best pleased at being left alone all night, and pick up some fresh clothes. Fresh in the sense they hadn't been worn for a while. The ones he'd worn the night before were caked with mud and dirt, and another load was still in his room in the main block awaiting his attention. He was rapidly running out of things to wear.

Room 327 was his next stop, where he grabbed a quick shower. There were no more warning notes. But despite it being the cold light of day and the bizarre events of the night before already retreating into his memory, he couldn't help feeling uneasy.

The moment he was dressed and his hair semi-dry, he headed off to his latest scheduled meeting with Christine. He was so eager to find out what information she had about Beth White that he was actually early.

It may have been his imagination, but even on the short walk to the resort manager's office, he detected a kind of understated dread hanging in the air. There were only a few people on the road, and the ones Ben made eye contact with seemed to regard him with veiled suspicion and dis-taste, almost as if they all knew what had happened that morning and the night before.

That was ridiculous, he scolded himself. How could anyone know?

Besides, in his mind, he hadn't done much wrong. Of course, it depended how you presented it. He and Tim were either responsible for at least partially solving one of the area's greatest mysteries, or they were just pair of thieving, trespassing grave robbers. There are three sides to every story. Your side, their side, and the truth, which was usually somewhere in the middle. More than likely, people were just a bit unnerved because of the recent murder. That was enough to put anyone on edge.

An even more likely explanation was that it was all in Ben's imagination. The somber atmosphere and general uneasiness, combined with pre-existing paranoia and elevated stress levels, nearly paralyzed him with anxiety and trepidation. By the time he finally knocked on Christine's door, he was shaking with nerves.

"Come in!"

"Good morning," Ben said, striding into the office as confidently as he could. Over the years, he had become adept at masking his insecurities.

"Ah. Morning, Ben," Christine said, lifting a coffee mug emblazoned with the words **STRONG INDEPENDENT WOMAN** to her lips. Nothing could be more fitting. "Take a seat. I hear you had an eventful night."

"How did you know about that?" Ben asked, sinking into the offered chair.

"I had a very, very early morning phone call from the charming Detective Carter," Christine began. "He said you and one of our guests, a Tim Norgood, were arrested and taken into custody on suspicion of theft and desecrating a grave or something along those lines."

"It wasn't as bad as all that," Ben said, feeling his cheeks redden with embarrassment.

"Well, I'm happy to hear it. What was the upshot of it all. Will you be continuing your work from prison?"

"Admittedly, we did get caught red-handed doing something we probably shouldn't have been doing," Ben said. "But they were trumped-up charges, largely due to the owner here pushing for them. I'm pretty sure he would've had us both hung, drawn, and quartered if he'd had the power to do so."

"Are you talking about Glenn? Glenn Davenport?" Something resembling distaste passed over Christine's face as, for the briefest moment, her normally professional guard slipped.

"The very same. Why? Is there a problem?"

"No. Not unless you call pissing off one of the most powerful men in the country a problem. He's on site for a few days. Chose the right time, too, with the murder and now this debacle to keep him busy. I'm sure he was very pleased about it. If this continues, he'll probably run off back to London before the day is out. He can be quite…"

"A dick?"

"Well, I wouldn't use exactly that turn of phrase."

"You can't. You'd probably get fired."

"Probably."

"So what kind of man is he?"

"Not the kind of man you want to be on the wrong side of. I don't really have many dealings with him. My job is here, while he has dozens of other business interests. But I know he can be ruthless."

"Roger that," Ben said, heeding the warning. "Anyway, what did you want to see me about? You said you have some information about Beth White?"

"Mister Shivers. In light of recent events, I'm not sure it's such a good idea to be discussing that. I may have been getting ahead of myself. In fact, I've been reassessing the terms of your employment here at the R.R. and it might be better for all concerned if we part ways. Is there anything you can say that would convince me otherwise?"

This didn't exactly come as a shock to Ben. "Christine. Don't make me beg for my life here. I understand you have to do what you think is best for the resort. But in only two days I've made real progress here. The visit to the island last night was the culmination of my research so far, and a real watershed moment. Things are just beginning to slot into place. I've come too far to just walk away."

"Indeed. I have to do what I think is best for the resort, as well as what I think is right on a personal level. And that's exactly what I intend to do."

Christine paused, chewing her bottom lip as she turned things over in her mind. Finally, she said, "Listen, I might regret it, but I've decided not to terminate your employment. This has gone on long enough, and it's high time the situation was resolved one way or the other. To that end, we need to be both frank and totally honest with each other. What exactly happened last night? I know you found a burial site. What's the significance of it?"

"Are you sure you want to hear this?" Ben asked. "It's not too late to just knock it on the head and leave it in the hands of the police. I can walk out of here and you'll never see me again. I won't even cash the check, should you decide to send one."

"I'm sure," Christine said. "The police are good at reacting and solving crimes after the fact. Usually. I mean, they do their best. But that isn't enough for us anymore. We need to be proactive and get to the heart of the matter, find out *why* these terrible things keep happening, and how we can stop them. If this find of yours is connected to something that might help us achieve that goal, then I want to know about it."

"Fair enough. Tim Norgood, the man I was with last night, is a local historian. Between us, we developed a theory that most of the deaths here can be traced back to a woman called Elizabeth Thrower, who was drowned in the lake during the seventeenth-century witch trials."

"The Gray Lady?"

"Precisely. I couldn't find too many substantiated reports of any sightings, and certainly no documented evidence of this Gray lady stuff. But it stands to reason that the sightings might be tied into everything some-how. Perhaps they are an omen, or a way of making her presence felt."

"And you think this burial site you found on the island belongs to her."

"Still to be made official, but we're almost sure of it. We found a body where Tim said there'd be one, and it all fits in neatly with the legend, which says that after surviving being tortured and thrown in the lake, Elizabeth made it to the island. There, she laid some kind of curse before finally dying of her injuries and being buried on the spot by some fishermen."

"God," Christine said, her top lip curling slightly as if she'd just eaten something sour.

"Wait. You haven't heard this story before?"

"Of course, I have. But I didn't know it was bloody real."

"What did the police tell you?"

"Not much more than you, really. In fact, a lot less. Detective Carter says an investigation is underway but wouldn't go into too much detail. Given the length of time the body has been there, I doubt there'll be any sense of urgency. I suppose it all means that instead of having dozens of police roaming about the place, we'll have dozens of archaeologists and the like instead. Never a dull moment at the R.R."

"You should try to capitalize on it."

"How?"

"After, or maybe even while the site is being excavated, there's certain to be fresh media interest. It'll be a huge story. Not quite on a par with King Richard the third turning up under a car park in Leicester, but not far off. The news crews will spread the word, then the documentary makers will take over. You'll be able to name your price. Plus, you might be able to turn the island itself into a memorial and charge people money to visit it. Pick people up in a boat a few times a day, ferry them around the lake, throw in a visit to the grave site and the services of a tour guide, and you'd make a killing. Pun not intended."

"It might be something worth thinking about."

"Now, if you wouldn't mind telling me, what am I doing here this morning?"

Christine paused, as if considering her response. Then she opened a drawer in her desk, reached in, and brought out a plastic zip-lock bag. Inside the bag was what appeared to be an old, faded, off-white piece of paper. Ben watched as she opened the sealed bag, took out the piece of paper, and put it on the desk.

"What's that?"

"You wanted to know what happened to Beth White? There it is. Have a read. But be careful with it. I think that's what the police call 'evidence.'"

Ben picked up the piece of paper and gently unfolded it. It turned out to be two sheets, both seemingly torn from the same notepad and both sides of each sheet covered in an elegant, left-leaning scrawl written in black ink. The handwriting made the gears in his mind suddenly shift as another part of the puzzle fell into place. But he couldn't think about that.

Not now.

Instead, he started reading.

To Whom it may Concern,

I am Michael Davenport, owner of Davenport Enterprises Ltd, and this is my confession. I thought I could escape the consequences of my actions, but after years of living this lie, I've decided I cannot do it any longer. I feel drawn to this place. The Retreat. Everywhere I go, I feel something calling me back. And when here, I have to suffer the dreams. The awful dreams, making me re-live that night over and over again. Sweet Beth. Lovely Beth. I never wanted to hurt her. I wanted to make her a princess. But life was complicated. Isn't it always?

I was already on my third marriage so there was no chance for us. I tried to persuade her, and I do believe we had a chance in the beginning, but I don't think for a moment she ever loved me. She was just flattered that someone like me had taken an interest in her. But I digress. As I said, this is my confession.

Beth White agreed to meet me near the lake, after I arrived back at the resort after a business meeting in Ipswich. It was cold and wet. I should have stayed at a hotel as usual. But I wanted to come back here for her. I wanted to see her, and make my feelings clear once and for all. I wanted to tell her I was willing to sacrifice everything, if she would only agree to be mine. At that point, nothing else mattered.

She didn't believe me. And why would she? I was a cad, a philanderer, a man more than fifty years her senior. What could we possibly have in common? Despite the march of time, I never had any problem attracting women before, though I always knew it was my money they really loved, not me. To many, I was little more than a doorway, an entry point to a better life. I grew to accept it.

Beth was different. She didn't care how rich I was. She said she sought real love, not some awful, twisted mockery. She couldn't be swayed. I had to have her. I was used to getting what I wanted. But there was no way I could ever get her. First, I pleaded. Then I offered her money to spend the night with me. A few thousand pounds. It was stupid, I know. But I thought if I could only buy some of her time, she would relent and see how happy I could make her. She rejected my offer, and more than that, she told me off. Called me a creep and said she would report me to human resources, at my own company no less, if I didn't leave her alone.

That's when I snapped.

That prim little bitch telling me what to do? When I was the one paying her wages? Not in my world. Not in the empire I created.

There was an engraved silver letter opener in my pocket, a gift I received at the function. Without thinking, I pulled it out. I don't even know why. I just wanted her to listen to me. She saw it and ran. I had to give chase, and when I caught up with her, I lashed out to make her stop screaming. But she just screamed louder, so I stabbed her again. And again. It was like something took over my body, some malevolent force, and I couldn't stop. I was in a frenzy.

When Beth was dead, I could finally get what I wanted from her, and I took it. Right there next to the lake. I know how immoral and unnatural that act was. It was wrong on every level. And believe me when I say that moment of madness has haunted me every day since. I felt caught up in a maelstrom. One deed led to another, each one taking me further down the dark path to hell.

I can't take it anymore. The guilt, the shame. The constant fear of my past catching up with me. For years I was able to lose myself in work and my business interests blossomed as a result. More money came, but what use is it? No amount of money can bring me what I want. It can't bring Beth back, and it can't make her love me. Now my health is failing I am afraid quite soon I will be completely alone with my thoughts. My guilt. My horror. That would drive me insane.

While I am still capable, I have decided to end my life on my own terms. It is mine to do with what I wish, isn't it? I know nothing I can do will ever bring Beth back, but I hope my last act on this earth, and this confession, will help atone for my sins.

M. Davenport

After reading the letter, Ben took a few moments to let the magnitude of it all to sink in, before saying, "So Michael Davenport, owner of the R.R. and father of our mate Glenn, murdered Beth White, then committed suicide?"

"It would certainly seem that way," Christine replied.

"How do you know this letter is genuine?"

"I don't. Not one hundred percent. But I'm sure the right experts would be able to date the paper and analyze the writing to remove as much doubt as possible should we choose to go that route."

"How did you come across it?"

"I found it in the office safe not long after I started working here, hidden in a folder with some old invoices."

"Hidden? By who?"

"My guess would be the man you met last night, Glenn," Christine said. There was an air of certainty in her tone, as if she'd spent a long time thinking about it before arriving at that conclusion. "He would be the one who stood to gain the most by covering up the truth of his father's death. If word got out the owner of the Regal Retreat was a murderous rapist, there's no telling what it would do to the resort's reputation. It would be left to him to deal with the fallout, as well as potentially pay a hefty amount of compensation to the murdered girl's family. The whole thing would be both costly and messy."

"Much easier to just brush it all under the carpet," Ben said.

"Indeed," Christine continued. "My guess is that when the body was found, the letter would have been found along with it. Glenn Davenport would naturally have been one of the first on the scene. Probably before even the police and emergency services arrived. He spent a lot of time here in his younger days, virtually living in one of the villas. He could easily have taken possession of the letter and hidden it."

"But why keep it at all? Why not just destroy it?" Ben asked, frowning. As convenient as the scenario may be, he wasn't quite buying it. Not yet.

"Who knows. Sentimentality? Maybe he just couldn't bring himself to do it. Apparently, Glenn Davenport had a rather tumultuous relation-ship with his father. Maybe this letter served as a final link to his past. An-other possibility could be that it wasn't Glenn who took the letter at all, but an employee who planned to stash the letter until they were in a position to blackmail the Davenports."

"If it had been an employee on the make, you can be damn sure they wouldn't keep the evidence in the office safe."

"Why not? It would be the last place anyone would think to look."

"Possibly," Ben said. "I have another question. Didn't anyone think to do an autopsy on Davenport to determine the cause of death?"

"Why would they?" Christine said, "There's nothing unusual about a man in his eighties having a heart attack. And there's something else. When housekeeping found his body, they found two other items. The first was a box of ibuprofen."

"Maybe he had a headache."

"The box was empty, Mister Shivers," Christine said.

"So maybe he had a headache and found a box of ibuprofen with only two pills left in it."

"That would be convenient, wouldn't it? We'll never know. But I've done some research on this. Ibuprofen is an over-the-counter NSAID."

"A what now?"

"An NSAID, a non-steroidal anti-inflammatory drug. These are used mainly for pain relief, but they also make your body retain water and salt. This disrupts blood flow, hugely increasing your chances of a heart attack. Plus, if you take a bunch at once, the shock to the system, especially an ageing system, could be enough to induce a heart attack all on its own."

"So Michael Davenport decides to top himself by swallowing an entire box of ibuprofen, knowing that if he didn't die from a chemically-induced heart attack, the pills would poison him?"

"Precisely."

"Why not just hang himself?"

"Who knows? Why does anyone take an overdose? Probably because it's a lot less traumatic than hanging."

"What was the second item you mentioned?"

Christine reached into the drawer again and put something on the desk between them. The object was so unusual, and unexpected, that for a moment Ben's brain couldn't process what it was. It looked like a miniature curved sword, four to six inches long, in a fancy decorative scabbard.

"What's that?" Ben asked, frowning. Then he suddenly felt as if he'd been punched in the stomach. It was a silver letter opener. "The letter opener used to kill Beth White?"

Christine nodded solemnly.

Chapter Twenty

As Ben walked out of Christine's office, he didn't feel quite so over-joyed at finally unmasking Beth White's killer as he probably should have. Instead, he felt only frustration and an overwhelming sense of helplessness, almost as if he'd been cheated. Michael Davenport would never be brought to account, and never be punished for his crimes. Where was the justice in that? Even if his transgressions were exposed in all their horrific detail, it wouldn't change anything and it wouldn't bring Beth back. The only good it could possibly do would be to give her family some closure. The question that had undoubtedly dominated the past thirty-odd years of their lives would at last be answered. And presumably, after that would come the same crushing disappointment and sense of disillusionment Ben was experiencing now.

Plus, even with Michael Davenport's written confession, it wouldn't be easy for anyone to actually prove anything this long after the event. It was a legal minefield, and any good lawyer, the caliber of which the Davenport estate now headed by Glenn would be more than able to afford, could make things extremely difficult. Letters can be faked. Even if it was genuine, it could be argued whether or not Michael Davenport was of sound mind when he wrote it. He was an old man, and his mental state was deteriorating by then. The whole thing could just have been some whacked-out fantasy.

Having not only been up all night, but coerced into strenuous physical exercise for half of it and being subjected to intense levels of scrutiny for the other half, Ben was exhausted. He'd already decided to grab a few hours' sleep in the VW rather than his room, and was sure he'd be far more comfortable in familiar surroundings. There was just one more chore to take care of first.

As Ben approached the lakeside villa, he was glad to find the red Plymouth Fury still parked outside. So at least Tim and Sheila hadn't been frightened away. He felt he needed a debrief with Tim, if only to compare notes about what had happened to them both at the police station. Taking a deep breath, he knocked on the door.

It opened almost instantly, and a bedraggled Tim Norgood stared back at him. "Wow. Ben," he said. "I didn't expect to see you again so soon. If at all."

"Surprise," Ben said, busting out the jazz hands. "Yeah, it was touch and go there for a while. I almost got myself thrown in jail for being rude to the Detective, then I almost lost my gig here."

"'Almost' being the operative word, I assume?"

"Exactly. It all worked out in the end," Ben said with a wink. "Listen, I just wanted to touch base with you before I grab some sleep. Is this a good time? It won't take long."

"Sure. Come in. We have the place to ourselves. Sheila has just gone to the shops to pick up some milk. We love making our own lattes. Can't do that without milk."

So the elusive Sheila was nowhere to be seen. How convenient. A dark thought crossed Ben's mind once again, and once again he swatted it away.

The interior of the villa was just as impressive as the outside. A bay window facing the lake took up most of the far wall, and the open-plan ground floor featured a breakfast bar and two large cream-colored sofas positioned around an expensive-looking coffee table.

Tim sat and motioned for Ben to do the same.

"I don't know how good your duty solicitor was," Ben said, inwardly marveling at how luxurious the sofa felt. "But mine was hot shit.

He got the charges downgraded to what amounted to going on the island without permission. I might get a fine, but there's a chance I might escape even that."

"Same here," Tim said, running his fingers through his thinning blond hair. "I knew that the Burial Act was a complicated piece of legislation, so I was quietly confident we'd be able to crawl out through some kind of loophole. I just wasn't familiar enough with it to be able to speak with authority on the spot like that. Thank God for capable duty solicitors."

"Indeed. Listen, there's something I didn't tell you about before," Ben said. "I didn't think it was relevant. We had enough to be going on with. I'm still not sure it's relevant, but it might be, and if nothing else, I'd like to get it off my chest."

"Listening," Tim replied.

Ben then told his friend about his meeting with Beth White on his first day at the Regal, and the subsequent realization that she was not of this world. He thought Tim might dismiss his story as a case of mistaken identity—or just plain bullshit. Instead, he waited until Ben's account was over, nodding in all the right places, then said, "This doesn't surprise me. The Regal has quite the reputation in some circles, as I'm sure you know, given your line of work. The thing is, the paranormal stuff is usually overshadowed by the real-life tragedy that goes on here. It's easy to see why some people might think one is a byproduct of the other. Supernatural encounters, ghost sightings and the like, are often synonymous with locations that have suffered some kind of large-scale catastrophe. Or a series of little ones. I can't help thinking there must be a link."

"And I can't help agreeing with you," Ben said. "Pretty soon, that whole island is going to be dug up, scrutinized, and analyzed. We'll lose any chance we might have of ending this forever."

"So what do you suggest?"

"I don't know. I was hoping that between us, we could thrash out a solution."

"Actually, this morning I looked a few things up," said Tim.

"Find anything?"

"Nothing concrete. But I have a few ideas. We've established that these dreams people have, including us, seem to be the root of everything. So the question is, are they connected in some way to either the Regal Retreat or Elizabeth Thrower?"

"I think 'established' would be a leap," Ben said. "But that's our current working theory, and it will do until one of us can think of a better one."

"Let's suppose Elizabeth did manage to invoke a spirit or curse or something out of revenge. The 'how' and 'why' isn't important at this point. But maybe there's some way to fix it. Neutralize it and make this place safe for future generations of rich people."

"How?"

"It would mean…"

"It would mean what?"

Tim remained silent, obviously waiting for Ben to put the pieces together himself.

"Oh, no. You're not thinking… You can't be thinking… You don't want to go back there, do you?"

"I don't see what choice we have," Tim said with an air of resignation. "Admittedly, I'm kinda making this up as we go along but I really feel those remains are key."

"That's not especially helpful, Tim. Fucking hell. Didn't the police seize your tools as evidence?"

"Some. But there's plenty more where they came from," Tim said with a shrug. "First, we have to try to figure out what we're dealing with. It'd help greatly if we could at least ascertain what deity Elizabeth worshiped. It's a reasonably safe bet she was pagan, but during and after the Middle Ages, the term 'paganism' was hijacked and applied to any unfamiliar religion. All those weird little cults and offshoots, not to mention the existing equivalent religion, were shoehorned into one big category and the whole thing demonized. It was the equivalent of banning all music except the Backstreet Boys."

"The Backstreet Boys? Really? That's the best example you can come up with?"

"On such short notice, yes," Tim said, looking deflated. "Are they not cool anymore?"

"Hardly," Ben said. "Were they ever?"

"That's hurtful, Ben. Anyway, you get the point, don't you?"

"Christianity, good. Anything else, bad."

"Precisely. In church circles, 'paganism' pretty much came to stand for a belief in false gods, as deemed by the Christian faction who were determined to stamp out anything that didn't fit into the little box they created."

"Anything that wasn't the Backstreet Boys."

"Yep. Most of these ancient religions had certain similarities, though. If you look at the clues they left in different parts of the world, there are a lot of commonalities. On a religious level, many of these ancient civilizations perpetuated what essentially boils down to pantheism and polytheism."

"Eh? Were they some nineties pop duo I missed? Like Robson and Jerome?"

Ignoring the quip, Tim plowed on, "Pantheism is the belief that reality and divinity are one and the same. In other words, that all things are connected and all-encompassing. Therefore, they didn't install any one deity as some all-powerful divine presence, instead following a wide-ranging set of doctrines, although the Irish did have Dagda, who was considered the Chief of Gods. This is where polytheism, the worship of multiple deities simultaneously, comes in. They were usually assembled into a pantheon of gods and goddesses, each having their own religions and rituals."

"I don't see how any of this is helping," Ben said.

"Stay with me."

"I'm trying, but how can we even begin to find out which god or goddess Elizabeth followed?"

"Making an educated guess, I assume what Elizabeth adhered to was something akin to what we now call Celtic mythology. Within the sphere of Celtic mythology, there were, or are, literally hundreds of deities. There were different embodiments in each Celtic outpost, or perhaps they were the same thing known under different names. Who knows? When Christianity arrived on the scene, a few of these deities were inducted into the church as Saints, but most were eradicated. Some were even demonized."

"Please get to the point," Ben said with a roll of the eyes. "This is like being in R.E. class."

"Okay, okay. Now this pantheon of deities in Celtic mythology was basically split into two categories: general deities and local deities. General deities were widely known, while local deities were more regionalized and specific to one area or feature of the landscape in any given location. For example, a mountainous area might have a general god or goddess of the mountains, and then each mountain might have its own specific god or goddess known only to locals. Now, are you thinking what I'm thinking?"

"The lake?"

"Yes. What if the lake is the thing binding all this together?"

"That lake should definitely come with a health warning," Ben conceded. "But technically, Elizabeth Thrower died on the island…"

"The island *in* the lake," Tim corrected.

"I've been thinking for a long time that the lake must be central to everything," Ben said. "It's the only constant. People come and go, buildings are built and demolished, but the lake was here long before the Retreat, and long before Elizabeth. That body of water, and whatever it contains, has probably been here for millennia. What if all these places, like large bodies or water and mountains, have some kind of unique power? Our ancestors knew it, but it was easier for them to interpret it a different way."

"Hence all the gods and goddesses?"

"Yes! They needed a frame of reference. If you give a cellphone to a Neanderthal who has only ever seen rocks before, he'll just see a shiny rock because he has no concept of technology. It's alien to him. Now think one step further and imagine that Elizabeth Thrower found some way to harness this power or energy of the lake."

"But all this Celtic mythology mumbo jumbo, it's just superstition without any scientific basis, isn't it? Same as conventional religion?" Ben said.

"I'm in no position to definitively answer that question, Ben. Nobody is. I am aware of the scientific argument, but my personal opinion is that though religion has morphed and changed over time, there has to be some fundamental truth in it. How can so many people be wrong? You could also make the case that if someone believes in something enough, it *becomes* true. At least to them. How that would affect the wider world is, of course, open to debate. But let's not lose sight of the objective.

"What I really mean to raise is the possibility that perhaps somehow all those years ago, in all her pain and fury, Elizabeth tapped into something primal. Either something present here in the lake, or some latent ability buried deep within herself. In the case of the latter, perhaps she channeled her abilities through what she believed was an outside entity as a coping mechanism. Another possibility is that some kind of perfect storm occurred, and a combination of factors were responsible for what we're now dealing with. Whatever happened can't just be the result of an individual's ability, even considering otherworldly or psychic abilities, for the simple reason that long after she drew her last breath, the curse was still active. If it were attached only to her, then it would have died when she did. Would it not?"

"Seems reasonable."

Ben could tell by Tim's demeanor that even if he was reluctant to openly admit there was some supernatural entity attached to the lake, that was what he believed. Being so used to rational analysis dressed up as academic study, it must be difficult for a man of his background and standing to own up to something like that, which only gave the theory more credence.

In Ben's mind, it confirmed the suspicion he'd held all along that everything centered around the lake. He didn't think there was an actual monster living in it like in the movie that had been filmed there, though that wouldn't come as a complete shock. Rather, he'd come to believe that the monster represented something less tangible in the public consciousness in much the same way as fear of outside influences like communism or nuclear war were played out in all those 1950s B-movies.

In this case, perhaps the monster was a manifestation of the perceived threat to Christianity, something forever synonymous with the lake and the fate of Elizabeth Thrower. He wondered if the makers of *From the Depths* had been aware of the legend, and that was why they made the movie here, of all places. "So, what's the plan?" he said. "Will giving Elizabeth a pagan burial put a stop to it?"

"I thought of that," said Tim. "The problem is because the term 'pagan' encompasses so many disparate beliefs and religious practices, we'd be hard pressed to find the specific ones Elizabeth adhered to. We would only be able to take the scattergun approach and hope we hit the target. And there could be consequences to doing that."

"What kind of consequences?"

"Best-case scenario would be choosing the wrong burial ritual and it having no effect whatsoever. That would just be a lot of effort for nothing. Worst-case scenario would be that it could anger her, or the lake spirit, or whatever is causing this, even more. While I was researching all this, however, one thing did occur to me."

"Which was?"

"The crucifix the fishermen laid her to rest with. Being buried for all eternity with a permanent reminder of an enforced religion that had eventually been the death of you must have been like having a pebble in your shoe. That could be why she never found rest."

"So you think we need to find the crucifix? And then what?"

"And then we destroy it with fire? Believe me, such an act of willful vandalism on a potentially significant historical artefact, assuming there is anything left of it to find, would be against my sensibilities. I would like nothing better than to keep it, or maybe donate it to a museum where it can be properly studied. But I really feel this could be our best shot at ending this. Unless you can think of something else?"

"I'm out of ideas," Ben replied. "And we're already criminals, so it's not like we have anything to lose by putting your theory to the test."

"We can't do much until darkness falls," said Tim. "Come back at midnight. Until then, I'm going to spend the day resting and looking around for anything else that may help us. I'd advise you to do the same. We might need the energy."

Chapter Twenty-One

Ben's entire body was screaming out for rest, but he couldn't sleep yet. He knew he should try to grab a few hours before he met up with Tim again, but he needed to decompress a little first.

He wasn't especially hungry, but as Ground Zero was so close and he was still entitled to free meals courtesy of Christine and her vouchers, he thought it would be a pity to waste the opportunity. Stepping inside the place filled him with dread, as well as a strange sense of anticipation. This was his first visit since he'd discovered what Beth White really was. He was mildly terrified, but at the same time excited to see whether the ghost would be there to greet him again. He didn't know how he would handle such an eventuality, but he wanted to at least try to explain that he hadn't forgotten about her, and that the Davenports would soon get what was coming to them.

The ghost of Beth White wasn't there. Which, despite his initial apprehension, was a touch disappointing. There was no proof the encounter had even happened, outside his own questionable memory and a hole punched in a meal voucher. But as attractive as that idea was, he knew it wasn't true. The encounter with Beth had been as real as his encounters with Christine, Tim, Detective Carter, or any of the other people he'd met during his short stay at the Regal.

The restaurant was mostly deserted, and he didn't see anyone he recognized, which suited him fine, as he was still wrestling with pangs of paranoia. Nevertheless, his gaze fell on a middle-aged Asian couple seated at a table he had to pass to get to an empty one in the corner. They were looking at him furtively and appeared to be hiding their mouths with their hands while they talked. Ben concluded that he'd probably caught their attention purely on the basis of being a lone, unshaven, haggard-looking guy eating breakfast alone at an upper-class establishment. Either that or they were captivated by his dashing good looks.

After a quick, simple meal of scrambled eggs, sausage (half of one wrapped in a napkin and stuffed in a pocket for Mr. Trimble), and coffee, Ben made his way back to his van. It was an overcast day, the sun's rays only intermittently penetrating the dense cloud cover, and a gentle breeze ruffled his hair. As he walked, he was almost in a daze. His legs and shoulders ached, and his mind felt foggy and labored. Everything was far more work than it should have been.

Opening the side door, he climbed into the VW's living area, his entrance greeted with a dramatic show of affection from his cat, whose sixth sense must have told him there could be a treat in it for him if he played it cool.

Ben turned on his radio and fired up his laptop. As the sounds of Belinda Carlisle and Roxy Music swept through the van and Mr. Trimble curled up into a hairy ball next to him, he checked his email, social media notifications, and news reports like he did every morning. A few things required his attention: there were several new comments on his blog he needed to check out before approving and a couple of leads to new assignments, but nothing that couldn't wait until he was in a better frame of mind.

Then he had an idea. The bulk of the research may have been finished and a plan of action conceived, but there was still an important piece of unfinished business to attend to before he left the Regal. He turned off the radio, typed four words into a search engine, hit PLAY on the video that came up, and then sat back on the bench as the opening scenes of *From the Depths* began playing. Watching old horror movies was one of Ben's guilty pleasures.

Despite being filmed over half a century ago, the landscape was unmistakably that of the R.R. The film was set in the 19th century, so in the days before CGI clever camera work avoided any of the buildings being in shot, but the nearby hill was clearly visible, and there was the lake, every bit as mysterious and beguiling as it was in real life. With the dramatic soundtrack and overwrought dialogue reverberating gently through the van, he closed his eyes and drifted off to sleep.

This time, Ben knew he was dreaming. It didn't make the experience any less terrifying.

He was being chased along the bank of the lake, his feet padding on the concrete path, his own labored breathing and feverish gasps the only other sounds he could hear. He could feel the horror flowing through him in waves and developed something akin to tunnel vision as the panic threatened to consume him.

This couldn't be happening.

Shouldn't be happening.

But it was.

He had to get away.

Find somewhere safe.

He sensed his would-be attacker gaining ground but didn't dare turn around to see how much.

Underlying the panic and sense of impending danger was anger. Not at the person chasing him, but at himself. His own stupidity. On some level, he'd known his attacker's intentions for a long time, yet he ignored his instincts. What did he think was going to happen?

It was his own fault, and that's what hurt most.

This powerful man…this monster…was used to getting what he wanted and had made it clear in no uncertain terms that he could make life very difficult for people if he didn't get his own way.

As Ben ran, an understanding settled over him.

He wasn't Ben anymore.

He was Beth.

Beth White.

A crushing sense of hopelessness enveloped him. This was futile. There could be no escape. He already knew his fate. And even if he did manage to evade his pursuer tonight, there would be a next time. He would never let it go. He had too much to lose. He would be back. Maybe tomorrow, maybe the next day, or the day after.

The awful realization made Ben's steps waver. He lost his balance, and the next thing he knew he was flying through the night air with his arms outstretched to break his fall.

He landed with a thud, skinning his hands and knees as he rolled on the concrete. Disoriented, he saw a dwelling in front of him. One of the villas next to the lake.

The upstairs lights were on.

Taking a deep breath, he opened his mouth to scream.

He had to draw somebody's attention. Get help.

But before he could give voice to the terror engulfing him, the pain came; an awful, crippling, devastating pain, emanating from a point somewhere between his shoulder blades and radiating through his body in waves with such intensity that it simultaneously caused his eyes to widen and his mouth to drop open.

With the pain came the cold. A terrible, pervasive chill. It was cold *inside,* as if the night itself had reached out its icy fingers, penetrated his body, and was now probing around inside him.

He'd been stabbed.

As the awful realization began to settle, the pain came again. The same icy sensation, this time coming from a different point in his back.

Again and again, each strike bringing fresh waves of agony.

He was being stabbed to death.

The whole world now was pain. He was drowning in it. He could feel the blood draining out of his body and knew he was dying. But his fevered mind couldn't process the information. It was too bizarre, too far removed from how things should be. A tiny shred of his being still clung stubbornly to the notion that this couldn't really be happening.

Then, something struck the base of his skull from behind, jarring his vision and making his eyes roll back in his head.

There was a hand on his shoulder. A big, strong, masculine hand. It effortlessly flipped him over. For a few moments the world was askew. Ben had time to gaze up, admire the spectacular array of stars and planets overhead and wonder if they would be the last thing he would ever see. It all seemed so…. Fitting. Preordained, even.

A hulking silhouette suddenly blocked out the view. Ben couldn't make out any features; they were hidden somehow, but the sheer size of the shadowy figure was overwhelming.

His, or Beth's, attention was captured by the object the huge, dark figure held high in the air with one hand. There was a silvery glint as the effervescent starlight reflected off something metallic.

A knife?

It was curved, like a little sword.

A single drop of dark liquid ran down the length of the blade and fell to the ground.

Blood.

NO!

He tried to summon his fading energy for one last fight, but it was too late. All too late.

The blade came crashing down, making a *whoosh* sound as it cut through the night air.

When it landed, it felt like a punch to the chest. Ben inhaled sharply, his lips pulled back over teeth, and then everything went black…

He awoke with a start so pronounced it woke Mr. Trimble who had been sprawled on his lap. The cat yawned in his face, gave him a dirty look, then promptly put his head down and went back to sleep. Ben lay still for a few moments, waiting for the panic-inducing effects of the dream to wear off and for reality to fully rouse him.

That's what you get for dropping off to sleep watching cheesy horror movies.

He should be used to the weird dreams by now. Except this hadn't just been a dream. It was more than that.

Was it the latest manifestation of whatever dark presence had taken hold of this place?

Or another cryptic message from the spirit of Beth White?

If that were the case, he was missing the point. The culprit had already been identified. And furthermore, was already dead. What more could there be?

Ben frowned and sat up on the bench, the action drawing yet more angry glares from Mr. Trimble, who was obviously getting tired of his human's shit. His laptop had powered off, so he checked the time on the wind-up clock he kept on the shelf beneath the window. It was 7:50 p.m. He'd been asleep for hours. It was already getting dark outside.

It was still too early to meet Tim, but he felt restless and claustrophobic and wanted to stretch his legs. Plus, there was something he wanted to check out.

Before leaving the sanctity of the van, he did a quick inventory; all he really needed were his phone and the Maglite flashlights. The battery level in his phone was at 77%, which should be more than enough.

Stuffing the device in the front pocket of his jeans, he quickly replaced the batteries in both Maglites and checked they were working before grabbing his jacket and exiting through the side door. He locked it behind him, and headed out into the evening, again cursing his luck that he'd managed to land a gig at one of the few "dry" resorts in the country. At that moment, he wanted a drink more than anything.

With time to kill before his appointment with Tim and a lot of nervous energy to expend, Ben decided to go for a walk. He had no destination in mind. This was something he often did when time and circumstances allowed. He found just wandering around any given area liberating, and it counted toward his daily exercise. It was all the better if he managed to get himself lost, because there was no better way to find yourself than getting lost.

Inevitably, he found himself drawn to the lake and the narrow concrete path running around it. The water looked calm and tranquil, an eerie mist clinging to the surface. He could just make out the outline of the island. In the fading light, it looked no more substantial than a collection of crawling shadows. He shuddered as images of the horribly mutated, bloodthirsty creature of *From the Depths* emerging from the water to stalk its unsuspecting victims resurfaced in his mind.

As he walked, Ben tried to detach himself and look at things objectively. Even so, he was pulled irresistibly toward the villas lining the shore. The place where Beth White had been murdered. The place, he now realized, that had featured so prominently in his latest nightmare.

As he made his way along the very same path down which he had ran for his life, he was buffeted by a stiff breeze studded with tiny droplets of water and was forced to wipe moisture from his face with his sleeve. Despite the typically British weather, he was surprised by how few people he saw. He didn't expect the place to be alive with holidaymakers, but to find it completely deserted was another shock. It was almost as if their instincts were telling guests to stay away from the water after dark.

Ben made a conscious effort to keep his pace slow and steady, his stride almost methodical. The time passed incredibly slowly. So much so that he was compelled to constantly check his phone, only to find that barely a few minutes had passed since the last time he'd checked it. He came to suspect he'd been sucked into some kind of vortex that distorted time, turning hours into minutes and minutes into seconds. With all the other weird shit that happened at the R.R. on a regular basis, it would be totally beyond the realms of possibility.

Finally, he reached a point on the path that felt so eerily familiar he came to a complete halt. The spot was adjacent to the lake and within sight of the villas. And just like in his dream, the lights were on.

This was the exact place where the killer had struck, where Beth White's life abruptly ended.

He paused, took a long, shuddering breath, and welcomed the dull sense of sadness into his heart. After the anger was gone, sorrow was the only thing left. Who was there to be angry with?

He turned around and looked at the path down which he'd walked, then back up at the villas lining the edge of the lake.

It was wrong.

It was all wrong.

Why hadn't he thought of it before? It was so fucking obvious, yet he'd needed the dream to sketch it out for him.

In 1987, Michael Davenport had been an eighty-two-year-old man, and his health was already beginning to fail. There was no way he would be physically capable of chasing down a fit, teenaged girl who was running for her life. She would be able to outpace him easily. Even if he succeeded in catching her, as big and threatening as he was it was doubtful he would have enough in the tank to be able to overpower her, let alone hold her down and stab her multiple times.

It could only mean one thing.

Michael Davenport wasn't the killer.

That was what the dream had been trying to show him.

Once he had made the connection, he wondered how on earth he'd managed to miss it before, and the knowledge suddenly made him feel very vulnerable. If Michael Davenport wasn't the killer, it meant someone had gone to great lengths to imply he was. And they'd been very clever about it.

Furthermore, there was a good chance the real killer was still alive.

After paying his respects at the spot where Beth died, Ben continued his pilgrimage. There was one more place he wanted to see before he met up with Tim.

He'd never walked the path on the other side of the lake before. As it turned out, it was just as impeccably kept as the more public side where the main buildings were located, and illuminated with sodium streetlights that kept the darkness at bay.

However, it was very different on the other side of the lake. It felt more authentic, rustic, and closer to nature, though a more pragmatic person would perhaps just call it more secluded and isolated. Crawling with shadows and devoid of life, it was like the dark side of the moon.

Now, out of sight of the main thoroughfare, Ben quickened his stride, his breath coming in steady gasps. He soon developed shin splints and made a mental note, as he did most days, to start a new exercise regime, or any exercise regime come to that, sooner rather than later. He kept up the punishing pace until his route took him parallel to the island. Conveniently, there was a bench, one of many installed at intervals around the lake.

In spite of the spitting rain, Ben sank onto the bench and gazed out across the stretch of black water at the island. This was the east side, where the corpse of Elizabeth Thrower was buried, and where he and Tim would be returning later. Ben couldn't distinguish much detail, but all appeared to be quiet over there. No disembodied colored lights "dancing" in the air, no Gray Lady gliding around, and no torch beams or police.

The lack of activity made sense. The police didn't have the manpower to waste on a centuries-old cold case and the Powers-That-Be at the Regal wouldn't dare draw any more attention to it. Nobody wanted to spend their holiday watching corpses be dug out of the ground.

Then he noticed something else: an angular shape a few yards down the path sitting at the water's edge, half-obscured by shadows and mist. Ben rose to his feet and approached cautiously. As he drew near, he saw that it was a tiny rowboat with a tarpaulin thrown over it, either to protect it from the elements or hide it from view. He couldn't tell if it was the same boat he and Tim had "stolen" before. They all looked basically the same to him. But this was too good to be true.

He looked around, half-expecting to find Detective Carter or a film crew waiting to leap out at him. But there was nobody in sight. Of course, that didn't mean they weren't there. What was the T-shirt slogan?

It's not paranoia if they really are watching you.

Ben couldn't think of anything more fitting.

Just in case, he decided to continue his circuit of the lake, even doubling back to the bench under the pretense of looking for something he'd supposedly dropped, all while thoroughly scoping out the area. If he was being watched, and the rowboat had been left there as some kind of honey trap, there were no tell-tale signs: no sounds or movement, no blinking LED lights.

He could only conclude that the rowboat had been carelessly left there by someone, probably the police themselves, who would no doubt be needing quick, easy access to the island in the near future. How ironic.

They were probably under the impression that no lawbreaker would be so stupid as to steal it. If that were the case, they had no idea how stupid Ben could be.

Just before midnight, Ben was back on the doorstep of Tim Norgood's villa. This time, before he could even raise a fist to knock on the door, it opened and out strode a confident, purposeful-looking Tim carrying a blue plastic bag. "Glad you made it. The past few hours have been agonizing," he said, mirroring Ben's own feelings. "Let's get this over and done with. First thing on the agenda, finding a boat, because we can't fly over to the island. There might be one near the lake. I had to hold myself back from going on a reconnaissance mission so as not to arouse suspicion."

"I don't have that much self-control," Ben replied. "I went out earlier and found one on the other side of the lake."

"Good man," Tim said as he walked. "Were you spotted?"

"If anyone saw me, they would have just seen me going on a late-night stroll. Carter probably thinks he's already done enough to frighten us into being model citizens for the rest of our lives. What's in the bag?"

"A spade, and some other odds and ends we might need. Not a full-size spade. That would be impractical. This one is a travel spade, would you believe? I think they're used by dedicated campers and other outdoorsy types. I figure we wouldn't need a big one, or a pick, seeing as we've done most of the work already, and this size is easier to conceal."

The night felt colder, the rain heavier, and the wind stronger than before. The weather seemed to deteriorate with every step the men took, and by the time they arrived at the boat, they were being viciously buffeted and had to raise their voices to be heard above the storm.

"Do you think it's a good idea to go out there in these conditions?" Ben asked, surveying the increasingly choppy waters.

"Of course, it's not a good idea," Tim scoffed. "None of this is a good bloody idea. We should leave well enough alone. You know it, and I know it. But we also both know we aren't going to do that. We've come too far to turn back now."

"Fair enough. Let's get it done, then," Ben said, grabbing the tarpaulin and casting it aside to reveal the rowboat beneath. "It's not exactly a luxury liner, but it'll do the job."

"Certainly will," Tim replied, wasting no time in pushing and maneuvering the tiny vessel into the water.

On the short trip to the island, both men were resolute. Neither of them talked, focusing instead on getting across the water as quickly as they could without incident. The water was turbulent, the waves periodically picking up the boat and plonking it back down again with a hefty splash. Pretty soon, the bottom of the craft was filled with several inches of water. It felt as if they were paddling against the tide and directly into the face of the wind, almost as if the lake itself was doing everything it could to repel them.

Despite the adverse conditions, Ben and Tim reached the island, soaked to the skin but otherwise unscathed, in record time. Another bonus was landing on the east side, meaning they didn't have to risk their lives crossing the island again. Ben still wore the scars of the last attempt.

Even as they approached, Ben could see the blue and white tape marked with the sobering words POLICE LINE: DO NOT CROSS flapping in the wind. Tim noticed it when he turned around and paused in the act of heaving the boat onto dry land. "At least there's no welcoming committee," he said. "The only police presence seems to have come out of their stationary box."

Ben switched on one of the flashlights and ducked under the tape, with Tim following close behind. They were relieved to find what was left of Elizabeth Thrower's body lying where they'd left it, the domed white skull still protruding rudely from the ground. Ben never thought he would ever be happy to see a dead body in the middle of the night, or any other time, for that matter, but there it was.

Before they could even discuss how to approach matters, Tim took things into his own hands by liberating the miniature spade from the plastic bag and digging into the sodden, sandy turf immediately adjacent to the skull. He was careful and methodical, and as if searching for something rather than trying to uncover more of the body.

"What are you looking for?"

"The wooden cross. We have to get rid of it. I think it's the only way."

His task was made more difficult by the consistency of the waterlogged soil, which was like quicksand. The moment Tim extracted a spadeful and made an indentation, the sides fell in and he would be back where he started. Even just standing over him under the pretense of keeping watch, Ben could feel his feet sinking into the earth. He had to constantly change position to prevent them from doing so and turned up his collar to guard against the chill.

Maybe it was the weird situation he found himself in—he'd never dug up a body on an island in a lake before so had very little experience in such matters—but something about the situation didn't feel right, putting him on edge. Not only was the island in near-total darkness apart from their Maglite beams, but it was also enveloped in a thick, oppressive coat of silence. There were no birds, no insects, no wildlife of any kind. Almost as if Mother Nature herself was respecting the sanctity of the grave site.

The minutes ticked by until Tim suddenly whooped with joy. "I think I found it!"

"The crucifix?"

"Yes!"

Ben leaned in for a closer look. Tim had discarded the travel shovel and now held up a chunk of darkened wood for Ben to see. It was small, barely the size of a cigar, and caked in mud.

"It's rotten and is hardly more than a twig now, but I found it near her chest, and it's the only thing around here that resembles what we're looking for."

"Could it really last all this time?" Ben asked.

"Why not?" Tim replied. "There are stories about fragments of the True Cross still surviving, and they would be over two thousand years old if genuine."

"Yeah, but still…"

"Hold on," Tim said, putting his spare hand on his hip. "Let me get this straight. You believe in ghosts, an ancient curse, magic and witchcraft, and all manner of other paranormal activity, but draw the line at accepting a piece of wood can survive in the ground for a few centuries?"

"Okay," Ben said. "Point taken."

At that moment, he suddenly sensed activity.

Close.

He heard the approach before he had time to look up, and by the time he reacted to the threat, it was too late. He saw a figure out of the corner of his eye. A huge, hulking figure.

Like in the dream.

As he turned, something struck his solar plexus, hard, knocking the wind out of him and sending him reeling.

He collided with Tim, both men falling to the ground in a tangle of arms and legs. Tim grunted in surprise as he was flattened under Ben's weight.

Ben now found himself on all fours, his hands sinking into the soft earth. A wave of revulsion washed over him.

He was *inside* the grave, in amongst the bones and rotted flesh.

Something was in his mouth. Something gritty, cold, and bitter.

Mud.

Tainted, dirty mud.

He spluttered, spat, and gazed up to see what the fuck had just happened.

The huge, hulking figure was now standing over them, silhouetted in the shadows. It was within touching distance. From Ben's position on the ground, it looked easily ten feet tall and emanated pure evil.

It couldn't be a flesh-and-blood entity, could it? It had to be some kind of nightmarish, mythical creature like the one in *From the Depths*.

When he replayed it in his mind later, Ben thought coming face-to-face with a monster straight from a film set might actually be easier to deal with than the truth.

Because when the shadowy mass shifted slightly and its features were illuminated by flashlight beam, the bulky frame and hooked nose was unmistakable.

It was Glenn Davenport.

This time, he was alone.

And he was pointing a handgun at them.

Chapter Twenty-Two

"Next time someone gives you a friendly piece of advice, take it," the owner of the Regal Retreat and latest in the Davenport bloodline sneered through gritted teeth as he towered above the two men.

Ben fought to free himself from the tangle of limbs and struggled to his feet, frantically wiping at his clothes as if that would be enough to eliminate the stink of Elizabeth Thrower's makeshift grave.

Tim wasn't far behind. "What the…" he gasped, looking around as if still trying to work out what had just happened.

Though winded and disoriented, this latest development didn't come as a complete shock to Ben. He'd been quietly piecing things together in his mind all day. "Are you referring to the warning note?" he said, feeling the anger bubbling inside him.

"I am." There was an element of arrogant self-satisfaction in Glenn Davenport's tone, as if he spent a lot of time reveling in the misguided notion that he was far superior to everyone else and the people he shared the world with just weren't on his level.

Ben's heart rate increased tenfold as his mind flashed back to the note he'd found slipped under his door, then fast-forwarded to the letter Christine had shown him. There was something he'd shied away from. Something he hadn't wanted to confront at the time. There were just too many other things going on. Now, it seemed like his mind had no-where else to go and the answer was staring him in the face.

The warning note and Michael Davenport's suicide letter were writ-ten by the same hand.

Those looping, elegant, left-leaning strokes. It was a distinctive style. If the notes really had been written by father and son, there might be a passing similarity, but no more than that. The two specimens wouldn't be virtually identical.

"There was nothing friendly about that piece of advice," Ben replied, hoping to distract the man with the gun enough so he could slip his hand in his front pocket and push a button on his phone. "You were warning me off."

"Believe me, it could've been a lot less friendly," Glenn Davenport countered. "Now get your hands where I can see them. You, too, professor."

"I'm not actually a professor," Tim said. "But we'll forget that over-sight for the moment and focus more on where you just came from and what the devil is going on here."

"I'm sure you'll catch up soon," Davenport said. "The truth is, you both played into my plans like a pair of mice on a wheel. I knew you'd come back here. You wouldn't be able to leave well enough alone. Do you think that rowboat you found so conveniently was left there acci-dentally? Nope. I was giving you enough rope to hang yourselves with, as the expression goes, and you just couldn't wait to oblige."

"What the hell is all this about?" Ben heard Tim say, his voice full of bewilderment. He couldn't help but feel a twinge of sympathy for the man. He was truly out of his depth.

For Ben, the penny had dropped long ago. After that, it was simply a case of filling in the blanks. Tim had no such luxury. For him it must be like trying to finish a jigsaw with only half the pieces. "He's a murderer," Ben chimed in helpfully.

"Ridiculous," Tim replied. "Elizabeth Thrower was killed centuries ago. He couldn't have done it. Could he? Is he immortal or something?"

"I think 'immortal' is pushing it," Ben said, rolling his eyes and strug-gling to suppress a chortle despite the gravity of the situation.

Tim had apparently reached the watershed moment where he would now believe literally anything, even if he knew it would fly in the face of reason. A UFO could land next to them and he would probably ask the occupants back to his villa for a cup of tea and a chat. "I doubt if he was personally responsible for that monumental fuck-up, but his ancestors undoubtedly played a starring role. We're not actually talking about Elizabeth Thrower, are we, Glenn? That isn't the only monumental fuck-up to have occurred in these parts."

"Shut it," the resort owner said, jabbing the handgun in Ben's direction.

"A man of wealth, power, and good social standing. A pillar of the community, and the main employer in the area. Nobody would dare sling any mud in your direction without proof, and you made sure there was none of that. Didn't you?"

"Care to catch me up?" Tim said, weakly.

"Remember the Beth White murder?" Ben said, without taking his eyes from Glenn Davenport.

"The unsolved murder case from thirty-odd years ago?"

"Yep," Ben said. "Except it's not unsolved anymore."

"It was this fuckwit?"

"It seems that way. Even had the audacity to try to frame his own old man. Except that didn't work out so well."

"Wait," Tim said. "Michael Davenport is his father. He died of natural causes, didn't he?"

"Maybe, or maybe this psycho killed him, too. I'm not sure about that. What I am sure about is that after he was dead, our friend Glenn here tried to make it look like a suicide. He even wrote a suicide note and left it at the scene."

"Whatever for? To take control of the Regal Retreat?"

"That might've had something to do with it," Ben began. "The benefits of not having his father around anymore were many. Yes, he stood to inherit the Retreat and the rest of the family estate. Glenn here couldn't wait for the old man to retire, knowing that even then he would still be involved in the businesses. A man like that wasn't the type to just fade into the background. As long as he was alive, he would overrule every decision Glenn made. But there was another, more pressing concern, wasn't there?"

"Shut your fucking mouth," Glenn Davenport snarled. "You two have already stirred up more trouble than you can handle. Certainly more than you're worth. Don't go making it worse for yourselves."

"How can it be worse?" Ben said, reflexively taking a step backward. As he did so, his eyes shifted to a spot off to his right. There was something there, lying on the ground a mere three or four feet away. He didn't know why he hadn't seen it before, but he knew instantly what it was. The baton he'd left behind on their previous visit.

Realizing he couldn't let Glenn Davenport's see it, Ben said, "We're being held at gun point on a secluded island in a lake in the middle of the night by a cold-blooded murderer who'll probably kill us next and get away with it. I don't think it can get much worse than it already is."

"Oh, I disagree with that," sneered Davenport. "It could get much, much worse. Interesting point you made about killing you both. It would certainly make things easier. Help tie up some loose ends, so to speak."

"Okay," Tim said, sounding like he was finally losing his composure. "If I'm about to die out here, I would like to know why. What does all this have to do with Beth White?"

"The suicide note Glenn left was also a confession," Ben said. "It was written in his father's name, obviously. Admitting to killing Beth White."

"Not following. Why on earth would he do that?"

"Because Glenn here is the one who really killed the poor girl. My guess is that his father knew about it somehow. Either Glenn confessed to him, or he found out by some other means. Maybe he saw what a loose cannon his son had become and threatened to go to the authorities."

"Ha-ha!" Glenn Davenport bellowed, the laugh containing no humor. "You must think you're so clever. You're not even half right. I didn't kill my father. I'm not a psycho. He worked himself to death, and when the staff found him, they called me first. I just saw an opportunity and made the most of it. My dad would've been proud."

"Yeah, that arrogance came shining through in the letter you wrote," Ben said. "So why did you take the letter back from whoever found it and store it in the office here where anyone could find it? Because someone *did* find it, and they showed it to me."

"They only thought what I wanted them to think," Glenn Davenport replied smugly. "I was in control the entire time. As far as anyone was concerned, that letter was a confession from my father. It was my insurance. Naturally, I hoped the murder would remain firmly in the 'unsolved' category, but if anyone ever pointed the finger at me, I could produce the suicide note and claim to be the dutiful son protecting the family name. Who would doubt it? The only person who would have a problem with that scenario would be my father, and he isn't around any more. Perfect."

"You evil bastard," Ben said. He couldn't help himself; it just slipped out.

"Anyway," Davenport said. "It's been nice catching up with you both and all that. Now we have to get a move on. I'm a busy man, you know." There was a brief pause. And then Davenport motioned at the remnants of the cross Tim still held. "What do you have there?"

"It's…a crucifix," Tim replied hesitatingly.

"Doesn't look like one."

"Yeah, it's been in the ground for a while," Tim said.

"How long?"

"Three-hundred years. Give or take."

"So that's why you came back here? For that?"

"Yep. Pretty much. We certainly didn't come for the company."

"Why is it so important?"

"Long story, but we think destroying this might just put a stop to all the ill-fortune blighting this place."

"Come again?" Davenport said, as if this was the first he was hearing of such a thing.

"It's not the time or the place to explain," Tim said with a roll of the eyes. "All you need to know is we have to burn this thing."

Davenport paused, as if in deep contemplation, his eyes going from Ben, to Tim, to the cross, and back again. Finally, he said, "Is it worth anything?"

"Money?"

"What else?"

"Probably," Tim shrugged. "It's an ancient artefact with documented historical relevance, so I assume it would be of considerable value to interested parties like museums or collectors on the open market."

"How much?"

"Who knows? Selling it at auction would probably start a bidding war. I've seen similar items go for twenty or thirty thousand."

"Thirty grand for that? That's another reason to kill you both."

"No doubt you'll make it look like an accident," Ben hastily countered.

"Good idea. Your little escapade last night set the scene perfectly. When the two of you are found floating in the water, people will assume you tried to come back here for reasons only you pair of simpletons were aware of. Except, on this occasion, you met with some bad luck out on the lake. As you rightly pointed out, such a thing wouldn't be unusual here. And actually, it wouldn't be that far from the truth."

"What about the sound of the gun shots? And the bullet holes?" Tim interjected. "That might cause a few suspicions."

"Way ahead of you, Champ," Davenport said. "The security detail is on high alert. But if they hear shots, they'll follow protocol and call the police. By the time they arrive, I'll be long gone. I'll wipe my fingerprints off the gun, which is untraceable by the way, and eradicate any sign of my being here. I already made sure there would be no witnesses. My P.A., wife, and all my staff think I'm spending the night at my London apartment. I even had a friend make an order at Pizza Hut in Covent Garden using my debit card. He doesn't mind. He's getting a free pizza out of it. When, or if, the police run any checks, to all intents and purposes I won't even be here. When they come back to the island in the morning to deal with this ancient grave nonsense, they'll just find two dead bodies and a smoking gun. They'll probably assume it was a murder/suicide. That would be the most convenient solution all around."

"That is the very definition of heinous," Tim said.

"I couldn't agree more," Ben chipped in. "Even with a stuffed crust, Pizza Hut produces a poor imitation of a pizza. Isn't there a Domino's in London?"

Davenport ignored him and plowed on. "Of course, the police will investigate. That's what they're paid to do. They'll probably assume you fell out over something you found in the grave. Or rather, something you didn't find, because I'll be taking that little trinket of yours with me. Thirty grand is thirty grand. But you obviously came here looking for something. You even brought that cute little shovel. Our friend Detective Carter and his buddies will spend untold amounts of man hours and tax-payer's money looking for answers in all the wrong places before finally concluding that they don't have the faintest sodding idea what happened. After that, they'll move on and you'll be just another mystery to add to the Regal's collection. You'll become a footnote in history. They might even write articles about you. How does that sound?"

"It sounds like you're a villain from *Scooby Doo* and we're the pesky kids," Ben said.

Davenport threw back his head and laughed, then pulled the hammer back on the handgun with his thumb. "I won't even be sorry. I'll be doing the world a favor by permanently closing that mouth of yours."

The heavens chose that precise moment to open and the rain started coming down in huge droplets.

Ben realized Davenport held a revolver rather than an automatic weapon. That was to his and Tim's advantage, with revolvers being slow and cumbersome compared to their more-advanced counterparts, which could rattle off a dozen or more rounds in seconds. "I have another question, if you wouldn't mind answering before you commit murder again."

Glenn Davenport sighed impatiently. "This is getting tiresome. I should just shoot you. But I'm curious about what you deem important enough to waste your last breath on."

"If you didn't want anyone digging around in your personal affairs and stirring shit up about unsolved murders, why did you bring me here?" Ben asked, genuinely mystified. "To the Regal? Your people sent for me; I didn't volunteer. Don't you know what I do? I stir shit up for a living."

"Christine pitched the idea," Davenport said, wiping the rain from his face with the sleeve of his jacket. "She really cares about the brand, the poor woman. In many ways she's the perfect employee. I tried to dissuade her at first. But I couldn't try too hard or she would want to know why. Besides, I thought you'd just spend a couple of nights here, take advantage of the facilities, fail to provide any answers, then take your payment and leave. How was I to know you'd turn out to be such a gigantic pain in the arse?"

"I aim to please," Ben said with a wink.

Then he made his move.

Taking a long stride toward Glenn Davenport to close the distance between them, he thrust out his fist in a downward motion, connecting solidly with the hand holding the gun.

There was an impossibly loud *BOOM*, and a flash illuminated the night like a firework. Ben paused for a fraction of a second as he waited for the pain to hit him, but it never did. When he realized he hadn't been shot, he tried to resume his assault.

But it was too late.

Momentum had been lost.

His hesitation had given Davenport enough time to re-adjust himself and use his size and weight advantage to grapple Ben to the ground again.

He landed flat on his back, his head smashing against a rock sticking out of the earth, and he found himself looking up into the inky black sky wondering if it would be the last thing he would ever see.

As if in slow motion, Ben watched Glenn Davenport pull back the revolver's hammer and raise the barrel once more. His mind flashed back to the dream where he'd been Beth and seen Glenn Davenport towering over him in the act of committing cold-blooded murder. It was turning out to be almost prophetic.

Never forget, history repeats.

Suddenly, as if on some signal, Tim erupted into life and rushed at Davenport with a yell of fury. Bizarrely, he brandished the small chunk of wood he'd found in Elizabeth's grave like a wholly inadequate weapon, probably because it was the only thing he had.

There was another *BOOM*, a second blinding flash illuminated the clearing, and Tim slumped to the ground.

Before Davenport could train the gun back on him, Ben reached out, snatched up the telescopic baton off the ground, flicked his wrist to open it, and swung it hard and low. Time seemed to slow down to a crawl as the weapon traversed the short distance between the two men and connected just above Davenport's right knee. He let out a squeal of pain, losing balance as his legs gave way beneath him. The revolver fell to the ground.

Seizing the opportunity, Ben scrambled to his feet and swung the baton once more. This time, he aimed for Davenport's head. He didn't just want to slow the man down or incapacitate him. He wanted to kill him.

However, Davenport saw the threat and deftly rolled out of the way. In the next motion, he sprang to his feet, simultaneously throwing a wild right hook. The strike sailed harmlessly past Ben's chin, which was just as well because Glenn Davenport had fists like concrete blocks.

Ben instinctively knew the best form of defense was attack, and without giving his adversary time to settle, he swung the baton again, grunting with the exertion. This time it connected high on Davenport's right shoulder and appeared to do some actual damage. The man doubled over, screaming with a mixture of pain and rage.

There was now a distance of several feet between them, and the pair stood off for a moment's respite, each one taking the opportunity to assess the other like two boxers in a ring. Davenport was a good six or eight inches taller than Ben and probably three or four stones heavier. He was also no stranger to violence of the worst kind. Even armed with the baton, in a one-on-one confrontation, Ben was hopelessly outgunned. Not that it phased him. He had always flourished in the role of underdog, when there was everything to gain and nothing to lose.

Somehow, in the scuffle, they'd switched positions. The lake was now behind Ben and Davenport stood near the open grave, light wisps of steam rising from the top of his head. The wind howled, and the rain still pummeled them.

Ben stole a glance at Tim, who was still lying where he'd fallen with water running down his ashen, upturned face. He hadn't moved. Ben's heart sank a few notches. Though tormented by his past, Tim had proven himself a worthy partner in crime, his last selfless act a desperate attempt at redemption and salvation. Despite only knowing him a short time, when he looked at Tim, Ben saw a kindred spirit and was acutely aware that without him around, the world would be a few shades darker.

Then, as if by some miracle, Tim's eyes fluttered open and his head moved almost imperceptibly.

He was alive!

Ben felt a rush of relief so powerful he momentarily forgot he was embroiled in a life-or-death stand-off with a man who might well be the very embodiment of evil.

Regardless of his size, Davenport was quick. Seeing Ben was momentarily distracted, he reached down, grabbed the revolver, and aimed it once more.

Raising his voice to make himself heard over the growing squall, he said, "I really do appreciate you putting up a fight. It's no fun otherwise. I take no pleasure in killing in cold blood. It's a bit like drowning defenseless puppies. You want them to at least struggle a bit. Or at least make a run for it like that bitch Beth White, who you seem to care so much about. It makes it all so much more entertaining."

Ben had just enough time to reassess his options before realizing that he didn't have any. He was all out, and he cursed his own naïveté. Had he lived his entire life just to be led to this point and have it all snuffed out by a homicidal maniac on a power trip?

He quickly banished any thoughts of a last-second frontal attack. Such a move would undoubtedly result in a bullet to the face. That tactic hadn't ended well for Tim. Another quick glance at his stricken friend revealed that the man's eyes were closed again. What Ben had seen must have been just a trick of the light or some kind of post-mortem reaction.

A maniacal smile passed Glenn Davenport's lips before morphing into one of smug self-satisfaction. Ben and Tim had put up the expected token resistance, and now he was going to kill them. End of story. To him, this was little more than a bloodsport.

Ben closed his eyes and prepared to answer the greatest question of all.

As perverse as it might seem, he was looking forward to it. Life without Amy and Louise wasn't worth the hassle, anyway. A banal, gray existence chasing shadows and ghosts was a poor substitute for the vibrant, colorful life he'd once known, and he welcomed the opportunity to see beyond the veil. He'd settle for a wide expanse of nothing, but a fresh start free of guilt and pain would be a bonus.

However, the shot that would end the misery and bring blessed relief didn't come.

Ben felt he was in a time warp again, every nanosecond being stretched to impossible lengths.

It was beginning to get awkward.

Then came the scream. An inhuman howl straight out of a video nasty. Ben had never heard a person make a sound like that before. He didn't even think it was possible. His eyes flew open again, and what he saw would haunt his nightmares forever.

There was something coming out of the ground. More precisely, there was something coming out of the shallow grave over which Glenn Davenport stood. Two skeletal arms, the bones brittle and discolored after spending so long in the damp earth, were reaching up and grasping at the man's trouser leg.

Ben watched on in horror as Davenport screamed again, his mouth opening impossibly wide in an attempt to convey the raw terror he must have been feeling. The scream ended in a series of fevered gasps, his mouth hanging open in shock as he tried to comprehend the incomprehensible; the corpse of Elizabeth Thrower, forgotten and neglected all these years, sensing long-promised retribution and returning from the grave to claim it.

As the rain lashed down, the skeletal arms reached ever upward, clawing at Davenport's clothes as they pulled themselves out of the cold, clammy earth. The skull was entirely visible now, not just the rounded dome Ben and Tim had already uncovered. The empty eye sockets were cavernous, and the lower half of the skull horizontally split in two by a wide, toothy mouth. It appeared to be grinning, the teeth chattering as they clashed noisily into each other.

Eyes wide, Davenport looked down, turned the gun on the creature emerging from the grave, and aimed the barrel directly at the thing's head. From a distance of mere inches, he pulled the trigger.

BLAM!

The head jerked back on skeletal shoulders and white slivers of bone flew off it in all directions. When the skull came back into view, there was a neat hole near the center of the forehead. Ben guessed there would be a much larger one in the back. However, the bullet did nothing to slow Elizabeth's relentless assault. If anything, she seemed to set about the task with increased urgency.

Or maybe it was fury, now unrestrained.

Davenport pulled the trigger again. But this time there was only a dry *click*. Either the gun had malfunctioned, or he was out of bullets. With a wail of frustration, he resorted to using the revolver as a kind of bludgeoning tool instead and started raining blows down on the creature's head, each one making a hollow-sounding *thud* as it landed.

Still, the reanimated corpse was unperturbed and finally succeeded in dragging Davenport to the ground where he sank first to his knees, and then onto his back. "Help! Help me!" he screamed, holding out a hand in Ben's direction, his eyes so wide the eyeballs looked as if they were about to pop out of their sockets.

For a moment, Ben actually considered stepping in.

That's probably what would have happened had this been a movie.

But it was no movie.

Ben couldn't move a muscle. He was rooted to the spot. What was more, he found he didn't even want to move. He wanted a ringside seat. Davenport had this coming.

So instead of going to help, Ben simply stood and watched as the corpse clambered over him, its teeth chattering ever more ominously until it finally succeeded in hauling itself far enough out of the ground that it could sink its grave-blackened incisors deep into Davenport's cheek.

The man screamed again, even louder than before, if that was possible, and thrashed his arms as the thing that used to be Elizabeth Thrower bit down hard and shook its head from side to side like a rabid dog, tearing a mouthful of flesh from his face. It came away with a wet, ripping sound, and the scream soon trailed off into a gurgle as Davenport began choking on his own blood.

As Davenport continued to splutter and whimper, the creature took hold of his collar in a talon-like grip and began pulling him inch by dreadful inch toward the water's edge. Its lower body didn't seem to work correctly, or at all, forcing it to drag itself across the ground in a stop-start lurching motion. Davenport was too weak or shocked to fight back, and instead seemed resigned to his fate. His ruined face was ashen white as he stared straight up at the sky.

He left his gun in the mud.

The last thing Ben saw was Davenport disappearing beneath the surface of the lake with the creature's arms still wrapped around him like the embrace of a long-lost lover.

Chapter Twenty-Three

Here, now

With a sudden rush of what can only be described as awareness, Elizabeth came alive again.

No, not alive. But not dead, either. Some place in the middle, between light and dark. Twilight.

She was dimly aware that the spells and incantations had served their purpose and brought her back.

She'd been waiting a long time. Years. Centuries.

Lying still.

She always knew this time would come. The universe, and the gods she prayed to, would see to it. Sooner or later the planets would align, the forces would conspire, the circumstances would arrange themselves, and justice would be served as cold as her long-dead fingers.

And that time was now.

She couldn't see or hear. She couldn't feel the multitude of wounds in her flesh anymore, nor the chill seeping into her bones. Her heart was no longer broken.

She felt nothing except this compulsion, driving her forward. The same blind urge she'd felt when she'd survived the lake. It had served her well then, and it would do so again.

Davenport, her nemesis, was close. She could feel him. Sense him. The evil emanated from him in waves like the stench of rotting meat. The closer she was, the more powerful it became. She didn't need eyes, or ears, or even thoughts. This was something more primal.

Instinct.

Now, he was close enough to touch.

Close enough to hold.

Close enough to kiss.

She reached out in the perpetual darkness. Probing, exploring.

Her fingers found something, and she knew it was him. She clung on tightly. When he was finally within her grasp, she was never going to let him go.

Never.

She knew what had to be done. Balance must be restored.

He was going to pay for his sins, and the sins of his ancestors.

As she tugged and pulled at him, his resistance wilted, and his ragged, throaty screams were like sweet music to her ears.

Now she could sleep.

After watching what was left of Elizabeth Thrower drag Glenn Davenport to his watery demise, Ben felt an overwhelming surge of relief.

It was over.

Events had come full circle and ended exactly where they had begun. In the lake. As if even the elements were aware of this latest plot twist, the pounding rain abruptly subsided to a drizzle and the wailing wind dropped to barely a whisper.

Finally, justice had been served. The latest head of the Davenport family hadn't been personally responsible for what had happened to Elizabeth all those years ago, but he was certainly responsible for what had happened to Beth White. There could be little doubt that both Davenports, and probably all those that came between them given the evidence, were thoroughly despicable human beings the world was better off without.

You reap what you sow in life.

Reaching into his front pocket, Ben pulled out his cellphone and checked to make sure the voice recorder was still running. It was. He quickly pushed a few buttons and played back a brief section of the audio file. The voices were slightly muffled due to the device being in his pocket the entire time, but Davenport's voice could clearly be heard over the hiss of the rain and wind. A little sound editing and the confession would be crystal clear. That was what Ben wanted. When he'd first pressed "Record," he was thinking the sound file might serve as some kind of document should Davenport kill both him and Tim, and he planned to discreetly leave the phone somewhere it could easily be found before Davenport did them in.

"Is it over now?"

The voice almost made Ben jump out of his skin. He whirled around to find Tim sitting up on the ground and looking around.

"What the fuck?" Ben said. "I thought you were dead."

"Playing dead. And doing a mighty fine job of it, too. I stole that line from *Lost Boys*, by the way. A seminal comedy horror film from nineteen-eighty-seven with a great soundtrack. The only thing missing is a red Plymouth Fury. It seems fitting, don't you think? I knew all those am-dram classes would come in handy one day," Tim said, getting shakily to his feet and looking around as if fully expecting a round of applause.

"Is that what you call it?" Ben said, still trying to process what was happening.

"I'd go one step further and call it the performance of a lifetime," Tim said. "It could even trump the time my group put in world-class renditions of *Joseph and the Amazing Technicolor Dreamcoat* over three consecutive nights at Scarborough Open Air Theatre five summers ago. It was quite the undertaking, but all was going swimmingly right up until rehearsals for the final night when Enoch, who until then had been playing Joseph—and with some aplomb I might add—was suddenly taken ill with food poisoning. Wouldn't you know it, all eyes fell on me. Until then, I'd been playing the part of Judah. It was one hell of a step up. Of course, it was a topic of hot debate among the members whether or not I should have been awarded the role of Joseph in the first place, but that's a whole other story. It took quite the reshuffle, let me tell you, but the crisis was averted and that particular performance was widely regarded the best of the run. You could say it was career-defining. Of course, I realize it was a team effort, so I wouldn't dream of taking *all* the credit, but I do look back upon that night with particular fondness."

"Well, I'm glad you're in such fine fettle," Ben said. "And thanks for all the help and support back there. I really couldn't have done it without you."

"Ouch!" Tim said. "Your sarcasm is positively biting. I'll have you know that when I initially hit the deck, I was just playing for time. I thought if Davenport thought I was dead, we could have perhaps used it to our advantage. I could have blindsided him when he wasn't looking or something. Thank God that man is such an awful shot. He almost missed me completely, and at point blank range, too!"

"Almost?"

"Yeah, I think I got shot a little bit," Tim said, inspecting first his chest then his left arm.

"You got shot but it was just a little bit?"

"Yeah. It seems the bullet just grazed my elbow. Bleeding a bit. Still hurts like heck, though."

"At least that's one more thing to cross off the bucket list. Haven't you always wondered what it feels like to get shot?"

"Not really, no," Tim said. "I wasn't playing dead the entire time, but I must have drifted in and out of consciousness because I'm not sure if everything I saw was real."

"What did you see?"

"I heard some awful screams, opened my eyes, and saw the skeleton from the grave chowing down on Davenport's face. It was like something out of a zombie film. I remember thinking how ironic it was for a sin eater to be literally eating a sinner."

"I'm so glad you saw that. Now I know I wasn't hallucinating," Ben said.

"It was for real?" Tim said, looking around and then down at the now-empty grave.

Ben nodded.

"But…that's impossible."

"How so? Because everything else that has happened here over the years has been so plausible?"

"Point taken, but what I saw was some next-level fuckery. Such a shame there was no camera crew here to capture it."

"Indeed, it is. But I have some audio footage," Ben said and played a few more seconds of the recording for Tim's benefit. "Nobody would believe us otherwise. Saying that, they probably wouldn't believe us even if we'd captured the whole thing in high def."

"Do…people have to know what happened here tonight?" Tim asked. "I mean, I know a man died, but he was a dick. I don't feel we owe him anything. Nobody would believe us, anyway. And as you say, that audio recording alone won't be enough to convince anybody that a woman killed and buried hundreds of years ago rose from the grave and took her revenge on a modern-day murderer, who just happened to be a very rich and powerful man. At best, we would be ridiculed, and at worst they would try to make us scapegoats. The police have fitted people up before, you know. It would be a convenient way to tie up some loose ends. We're already in Detective Carter's bad books."

"I just don't see what choice we have. He's bound to be reported missing," Ben reasoned.

"Oh, for sure, but he's supposed to be in London tonight, remember? He let it slip during one of his rants. The authorities would probably think whatever happened to him happened there. He'd just be another statistic."

"And what about when the boat he must have used to get here is discovered. Or when the body is found in the lake?"

"There won't be anything connecting the boat to our friend, and somehow I don't think his body will be showing up any time soon," Tim said solemnly. "Even if someone did find his body here, it would just be another mystery for someone to solve. We'll both be long gone by then, and there will be nothing to link either of us to it. The water will take care of any trace D.N.A. evidence."

"You might be right," Ben agreed, thinking of the people who had gone missing in the lake before, never to be seen again.

"Ironic that's exactly what he had in mind for us."

"Very," Ben said. "But we can't just brush it under the table for the simple reason that Beth's family deserves to know the truth. I think that's the main reason she showed herself to me. If it were your daughter, wouldn't you want to know what really happened?"

"I suppose you're right," Tim conceded.

"Look," Ben began. "If you don't want to be involved, I'll just say I came out here tonight alone. There's no need for anyone to know the whole truth."

"You'd do that?"

"Why not? You have more to lose than I do should everything go tits up."

"It wouldn't work. I'm all over the tape. At least, I was until I got shot."

"Oh yeah," Ben said. "There's no getting around that."

Tim sighed. "To heck with it. We were in this together, and we still are. Bring it on. If people leap to conclusions or I end up in jail, I wouldn't be the first academic and amateur thespian with something of an eccentric reputation. It would all add to the enigma."

"Welcome aboard," Ben said. "We needn't make a huge deal of it. I was thinking I could just send Beth's parents an email. That way, the information will be theirs to do with what they want. How do you think she came back like that?"

"Beth or Elizabeth?"

"Both. Either."

"Who knows?" Tim shrugged. "You're the paranormal expert. Perhaps the same weird force that brought all the tragedy here? That man Davenport may have been directly responsible for a small portion of it, and his father before him. Maybe being a cunt was a family tradition going back generations. But there's no way even they could do away with that many people over such an extended period and get away with it every time. Something else was at work. Something inexplicable. Regardless, I have the feeling poor Elizabeth got what she wanted in the end, so things might calm down a bit around here."

"I certainly hope so. For everyone's sake."

"There's one more thing we can do. Kind of an insurance policy," Tim said.

"What's that?"

But Tim had vanished. Ben turned to see where his friend had gone and saw him hunched over peering at the ground. He was hunting around the clearing for something. He came back a short while later holding the remnants of the wooden crucifix they'd found in the grave and the plastic bag they'd brought with them. Ben watched as Tim pulled out a small container of lighter fluid and a Zippo lighter. "Let's make a fire," he said.

Tim laid the crucifix on the ground as close to the water's edge as he dared, squirted a generous helping of lighter liquid on it, then ignited it.

"Is that thing really worth thirty grand?"

"Nope," Tim said. "It's just a lump of old wood. There's no way anyone can prove it has any cultural or historical significance, even if it does. I was just trying to provoke a reaction from our angry friend. I knew that greedy bastard wouldn't be able to pass up some easy money. And I was right."

As Ben watched the flames consume the object, he couldn't help recalling once again the dreams he'd had of being burned alive. Given his past, fire was proving a constant in his life. The synchronicity was striking, making him even more inclined to believe there was some mysterious force at work in the universe knitting everything together.

Never forget, history repeats.

"We need to get out of here," Ben said. "These flames might attract some unwanted attention. Not to mention the gunshots. The police are probably on their way as we speak, and I don't know about you, but I could do without another run-in with Detective Carter."

"I second that."

With a series of grunts Ben and Tim pushed and pulled the tiny rowboat into the inky black water and cast off.

CHAPTER TWENTY-FOUR

en woke up and stretched as the fog of sleep slowly dissipated. He felt revitalized. That was what a good night's sleep could do. Or, more accurately, half a night's good sleep. It had been after 3:00 a.m. by the time he'd finally staggered through the door of Room 327 following his and Tim's latest island escapade. He remembered taking off his shoes and clothes, then finally collapsing in bed. His rest hadn't been fitful or broken at all, and there had been no dreams about burning. In fact, there had been no dreams whatsoever. Just a serene tranquility. You could say he'd slept like the dead.

Kicking off the bed sheets, he went into the en suite to examine the most recent damage his body had sustained. He'd accumulated a few more superficial bumps and scratches, probably in the scuffle with Glenn Davenport. The ribs on his left side hurt where the shadow of a bruise was beginning to form, and his right shoulder was sore. He must have strained it somehow. All this just underscored what Ben already knew: there were no winners in physical confrontations. The winner usually goes to the police station and the loser goes to the hospital. This time the stakes had been even higher.

That said, at least he'd walked away. Davenport hadn't been so lucky.

After a quick shave and a hot shower, which might be his last for a while, he got dressed and exited the room. On the floor outside, next to the door, was a black refuse sack. He stopped and cautiously peered inside, not knowing what he might find in there. A severed head wasn't completely beyond the realms of possibility.

Thankfully, the bag contained only the dirty clothes he'd brought over the day before, except now they were clean and neatly folded. The maid must have taken them, had them washed and dried, and then brought them back.

"That's what I call service," he said, picking up the bag.

Next port of call was Christine Turner's office. He thought about sending her a text message telling her he was on his way but decided to save himself the trouble. What he wanted to say wouldn't take long.

Outside, it was a lovely, bright spring morning. There wasn't a cloud in the sky, allowing the sun's rays to blaze down unhindered.

Christine didn't look surprised to see him. It was probably his imagination, but Ben could have sworn she looked almost happy about it. She looked resplendent in a cream-colored blouse with a plunging neckline and seemed in good spirits.

"I just came to say goodbye," Ben said upon being invited into the office for the last time.

"Really?" the resort manager said, looking up from her work. "That sounds so…final."

"I'll be in touch, of course. But Mister Trimble and I will be hitting the road in a couple of hours."

"Has something happened I should know about?" Christine asked, a look of wary anticipation souring her good mood.

The subtext was clear.

Did you solve the problem?

"There are just one or two things we probably should discuss," Ben said. "May I sit?"

"Please," Christine said, motioning to the chair on the opposite side of her desk.

Ben sat, plopped the bag of clean clothes next to the chair, took a deep breath, and related the events of the past day or so as quickly and accurately as he could. He started with the revealing dream he'd had about the murder of Beth White and his and Tim's theories about the lake and ended with their second trip to the island, Davenport's confession, and Elizabeth Thrower coming out of the ground and dragging him to his watery end. Things had already taken on a surreal quality, and for the most part, it felt more like he was describing a book or a movie rather than real life.

Christine listened intently, the expression on her face varying from mild amusement to absolute shock and disgust. Understandably, the last part of the story elicited the most response, and it was here that Christine began to argue, even going so far as to say Ben and Tim must have been duped or tricked somehow. But Ben could tell that the more she thought about it, the more everything slipped into place. He stayed calm, appreciating it must be a lot for someone who hadn't been there to take in. Acceptance was rarely instantaneous, but it was difficult to argue with the facts.

Even so, he was doubly glad he'd succeeded in capturing Glenn Davenport's final horrific moments. Apart from the body mysteriously going missing from the grave site, it was the only real proof they had. Not only did it help assuage any lingering doubt in Christine's mind, but without it, Ben himself might not believe what had happened.

Together, Ben and Christine listened to Davenport admit to not only killing Beth White and trying to pin the blame on his own father, but also giving Ben the warning note in Room 327 and outlining his intention to kill both him and Tim. Despite the questionable sound quality, there was more than enough incriminating evidence. Finally, the recording finished.

"Wow," Christine said. "I always thought there was something 'off' about the bloke. I just wish I'd put it all together before. It's painfully obvious now."

"Don't beat yourself up about it too much," Ben said. "Everything's easy with hindsight. Psychopaths like him spend their entire lives pulling the wool over people's eyes."

"So, what's the plan?"

"I think I need to present this evidence to our friend Detective Carter. No doubt the revelation will help Beth White's family finally get some closure. I'm also going to make some copies and send them to the press. Just in case anything should happen to the original. Of course, that will see an upsurge in media interest in the Regal. Everybody loves to see a cold case solved and justice served. The supernatural element would be the icing on the cake."

"I'm used to the media attention."

"I bet."

"It sounds like a solution we can all get behind. So that's the Beth White mystery solved. But let me just get this straight," Christine said, frowning deeply. "The murder of Elizabeth Thrower all those years ago was the crux of all this? The reason for all the deaths? How?"

"We're not entirely sure of the 'how,' but it appears that Elizabeth was somehow able to harness some kind of esoteric magic or ancient force and use it to influence people's dreams, where she turned any pre-existing guilt against them and brought it to the surface, essentially using it to drive them crazy. It doesn't answer every question. But it rings true in at least some of the cases."

"It certainly does. And can you guarantee it's over now? Finished? For good?" Christine asked hopefully.

"I wish I could," Ben said. "But unfortunately, there are very few guarantees in life. We do think Elizabeth Thrower had some vendetta against the Davenports. One of their ancestors probably had a hand in her death back in the seventeenth century. Whether the latest Davenport's death is enough to quench her thirst for revenge remains to be seen. Personally, I think it will be. Some of her original message may have been corrupted over the years, but I think she was basically a good person. All she wanted was to live a meaningful life, help people, and see good triumph over evil. And it seems that, ultimately, she got her wish."

Christine nodded. "I suppose we can't ask for more than that."

"Now I have a question, if you wouldn't mind answering," Ben said.

"Sure. Fire away."

"Since all this seems to have such a strong connection to dreams, did you have any while you were here? I don't mean normal ones about running around naked in fields and stuff. We all have those."

"Do we?"

"Or some variation," Ben winked. "But did you dream of something that dredged up regret or bad memories?"

"Don't we all have regrets?"

"I suppose so," Ben agreed. "But it seems that this place, especially any-where near the lake where Elizabeth was killed, emphasizes them or brings them to the surface."

"That's why I live in a house a thirty-minute drive away instead of stay-ing on-site," Christine replied. "It's easier to live with myself, and my regrets."

"We all get by any way we can," Ben said, picking up the bag of clean laundry and heading for the door. Hopefully Christine would be able to find peace now, too. And maybe even move closer to where she worked.

Given all that Ben had been through in the past few days, he thought it unwise to attempt anything strenuous, or anything at all, on an empty stomach. He was passing Ground Zero anyway, and the cheapskate side of him couldn't stand the idea of leaving with unused meal vouchers still in his pocket. There was no telling when the next time he might be able to get a free restaurant-cooked meal would be.

He could smell the intoxicating aroma of sausages and bacon wafting through the doors before he even crossed the threshold. It was that awk-ward brunch time again, and the restaurant was a hive of activity. The at-mosphere seemed to have completely changed. It was no longer ominous and vaguely oppressive, as if primed for something unpleasant to happen. Now, it was cheerful, bright, and breezy, with sunshine streaming through the windows and the sounds of laughter and conversation filling the air.

Alex, the Eastern European guy manning the desk, greeted Ben with a well-practiced, disarming smile as he took the offered voucher and scanned it with his handheld machine. If he held any bad will from their previ-ous encounter, it didn't show. Transaction completed, Ben made his way toward an empty table near the window.

Settling into the chair, he signaled the blonde waitress, who came bounding over with admirable enthusiasm, all past discretions apparently forgotten, and ordered a full English breakfast. There was no need to consult the menu. While he waited for his food to arrive, he gazed out of the window. With such gorgeous weather, the Regal was bustling with people walking up and down the road on their way to whatever activities they had planned. It seemed as if the newfound joviality and optimism on display in Ground Zero had spread throughout the entire resort. It felt like a new beginning, as if dawn was finally breaking after a particularly dark, fraught, and dangerous night.

"Ben?" said a voice from somewhere behind him. "Ben, is that you?"

Startled, Ben craned his neck and turned around. There, just two tables behind, was Tim Norgood. Dressed in a bottle green polo shirt. He looked relaxed and comfortable. And he wasn't alone. Opposite him was an attractive woman in her forties wearing a yellow sun dress that showed her long, slender arms. Ben stood and went over to the couple's table.

"Tim! Good to see you. Although I should really have spotted you when I came in. Sorry for the oversight. I was too focused on getting some food."

"No worries," Tim said. "That's perfectly understandable. This is my wife, Sheila."

The woman in the yellow dress smiled and dutifully held out her hand. Ben took it and said, "Ah, the famous Sheila. So nice to finally meet you."

"Likewise!" the woman replied.

Ben had to physically bite his tongue to stop himself adding how happy he was to see that Tim hadn't murdered her after all because there had certainly been moments when he firmly suspected as much. Instead, he went with, "I'd like to apologize for smuggling your husband away so much these past few days."

"Oh, that's quite all right," Sheila replied. "You can smuggle him away any time you want. Just put him back where you found him when you've finished."

As all three laughed at the quip, Ben met Tim's gaze and something unspoken passed between them. It was partly an acknowledgment of the bond they shared, and partly an expression of a mutual relief that it was all over at last.

Have we really done enough?

I hope so.

"Would you like to join us?" Tim asked. "We had a little lie-in today, so we just ordered a late breakfast."

Ben shuffled his feet, his social anxiety rising to the fore. "Oh, I really wouldn't want to impose…"

Sheila looked delighted about this unexpected turn of events. "Oh, don't be silly. Tim and I have spent almost every waking moment since nineteen-ninety-five in each other's company. It would be a pleasant change to have a conversation with someone else for a change."

"Do you have to sound so thrilled about it?" Tim said with faux disdain.

"Well, since you put it like that, I don't mind if I do," Ben said, pulling up a chair.

The next forty-five minutes passed in a blur. Tim and Sheila bounced off each other like a perfectly happy, contented couple. They appeared to have the kind of idyllic middle-class marriage most people craved.

Ben wondered how he could have ever doubted it.

As they tucked into their breakfast, the trio discussed everything from Tim's obsession with Plymouth Furys to Sheila's penchant for Dan Brown novels and Rich Tea biscuits. It was undoubtedly the most enjoyable meal Ben had had in months, the company making all the difference.

Tim and Sheila didn't even raise any eyebrows when Ben wrapped one of his sausages in a napkin and put it in his pocket, not after he explained the rationale behind it. He and Mr. Trimble's origin story always went down well. On this occasion it went down so well that both Tim and Sheila donated sausages and bacon rind of their own to the cause, thereby ensuring the cat would be enjoying a lunch fit for a king.

At one point, Sheila asked Ben what his plans were now his work at the Regal Retreat was effectively complete. He thought about it for a few moments, then said, "Mister Trimble and I are going to hit the road again. We'll find somewhere quiet to stay, maybe a campsite or a caravan park, then I'll spend a couple of weeks writing all this up. I have to produce a full report for the R.R.'s records, though I doubt it will ever see the light of day. No matter. I'll have a wealth of material for my website.

I'll make a couple of videos for YouTube, and also look at bashing out a few articles for the mainstream press. Maybe even start that novel I've been threatening to write since I was a teenager."

"It all sounds very exciting," Sheila said. "It must be wonderful to be so free of responsibility."

"To be honest," replied Ben, "I kinda hope all the excitement is over and done with. At least temporarily."

With breakfast finished, Ben bade farewell to Tim and Sheila, and this time they exchanged contact details. On the way out of Ground Zero, he grabbed a latte to go, then stopped at reception to hand in his gold R.R. card. After that, there was just one more place left to visit.

The lake looked just the same as it always did: a huge expanse of gently rippling blue-green water of varying shades. Sunlight sparkled on a surface studded with tiny rowboats and small pockets of people lined the banks. As he took a seat on a bench facing the water, Ben wondered if any of the boats were heading out to the island. He hoped not, though it would only be a matter of time before that happened. Not that there was much to see on the island anymore, apart from a big hole in the ground. There might be an investigation of sorts into where Elizabeth Thrower's remains had vanished to, but Ben doubted it was something that would bother the police too much, and soon the whole incident would be woven into history's great tapestry. Just another Regal Retreat mystery.

Even though the lake looked the same, it certainly felt different. There was no trepidation or nagging sense of dread, and even the island itself now appeared a lot less foreboding than it had before.

All things considered, Ben thought as he sipped his coffee, one could describe the scene as pleasant and dreamy in the best possible sense. It was already hard to believe that anything terrible could happen here, and he almost felt a pang of regret at having to leave.

Almost.

He didn't think Christine would mind if he stayed on a couple of nights, but now his work was done here, he wanted to make a clean break. The longer he stayed, the more difficult it might be. That much became apparent at the meeting with Christine that morning when he'd caught his eyes being drawn repeatedly to the woman's ring finger, which he belatedly noticed was bare. Not that it mattered anymore.

After dumping his empty coffee cup in a wastepaper bin conveniently placed next to the bench, Ben took a leisurely stroll back to the camper van. He half expected a welcoming committee consisting of Detective Carter and maybe a uniformed officer or two, but thankfully that didn't happen. The only welcoming committee was Mr. Trimble, who yelled at Ben for being a dirty stay-out, gobbled up his version of a full English, then noisily made use of his litter box while Ben prepared for departure. Fucking attention seeker.

Minutes later, the duo was driving slowly down the road bisecting the complex, with Mr. Trimble taking up his usual position riding shotgun in the passenger seat. Ben took his time, drinking in the scene, eventually arriving at the main gate. Coincidentally, it was being manned by the same overweight, balding, bad-tempered security guard with heavily tattooed forearms who had signed him in.

"Checking out?"

"Yes, pal," Ben replied, winking at the guard as the gate was lifted. He couldn't wait to park up outside the nearest pub.

<u>**By the same author**</u>

<u>**Novels / Novellas:**</u>

Devil's Island
Out of Time
Sker House
No Man's Land: Horror in the Trenches
Apartment 14F: An Oriental Ghost Story – Uncut
Human Waste
Dead of Night – Uncut
Tethered

<u>**Collections:**</u>

X: A Collection of Horror
X2: Another Collection of Horror
X SAMPLE
X3
X: Omnibus
X4
X5
Back from the Dead: A Collection of Zombie Fiction

Stalkers welcome:

<u>cmsaunders.wordpress.com/</u>
@CMSaunders01
<u>www.facebook.com/CMSaunders01/</u>

ABOUT THE AUTHOR

C.M. Saunders is a writer and editor from south Wales. His work has appeared in over a hundred magazines, ezines and anthologies worldwide, including *Siren's Call*, *34 Orchard*, *Phantasmagoria*, *Welcome to the Splatterclub*, and *Handmade Horror*, while his books have been both traditionally and independently published.

LIGHTS!

A killer is targeting TV and Film extras on various productions throughout the South West of England. The murderer leaves a macabre marker at each crime scene—a VHS video nasty, while the murders themselves mimic the killings depicted in the tapes.

CAMERA!

While the police are drawn into both the seedy world of nasties and the hierarchical system that thrives in the film industry, the killer remains one step ahead.

CUT!

It's an A–Z kill list, and the cops are in a race to stop the slayings before the murderer can chop their way through the 39 titles on the list of banned films, from *Absurd* to *Zombie Flesh Eaters…*

WALKING SHADOW
A Stone/Darke Mystery

www.ingramcontent.com/pod-product-compliance
Lightning Source LLC
Chambersburg PA
CBHW060911210726
48293CB00006B/2049